He'd managed to move to within a few feet of her, and it was all Brittany could do to keep from retreating a step. His shirt clung to his still-damp chest, and she noticed, in spite of herself, the way his powerful upper torso moved gently with his every breath ... He was utterly masculine—and Brittany's every instinct told her to run from him.

He reached out as if to touch her. "I am offering you a position here at Wildwood, Brittany. I think you would be happy here."

"Happy here? I think you misjudge me, my lord! How much need can you have for a housekeeper? It appears you seek a wench to warm your bed!"

He moved to within inches of her, his mesmerizing gaze delving into her. "Nothing that you are not willing to give, Brittany ..."

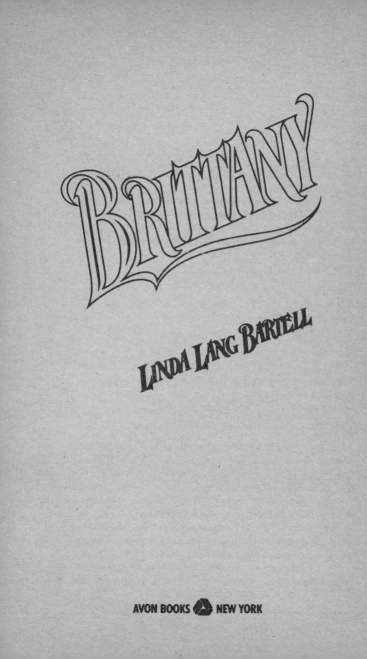

BRITTANY

LINDA LANG BARTELL

AVON BOOKS ◭ NEW YORK

BRITTANY is an original publication of Avon Books. This work has never before appeared in book form. This work is a novel. Any similarity to actual persons or events is purely coincidental.

AVON BOOKS
A division of
The Hearst Corporation
105 Madison Avenue
New York, New York 10016

Copyright © 1989 by Linda Lang Bartell
Published by arrangement with the author
Library of Congress Catalog Card Number: 88-92101
ISBN: 0-380-75545-9

First Avon Books Printing: January 1989

AVON TRADEMARK REG. U.S. PAT. OFF. AND IN OTHER COUNTRIES, MARCA REGISTRADA, HECHO EN U.S.A.

Printed in the U.S.A.

K-R 10 9 8 7 6 5 4 3 2 1

For Bob, with love

I would like to extend my gratitude to my friend and fellow writer Judith E. French for sharing her knowledge of Eastern American Indians; to Joyce C. Wells for her input when BRITTANY was still in the synopsis stage; to R. C. Tomas, M.D., for answering my medical questions; and to Keith Culver for guiding me through the sails of a ship.

Last, but not least, many thanks to my editor Ellen Edwards.

"Look for me by moonlight;
  Watch for me by moonlight;
I'll come to thee by moonlight,
  though hell should bar the way!"

Alfred Noyes
The Highwayman

Prologue

Geneviève Elise Chauvelin stared at the man before her, her fingers convulsed around the brass candle holder as she watched him sink slowly to the floor. The doll she'd had as a child suddenly came to mind in the midst of an unexpected and eerie impassivity. *He looks like a rag doll that crumples into a shapeless heap when dropped.*

With fascinated detatchment she studied the look of astonishment frozen forever on the once handsome features of her husband, and then slowly, stiffly, her right arm lowered to her side. The clenched fingers relaxed and the instrument of death clattered to the floor. It reverberated with a metallic *clink* against the raised stone hearth and rolled to a halt before the dancing flames in the sudden, enshrouding silence.

Minutes—or hours—passed. She knew not which. At some point, the horror of what she'd done penetrated Geneviève's benumbed mind as she stared at the unnaturally positioned body on the floor.

Murderess . . . Murderess!

The word splintered through her mind with lacerating impact. Then shock receded and emotion came reeling back as she opened her mouth to scream. Yet no sound came forth.

The once striking features of the blond, blue-eyed Raymond Chauvelin looked grotesque now, a carven death

1

mask with a trickle of ruby-bright blood threading its way down his left temple to pool obscenely in the hollow at the side of his narrow, aristocratic nose and at the corner of his thin, pale lips, which now merely hinted at his innate cruelty.

It did not occur to Geneviève to try to find a heartbeat, for it was obvious he was dead. And by her hand . . . She, a woman who could not bear the thought of a flushed grouse, had sunk to the level of the depraved man whom she'd wed by arrangement two years ago.

As the unnatural quiet swirled around her, she realized she had to get away—and quickly—for the few servants in their employ would appear with the first light of dawn.

She glanced at the clock on the mantel. She had much to do and little time in which to do it. With wooden steps she moved to a washbasin, cleaning her hands and rinsing her face to help restore some semblance of calm to her turbulent emotions.

Mechanically she ascended the stairs to the room they had shared and removed her nightshift, stuffing the blood-spattered garment beneath the mattress of the bed, her mind racing to form a plan to slip out of St. Malo and away from her beloved Bretagne, forever. Her life depended on it, she was certain.

She dressed in clean clothes and moved back down the stairs to the fireplace of the modest, half-timbered dwelling, then gazed down at her late husband one last time. No more would he debase her—use her for his own bizarre and insatiable appetites, with a total disregard for her own feelings and sensibilities. Images of his menacing approaches and lewd assaults on her person flashed before her mind's eye, and she lowered her lashes in pained remembrance, swallowing the bile that burned the back of her throat.

Those lurid scenes were etched in her memory for all eternity. At last she'd become convinced once and for all that there could never be even simple tolerance between them. After they'd retired this eve, the normally shy Geneviève, showing her mettle as never before, had refused his perverse advances. When he'd taken a knife to her, she had bludgeoned him in self-defense with a single death stroke. Never, she thought as her eyes opened to regard him, would she forget his brutal treatment of her. And never would she forget the crimson lifeblood that still trickled over his crushed temple and cheek, continuing to settle in the crevices and hollows of his face, crying out to all the world that he had been murdered.

The brilliant, blood-hued liquid trickled steadily, collecting in the crevices and hollows over which it passed, ruby-bright, along the uneven surface of the street.

Wine. It literally flowed through the streets. It geysered from myriad fountains, spewn heavenward in the bright May sunshine. The garnet liquid splashed onto the smooth, rounded stone sides and wended downward to splatter onto the cobblestones, unnoticed in the riotous celebration that held all of London in thrall.

The noise was fulminating—guns resounding with sharp reports, cannon booming, bells singing out in ceaseless hosannas, soldiers' horses clattering. But the greatest din came from the people themselves, over twenty thousand strong and from as far away as Rochester—shouting, laughing, crying, and jostling one another in their efforts to witness King Charles II coming into his own.

For today was Charles Stuart's thirtieth birthday, and, more importantly, the day the English monarchy was being restored after nearly two decades of radicalism and fanatacism—of rule by "saints" and model army major-generals. The English longed for the comfortable traditions of king, church, and Parliament.

Tristan Andrew Savidge, trusted friend and confidant of Charles Stuart, rode by choice well behind the main body surrounding the king. The cortege crossed London Bridge, preceded by the lord mayor, the wooden houses on either side of the structure so clogging the thoroughfare that only a twelve-foot-wide passageway was possible. From what

Tristan could see ahead of him, he was relieved not to be trapped in the immediate press of heralds, maids, and other attendants surrounding the returning monarch.

Their progress across the bridge was snaillike, and when at last they passed over it, the huge throng spilled out over the streets in a wave of cloth-of-silver doublets, multicolored velvets, purple liveries, uniforms of sea green and silver, against the vivid contrast of the sheriff's men in their red coats and argent lace, the richly adorned scarlet gowns of the aldermen of London.

No reminders of civil war. Everyone is royalist this day, Tristan thought wryly, for the buff-colored coats of the English army were adorned with sleeves of cloth-of-silver and other trimmings of like-colored lace. And it was just as well, he conceded, for Charles Stuart came not as a suppliant exile. Not only was a monarchy being restored, but a way of life as well.

Tristan could hardly see the back of the king's dark, bare head, yet now and then, because of Charles's unusual height, Tristan caught a glimpse of the royal profile when the monarch inclined his head to acknowledge the joyous acclamation, his snow-white mount picking its way along the flower-strewn, wine-washed streets. Dark-haired like his king, but several inches short of the latter's six-foot-four frame, Tristan, too, was an impressive sight astride his fine steed. But he was unconcerned as to the figure he cut, for it was not in his nature to set out to impress. And, in any case, this was Charles Stuart's day.

He suppressed a yawn and, in an effort to divert boredom, squinted up into the sunlight at the ladies posed in windows and on balconies. It was a pleasant enough game for a while, but he tired of it all too soon.

As he flashed a gracious smile at one last maid waving effusively in open invitation, it occurred to him how out of his element he was. He loved Charles, had nearly died for him on several occasions, yet he also loved the quiet solitude found so readily in the colony of Virginia across the Atlantic. That place, with its untouched verdant meadows, its primeval forests, was as much his home as the court of Charles Stuart. Sometimes the lure of the land of his birth tugged at him unmercifully.

With a rueful smile that threatened to send the exuberant girl still hanging over the iron-grilled balcony into a swoon, Tristan mentally chided himself for acquiring the staidness that came with age—no matter that he was five years younger than Charles. His self-imposed duty and freely given loyalty was to the restored king of England, despite the ties that bound him irrevocably to the magnificent wilderness where he'd been born.

Then, without warning, from within the press of humanity surrounding them, a young girl emerged smiling shyly and thrust a small flask of wine toward Tristan in jubilant offering. As he reached down to accept it, the girl was suddenly jostled by another zealous celebrant, and some of the bloodred contents spattered onto his breech-covered thigh, dribbling downward to trace a path of crimson against the immaculate white hose covering his lower leg.

The startled girl stammered in apology, but with a shrug of dismissal he laughed aloud, tossed down the contents of the flask with relish, and threw himself into the gala mood of the festivities with an enthusiasm that did Charles Stuart proud.

Brittany

Chapter 1

May 1662

The blue and gold painted wooden sign proclaiming the building to be the Hunter's Run creaked and groaned as it swung in the quickening wind. Portending a storm, the moisture-laden breeze swirled into the half-timbered edifice each time the door opened and shut, admitting a mixture of odors redolent of the nearby Thames.

To the occupants of the taproom on the ground floor, the fresh draughts of air were as welcome as the breath of spring in the stuffy, stale atmosphere of smoke, drink, cooking food, and closely packed, unwashed bodies. A diverse mélange of customers occupied the benches, tables, and stools scattered about the large room, with serving girls scurrying to and from the bar and kitchen area to serve their clientele.

Many men stood laughing, talking, gesturing, or ogling the young women serving them. A few pinched ample behinds in familiar jocularity or went so far as to pull a rosy-cheeked girl onto a lap for a brief tussle or flirtation—depending on the lass's inclinations and the innkeeper's mood.

Some of the wealthier patrons dined at tables set up before the small, diamond-paned windows on the wall facing the street. Men and their wives or, more often, mistresses, sat with their heads together in as much intimacy as the surroundings would allow. One could find men head

9

to head in similar private conversations as well, and it was an accepted fact that politics were as much discussed at the Hunter's Run as were romantic trysts.

The outside door suddenly swung open once more, allowing a cool rush of air to sweep into the smoke-hazed, crowded tavern. Two tall, impressive figures loomed briefly in the doorway, pausing a moment to assess the scene and, at the same time, drawing the curious stares of those close by.

"Gemini!" declared a tiny, lank-haired serving girl near the bar to the taller young woman beside her. " 'Tis the duke of Buckingham 'imself."

The other girl paid scant attention, having seen the pompous courtier before and, after a cursory glance toward the door, continued to load the mugs of ale and bottles of sack onto her heavy tray.

"Lord, 'e's a handsome one!" Janie Neggers continued.

The taller one shrugged negligently before hefting the loaded tray to her shoulder. "Perhaps you'll catch his eye this night, Janie," she said in an attempt at levity, for Janie was still very young—all of sixteen years—and as yet much agog with the flamboyant aristocrats who frequented the inn.

Janie looked at her friend, a wistful expression replacing her childlike enthusiasm. "Nay, Brittany. 'Tis more likely *you'll* be the one to catch 'is fancy."

At Brittany's frown, Janie hastened to assure her, "No harm meant, Britt . . . I'll see if I can find 'im a table and you carry on here."

Brittany flashed her diminutive friend a quick, grateful smile and began to turn away when a stentorian voice from near the door stopped her cold.

"We've come looking for the fairest maid in London, and I've reason to believe she's to be found right here."

A brief silence ensued and then, as the duke and his companion strode into the room, a cheer of approbation went up.

Brittany paled, her hands trembling under the heavy burden of her tray. *Dieu au ciel,* where could she hide before Buckingham made his way through the crowd and—

But Janie was nimbly dodging ale-happy customers and making her way toward the awesome, fair-haired duke.

"Look no further, yer grace, for here I be!" she said in her most provocative tones, and grinned impudently up at him.

Relieved by the deliberate diversion, Brittany quickly served the men awaiting their libations, replaced the empty tray, and retreated toward the stairs leading to the upper floors, dodging hindering arms and hands that seemed of a sudden to entrap her within the milling throng.

"A bet with the king I've made, my good fellows," bellowed Buckingham. "Yet, dammee, I cannot recollect where I've seen an amber-haired vision of loveliness. Which inn was it? Hunter's Run, perhaps?"

At the imperious query of George Villiers, second duke of Buckingham, Brittany felt faces turn toward her and her feet turned to lead. Panic clawed through her as the relative safety she felt in her anonymity crumbled into ashes.

"Here's a fair enough one fer ya, yer grace," called a voice from nearby, and a hand yanked at the tight knot of hair at the nape of Brittany's neck.

She slapped away the offending hand, galvanized into motion by the good-natured yet infinitely unwelcome attack. Whirling free, she fled for the stairs, the light from the fire in the great hearth and myriad wall sconces highlighting the honey-colored cascade of her long hair. Like a signal flag to the duke across the room, it jogged his wine-blurred memory with startling effect.

"Stop her! Stop the wench!" he shouted.

"Yer grace, she's not the one! She's—she's had the pox," interceded Janie. "Her face—her face is marked . . ."

Her words died as the duke's narrowed eyes impaled her. "You lie," he said, then turned his gaze once more toward Brittany. "Five pounds to the man who catches her!" he roared.

Hands reached for Brittany as she nimbly sprinted up the stairs. But she was too quick for most of the now-earnest but half-tipsy grapplers—until the sound of her green overskirt rending in twain brought her up short. Half the skirt was torn away and, without even glancing around, she knew the yellow and white striped petticoat beneath was completely exposed in the back and on one side.

The tension on the garment abruptly eased in the sudden silence. Slowly, with the beginnings of an outrage born of humiliation building inside her, Brittany turned to face the roomful of patrons. With her hair swirling around her expressive features in curling disarray, her eyes mirroring her ire, she met with quiet dignity Buckingham's stare across the room.

The crowd parted as the duke strode toward her. "I knew it!" he exclaimed, his eyes taking her in from the top of her head to the tips of her shoes. In a trice he was on the step below her and, before Brittany could protest, he lifted her petticoat to expose her legs to well above the knees. "And by God, his majesty is mightily taken by long, fine-shaped limbs, I warrant you!"

Two years of marriage to Raymond Chauvelin, culminating in his death by her hand, surfaced within her mind like scum in a simmering cauldron, with all the accompanying soul-shaking memories and, without thought, the girl who was now known as Brittany Jennifer St. Germain knocked away his blue-blooded hand.

"How dare you!"

The words were quietly uttered, the natural musical lilt replaced by anger, the faint French accent thicker now.

The egregious Buckingham grabbed her wrist and pulled her down so violently that she lost her balance and came up hard against his chest.

"Tavern jade," he accused into her startled face, "how dare *you?* I should have you flogged for raising your hand to me."

Strained silence reigned until a hand clamped onto Villiers's shoulder and another masculine voice interjected,

"Can't you see, Villiers, that you've been duped? The wench was only using this charade to further her chances of being presented to the king."

Buckingham's grip on Brittany relaxed slightly as he studied her face with a deepening frown, his alcohol-muddled mind hindering his thoughts. "Duped? How so, Savidge? She is fair enough to have no need of such tricks. Why, she's even more handsome than my cousin Barbara."

Brittany took advantage of his momentary uncertainty and pushed away from him. Straightening to her taller than average height, she awaited the outcome of her rash actions, her eyes still locked with his.

"I can overlook your outrageous behavior, girl, if you will docilely come with me to see the king. I would claim my hundred pounds."

Sudden fright lanced through Brittany. It was bad enough to have been brought to the attention of everyone in the taproom, but to be presented to the king himself!

And then her fear-shadowed eyes met those of Buckingham's companion—the owner of that other cultured masculine voice. Brittany caught a flicker of something indefinable in the sapphire gaze before it swiftly disappeared. "I believe the bet was the fairest *maid* in London, Villiers, and this one is no maid."

Again his grace ran his eyes consideringly, insultingly, over Brittany. "I did not understand that to be a condition, Savidge. It is doubtful there is a virgin left in the entire city." He captured her wrist and none too gently started pulling her down the steps. The room began to hum with activity once more, the game over now with Brittany's capitulation. But the young woman was frantically scavenging her mind for a way out of her predicament.

Savidge provided it—brutally but effectively.

"The girl is no maiden, Villiers, and his majesty will be most disappointed."

Buckingham turned abruptly to the other man, his expression scornful, Brittany's wrist still imprisoned within his powerful fingers.

"You doubt my word?" Something in Tristan Savidge's eyes gave Buckingham pause.

"And what if I do?" The words were barely audible above the increasing din in the tavern.

Tristan looked at the young woman standing so close to him. She was statue-still, yet trepidation was written across her fine features, and the fingers of her free hand still clutched the banister. Obviously she feared not so much Buckingham as the prospect of being brought before the king, and for some strange reason, something about her unshakable stoicism in the face of her humiliation struck a sympathetic chord deep within him. He regretted that she would now associate him with the duke of Buckingham.

"Then you are a fool, Villiers, for I have had my way with her—many times."

Buckingham knew Tristan Savidge was many things, but even he had to admit that prevarication and intrigue for self-gain were beneath the quarter-breed Indian from Virginia. As jealous as Villiers was of the king's affection for the steadfast, loyal colonist, he knew Savidge would not lie under ordinary circumstances. And what could be more ordinary than bringing a pretty wench before Charles Stuart? Heaven knew Edward Progers, the page of the backstairs, did it often enough for his sovereign.

George Villiers ignored the fact that Tristan Savidge had addressed him so familiarly, though the Virginian had attained knighthood the year before, and also that Tristan had named him a fool. Rather, the duke concentrated on the matter at hand. What had Savidge to gain by thwarting him over a common serving wench?

Buckingham studied Brittany with renewed interest, looking for a sign of affront or indignation over being named a harlot. But her expression remained cool, maddeningly aloof.

"Very well, Savidge," he conceded with great reluctance as he envisioned his hundred pounds literally sprouting wings and taking flight.

At an all but imperceptible look of warning from Tristan, Brittany turned and went upstairs, wrapping her torn skirt around her as if it were a royal mantle.

Once in her room, however, a rush of conflicting emotions swept over her, for at last the thing she dreaded most had come to pass. She had inadvertently drawn attention to herself. That the one to notice her had been the duke of Buckingham, a powerful and influential friend of the king, brought tears of vexation to her eyes, despite her efforts to maintain some semblance of calm.

Unable to return to the scene of her debasement downstairs, Brittany slowly undressed and pondered her situation. Although she'd taken pains to change her given name to Brittany in remembrance of her homeland, she'd merely anglicized Geneviève to Jennifer and taken her mother's surname. But Janie was the only one aware that her Christian name was really Geneviève and that she'd fled France. There was no way anyone could guess that Brittany Jennifer St. Germain was Geneviève Elise Chauvelin . . . unless someone she'd known in France saw and recognized her. And to avoid that possibility—slight as she'd hoped the chances would be—she'd been forced to lie to the innkeeper Dobbs and his wife to gain employment.

She moved to the window in her bare feet and nightgown and stared unseeingly into the night. For just under two years she'd managed to retreat behind her shyness, keeping to the shadows as much as she dared and dressing as modestly as possible—even pulling her hair severely back in a prim, outdated fashion. Yet less than an hour ago she'd become the very center of attention in the crowded taproom. And even if things could continue on as they had before, what of the duke of Buckingham? Had his companion succeeded in moving him from his purpose for good?

There was no way of knowing.

In the taproom below, Tristan continued to ply Villiers

with his favorite Rhenish until the latter's speech was so slurred that the Virginian was certain the duke had forgotten the beautiful, frightened creature he'd assaulted earlier. But when he finally led Buckingham out the door with an arm around his shoulders in feigned camaraderie, he discovered he'd underestimated the duke. "But—the wager, Savidge . . . What of—the wager?"

They stepped into the rain-washed night before Tristan answered, "Take heart, Villiers. There is a most fetching creature at Dagger Tavern who will not give *me* the time of day, but perhaps . . ." The words drifted upward into the cool, tangy night air, past the unshuttered window where Brittany lay in a troubled, restless sleep.

With a blearily skeptical look at Tristan—as if he could not quite believe he hadn't been the victim of some spur-of-the-moment chicanery—Buckingham allowed himself to be led to his coach.

"*That* is the fairest maiden in London?" the duke of Buckingham asked scathingly, now beginning to sober.

"Indeed," answered the young courtier, his chest puffing with pride.

Tristan restrained a smile as he pretended great interest in the "lady" Smith had produced.

Charles Stuart stood with his back to the window, leaning against the opened casement with a smile of lazy amusement on his swarthy features. "Lovely," he complimented the young woman, who was obviously an actress, with painted face and the garb of a youth to show off her figure to advantage. "You've represented us well, Smith, but"—his deep brown eyes went to the duke—"what of your night's search, George?"

"*That*"—Buckingham pointed a righteous finger at the girl, ignoring his sovereign's question—"is no maiden."

Charles raised a dark eyebrow and bent to scoop up one of his favorite spaniel's pups. "And what, pray, has that to do with it?" He straightened and stroked the miniscule animal's downy head.

Buckingham turned his baleful gaze toward the object of his increasing animosity. "Your majesty, if you say that virtue was not part of the wager, then Savidge tricked me this eve while I was less than sober."

The king looked at Tristan and, knowing full well the malice his childhood friend could harbor—the incisive sarcasm of which Buckingham was capable when in control of his wits and his words—Charles, ever the peacemaker, interceded. "Well, I suppose Tristan spoke truly, after all, George. Would not a chaste beauty be of more value? Begging your pardon, madame," he added with an apologetic look at the actress as he addressed her in the manner befitting a female of her profession.

"Sire, the woman I had in mind was worth a score of the likes of her," the duke stated baldly, heedless of the insult to the young actress. "And I intend to fetch 'er."

Grim determination stamped across his features, he turned toward the door. Inadvertently he trod on the paw of one of the other puppies roaming about the room—this particular one pausing to sniff curiously at the duke's foot— and swore under his breath. He recovered himself with alacrity, feeling like a fool after the king's defense of Tristan and his own clumsiness with the bothersome canine.

"Oh, come now, George," said the king. "It's not as important as your anger merits. You can well afford one hundred pounds and, you must admit, Smith here has done an admirable job."

But Buckingham refused to be moved from his purpose. He continued toward the door since he'd not been given a royal command to do otherwise.

"I wouldn't if I were you."

Softly ominous, Tristan's warning stopped him, as much because of the unexpectedness of his words as for the barely leashed menace in the tone. It made Villiers's blood run cold.

It did not help matters that "the savage," as Buckingham had privately named Tristan long ago, was blocking the doorway.

"Oh? Now don't tell me you are so taken with a common tavern bawd that you'll not share her with his majesty—even for a wager?"

The tension between the two men was suddenly palpable. Yet while the duke's anger was obvious, Tristan's well-schooled features maintained a deadly lack of expression. Fortunately, Buckingham knew the colonist well enough to realize that the consequences of crossing him when he wore that look could be disastrous.

"Your must consider the circumstances under which it was thought up, George," said the king into the sudden silence. "We'd all had a bit much to drink and, at the moment, I can ill afford the hundred pounds with my bride-to-be sailing for Portsmouth from Portugal even as we speak. I have a marriage ceremony and a queen's coronation to consider." He replaced the pup and traversed the black and white marble paving toward the huge four-postered bed. At a signal from Charles, a page hurried to remove his shoes. The monarch studied the two men still rigidly tableaued before the door. "I hereby cancel my part in this bet, which has obviously been the cause of this, er, misunderstanding."

"But your maj—" began Buckingham, then stopped as Charles continued nonchalantly.

"We thank you for coming, madame." He bestowed his most charming smile upon the disappointed girl. "Indeed, you are enough to turn the head of the least observant of men, but please take this small recompense and leave us." Another hovering page placed a small pouch in her hand.

Deflated, Smith led her away.

As the courtier passed Buckingham, Tristan obligingly moved aside.

"George, you may leave as well, for I find I am weary with the aftereffects of our celebration earlier." Again, the king's gracious smile did not quite hide the melancholy that had been present in the dark eyes ever since his return to England.

Knowing he was temporarily defeated, Buckingham bowed stiffly to Charles and, with barely a glance in Tristan's direction, exited the room.

Charles closed his eyes wearily and gave himself up to the ministrations of his servants. "I hope it worked, Savidge."

"I apologize, sire, but in truth the girl was terrified of—of Buckingham. He mauled her publicly with no concern for her . . ."

Charles dismissed Tristan's explanation with a wave of a hand. "I know very well how unfeeling George can be, especially to women. 'Tis unfortunate that a man of his looks and position is not only squandering the largest fortune in England, but also prefers men." He opened his eyes again to regard Tristan squatting near the doorway and wrestling with the mother spaniel. "Was she as beautiful as I suspect?"

Tristan remembered the terror in the girl's eyes at the Hunter's Run and could not prevent the untruth that sprang to his lips. " 'Tis hard to say, your majesty, when fear distorted her features so." He stood up, awaiting permission to leave.

"Until the morrow, then."

When Tristan had gone, Charles leaned back on his elbows and thoughtfully studied the rich canopy. "Ah, my Tristan, what downtrodden soul do you champion now, I wonder?"

"So you do not approve of my attentions to Garrard—a mere stable boy, chère Geneviève? Tsk, Tsk." He clucked his tongue in feigned resignation. "You have much to learn of life and loving, my innocent wife."

"You know naught of love, Raymond, if you think what you forced Garrard to endure has anything to do with it. You sicken me." And she turned from him lest he see the apprehension in her eyes, for when he was in a mood like this it only boded ill. This time she was determined to avoid his attentions at any cost.

He came up behind her and grabbed her cruelly by the arm before she could retire behind the dressing screen. "I want you to disrobe while I watch, Geneviève, and then I have something very special in mind for us."

Knowing it was useless to struggle, and dreading the final confrontation she knew must come, she reluctantly obliged him, hurrying through the motions lest she increase his lust unduly.

"And now," he purred when she'd donned a diaphanous nightgown which he'd handed her in unspoken command. He forced her to her knees right there on the floor before the screen and began to mount her from behind, with no preliminary preparation, like an animal.

Panic sheared away all thought save that of getting away, and wildly she flung her elbow up and outward, striking him soundly on the side of his jaw. Barely aware of the faint grinding sound of the dislocating bones, she took advantage of the unexpectedness of her attack and fought her way clear before he could regain his hold on her. Leaping to her feet, Geneviève fled the bedroom and ran down the stairs, tripping on the last step in her haste and losing precious moments as the angry clump *of Raymond's footsteps signaled his presence close behind her.*

Despite the piercing pain in one ankle, Geneviève made it as far as the fireplace before he snatched her wrist in a viselike grip and flung her around to face him before the lowering flames in the hearth. But it wasn't the look of malevolent fury in the pale eyes as much as the glint of firelight caught by the steel tip of a dagger held in his free hand that froze her heartbeat in her chest.

"Ray-Raymond, this is madness!" she found her tongue long enough to exclaim softly.

His speech was slightly slurred as his lips twisted unnaturally in pain with his reply. "You dare to refuse a husband's conjugal rights—to actually strike me? You, a country mouse, a nobody? Killing you would avail me little, but perhaps a few scars on that unblemished skin will serve to remind you of your place."

He swung the knife menacingly toward her face once, twice, and then with the swiftness of a striking snake lashed out at her cheek.

The whoosh of the weapon slicing through the air sounded like the roar of thunder in her ears, and her eyes widened in horror as the soft rush of air caused by its flashing flight caressed her cheek in deadly warning.

He swung again, knocking a brass candlestick from the mantel on the backswing, and as the knife returned for the fourth pass, Geneviève ducked to avoid its razor-sharp blade. Her right hand came in contact with the cold metal of the fallen candle holder, and her fingers automatically curled around it, a prayer of thanksgiving upon her lips.

"Afraid, pet?" he grated through barely separated teeth, and as she straightened and skipped backward, the candlestick hidden behind her, he made to strike once more.

Geneviève raised the weighty object in her hand. The edge of a low table digging into the back of her knees and preventing her from further retreat gave her the final impetus to bring down the weapon with all the strength she possessed.

He started to turn his face aside in a last-minute attempt to avoid being struck, but the instrument took him in the side of the skull. And then, unthinkingly, she raised it again, prepared to repeat the motion . . .

She awoke with a start, a low cry of distress escaping her lips. Her head thudded against the beam directly over her bed in the stuffy, low-ceilinged attic room she shared with Janie. The younger girl stirred. "Brittany? Brittany, are you 'aving a bad dream again?"

Wide awake as a result of the sharp bump to her head, Brittany nodded before she realized Janie couldn't see in the darkness. "*Oui, chère.* But it's nothing. I'm sorry I woke you."

"Uds lud, Britt!" Janie sat up and fumbled for the tinderbox to light a taper. " 'Twas Buckingham, wasn't it?"

The flame she coaxed from the cheap tallow candle threw an eerie mixture of light and shadow across the small room. "Lord, 'e was enough to put the fear o' God into *any* female, let alone one who's been as ill-used as you." She slipped from beneath the light cover on her pallet and sat down beside Brittany.

"Do you think he'll be back, Janie?" Brittany asked, a frown marring her smooth brow.

Janie put a comforting arm around her friend, having suspected all along that Brittany was hiding from more than a cruel husband somewhere in France. "I think that other—whoever 'e was—was very clever. I guess you should thank your lucky stars that 'e saw fit to insult you— 'many times,' indeed!"

A ghost of a smile flitted across Brittany's features. "However he accomplished it, if he has succeeded in saving me, it matters not what he said."

Janie sighed, relaxing as she felt the tension begin to ebb from Brittany's body beside her. "Well, 'e *did* have the very bluest eyes I've ever seen."

A sudden unease crept over Brittany at the thought of that intense gaze that seemed to reach into her very soul. *"Eh bien,* his grace has blue eyes, as well."

Janie shook her head. "Not like that other's, I tell you. And the duke isn't 'alf as 'andsome, either." She glanced at her friend, an impish light in her eyes. "I think I'm going to find out more about 'im—like his name . . . You know, just curiosity."

Savidge is a good start, Brittany thought, but kept her silence. As the stern details of his face and bearing filtered back into her memory, she wondered if his name was any indication of his temperament.

Janie stood up. "Are you all right now?" At Brittany's nod she snuffed out the candle, plunging the room into blackness. "I know how you feel about men, Britt, but maybe, if you get the chance, you should thank 'im."

Chapter 2

Brittany mucked out the last stall and, setting down the shovel, led the great golden chestnut stallion back into place and tethered it securely before giving it an extra handful of oats from a pail. She smoothed her hand down its sleek, satiny sides, reveling in the feel of such power beneath her fingertips. What would it be like to be so strong, yet as a man rather than a beast?

The animal swung its majestic, white-maned head toward her when she removed her hand to clutch her own aching back in weariness, and whickered softly in protest. "No more, Gorvenal," she murmured. "You've had more than your share of attention, and I can hardly stand for want of rest."

For the past two weeks she'd been working in the stable in an effort to avoid the taproom, while still earning her keep. She'd donned one of the other stableboy's breeches and shirt, and pitched in with as much energy as if her life depended on it. And, indeed, perhaps it did.

"A fortnight?" Jack Dobbs had exclaimed in bemusement. "I took you on without a recommendation from anyone. Fer all I knew you could have been an escaped felon from Newgate or a criminal from the Friars . . ."

"With 'er looks and bearing? With that French accent?" demanded Maude Dobbs with equal determination. "Come now, Jackie, what harm can two weeks do to the inn? Willie's injured and we can't manage the stables with only one other boy."

"And what of the taproom, eh? Yer addled, Maude, if ye think we can meet the demands of our customers with one girl less."

"And what of yer own daughter? There's no reason that the high 'n mighty Katie Dobbs can't take on more of the responsibility."

And so, with Maude taking her side, Brittany had been granted stable duties for two weeks. If Willie was unable to return after the second week, she would be granted another few days' reprieve from working in the taproom with its myriad customers and the dreaded chance that Buckingham would reappear.

Yet it was backbreaking labor, and each night Brittany tumbled into bed bone-tired, asleep before her head hit the pillow.

Now, as she made one last round, the other stableboy already asleep in the loft above, she thought of how she'd miss the beautiful animal that had appeared several times this last week, his owner unknown to her. She loved horses, and the stallion seemed to sense her loneliness, her need for a friend, be it even a silent beast.

"*Bon soir*, Gorvenal," she bade softly with one final pat on its flank before turning away, lantern held high to light the way.

"So you've taken it upon yourself to rename my horse, have you?" came a deep masculine voice from the shadows.

Brittany started so violently that the lantern began to slip from her suddenly slack fingers and the owner of the voice emerged swiftly from the doorway to retrieve it. "I didn't mean to startle you." He hung the lantern from a convenient nail on a post beside him and studied her in its steady light, from the dirty cap which hid her glorious hair to her mire-caked shoes, from her dirt-smudged face to the long legs encased in Willie's breeches.

When Brittany finally found her voice, she responded quietly, trying to hide her alarm at being alone with a man—any man—in the relative isolation of a stable, despite the fact that this particular man had rescued her from the duke of Buckingham's attentions. *"Ma mère* repeated to me many times the legend of Tristan—of his faithful friend and companion-at-arms, Gorvenal. I-I would think a man would be well-favored to have such a faithful beast beneath him when danger threatened."

He gifted her with a smile that went all but unnoticed, so caught up was Brittany with the unusual blue of his thickly lashed eyes. As she ran the tip of her tongue over dry lips, she unexpectedly thought of the deep indigo of a clear sky at dusk.

He stepped forward and reached out to remove her cap. Fear made her retreat before him, and her hand automatically felt for the shovel propped up against the stall's partition. "I mean you no harm, mistress. I only wished for proof that you are the one whom I've sought almost every night for the last week—that you are a real woman in the flesh and not some figment of my dreams."

Essaying to change the direction of his thoughts, Brittany drew in a deep breath and said, "I-I wish to thank you, my lord, for what you did when the duke . . ."

He brushed aside her halting words with a wave of his hand. "George has a nasty habit of using others for his own gain—whether king or serving girl. I only regret that in coming to your aid I all but named you a lightskirt before the entire taproom."

Soft color suffused her face. *"Ce n'est rien* . . . It is of no import."

He studied her under a pretense of casualness, but Brittany had the distinct feeling he missed nothing—that he could read her very thoughts. She was suddenly conscious of how she must look . . . and smell. "I had hoped you would guess that he has been diverted permanently, and would grace the taproom with your presence once again. But, alas"—he gestured to the stable and horses—"to the loss of every man with any eye for uncommon beauty, you've deemed it necessary to avoid your usual tasks."

In the light of the lantern Brittany caught a momentary

glimpse of his sharply defined profile. He had beautiful features, with high cheekbones and . . . She immediately chided herself for such madness.

And then his gaze caught hers once more. "If you truly seek my acceptance of your thanks, then you will not be offended if, indeed, I name the steed Gorvenal, for in truth he is newly acquired—a gift from the king—and as yet unused to the name I've given him. His Majesty will be delighted with the choice for he has a streak of the romantic in him, as well as a wonderful sense of humor." He replaced his cavalier's hat and tipped it at her. "Until we meet again."

He walked past the nonplussed Brittany and untied the stallion's reins before leading it out the stable door.

This time Brittany did not fall asleep as soon as she hit the bed. And this time she washed more carefully than she had since beginning her tasks in Willie's place. Why had he come searching for her—if he could be believed—in the past week? And what had the king's sense of humor to do with naming the horse Gorvenal?

Ulterior motives, Geneviève, whispered a voice inside of her. *No doubt he had his own reasons for dissuading Buckingham—like satisfying his own desires . . .*

"Brittany!"

Janie burst into the small room they shared under the eaves, her hazel eyes alight with triumph. "This is the fourth night 'e's been here, and I have discovered some—"

"Who's been here, *chère?*"

"*Him!* The one who got Buckingham foxed after 'e'd persuaded him to leave off mauling you."

Brittany slipped a clean nightgown over her head. "*Oui,* I know."

Janie raised an eyebrow. "Well then, did you know 'is name is Savidge? Sir Tristan Savidge? And that 'e's part—"

"Tristan?"

"Aye."

That explained his remarks about King Charles's sense

of humor. His name was actually Tristan, the champion of her favorite legend, the knight she'd dreamed of as a young girl, still in love with the thought of love itself, until she'd married Raymond and had the eggshell fragility of her dreams crushed by the sledgehammer of her husband's perversion. And she'd actually told him . . . *Dieu!*

She looked at Janie accusingly. "And how did you learn his name, pray?"

Janie glanced down at the worn shoes peeping from beneath her skirts. "Well—well, I asked him."

"You *asked* him? *Mon Dieu,* but you are becoming brazen, Janie. Do you want to end up like the girls at Dagger Tavern—or any number of others—making a living on your back and then dying a slow death from the clap?"

Janie turned scarlet at the uncharacteristically sharp rebuke. "Well, I only asked 'im if 'e was looking for someone. 'Twas a harmless enough question after 'e'd come in here three or four nights an' searched the taproom with those gorgeous eyes of 'is as if 'e were looking for someone special."

At Brittany's continued silence she added, "An' I just said, 'Can I help you find someone, m'lord—?' He just smiled at me—Lord, Britt, I thought I'd die from the beauty of it!—an' said, 'Tristan, little sparrow. Tristan Savidge, at your service, and nay, you cannot help me, but I thank you all the same.' But I watched him, I can tell you that, an' although 'e kept to 'imself most of the time, 'e was watching an' waiting. Every time someone came down the stairs or stepped from the kitchen, he saw . . . Britt?"

"*Oui?*"

"I think 'e was looking fer you."

Brittany walked to the open window, drew in a deep breath, and asked over her shoulder, "How do you know his title?"

"Katie told me. She thinks 'e's a handsome buck, too, and she's been asking questions." Caught up once more

in her exuberance over the handsome visitor, she added,
"Did you know that 'e's part—"

Brittany's voice cut across her friend's words without
ceremony, a warning implicit in the normally lilting tones.
"You must not speak to him again—or encourage any of
the other girls to inquire about him, Janie."

"But—but why, Brittany? What harm can there be in
that?" There was hurt as well as puzzlement in her voice.

Brittany turned from gazing out into the star-strewn
night to regard her friend. "Because if you continue, I
will be forced to leave here. Perhaps even leave London
itself."

Janie heard the edge of panic in her voice and immediately went over to Brittany and embraced her. "Oh, I'm
so sorry, Britt! What a ninny I am. We've been the closest
of friends—you're like a sister to me—and mayhap I've
placed you in jeopardy." She sniffed and held Brittany
away from her. " 'Tis far more serious than just running
away from your husband, isn't it?"

Brittany nodded, preoccupation creasing her brow, and
walked to the washbasin to run a cool, wet cloth over her
flushed face. "He accosted me in the stable this eve and
I fear he's only spared me from Buckingham for his own
purposes." She turned to face the astonished Janie.
"Please, *chère*, no more matchmaking. If he—or anyone
else—should inquire, I am wed to—to a very jealous husband and must work hard to feed my children. Say that I
have no time for dalliances—that I am older than the other
girls here, or have had the pox or the clap—anything that
will serve! Do you understand?"

"I—I promise, Britt. 'Twas just that Sir Tristan seemed
different than those others of Buckingham's ilk."

Brittany's mouth turned hard and the leaf-green eyes
suddenly glittered with past memories better left buried.
"I've run across his kind before, Janie. The sweeter they
are in the beginning, the more evil they become once they
have you where they want you. I saw my father turn into
a different man after years of seeming kindness. And then

my husband—well, his cruelty was there, lurking beneath the surface all along, but by the time I saw him for what he really was, 'twas too late.'' She slipped into bed, turning her back to Janie lest the young girl see the hatred in her eyes. "There may very well be decent men somewhere, but I've no desire to seek them out, and if you are smart, *petite,* you will not be so easily taken in by a sweet smile or a kind word . . . and least of all a noble title.''

Brittany tossed fitfully after Janie had doused the candle and fallen asleep. Everything seemed to be going awry of a sudden. Two years . . . Two years since she'd fled St. Malo, and just when she was beginning to think she was safe at the Hunter's Run, everything had begun to crumble down around her ears.

She'd had a difficult time deciding where to go once in England, but with no letters of recommendation, she would never have found work in a small town or village. Yet although Restoration London was teeming with people from all over—including France—Brittany had decided it was easier to get lost in the masses and find some kind of work without as much to-do about past referrals. Because of her education in a small convent school outside St. Malo, she was qualified to be a governess, but no one would ever entrust their children to a stranger with a nebulous past.

She sat up and swung her feet over the side of the bed. She just could not sleep. Rather than disturbing Janie, she soundlessly moved to the door in her bare feet and made her way down the back stairs and out into the yard. The moon and stars were now hidden by a veil of clouds and the smell of rain was in the air. Strangely drawn toward the stable, Brittany quietly let herself in, praying that Ned, asleep in the loft, wouldn't hear the creak of the heavy oaken door.

As her eyes adjusted to the dimness, some strange force compelled her to return to the empty stall where she'd fondly fed and groomed the great stallion she'd whimsically named Gorvenal. She sat down on a fresh bale of hay, heedless of the prickly straw beneath her feet and under her thin gown.

Why am I here? she wondered to herself. But only the sighing wind coming through the open door, and the soft sounds of the animals stabled around her, answered her.

And then, after what seemed hours, revelation struck. She was lonely. She needed someone to whom to unburden her soul—someone whom she could trust implicitly. Tears slipped down her cheeks in the gloom of the byre as she remembered how much her mother had loved her and how much she had loved and trusted in return. Even her father had held her in his affections for a while—until his beloved Angelique had passed on.

Brittany closed her eyes and rocked back and forth in her remembered sorrow. Rather than turning to his only daughter in his pain, André Renault had blamed Geneviève for her mother's slow decline after Geneviève's birth, and then her eventual death eight years later. He'd forced his daughter to remain in school, seeing her only on rare occasions so as not to alarm the good sisters who ran the school. And when at last Geneviève had come home to stay, her father had managed to find a husband for her—a husband who'd been so eager to wed Geneviève that his family had actually paid André Renault handsomely to "sell" them his dowryless daughter.

Nineteen years old and still innocent, Geneviève had been swept away by Raymond Chauvelin. Here, it seemed, was her Tristan in the flesh—the hero of Angelique's oft-repeated legend come to take her away from her bitter father and keep her safe and protected within the shelter of his love.

Now he was dead, and by her hand. And with him had died her hopes, her dreams, her innocence. Now she had only herself to rely upon. And with the burden of his death on her conscience, Brittany had an almost unbearable load to carry.

Bah! her conscience whispered. *'Twas no less than he*

deserved! You must hold your head high and face down men like Savidge. Think of the name St. Germain—an old and honorable one, older and more revered than Chauvelin could ever be, despite hard times. St. Germain blood runs through your veins, and you must be strong or you will end up like your mother—a dreamer, weak-willed, and easily won over by a man with a handsome face and empty promises, an offer of love everlasting . . .

''But I'm so lonely,'' she whispered into the darkness. ''So lonely.''

''Oh, come along, Brittany,'' urged Katie Dobbs. ''Wouldn't you like to hear the gossip about the new queen from Portugal? I hear she still wears those horrid farthingales that stand out like so''—she made a comical face and gestured outward from her hips as far as her arms would reach—''and is ugly as a bat!''

''Do come with us, Britt,'' implored Janie. ''The court is still at Portsmouth and the 'Change will be almost deserted. You never get out of here. Why not come now?''

''Eh bien,'' Brittany sighed in resignation. Indeed it *was* fairly safe just now, with most of the king's entourage in Portsmouth for the royal wedding. The honeymoon would then take place at Hampton Court, and the locals were betting Charles and Catherine would not return to Whitehall in London until some time in August.

And Brittany was tired of hiding like a frightened rabbit.

The three of them set off on what promised to be a beautiful day once the mists were burned off by the morning sun. Brittany determined to treat herself to a trinket or two at the Royal Exchange, or 'Change, a fashionable lounge and meeting place for ladies and young gallants. She was impressed by the huge quadrangle building near the intersection of Corn Hill and Threadneedle Street. It enclosed an enormous courtyard where merchants talked animatedly of stocks, mortgages, and their sea ventures. The galleries along the sides were divided by pillared arches into numerous, tiny shops attended by pretty young women who called out to the shoppers to hawk their wares. Young gallants flirted openly with the Exchange girls or lounged about, eyeing the ladies and often brazenly calling out to those who were exceptionally fair or even discreetly receptive to their attentions.

The three young women from the Hunter's Run produced vizards to cover their faces in imitation of the gentry. But while Katie had assumed they were wearing masks for fun and to get into the spirit of things, Brittany knew that when Janie had suggested they use them, she'd been thinking of Brittany, and the French girl was grateful.

Soon they were giggling like any young girls with a free morning surrounded by all the things a female, wellborn or not, loved, listening avidly to the gossip from the 'Change girls and other shoppers. Brittany bought a tiny vial of perfume, in spite of her habit of hoarding every last coin she earned for the time when she could leave England for the Colonies—dim as her future might seem at the moment.

"—and my lady Barbary had nerve enough to insist on lying in at Hampton Court itself! During the honeymoon!"

Brittany couldn't help but hear the rest of what the girl was saying to Janie and Katie, their mouths agape at this bit of news. "Of course everyone knows 'tis the king's brat she'll bear, but the nerve of that woman!"

Barbara Palmer, newly titled countess of Castlemaine, was a favorite subject of gossip, and much speculation had been aroused concerning how the king would handle his beautiful, ebullient, and often uncontrollable mistress after his marriage.

"The queen will never even notice 'er, no doubt, so caught up is she in 'er devotions. Did ye know she was raised in a convent and is already three and twenty?"

Brittany hid a smile as she discovered that she had at least one thing in common with the new queen. To Janie and Katie, neither yet a score of years old, three and twenty must, indeed, seem ancient.

"But I've heard she is very petite, with large brown eyes and lovely dark hair, that she looks not a day over eighteen."

All three girls swung their heads toward the up-till-now silent Brittany, surprise written across their youthful countenances. "Indeed?" replied the girl selling perfumes. "Well, she'd have to be Venus 'erself to take Castlemaine's place in the king's affections."

Brittany moved on, more interested in the colorful display of ribbons and hair bodkins than the gossip about Catherine. In her efforts to better see the array of goods spread before her, she removed her vizard and immediately received a whistle of appreciation from one of the young bucks not sufficiently wealthy or in enough favor to have accompanied the court to Portsmouth.

Ignoring the unwelcome attention, Brittany nonetheless replaced the mask to discourage any more such incidents. But when she couldn't decide between a red velvet or a green satin ribbon, a voice behind her suggested, "The green satin matches your eyes, mistress."

She spun around so quickly, the vizard went flying. "Well, then, ye can buy the lady both—and several to spare," added the girl behind the counter, quick to pick up on a prospective sale.

Embarrassed by her overreaction to a man's voice, Brittany bent to retrieve the mask, her cheeks pink. But a large, tanned hand brushed hers as the owner of the voice gained hold of the object first. Even as she raised her eyes, she knew whose gaze she would encounter, and as green eyes met blue, as bronzed skin touched peach, an odd flicker of some heretofore unknown emotion went streaking through her, leaving her unsettled and shaken in its wake.

"Thank you, sir . . ." She could not say his name.

Tristan's mind was on other things, and he failed to relinquish his hold upon the vizard, thus forcing Brittany to maintain contact with his hand until she realized, belatedly, that he had no immediate intention of letting go.

"I hail from the Colonies, mistress, and I cannot help but notice that your eyes are the most beautiful hue—the shade of a lush Virginia meadow in spring."

If Brittany had had any inkling of how very much he was reminded at that moment of the place he loved most in the world, she might have been flattered; but she only knew that her hand had become entrapped under his in her efforts to retrieve the vizard.

"My hand, good sir," she murmured. "My . . ."

Recovering himself, Tristan gave her a rueful smile. "I beg your pardon, mistress—?"

Her gaze met his again. There was, it seemed, no way out but to tell him. "Brittany."

So that explained the melodic French accent, he thought. "You are French, then? From Bretagne?"

How much more would he want to know? Brittany wondered with growing uneasiness. And what was he doing here now?

"She's married, Sir Tristan," broke in Janie as she came up behind them. A gleam of fire shone in her eyes as she came to her friend's defense. "And a hulking, jealous lout 'e is, I can tell you! If 'e catches any man even looking cross-eyed at 'er, he'll kill 'im! And Brittany, too! Then who'll tend to 'er five little ones?"

Tristan took one look at the tiny girl who'd served him many times at the Hunter's Run, her fists doubled at her sides, and a corner of his mouth quirked with good humor. He checked his urge to laugh, however, in light of what he'd surmised by the lovely Brittany's behavior since Villiers's assault, and assumed an expression of sobriety. "I have no intention of causing trouble between the lady and her husband. I merely intended to buy her a few ribbons in payment for the excellent care she gave Gor— er, my horse while he was stabled at the Hunter's Run." He turned to the 'Change girl and paid for the ribbons Brittany had been deciding upon, and several more as well. When he swung around and presented them to Brittany with her mask, the two young women had been joined by Katie, the latter's eyes upon him in open admiration.

"Oh, but I couldn't," Brittany protested softly.

"I will not take no for an answer, as they are well earned. May I escort you ladies anywhere?" he inquired politely, his eyes remaining on Brittany.

"Why, yes," began Katie, only to be cut off by Janie.

"Thank you, no, Sir Tristan. We 'ave more shopping to do here and then . . . and then we are to meet Brittany's husband outside the 'Change."

With a straight face, Tristan nodded in understanding, and Brittany guessed instantly that he wasn't taken in by Janie's fabrications. He stood where he was, seemingly reluctant to part company. At Janie's frown and Brittany's obvious discomfiture, he nodded politely at Katie and, with one last look at Brittany, bowed and returned with long, lithe strides to a small group of men deep in discussion in the center of the courtyard.

"If I were you, I wouldn't have nothin' to do with Sir Tristan Savidge," warned one of the 'Change girls behind them. "He may be a handsome devil, but did ye know 'e's part Indian?"

Janie's eyes went to Brittany in anticipation of her reaction.

"Indian?" echoed Katie in surprise. "What do you mean?"

"Indian—as in savage. You know, one of them redmen from the Colonies."

Brittany felt suddenly queasy at the word *savage,* and the picture of an Indian with feathers and paint-smeared face flashed before her, bringing to mind Tristan Savidge's high cheekbones and lightly bronzed skin.

"But 'is grandmother was some relative of that Indian princess what married John Rolfe—Pocy, er . . ."

"Pocahontas."

The girl looked at Brittany suspiciously, obviously wondering how she knew the answer so readily, then continued. "But at least she was a princess, not just a mere commoner, or whatever they call 'em."

Katie drew nearer, lowering her voice. "But what of his grandfather? Who was he?"

The girl scratched her head and screwed up her eyes. "Seems to me 'e was some lord—an earl or somethin'."

"Gemini, but it sounds farfetched to *me*," sniffed Janie disdainfully, for Brittany's sake. "You probably heard wrong or just made up the tale."

"I did not!"

"Well *I* think 'tis a most romantic story," Katie sighed wistfully. "The grandson of an Indian princess's kin and an English earl."

But Brittany was remembering what she'd learned at the convent school of St. Monique. As well respected as were those at the top of the colonial Indian hierarchy, even in England, the nuns at St. Monique had been horrified at John Rolfe's marriage to a heathen savage.

A frisson of terror rippled through Brittany—not because she was particularly prejudiced, but rather because the word *Indian* conjured up visions of the horrible Jamestown massacres.

And Tristan Savidge was an Indian.

Chapter 3

Tristan was weary of the endless round of balls and banquets, cockfights and picnics, rides on the canal in the lavishly appointed royal barges, plays performed by London actors . . .

He had been spared several weeks of the endless-seeming festivities, first by an unexpected message from his boyhood friend and business partner, privateer ship owner and captain Matthew Stark. This had brought him most eagerly to London in June and to the Royal Exchange the day he'd come across Brittany. Then in July, much to his surprise, he was summoned to Surrey by his ailing grandsire, Richard Carlisle, the earl of Weyrith.

In spite of the earl's refusal to publicly acknowledge his son Richard by Running Deer, Tristan's grandmother, Tristan could not in good conscience return the snub and, glad of any excuse to escape the neverending revelry at Hampton Court, he rode to confront his paternal grandfather with a mixture of wry curiosity and wariness. What could the old earl possibly want after almost fifty years of silence? Tristan knew that in later years Carlisle had made overtures in the form of funds to his half-breed son, but Richard Savidge would have nothing to do with the earl's belated attempts to salve his conscience.

As Tristan approached Surrey, he wondered if he were doing the right thing—acknowledging a man who'd refused to recognize or claim his natural son. Not one to hold a grudge, or make hasty judgments—especially since it was more his father who was the injured party than himself—Tristan pushed aside his doubts with a mental shrug and tried to prepare himself for the coming meeting.

The huge, sprawling Jacobean structure that served as the earl's home was situated on a vast tract of land. Carlisle Hall, as the earl had called it in the brief missive to his grandson, was as grand a manor as could have been expected for an earl. Many peers of the realm had lost everything during the civil wars, especially if they'd been staunch Royalists. Although in Tristan's mind Richard Carlisle, earl of Weyrith, might be many things, he was first and foremost a Royalist, and Charles had been attempting to restore most of the earl's lost assets. That Carlisle Hall itself had been returned to the earl said much about the esteem in which Richard Carlisle was held by Charles Stuart.

The grounds needed tending, but the magnificent stone edifice appeared unscathed by the struggles between Roundhead and Royalist. Myriad square-paned windows reflected the sun's rays beneath the azure sky, the fanciful cupolas and graceful spires bringing to mind a sense of the theatric in an age of plays and masques.

Tristan squinted against the brightness and, against his will, was impressed.

He was met by a stableboy, and as Gorvenal was led away, he strode up to the great door and raised the brass knocker. It barely touched the oak-paneled portal before the door swung open to reveal a gnarled old butler standing at attention before him.

"Sir Tristan Savidge?"

Wondering how the servant had known with such confidence that he was, indeed, Savidge, Tristan nodded slightly and imitated the old man's formality with a practiced ease acquired after almost half a score of years in Charles Stuart's service.

"A bit of refreshment, sir, before you see his lordship?" the butler inquired in a voice that reminded Tristan of the rattle of dry leaves in a brisk wind.

"Thank you, no." He'd spent the night at a nearby inn rather than taking advantage of the earl's hospitality—especially in the face of such uncertainty—and it would be just as well to get this interview over with as quickly as possible.

The butler led him up a winding staircase with a carved oaken balustrade and down a wide corridor, passing numerous chamber doors. And then, after a brief announcement by the butler in his thready voice, Tristan found himself alone with the earl of Weyrith. The bedroom was dim, and his eyes narrowed to adjust and focus on the figure that seemed to be engulfed by the huge, eight-foot-high, four-postered bed.

"Well, boy, open them drapes and let in some sunlight," was the first command to leave the old earl's lips. "Let me get a look at you."

Tristan did as he was bid and turned back toward the bed.

"Now come closer . . . Ah, there!"

Richard Carlisle pushed himself up against the pillows. When Tristan made to help him, he barked, "I'm not that helpless yet, young pup! 'Tis just one of my bad spells, is all."

Deep blue eyes met faded blue and noted the keen intelligence that still shone in the latter. "Why have you summoned me here, your lordship?"

"And after all these years—civil wars aside—when I've never even seen your father? 'Tis a fair enough question, I'll grant you." He patted the edge of the mattress beside him with a gnarled, blue-veined hand. "Sit and let me see if you're a Carlisle or nay."

After a brief hesitation Tristan sat, if for no other reason than to humor the old man, for whom he was beginning to feel the stirrings of a grudging respect.

The earl studied the younger man for a few moments. "Your looks are a combination of myself and your grandmother Running Deer—the best of both. Those eyes—just like mine when I was young. The color of lapis lazuli, my

father used to call 'em.'' He paused and settled himself
more comfortably against the pillows. "Carlisle eyes—a
very unusual blue. Did you know the Egyptians used them
stones for their jewelry? 'Sdeath, but how I'm rambling
on—just like a dying old dotard.'' He narrowed his gaze
shrewdly. "And you've the patience of few, by God. 'Tis
the Indian blood. You've more patience than your fool half
cousin John ever shall—I can see that just within the few
moments since you've been here.''

Tristan couldn't help but smile. "So you think to win
me over with compliments? Be warned—the part of me
that is Powhatan is very stubborn.''

Carlisle nodded. "I never meant to get your grandmother with child, ye know,'' he admitted unexpectedly.
"When Rolfe presented his Pocahontas at court, I was
there. But Running Deer had her own kind of dignity—as
if she were looking us over and not the other way around.''
He paused, his eyes leaving Tristan's face, to gaze toward
the opposite wall, looking back into the past. "And, of
course, she was the most magnificent woman I'd ever
seen—Indian or no.''

"So you set out to seduce her.''

The faded eyes flicked back to Tristan. "Well, you im-
pudent brat, I cut a fine figure back then myself! It was
more mutual than you'd imagine.'' He closed his eyes momentarily, whether in regret or weariness Tristan couldn't
discern. " 'Tis too late to correct past errors, and I regret
never having sent for my namesake—my son. Any funds
I sent to the Colonies were always returned. And then
Richard made it obvious, you see, that he had no use for
me—he took his wife's name and forsook a fine and ancient family like the Carlisles . . .''

Tristan glanced out the window at the glorious, sun-
filled day before he answered. "With all due respect, your
lordship—''

"Grandfather.''

Slightly taken aback, Tristan met Weyrith's gaze. "With

all due respect, *he* was the one forsaken and there is no way around it.''

"Touché," said the earl with a sigh. I s'pose you've every right to see it that way.'' He cleared his throat in the awkward pause. ''I don't intend to try and insinuate myself into your—or your father's—good graces, boy, but I am leaving a decent amount of money to you after I'm gone . . .''

Tristan stood abruptly and stared down at his grandfather, a stony look stamped across the sculpted features. ''I want nothing from you.''

The earl held up a hand placatingly. ''I knew I'd get no cooperation from you, but did it ever occur to you that if anything happens to John, my legal grandson—if he should follow in his wayward father's footsteps and get himself killed in the service of anti-Royalists or some other such treasonous nonsense—you would be the only surviving heir to the title?''

Tristan went over to the window and stared out over the grounds, blind to the riot of summer flowers blooming in less than perfect array. ''My father would be your heir in that case.''

''And he will have naught to do with me or England. He was quick enough to relinquish his rightful surname.''

Tristan spun around, exhibiting the first real anger since he'd walked into the room. ''He had *no* surname.''

The earl of Weyrith sank wearily against the pillows and did not see the quick flash of concern appear briefly in his grandson's eyes. ''I did not think this would be easy, but I am prepared to do anything—*anything*—to preserve the Carlisle heritage.''

Tristan's features twisted with irony. ''You are prepared to have a 'breed' carry on in the event of John's untimely death, if he should produce no heirs? Surely you cannot wish to taint the pure blue blood of the Carlisles?'' He could not hide the note of sarcasm that had crept into his voice.

But the earl was adamant, a fist clenched upon the sheet.

"The Carlisles need new blood—be it Indian or otherwise. Surely *you* can see that simply by the fact that I had only one son by my late, lawful wife, and *his* son has had no issue thus far. And"—he raised a thick gray brow with his final thrust—"the Carlisle blood is as mixed as the king's. That's what makes a line thrive—continue to produce healthy, virile heirs! How many by-blows have *you* sired, grandson?"

The expression in Tristan's eyes gave force to his clipped words. "None. I would never subject a child—or its mother—to that kind of ridicule. Now, if you will excuse me, your—"

"I will not excuse you! Have you met your half cousin John yet?"

"Briefly. We try to avoid each other whenever he is at court."

Carlisle nodded. "Then you've undoubtedly seen that he's not fit to be successor to the earldom—to any title of consequence."

Tristan shrugged. "That is not for me to say."

The earl ignored his words. "You will remain here the night and on the morrow we will resume our discussion. After you've had a night to sleep on it, I'm certain you will be more reasonable and swallow some of that damnable pride of yours."

Tristan opened his mouth to protest, but the sudden grayish cast to the old man's face gave him pause. What harm could one night do? No one could force him to take on any title he didn't wish to accept—not even the earl of Weyrith. And this would only be in the event of John Carlisle's early death, rather unlikely.

He stepped closer to the bed, wondering if his grandfather could turn pale at will. He wouldn't put it past the wily old devil. "Very well. I will remain at Carlisle Hall the night." He turned and moved toward the door, swearing to himself that the dimmed eyes had lit up with triumph. "But no matter the outcome of tomorrow's talk—no matter what you write in your will—no one can force a man to accept aught. Not lands, not wealth, not a title. Not even you, *Grandfather.*''

With that parting shot, he quit the room.

Brittany watched the eagerly awaited return of King Charles with his new bride from her open dormer window. Against her will she'd been drawn to witness the sight of thousands of spectators packed along the riverbanks, of hundreds of boats and smaller barges surrounding the canopied barge carrying Charles and Catherine. Brittany knew in her heart of hearts that what she really sought was a glimpse of Tristan Savidge, despite the contradictory emotions he had aroused in their last two encounters. Yet it was all but impossible to discern the king and queen, so crowded with people were the myriad craft moving down the Thames on this August day. Even the water itself was completely covered, so thick with traffic was the river. Garlands of flowers trailed in the water, banners snapped in the wind, bells pealed from every bell tower in joyous acclamation.

Brittany was only just able to make out the landing at Whitehall Bridge. The thunder of cannon from either side of the river at that point announced the royal couple's arrival.

With a shake of her head, as if to scatter her errant thoughts, the foolish imaginings, Brittany pulled away from the window. There was much to do in preparation for this eve. Those who could not join the revelry at Whitehall would pack the taverns and inns around the city in celebration of the king's arrival and, it was to be hoped, the ultimate conception of an heir by his new queen.

Caught up in the bustling arrangements for the anticipated festivities only hours away, Brittany found that time flew, and before she knew it, the taproom was filled to bursting with laughing, shouting, and increasingly boisterous patrons, all seizing this special opportunity to enjoy themselves to the utmost.

Too busy serving and dodging wandering hands and

leering come-hither looks, cleaning and clearing up to make room for new customers and keep some semblance of order at the tables of those who had no intention of leaving until the inn closed its doors, Brittany never noticed the duke of Buckingham enter and belligerently commandeer a table near one of the front windows.

"Uds lud! Buckingham is here!" Janie exclaimed to her friend in dismay and inclined her head toward the duke and several companions.

A knot of anxiety instantly formed in the pit of Brittany's stomach as she glanced in the direction Janie indicated. Indeed, it was Villiers himself, bewigged and beribboned in the latest French fashion. From the tips of his high-heeled leather shoes to the top of his fair head, he was the epitome of wealth, urbane sophistication, and arrogance, and Brittany vowed she'd as soon approach the edge of a yawning chasm of fire and brimstone as go near him or his companions.

"I'll handle 'im, Britt," the dark-haired girl declared with unaccustomed grimness. "You stay as far away as you can. Let the two extra wenches Dobbs called in for the night take up where you left off. I'll tell 'em to help me serve that section." And she disappeared into the crowd.

As she began working her way toward the rear of the tavern, Brittany realized with an uncomfortable jolt that she was allowing a girl seven years her junior to fend off the man she perceived to be her enemy. Coward! she thought, and determined in that moment to act as if nothing were amiss. If her help was needed toward the front, she would not hide in the shadows like a dog with its tail between its legs.

An hour or so later, a brawl began in the vicinity where Janie was working. More concerned about the young girl than a face-to-face encounter with the duke, Brittany pushed her way through the tipsy, cheering onlookers just in time to see Janie being shoved roughly aside by one of the men involved in the altercation. As she lost her footing on the slick, ale-soaked floor, Janie's feet shot out from under her and her head hit the corner of a bench as she went down.

Brittany gained her friend's side just as several burly men in Dobbs's employ began to haul the miscreants apart. Brittany gingerly felt the back of Janie's head before lifting it into her lap. Her fingers came away from a sizable knot with blood smeared over them. "Oh, Janie!" she cried softly and, cradling the unconscious girl in her arms, she looked up in search of help . . . and encountered the pale, predatory stare of George Villiers.

"Here—let me, mistress." A man she'd never seen before blocked her brief, unnerving glimpse of Buckingham before scooping the inert Janie into his arms.

"Merci bien, monsieur," she gratefully acknowledged, reverting to her native French in her relief. "Follow me, *s'il vous plaît."*

Kind hazel eyes met hers reassuringly and as the man stood, Brittany did likewise and turned to forge a path through the crowd.

Once in the attic room she and Janie shared, Brittany motioned to Janie's bed and the stranger gently laid the girl down. "Matthew Stark, at your service, mistress," he introduced himself, and then his gaze went to Janie. "I would guess she's only been knocked out. If you see to her head, she should be fine aside from a headache in the morning." He smiled and Brittany instantly liked him—something almost unheard of since her marriage to Raymond Chauvelin. "I regret that I couldn't have prevented the accident," he continued, "but I'd only just entered the taproom in search of a friend and caught the tail end of the scuffle."

She nodded and immediately began tending to Janie.

"Is there aught I can do?" he asked.

"Merci, mais non," she answered, and turned her full attention to Janie.

After he'd gone, she cleaned the laceration as best she could, bloodying her white shift and darker laced bodice in the process. As she worked quickly and silently, her thoughts returned to Buckingham and the malevolent look in his eyes. Surely he'd had something to do with the brawl. It would have been an easy thing to stir up any of the half-fuddled men around him—through sly innuendos or down-right insults. Because he was a duke, no commoner would dare raise a hand to him, and the more likely result would be one man taking out his anger and frustration on another scapegoat.

And from what Brittany knew of him, Buckingham was shrewd, calculating. He'd undoubtedly guessed that Janie was close to Brittany—if for no other reason than the way she'd tried to interfere that first night. Was he deliberately trying to get to Brittany through Janie?

After seeing that Janie was as comfortable as possible, Brittany washed her hands and began to change her shift. She would be missed down in the taproom and, certain that Maude would be up to see how Janie fared, she tidied up quickly. Growing feelings of guilt and anger began to assail her. If she had stayed where she was, despite her fear of Buckingham, Janie wouldn't have been hurt—of this she was almost certain. *"Eh bien,* I will go back and take her place,'' she decided aloud. After checking the cool, wet cloth she'd placed over Janie's forehead, she turned to leave.

And there, looming ominously in the doorway, stood George Villiers, second duke of Buckingham.

"So, Pale Wolf, you think to slip away into the night like one of your wraithlike ancestors.''

The mirth in Charles's voice was unmistakable, and as Tristan swung around to face the monarch, an answering quirk of amusement played about the corners of his mouth. "Indeed not, majesty. With all the noise coming from within, a regiment of Roundheads could pass through these gardens unnoticed.''

"Your majesty?'' called a husky feminine voice.

"Quickly—here . . .'' Charles guided Tristan by the elbow to a place deep within the shadows. Only the silvery disk of the moon and a liberal sprinkling of frosty white stars betrayed their position among the tall hedges.

"Are you still playing hide-and-seek with Barbara Palmer, majesty?"

Charles frowned, obviously more than a little troubled—something he could not hide from his close friend. "A king ought not to have to skulk behind the shrubbery for fear of offending his wife."

"Then mayhap the king should seek his pleasure only in his wife's bed."

Only Tristan would have dared make such an observation. Knowing the colonist was usually right, Charles answered, "They are as different as day and night, and I've discovered Catherine can never see to my needs in the same way as Barbara."

They moved through the night until Charles led the way safely back to one of the paths. "Why did you seek me out, sire?"

"I've wondered why you've stayed away these past weeks. Can it be that you've at last made your peace with Weyrith?"

Tristan remained silent for long moments, choosing his words. "I found myself actually trying to understand his position all these years—although I could never have treated my natural son as he did his. But," he added softly, "neither have I ever been an earl."

Charles nodded in silent accord. "And so, what has he asked of you? John Carlisle is his rightful heir."

"After my father, if you wish to be scrupulously legal. A son—even a bastard—is more directly in line than a grandson."

"Only if acknowledged. And so, let me guess . . . You have agreed to accept the title in the case of John's early demise?"

"Only in that instance—and if he does not produce an heir of his own."

"Then you would remain in England?" There was a

guarded yet expectant note in the king's voice, for he had hoped to persuade Tristan to remain in England indefinitely and had hesitated mentioning it for fear of the Virginian's answer.

Tristan looked askance at his king, gauging Charles's reaction to his next words. "There will come a time, your majesty, when only a royal command will prevent me from leaving these fair shores."

"Then I hope that time is in the distant future, for I would be as reluctant to see you go as to give such a command." He abruptly changed the subject. "Is your friend Stark still in London?"

"Aye," Tristan answered as they headed back to the banquet hall. "I was to meet him at the Hunter's Run this eve."

Charles's full, sensual mouth hardened. "Hunter's Run? I could have sworn I heard Buckingham say earlier he was headed that way with Sedley and Sackville. You may want to avoid that particular inn tonight, for I believe George is still smarting from the wager incident back in May."

The names of Sedley and Sackville, two of London's most notorious rakes, barely registered in Tristan's mind in the wake of the king's mention of Buckingham . . . *Buckingham!* "Are you quite certain he said Hunter's Run?" Tristan felt the beginnings of a cold fury wash over him at the man's audacity.

"Indeed. But have a care, Savidge, for—"

"Your majesty?" came that throaty, feminine voice again. The countess of Castlemaine.

"I bid you good night, sire," Tristan said softly and, disinclined to encounter another audacious—and persistent—Villiers relation, he drew back from the light streaming out of the tall windows and open doorway, where Barbara stood silhouetted, and slipped away.

"So Savidge's doxy has a heart after all—especially when it comes to a fellow whore."

The deceptively silken tone of his voice, the opaque

blue eyes, the careless-seeming yet vicious verbal attack—
all combined with staggering force to render Brittany incapable of moving, a torrent of unwelcome emotions and
memories sweeping over her.

It was Raymond Chauvelin all over again, come back
from the dead to take the form of the duke of Buckingham.

He stepped into the room and closed the door behind
him with a soft *click*. To the girl rooted to the spot before
him, it sounded like a heavy stone portal sealing the vault
of a tomb.

"What—what do you want?" she whispered, finally
finding her tongue.

He smiled with deadly benevolence. "What do I want?
Why, I would sample that which our friend Savidge values
enough to keep from the king himself."

"I—I am no whore! If I give my favors to a man, 'tis
of my own free will and for no other reason!"

He was before her now, and he reached out to touch the
peach-tinted skin above her bodice, making her flesh crawl
even as she forced herself to remain unmoving. "You
would willingly lie with a mere knight when you could
have a duke, a king?" His finger dipped lower, smoothing
over the gentle upper swell of one firm breast. "What is
it about that breed that could possibly keep you so
staunchly loyal?"

Inadvertently Brittany verbalized the first thought that
came into her mind. "He prefers women."

The room exploded as the sharp crack of his open palm
across her cheek sent Brittany staggering backward until
she came up against the window ledge. *"That* is for the
insult to the king," he said calmly, "but since your observation concerning *my* tastes was so perceptive, you shall
be rewarded accordingly."

Brittany shook her head in genuine terror, causing the
world to tilt crazily in the aftershock of the stunning blow.
But the panic in her eyes only spurred him on, whetting
his appetite. "This night you shall learn what love is like

between men—that true and perfect union practiced by the ancients.''

Brittany's glance flicked to the bed where Janie lay, but there was no movement to indicate the girl had regained consciousness. She opened her mouth to scream, knowing in advance that the chance was all but nonexistent that anyone in the taproom would hear her. But Buckingham was quicker. His hand closed over her mouth before she could utter a sound, and he brought her up against his chest, crushing her in a bruising embrace. ''But first, a bit of a lesson for foiling me this past spring and making me look the fool before Charles.'' His mouth slammed against hers with such force that Brittany tasted blood on her lips.

One arm clamped around her upper torso, pinning her against his tall, powerful frame like a trapped butterfly. The other roamed under her skirts, pinching and plundering tender areas until Brittany thought she would swoon from the humiliation—or the pain of his savage, unnatural travesty of a kiss. Her lungs labored to draw in air as he all but sucked the breath from her body, his large face and nose pressing against her nostrils to ensure her capitulation. The world began to recede, and the ragged, stygian edges of oblivion fluttered about the periphery of her mind, dimming her awareness.

Then, miraculously, the pressure around her torso, against her nose and mouth, was gone. But it was too late. Brittany felt herself falling in slow motion, sinking into the soundless abyss that loomed before her, while eyes of deepest sapphire bored into hers, reaching out and calling to her, beckoning her back from the precipice of blissful unconsciousness.

Non! her recalcitrant will screamed. *Laissez-moi!* Let me be!

Then there was nothing.

Chapter 4

Tristan slipped silently through the partially opened door and froze at the sight before him. Brittany was caught in the rough and crushing embrace of George Villiers. She was struggling futilely against his bruising strength, and it took only a moment for Tristan to realize that her efforts to free herself were growing more feeble. She was losing consciousness.

Outrage surged through him.

He motioned to Matt to stay back and slipped a dagger from his waistband. With the quiet stealth he'd learned from the Powhatan, he approached Buckingham from behind and raised his arm to strike.

As the hilt of the weapon connected with the duke's skull, Buckingham's grip on Brittany immediately loosened and, without support, her knees began to buckle.

Sidestepping Buckingham as he crumpled into a heap, Tristan deftly caught her just before she hit the floor and swung her clear of her foiled attacker.

"Well done," Matt said softly from behind him.

Tristan critically examined the face of the woman he held in his arms, noting the darkening bruise across her right cheek. The sight of it added to the flame of his fury at Buckingham, and his mouth tightened.

Behind him, Matthew Stark was swiftly yet gently tying Janie's hands behind her back. "We can't let her take the blame. God only knows what he'd do to her." He deftly gagged the unconscious girl, avoiding the injury at the

51

back of her head, and turned toward Tristan. Stark gazed for a moment at Brittany cradled securely in his friend's arms, her loose honey-brown hair obscuring part of her face. Not so much, however, to hide the fact that she was reason enough for any man to dare raise a hand against the duke of Buckingham. "He'll come after you, you know."

Tristan strode toward the door. "Then let him come."

Stark shook his head. "I can see I'll have to be sensible enough for both of us. We'd better use the back door downstairs. I'll get you a hackney and follow with the horses—"

A muffled cry interrupted his next words. Both men looked up to see Maude Dobbs standing on the landing at the top of the stairway, her hand over her mouth.

There was a moment of tense silence before Matt said quietly, "I'll take care of her. Just get out of the inn and I'll meet you in the yard."

Tristan nodded and moved past Maude with his precious burden. The last thing he heard was the low, urgent tone of Stark's voice and the metallic *clink* of coins being exchanged.

He reached the bottom of the stairs and paused, listening. There was no time to be lost by waiting for Matt in the yard behind the inn—time needed to get Brittany away from Buckingham and to safety. Buckingham be damned, he decided suddenly. He'd walk straight through the taproom and hire a hackney. Let them all think and say what they would. He would deal with Villiers in his own good time and in his own way.

Tristan strode swiftly through the noisy taproom, Brittany's hair flowing over his upper arm like an amber curtain, an impressive and curious sight to those who cared to take notice—although it was not an uncommon occurrence for a man to carry off a tavern wench in the midst of such revelry. Any who had the presence of mind to consider interfering need take only one look at the closed, forbidding expression on Tristan's face—the unflinching determination in his long, effortless strides—to have second thoughts.

Once outside the Hunter's Run, Tristan found luck was with him. As if conjured up, a coach for hire stood before the entrance. "I'll triple your fare if you take me to Chelsea," Tristan said in a low voice to the man who sprang down from the driver's seat and opened the door for him. "And at top speed."

"Agreed, m'lord," answered the man with a knowing grin. "Chelsea it is."

As he settled himself back against the squabs, Tristan shifted Brittany more comfortably. Once he got to Chelsea, he hoped Matt would catch up with him with Gorvenal, for his home away from London was midway between Chelsea and Brompton, with nary a path wide enough for a coach and four.

Brittany stirred in his arms as they hit a particularly nasty rut, and Tristan studied her pale face by the vague light shining into the coach as they passed through the west end of London. Lowered lids and lush, long lashes hid the eyes that had haunted him relentlessly. The high cheekbones proclaimed aristocratic blood somewhere in her past, and the slim, retroussé nose with delicately flaring nostrils hinted at the quiet courage he'd only glimpsed that first night she'd dared to defy Buckingham. And the mouth . . . He glanced away then, lest he dwell upon the beautifully molded, provocative mouth—despite the slight swelling of the lower lip—and be forced to kiss her as he'd longed to do for the last several months.

Soon, however, his gaze was drawn downward again, a slight frown pulling his dark brows together. What was she hiding from at the Hunter's Run? The bawdy surroundings in which he'd first found her had only emphasized her rare and delicate beauty, an intelligence and nobility of character—and the obvious fact that she was hiding from something or someone.

"And now, indeed, you do well to hide," he murmured to the sleeping young woman.

His gaze left the pure oval of her face and returned to the darkness of the night as London went rushing by. Aye, he mused, now she had reason to hide from yet another threat—Buckingham. Tristan's lips compressed and anger pulled his thick, jet brows together. His grip on Brittany tightened almost imperceptibly and she stirred, but he was so deep in thought, his ire mounting with every turn of the wheels of the coach, that his gaze remained fixed unseeingly out the window. Buckingham's wrath when he realized who had taken the girl from beneath his nose would be the least of Tristan's concerns. Rather, how could he keep the duke from searching for her—from finding her at Wildwood and whisking her away? Even, perhaps, with the king's writ in hand?

He ruminated silently for long moments, ideas flitting through his mind only to be discarded just as swiftly as they took shape. And it was while these ominous thoughts occupied his attention, while his expression was as black as the night sky above, that Brittany awoke.

Tristan's regard returned to her face and met disoriented green eyes. Slowly the fog dissipated and Brittany's eyes widened as comprehension began to dawn. She caught the fierce look on his features before he could smooth his expression back to normal. Dismay and then fear surged through her. *Dieu au ciel,* she thought in growing panic. Buckingham was bad enough, but to be . . .

"How do you feel?" he asked, his look now one of concern.

Brittany ignored his query and struggled to free herself from his embrace.

"Ah, ah, ah . . . not so fast, mistress. You have a nasty bruise on your cheek and your lip is swollen. My guess is that your head is already throbbing, and any quick or unnecessary movements will only increase your headache."

"Then you consider my desire to escape your—your unwanted attentions unnecessary?" Her accent was strikingly melodic, heavy in her agitation. "If so, then you are no better than Buckingham."

He allowed her to sit up, and Brittany pushed away from him as if he were a viper, positioning herself rigidly on the seat across from him, her locked arms bracing her body on either side. He was right, she acknowledged silently, in guessing at the ache in her head, which was augmented by her movements. And her vision was hazy one moment, as if looking through a veil, and clear the next. But she admitted nothing, asking instead, "By what authority do you abduct me from my home and carry me off like some trophy?"

He smiled faintly in the muted light, his face cast in a crazily dancing pattern of light and shadow as the lantern swung gently with the movement of the coach. "I was under the impression that I'd rescued you, Mistress Brittany, rather than abducted you." The smile faded. "Do you not remember what happened at the inn?"

She remembered all too well, and as images of Buckingham's marauding hands invaded her memory, she closed her eyes and bit down upon her tender lip, heedless of the pain. Drawing in a steadying breath, she met his gaze head-on. "*Au contraire*. This amounts to kidnapping, despite your self-serving eloquence to convince me otherwise. You *must* take me back."

In an effort to get hold of herself by briefly turning her attention elsewhere, she pushed back a heavy hank of honey-hued hair and then moved to straighten her bodice. As she looked down, she realized to her mortification that the lacings that normally closed the garment over her breasts were torn, and the vee of her shift directly above the top of the bodice gaped open, the fastening evidently lost in her struggle with the duke. Her fingers moved to pull the material together, then stilled. It was useless, she knew. With a dignified straightening of her shoulders, she leveled her gaze at Tristan once more, in spite of her flaming cheeks, refusing to act the cowed wench before him. "I am grateful for your rescue, Sir Tristan, but that you are taking me away against my will must surely be apparent to you. The fact that the coach is moving as if the hounds of hell were at our heels does nothing to lessen that impression.'' She paused, warily watching him pull up one knee as he settled himself more comfortably in the corner diagonally from her.

''Surely you don't believe I wish to encounter your, ah, 'hulking jealous lout' of a husband?''

Brittany, however, could summon no answering amusement to match that which shone in his very blue eyes. ''If you don't stop this coach immediately and let me out, I swear I shall jump without benefit of your permission.'' Her voice rose slightly and her hand went to the handle of the door.

In a trice he slid to her side of the coach and entrapped her hand beneath his. ''Don't be a fool, Britanny. Surely you can't wish to return to the Hunter's Run to be mauled again—and worse—by Buckingham. I intend you no harm, believe me. I only thought to get you out of London and away from the duke . . . perhaps find you work elsewhere, where you'll be safe from his brutal attentions.''

As Tristan leaned toward her in the narrow confines of the hackney, his eyes fastened intently on her face, his breath caressing her cheek, Brittany felt a faint stirring of some inexplicable and alien feeling deep within her, some flicker of life in the long-banked embers of her emotions. She stared at him for a suspended moment, caught off-guard by the unfamiliar feeling, spellbound by his compelling gaze.

His hand felt warm and firm over hers, and for one fleeting moment she felt oddly, unexpectedly, secure . . . until her eyes dropped to the same hand causing such foreign sensations to go streaking up her arm. The sight of his fingers securely over hers triggered a distasteful memory, a recollection of Raymond Chauvelin's hand clamped over hers as she'd desperately reached for the latch on the door to escape his brutality. His fingers had been warm and firm also, but the firmness had increased steadily with her refusal to withdraw her hand from the latch, until she'd cried out in pain as the fragile bones and knuckles had begun to crack under the pressure.

She jerked her hand from beneath Tristan's with such force and strength that his eyes narrowed in bemusement. "Are you so repelled by my touch, Brittany?"

She clutched her hand to her abdomen and cried, "Set me free! *Laissez-moi—*"

"Chelsea, m'lord!" shouted the coachman, and the vehicle slowed, then came to a jolting halt.

Brittany stared at the man across from her, her near-hysterical demands silenced by the unexpected pronouncement. "I will not go with you, do you hear? I'll make a scene—"

"Aye, and I'll act the wounded husband bringing home my prodigal wife from a tryst with her lover in London."

Brittany opened her mouth in astonishment, but no words emerged. Until now, he'd not threatened her. She glanced over as the coachman pulled open the door and she saw that they were at another inn, with light beaconing from inside the taproom and sleeping rooms. A stableboy ran toward the coach, holding aloft a bobbing lantern.

"Or I can take you peaceably to my home until I decide what to do with you. At least there you would be safe."

Safe? Perhaps from Buckingham, but what about safe from Tristan Savidge? Not only was he a man, but a man with Indian blood running through his veins.

Before she could think further, he was drawing her toward the coach door. As if in a trance, she allowed herself to be led down the steps and into the inn yard. Still holding her hand, Tristan reached into the pocket of his doublet and produced several gold coins for the coachman. "My thanks for a job well done."

The coachman gave a jerky nod and pocketed the coins. "My thanks fer yer generosity, m'lord." After a sharp "Have a care when you feed and water 'em, boy!" directed at the stablehand, the coachman turned and sauntered off toward the inn. The boy led the team away.

Tristan looked down at Brittany. "Are you hungry? Or maybe you'd—"

"As usual, Savidge, you took your time getting here."

Brittany turned to see Matthew Stark approaching with Gorvenal and another mount in tow. *Stark . . . Matthew Stark!* she thought disbelievingly. So much for my judgment of men. He's in this scheme with Savidge.

"I thought we made good time, considering we were in a hackney."

After a nod acknowledging Tristan's reply, Stark turned his attention to Brittany. "So we meet again, mistress."

"*Oui*. I cannot believe my good fortune this night." She turned her back to both men, frustration and disappointment forming a knot in the pit of her stomach.

Matt glanced at Tristan, eyebrows raised, but his friend merely said, "If the horses have been watered, we need waste no more time."

"Aye," agreed Stark. "There is the possibility that Buckingham could be hard on our heels if someone dropped your name . . . especially since you walked through the taproom and not out the back door."

Tristan ignored the sarcasm in Matt's words and lifted Brittany to Gorvenal's back. "If he decides to question anyone in the taproom, I doubt he will come charging after us. 'Tis more his way to lie in wait, nursing his grudge until he feels the time is right." He vaulted up behind Brittany without touching the stirrup, and she wondered at his unconventional way of mounting. "Will you come to Wildwood with us? The hour grows late, and you know you're more than welcome."

"By all means. I've not the slightest inclination to ride back to London." A corner of his mouth raised as he added, "Besides, I've a mind to see the fair Geneviève again."

Brittany stiffened momentarily in automatic reaction to the name. Then, just as quickly, she turned her attention to Gorvenal's striking white mane. As her fingers gently splayed through the silken hair, she prayed that the man close behind her had not noticed her unthinking response. She also wondered if she would ever be unaffected by the sound of her French name.

"Hold tight." Tristan's low words in her ear, his breath whispering over her neck and jaw, inadvertently aroused some untapped wellspring of pleasure within her. The new sensation vied with—and lost to—the familiar revulsion caused by a man's—any man's—touch, and Brittany felt sick inside at the thought that she would now be forced to endure Tristan Savidge's attentions as she'd been forced to endure those of Raymond Chauvelin.

Holding herself stiffly erect, refusing to allow her tired body to relax and lean back against his chest, Brittany sought refuge in dwelling on how she would escape Tristan Savidge. So fierce was her concentration, so steadfast her determination, that she never noticed when they left Chelsea's limits and entered a thick forest. So complete was her retreat into herself, she never noticed the narrow path through the living black wall of trees that swallowed them up as they made their way to Wildwood.

If she had escaped Raymond and St. Malo, surely she could escape Tristan Savidge.

George Villiers, second duke of Buckingham, regained consciousness to discover himself sprawled across the floor in a most undignified manner. To make matters worse, his head felt as if someone had cleaved it in two.

He pushed himself to a sitting position, the movement sending pain splintering through his skull. He took his aching head in his hands and balanced his elbows on upraised knees. Christ, it hurt!

After a few moments, he dared to raise his head and look at the bed across from him. The mousy-looking wench lay staring at him, wide-eyed, her hands bound before her and a gag tied over her mouth.

Buckingham frowned and immediately regretted it, groaning softly with the renewed pain caused by the mere change of expression. The girl hadn't been bound when he'd first entered the room . . . His mind began to work, in spite of his headache. Someone had bound and gagged her to make her appear to have been victimized, as well. But Buckingham knew better. He knew as surely as he was sitting there who'd struck him from behind and taken away the object of his pursuit.

The image of Tristan Savidge rose in his mind's eye with such clarity that the duke had a murderous urge to reach out toward the mirage and throttle the colonist until his last breath was expelled. So great was his rage that for a few moments he forgot his injury as he slowly rose to his feet and moved toward the door with unsteady steps. Pausing to lean against the jamb to marshal his wits and assess any further physical damage, Buckingham determined with a deadly calm, even in the midst of his fury, to repay Tristan Savidge.

It was bad enough that the breed had insinuated himself into Charles's confidence years ago in Europe, bad enough that he'd been allowed easy access to the king from the beginning—as much so as Buckingham himself. And it was outside of enough that Savidge had made him look the fool before Charles and Smith and even the puffed-up little trollop that Smith had presented to the king.

He leaned his head against his arm as his head throbbed anew and light-headedness assaulted him. "But now you've overstepped your bounds, Savidge," he whispered. "You dared to raise your filthy hand to me? To steal the wench from beneath my very nose? You—a lowborn breed from a primitive, uncultured colony on the other side of nowhere?"

He pushed away from the door. "You will rue the day you ever attached yourself to Charles Stuart, you stinking heathen. And you will have no peace until I am avenged . . . tenfold."

Brittany's first impression of Wildwood was hazy. As they emerged from the forest, she felt the first wave of exhaustion penetrate her ruminations. To her chagrin, she found herself relaxing against the man behind her, but only halfheartedly did she attempt to pull away.

Lights blazed through the windows of the half-timbered manor house. Evidently the master had been expected. They stopped before the steps leading to the door and, in one fluid motion, Tristan scooped Brittany into his arms from her sidesaddle position. Swinging his right leg over the neck of the stallion, he slid easily to the ground. Again, Brittany was struck by his seemingly effortless strength and maneuverability.

The stableman came running from off to the left, his hair sleep-mussed, his shirttail only half tucked into his breeches. As he reached them he muttered a sleepy "Eve-enin', m'lord."

"Good evening to you, Georgie," Tristan greeted with a grin. "Forgive us for disturbing your sleep."

The front door opened and a large-boned woman holding a lantern high squinted into the night. "Is that you, Master Tristan? Faith, but I told Georgie here I had a feeling you'd be returnin' this night, but the stubborn old goat wouldn't listen. Now, here he be, lookin' like some lowborn ne'er-do-well, half dressed and—"

Tristan had released Brittany immediately after her feet hit the ground, as if sensing her distaste at his touch. He turned to the woman now descending the steps, a younger girl following close behind her, and said, "I see your in-tuition is sharp as ever, Enis." He nodded solemnly at the servant and raised her hand to his lips with a flourish, failing utterly to fool her.

"Aw, get on with ye, master. Every time ye come home from court yer showing off them fancy manners. This is England, not France, with them foppy Frenchies!" But her eyes glowed with pleasure at his gallant gesture.

"Tristan spent too much time in France with the king, Enis," Matt said from close behind them. "Old habits die hard, as you can see."

" 'Tis not an old habit, Stark," Tristan corrected. "Enis loves every moment of it and would surely be crushed if

I came to Wildwood and dispensed with my 'fancy manners.' As would the fair Geneviève," he added as he took the younger servant's hand and pressed his lips to it, also.

"*Oui*, Sir Tristan. The manners of the English are deplorable compared to the French!" But her eyes went to Matt as she spoke.

"How are you, Enis, Genna?" he asked.

Genna's cheeks pinkened perceptibly in the light from Enis's lantern and her lashes lowered as Enis acknowledged Matt.

Before the girl could answer, however, Tristan introduced Brittany. "She will be staying here awhile and I want you to see to her every comfort." He glanced at the tongue-tied Genna. "She's also from Bretagne, Genna, so you'll have an ally when Enis spouts off about the French."

Brittany, standing statue-still as she tried to absorb everything that was happening, felt Genna's curious gaze on her. Evidently, Tristan had taken them all in with his winning looks and gallantry. But Brittany knew better.

"Humph," muttered Enis as she put an arm around Brittany's shoulders and guided her to the steps. "Old Louis what's-his-name never lifted so much as a finger to help 'is majesty roust them poker-faced Puritans from power. I'll never forgive 'im for that." But obviously her resentment didn't extend to every individual of French extraction, for she immediately asked Brittany, "Are ye hungry, Mistress Brittany?"

Before Brittany could answer, a bloodcurdling whoop rent the still night air, and Brittany whirled from Enis's light embrace just in time to see an apparition hurtling through the air toward Tristan. She stifled a scream just as Tristan slued around and met the flying human projectile. Quick as he was, though, it would have been virtually impossible to prevent himself from being flattened to the earth by the impact. Their bodies collided with a dull *thud* and down they went.

The advantage on his side, the attacker pinned Tristan

to the ground, wrists at either side of his face. Then, throwing back his head, the Indian shrieked again, a savage cry of triumph.

Tristan said something in a strange tongue and the Indian immediately released him and lithely sprang to his feet. He stood over the Virginian, his legs straddled, and motioned with his hands.

"By all the saints, redman, ye pick the strangest times and most god-awful ways to make yer presence known!" reprimanded Enis.

"He says he's proving how soft Tris has become since he's been gone," Stark explained to the older woman.

Genna, too, seemed unafraid, although her mouth was a rounded O; but Brittany's blood ran cold as the Indian's gaze raised to meet hers. All else faded from the scene but those mysterious obsidian eyes that bored into her. Tristan picked himself up from the ground and retrieved his plumed cavalier's hat, dusting it off against his leg, but she saw nothing of his movements.

Raw horror clawed through her, inching up into her chest and winding its talons around her heart, constricting until her breathing became labored. Never in her wildest musings had she come close to visualizing what a real Indian looked like. Nor, in her undiluted terror, was she capable of acknowledging much more than breechclout, partly shaven head, and painted face—a face straight out of hell.

" 'E won't harm you, Mistress Brittany," came Enis's soothing voice from far off. "Ikuuk's just funnin' with Master Tristan." She tried to turn the stricken young woman toward the open door, but to no avail. Brittany's feet were rooted to the stone step, her eyes locked with those of the copper-skinned savage.

Then Tristan was walking toward her, his long legs swiftly eating up the short distance between them. But to Brittany, who finally managed to drag her gaze from the Indian's face, Tristan moved in slow motion, as if he were under water. His eyes tried to communicate something to her, but what it might be, she was in no state of mind to judge. Despite the color of those eyes, indisputably blue in the faint light, she perceived them as black as those of his uncivilized cohort and took an unconscious step backward, only to come up against Enis's solid bulk.

"There, there, child," the housekeeper comforted. "Don't be afraid . . ."

But it wasn't Enis's voice that moved her to action. It was Tristan's, repeating softly, "Brittany, Brittany—" that banished the arrested look from her eyes, that brought a hint of color to her ashen cheeks. And it was his touch on her arm, as if to prevent her from sinking to the ground or taking flight, that made her spin on her heel and sprint up the last steps and into the manor house.

Don't run! her pride screamed. *Stand your ground!* But it was too late. Reason and pride were swept away by primitive fear.

"Brittany?" Tristan called from close behind her, and she ran for her life like a doe from the scent of hunters hot on her trail. Through the closest door she fled, slamming it shut and throwing the bolt.

The grandson of Pocahontas's kin . . . Indian . . . Indian . . . Tristan Savidge is an Indian . . . Tristan Savage—Savage—Savage . . .

Round and round went the words, her shocked mind reeling, threatening to close everything out in soothing oblivion. *Why this? To flee France for this! Why?*

"Brittany! *N'ayez paz peur, chère, je vous en prie. Il ne vous fera pas de mal . . .*" he assured her in French. "Open the door, Brittany. Open the door," he coaxed.

What manner of man was this? she wondered dazedly. Indian ancestry, connections at court, and he spoke French like a native. What kind of *sorcier* was he? Friend or foe? His voice was dangerously dulcet, threatening to lull her into obedience. But he'd abducted her . . . taken her against her will as his prisoner. No man could ever be friend to her.

Brittany turned back to the door, resting her perspiration-beaded brow against the carven oak panel, gulping in air and essaying to stay her thundering heart.

The murmur of voices beyond the door helped bring her back to her senses. "Obviously Ikuuk frightened her out of her wits," came the low murmur of Stark's voice. "And, for some reason, your touch caused her to turn tail and run . . ." More talk followed, in undertones.

Oh, what must they think? she had the presence of mind to wonder. She was not one to flee without just cause and, in truth, the redman had made no move toward her. But those eyes—stone-cold and unfathomable, just as Raymond's had been, and Buckingham's . . .

A sound to her right alerted her, and she swung away from the door, her body stiffening in reaction. *Dieu me sauve*, she thought. There is another entrance.

Slowly the other door swung open and, hands clenched at her sides, Brittany fought to get hold of herself. How foolish she had behaved over an Indian. How . . .

Instead of Tristan Savidge, however, it was Matthew Stark who appeared and closed the portal softly behind him.

Chapter 5

"Mistress?" Matthew queried softly.

For a moment Brittany remained unmoving, staring at him, and then she found her tongue. "Why did he not just send in his painted friend? I do not doubt that the Indian could have cowed me into submission without lifting a finger."

Matthew moved toward her, a hand extended in a conciliatory gesture. "Tristan knows we've met, that I helped you attend your friend at the inn."

"Oui, and I liked you—thought that you could possibly be trusted. It seems"—she turned away from the deceptively friendly gaze and glanced about what appeared to be the saloon—"that I misplaced my trust."

"Will you sit?" He motioned toward a velvet-upholstered settee.

She shook her head, refusing to be lulled into dropping her guard. "But, I pray you, feel free to do so yourself." The sting of sarcasm was not lost upon Stark. He stopped several feet short of her and remained standing. "I realize that Tris's method of rescuing you was unorthodox, but—"

Her gaze locked with his, the outrage in her eyes silently proclaiming how completely she agreed with him. "My English is far from perfect, but even I know that abduction is not another word for rescue."

Matthew blew out his breath softly. "And what was he to do, mistress? If he'd left you at the Hunter's Run, when Buckingham awoke you would have borne the brunt of his wrath which, I can assure you, would have made his first assault on your person child's play in comparison.'' He walked over to an intricately carved table and ran a hand absently over the polished surface.

Against her will, Brittany noticed that he eschewed the new wigs that were becoming the rage, as did Tristan, for his sandy hair was pulled back in a queue. He was nearly as tall as his fellow colonist and moved with a similar, loose-limbed grace.

''You can believe me when I say the duke is a master at nursing grudges and meting out what he calls justice. If you had escaped further injury at his hand, it would have been nothing short of miraculous.''

Brittany watched his every move, as if expecting his calm words and mien to change without warning, but her expectations went unrewarded. ''And you, of course, had nothing to do with this farce. You just happened to arrive at the inn in Chelsea with Savidge's horse in tow.''

He turned to face her, his patience obviously tried. ''Mistress, I do not know why you are so eager to vilify us, but I assure you that Tristan Savidge is not an abductor of women, nor will he keep you here against your will if you do not wish to remain. I can understand why you fear Ikuuk, although he will not harm you. But Tris is a good man. I have known him all my life and his honor and integrity are unquestionable.'' He paused before his final salvo. ''You would do well to think of what Tristan risked for you. He raised his hand to the duke of Buckingham for, some would say, no more than a tavern wench. Buckingham is very close to the king, a friend from childhood. There is no guarantee that Charles will side with Tristan, despite their friendship.''

''I did not ask him to interfere in my affairs. If he has put himself at risk with the duke, 'tis what he deserves for meddling where he was not welcome.''

Matthew raked a hand through his hair in an obvious effort to keep his temper in check. When he spoke, his tone was soothing, but it also carried a warning. ''It appears to me that you owe Tristan Savidge much more than you are willing to acknowledge. Or perhaps you welcomed Buckingham's advances.'' He looked pointedly at her bruised cheek and instantly regretted his words at the expression that crossed her face. ''If you are inclined toward Buckingham's brand of carnal pleasure and pain then, indeed, Tristan has misjudged you, as have I. If not, I would remind you that you cannot hide forever behind your unjustified outrage for, if naught else, you only make yourself look foolish.''

Brittany had the grace to blush. However, it did not change her wish to be released. ''I thank you for setting me straight, Master Stark,'' she said, though the look in her eyes proclaimed otherwise. ''Now, if you don't mind, I believe I am ready to act the grateful hostage and face my captor.'' She reached for the bolt on the door.

Matthew watched her pull in a calming breath and square her shoulders. Her chin lifted as she opened the door, and he wondered just how much good he had done. That she was willing to emerge from the saloon with some semblance of calm was to his credit but, he mused, just how much had he put her at ease? And just how honorable *were* his friend's intentions? Tristan had never before performed so unorthodox a rescue, not that Matt knew of.

Just what *did* Savidge mean to do with her?

Enis fussed over Brittany like a mother hen while Genna chattered in French, delighted at being able to speak in her native tongue.

''Good Lord, child, stop that magpie gibberish! Can't ye see Mistress Brittany's tired?''

Brittany smiled from the soothing warm water of the tub in which she was soaking. Through slitted eyes she leisurely took in what she could see of the beautiful bedchamber, decorated in delicate shades of green and gold. While the room was furnished in relative simplicity, by Brittany's standards it was sumptuous. Enis directed Genna to bring her best nightgown for Brittany's use, and the girl hurried to do her bidding, eager to do whatever she could for her countrywoman.

While she was gone, Enis rinsed Brittany's hair and wrapped a length of toweling around it before helping her from the tub. "Yer eyelids are droopin', mistress. We'd best dry your hair and get ye to bed." She began to towel dry the heavy tresses while Brittany sat before a small fire in the hearth, unexpectedly content to allow herself to be treated like a lady of quality in the home of her enemy. So euphoric did she feel after a bite to eat and the soothing bath that Brittany's conscience could muster up only a weak mental protest at her acceptance of Tristan Savidge's hospitality.

Genna returned with a frothy white creation that looked too short for Brittany's greater height but, out of a reluctance to hurt the petite girl's feelings, she allowed her to slip it over her head without protest.

"*Merci*," she murmured. "But you shouldn't have given me so lovely a gown."

"*Eh bien*, I brought it from France. 'Twas made by my *grandmère* for my wedding night."

Brittany's eyes widened and she shook her head. "Please, can you not loan me another, Genna? I have no wish to bring you bad luck by wearing it."

Genna shrugged. "*Ce n'est rien.* He ran off with some tavern jade and I ran off to England . . ." She paused, unaware of her insult to Brittany, and clearly recovered from the heartbreak that had caused her to leave her home. A dreamy look appeared in her dark eyes. "I shan't wear it on my wedding night after all. I've already begun sewing another."

Enis grunted. "And she's already got 'er sights set on poor Master Matthew."

Genna pinkened and her lips curved in a secret smile. "This gown will be worn, not on the night of my wedding, but on many others to follow."

Enis finished brushing Brittany's honey-colored mane

and said not unkindly, "What would a fine gentleman like Master Stark be wantin' with a maid, child? Yer settin' yerself up for another heartbreak."

Genna folded down the gold and green embroidered coverlet and then the sheet beneath. "Monsieur Matthew told me that class distinctions—I think those are his exact words—are not so rigid in Virginia. Titles are not so well defined as they are here."

"Humph" was the only comment.

When they'd gone, Brittany willed herself to stay awake. Here she was, ensconced in Tristan Savidge's home and allowing herself to be lulled into complacency by a kind word, a warm bath, and a sinfully comfortable bed. *Dieu!* What was she about?

She struggled to sit up and push aside her languor, but it was not easy. She had to think of the arguments that would set her free. She had to plan what she would do, where she would go when she was released. And, should Sir Tristan refuse to allow her to leave of her own free will, she had to think of a way to escape by her own devices.

She drifted off to sleep, half propped up against the pillow behind her, in spite of her determination to do otherwise. She never heard the soft *click* of the door opening. Nor did she see the tall Indian brave, who moved as silently as a soft gust of wind, come to stand beside the bed and gaze down at her in the feeble light of a single taper beside the bed.

His hand reached out to lift a strand of honey-brown hair from the pillow, rubbing it between his fingers, his black gaze thoughtfully on her peaceful visage.

She stirred slightly and the hand drew back, yet he remained standing over her, a dark, silent shadow spilling across her still form, breathing deeply of the feminine scent of her.

Then he was gone.

* * *

Brittany tossed restlessly, in the grip of the nightmare that had plagued her since the night of Raymond Chauvelin's death. Her limbs twitched spasmodically; sweat sheened her forehead and upper lip and finally bathed her entire body. She flung out an arm, as if to ward off a blow, and sent the taper clattering to the floor. Still she slept on, helpless to escape the horror of her dream.

Then Raymond's hands were pinning her wrists above her head on the bed as he prepared to—

"Brittany. *Brittany!*"

Her eyes flew open, releasing her from one nightmare, only to encounter another—the blurred figure of a man looming over her, his hands on her arms to prevent her from moving.

She fought wildly to tear herself from his grip, the moonlight streaming through the windows behind him limning his imposing form. "Let me go—" she cried, before one hand left her arm to cover her mouth.

"Hush, Brittany, you'll awaken the entire household."

That voice . . . Tristan Savidge, here, sitting on the bed, alone with her . . . She struggled to sit up, tearing her mouth away from its gag and digging her heels into the mattress, pushing herself up against the headboard and away from him.

"Easy, love," he murmured. He fumbled with the tinderbox and briefly left the bed to retrieve the candle while Brittany remained frozen where she was, her heart ricocheting through her rib cage.

God help me, she thought. Raymond, then Buckingham, and now him . . .

The wick of the righted taper flared brightly in the dim room, highlighting the patrician contours of his face before the dancing flame stilled and he turned to her once more. The bed creaked with his weight, and Brittany went absolutely still as her gaze locked with his.

"If you—if you but touch me again, I'll scream so loudly that they will hear me all the way to Chelsea."

Her voice was calm enough, although, Tristan guessed,

it was so only because of a rigidly imposed discipline. He could see the frantic pulse beat in the hollow of her throat as she clutched the sheet to her breasts with bloodless fingers. The hair around her face had curled into damp ringlets. Her eyes were glazed with fear—and something more. Tristan frowned as he interpreted that something as revulsion.

He reached out tentatively to touch her hand, and she recoiled as if he were a leper.

"I will not harm you, Brittany. Do you remember your dream?" he asked in an effort to steer his thoughts away from her obvious aversion to his touch.

She shook her head, her breathing slowing as she fought to get hold of herself, and then, without warning, she began to shiver—slightly at first and then with increasing violence until Tristan was moved to place the heavy, embroidered coverlet over her.

He stood and crossed the room.

At first Brittany breathed a sigh of relief, thinking he meant to leave, but her relief was short-lived as he bent to rekindle the fire. She watched in unwilling fascination the play of muscles beneath the terra-cotta-toned skin of his nude upper torso as he stirred the dying embers and coaxed them into flame with a brisk economy of motion. When he stood and faced her, Brittany dragged her gaze from his breech-clad form and, in an effort to avoid those penetrating eyes, turned her head away.

"What is your name?" he inquired softly, suddenly. "Your real name."

Taken aback, Brittany allowed her gaze to meet his, astonishment stamped on her features. "I-I've already told you . . . Brittany."

"Just Brittany?"

"Brittany Jennifer . . . St. Germain." She prayed he'd never heard of the St. Germains. "Of what interest is it to you?"

He shrugged, his eyes caressing her face. "I would know for whom I risked Buckingham's wrath." He studied her with unnerving thoroughness, seeming to delve into her innermost secrets. "St. Germain is an old and esteemed name in France. Are you of that family?"

How would he know of them if he hailed from the Colonies?

As if he read her thoughts, he explained, "I studied in France for some years before I pledged myself to Charles Stuart and his cause. I've spent almost half my life in France."

Despite her fear, Brittany couldn't prevent herself from asking, "If you are Indian, why would the plight of the exiled English king hold any interest for you?"

A faint smile curved his mouth. "I see my background is a subject of gossip even at the Hunter's Run. But, not to change the subject, your trembling has begun to subside. Are you warm enough?"

She nodded. "I would have you know I do not engage in idle gossip. After we met at the 'Change, one of the girls spoke of your Indian background."

Again Tristan was struck by her unconscious dignity. Now, more than ever, he was convinced that her origins were more noteworthy than her position at the Hunter's Run suggested, though she'd not answered his question regarding the St. Germains of France.

He unthinkingly reached out to smooth her disheveled hair and then remembered himself, but not before he caught the flash of panic in her hauntingly beautiful eyes. "You need not fear me, love. I won't harm you."

His soothing, reassuring voice lulled Brittany for a fleeting moment before she reminded herself that he was a man. And part savage into the bargain. Just because he dressed in English clothing, spoke in cultured English and French, and acted civilized did not mean he was any less of a heathen than the painted redman who'd given him so bizarre a welcome. The high cheekbones and lightly bronzed skin proclaimed his Indian ancestry as much as any breechclout or facepaint.

"Who—who is that Indian?"

The flash of a perfect white smile contrasted vividly with his burnished skin. "Ikuuk became my childhood blood brother in Virginia after Grandmother found him unconscious in the woods with his tongue cut out by white men. My grandmother sent him to me here in England when I came here with the king two years ago."

Brittany felt the blood drain from her face at the thought of the barbarism that had led men to cut out Ikuuk's tongue. "White men did it?" she queried.

"Aye," came the soft reply. "So-called civilized men can be as barbaric as their Indian counterparts. The whites commit atrocities for no reason other than fear of the Indian or simple viciousness." He turned to gaze into the single flame of the candle beside the bed, giving Brittany a clear view of his profile. "Through Ikuuk, Grandmother thought to remind me of my Powhatan blood, of the ways of her people." He turned back to her. "You see, by the time I was fifteen, I was more Indian than white in my ways and my mother, who is of English descent, persuaded my father to send me to France for an education."

Fascinated in spite of herself, Brittany supplied, "And there you met Charles Stuart."

"Aye, and I've been with him ever since." He ran his hand lightly over the coverlet, and Brittany could not help but notice how long and well shaped his fingers were. As were Raymond's . . .

"I-I wish to sleep now."

His gaze captured hers, and Brittany caught some flicker of emotion in his eyes that she could not decipher. So intense was it, however, that it intrigued her even as it frightened her.

"But *can* you sleep, little one?"

She nodded, sliding down beneath the covers and pulling them up to her neck, her gaze never leaving his face.

"Very well. But, just in case, I'll fix you something to help you relax. If, when I return, you are asleep, I'll leave you undisturbed." He stood to leave. "Shall I snuff out the candle?"

She shook her head and was instantly sorry she'd exhibited such childish behavior—as if she were afraid of the dark.

But he merely smiled and left the room.

Of course, just knowing he would return to look in on her made sleep impossible. Then, too, she feared the dreaded, recurring nightmare.

Don't be foolish, Geneviève! Sleep, so you will not have to deal with him again tonight. But her body would not listen and she lay stiffly, feeling tension creep through her limbs and torso, up her neck and into her head until the headache she'd had in the coach returned, full-blown.

In no time at all it seemed, he was back, holding out a steaming cup of a brew that exuded a pungent odor. Brittany sat up reluctantly and reached tentatively to accept the cup. Her fingers touched his and she almost dropped the mug, so unexpectedly jolting was the contact. And it had nothing to do with fear, she realized in bemusement.

Pushing aside her confusion, Brittany wrinkled her nose as she lifted the vessel to her lips and thought she caught a gleam of amusement in his eyes. " 'Tis an Indian brew for deep, dreamless sleep. Ikuuk usually fixes any Indian remedies we use, but I did not wish to disturb him, although," he added wryly, "one never knows where he is or what he's about at any given moment."

She drank down to the dregs and placed the cup near the edge of the bed to avoid his touch. "Thank you."

He nodded, a ghost of a frown creasing his brow, then just as quickly disappearing. He retrieved the cup and slowly ran a finger around the rim as he contemplated her upturned face. Brittany found the gesture oddly sensual and shivered beneath the covers, reminded against her will of Raymond's many innocent-seeming devices to elicit an arousal in her before he abused her body. In time, the ploys had lost their effectiveness, and any desire for sexual gratification Brittany might have felt was obliterated, her own needs buried beneath stifling fear and revulsion.

"Good night, Brittany. Sleep well." Tristan remained

standing over her as the drink began to take hold, enfold-
ing her in a delicious euphoria as her eyelids began to
droop.

The last thing she remembered was the back of his hand
gently grazing her cheek—and her utter inability to shrink
from his touch, to feel anything but a soothing, wondrous
lassitude . . . and peace.

Brittany awoke late the next morning, the mote-laden
rays of the August sun pouring through the mullioned windows in a glorious invitation to explore the new day. She
stretched contentedly, enjoying the luxury of having slept
well past the time she normally awoke at the Hunter's Run.
She felt rested and restored—and much too comfortable in
the home of the man who'd abducted her.

Yet the thought wasn't as threatening as it had been the
night before. After all, she reasoned, he *had* saved her
from being ravished by the duke. She closed her eyes and
shuddered as the bewigged, pale-eyed image of Buckingham invaded her memory. She knew exactly what he'd
meant to do, for she'd been so abused by Raymond Chauvelin many times, and her hands tightened into fists at the
thought.

Perhaps Tristan Savidge did mean to find her another
position. Perhaps, if he were truly sincere, he would con-
coct a story—even a recommendation—that would gain her
employment in some small town or in the countryside
somewhere, safely away from the prying eyes and wagging
tongues in the hustle and bustle that was London.

Careful, girl, warned the voice of caution. *Do not be
taken in by a bit of kindness. There is always a price to
pay when a man is kind . . .*

Well, she would be careful, but she certainly had not
been mistreated since her arrival. Why not give him a
chance to prove his good intentions?

*Your father was "kind" until after your mother's death,
fool. Only when you were away at school did you escape
his verbal abuse. And Raymond, was he not a wolf in*

*sheep's clothing, appearing to be all the things you'd
dreamed of in a lover—until your wedding night?*

A soft knock on the door interrupted her reverie and
Brittany raised her head from contemplating her legs dan-
gling over the side of the bed. *"Oui?"* she answered unthinkingly.

Genna opened the door and brought a tray into the room,
Brittany's clothing draped over one arm. "Good morning,
Mistress Brittany," she greeted cheerfully.

Brittany couldn't help but smile at the girl's infectious
happiness. "Good morning. Please call me Brittany."

Genna's dark eyes widened. She shook her head, her
brown curls dancing beneath her white cap. "Oh, no, mistress. Enis would box my ears if she ever heard me address
you so."

Brittany opened her mouth to tell the girl where she'd
been working before being brought to Wildwood, then
thought better of it. "Where is everyone? 'Tis so quiet."

Genna set down the tray and clothing and pushed the
tasseled velvet draperies farther aside, letting more sunlight stream into the room. "Master Stark and Master
Tristan went ariding. They should be back soon." She
motioned to Brittany to eat her breakfast. "Everyone else
is about their daily tasks." She picked up Brittany's white
cotton shift. "Enis washed out your clothing last night and
I mended the shift this morn." If she thought anything of
the fact that the clothing was that of a country lass or
maidservant, she said nothing, merely arranging the shift,
brown bodice, and russet wool skirt across a chair, with
Brittany's stockings and high-vamped, flat-heeled buck-
skin shoes underneath.

"Thank you, Genna." Color rose in her cheeks at what
the French maid must have thought as she sewed the rent
bodice.

Hoofbeats sounded outside and Genna ran to the window once again. "Oh, they're back!"

As if she realized how she must have sounded, she
turned distressed eyes to Brittany, but Brittany said quickly,

"I can manage quite well here, Genna. Why don't you see if you are needed downstairs?"

"Truly, mistress?"

"Truly."

With a quick bob and a grateful *"Merci bien,"* she scurried from the room.

Brittany smiled as she sipped the mulled wine. What must it be like to be young and innocent . . . and trusting?

Thrusting aside the thought, she dressed and ate everything on the tray, then wandered to the window. Peering down onto the lush green lawn, she saw that Matthew and Tristan were still outside, talking. Someone—probably the stablehand, Georgie—had evidently led away their horses and they were strolling about the manor grounds, deep in conversation.

When they turned and started back toward the house, Brittany found she couldn't tear herself from the window, although she drew back slightly. Both men were bareheaded, and the sun glinted off Tristan's sable hair, a sharp contrast to Matthew's dark blond head and the pristine white shirt Tristan wore above his black breeches and boots.

Brittany found herself studying him, unaware that she'd emerged from her hiding place behind the drapery to get a better view—until Tristan looked up at the window and caught her staring.

Yet even as her mind bade her withdraw, her gaze was caught and held by the vivid blue eyes for a moment that was both fleeting and endless. A frisson passed over her, breaking the spell and moving her to retreat to safety, blood heating her cheeks.

Suddenly a bloodcurdling yell rent the morning air. Recognizing the sound, the same sound that had made her blood run cold the night before, she turned back just in time to see the Indian—Ikuuk, she remembered—collide with Tristan, sending both men sprawling. Matthew laughed and moved out of the way of the two would-be combatants, now struggling earnestly, until Tristan cried something in the Indian's tongue and the latter leaped to his feet, freeing him. Tristan stood then and swiftly removed his shirt, a slow smile of challenge curving his mouth. Ikuuk gestured to him in what was evidently some kind of Indian sign language and Tristan nodded. He said something to Matthew, and the colonist came forward and helped Tristan remove his boots.

Then they stood facing each other, one pure Powhatan, the other only part, of an equal height, one with skin several shades darker than the light copper color of his blood brother. They circled slowly, like two graceful dancers, each taking the other's measure, all else forgotten in their intense concentration.

Brittany held her breath, unable to tear her eyes from the scene. The sun shone off the shaved side of Ikuuk's head, bringing out the blue-black highlights in the cock's comblike ridge down the center and the long lock he wore on the left side. His face was still painted, although the colors were a blur from this distance, and only a breechclout covered his loins.

Suddenly, with the speed of a springing panther, Ikuuk leaped across the distance separating the two men.

Chapter 6

What chance did Tristan have when faced with a naked, painted savage? Brittany thought as she bit down on a knuckle to swallow a scream. But her unexpected fear for the colonist proved to be unwarranted. Tristan neatly side-stepped Ikuuk and thrust out a stockinged foot, hooking the Indian's ankle and sending him sprawling on his back.

Her sigh of relief turned into a gasp as Ikuuk recovered with alarming swiftness and dove for Tristan's knees, bringing the Virginian into the grass with him. Over they rolled, grappling, straining, well-defined muscle and tendon thrown into sharp relief in the brilliant sunlight. Move for move, Tristan matched his blood brother, first one man on top and seeming to have the advantage, then the other.

Brittany hazarded a glance at Matthew, who was standing out of their way, an indulgent smile on his face. Perhaps this was a game the two engaged in regularly, Brittany thought, for Stark appeared not the least concerned for his friend. When Genna arrived at his side, then Georgie, Brittany allowed her gaze to return to the two men struggling on the ground.

Sweat sheened their bodies, and Tristan's queue had been pulled loose, making him even more closely resemble the redman he seemed intent upon besting. Brittany was certain that his close-fitting breeches were a hindrance and, unbidden, there rose in her mind's eye an image of Tristan Savidge in a breechclout, his splendid form exposed to her gaze.

Warmth bathed her face at the thought, and she mentally rebuked herself for such foolishness. The beauty of a man's body proved nothing; rather it was what lay in his heart that made him decent and honest . . . and trustworthy. If such a man existed.

Her attention was drawn back to the two combatants, who were on their feet again, circling once more, glistening and dirt-streaked.

Ikuuk straightened suddenly and signed to Tristan, the last gesture a slashing movement across his throat with a finger.

Tristan relaxed and threw back his head to laugh. Brittany couldn't hear his answer, but from their easy stances she guessed Ikuuk had called a halt to the match. Tristan turned toward Matthew to retrieve his boots and shirt when, without warning, Ikuuk leaped toward him once more with amazing agility.

But Tristan was ready. As if he had eyes in the back of his head, he spun around and, using his momentum, delivered Ikuuk a stunning, backhanded chop across his chest with his right arm, sending the Indian reeling backward and effectively foiling his sneak attack.

With a few words to Ikuuk and the same slashing motion the Indian had used earlier, Tristan grinned and made a sign of victory.

Brittany pulled herself away from the window lest she be caught staring once more. What business was it of hers if Tristan Savidge chose to cavort with that uncivilized creature? If the colonist possessed any decency, she would soon be gone from Wildwood. If he'd rescued her from Buckingham's rapacious assault, perhaps he had her best interests at heart after all, although only God knew why.

And if he doesn't?

"Then I will take matters into my own hands."

With those words to bolster her resolve, Brittany opened the bedchamber door and began to formulate a plan to secure a position of safety and anonymity, with Tristan Savidge's help.

* * *

She paused at the bottom of the stairs, uncertainty flitting through her. Should she find Enis and ask that the woman request an audience with Tristan? Or should she—

The door opened unexpectedly and, before she could retreat back up the stairs, Tristan walked into the hall— alone.

As he closed the door, he caught sight of her standing rooted to the spot. "A good morrow to you, Brittany." A guileless smile lit his features. He was still bare-chested, his shirt draped over his shoulder and strands of his thick, wavy hair hanging untidily around his face. The scent of mingled sweat, sandalwood, and masculinity hung about him like an aura, and Brittany stared unashamedly at the smooth expanse of his chest, marred only by some kind of medallion that hung from his neck. Odd, she thought irrelevantly, he has no hair on his chest.

"Good—good morrow, my lord," she answered, feeling like a naughty schoolgirl caught peeping through a crack in a door to a forbidden room.

She dragged her gaze upward to meet his.

"Forgive me," he apologized, and quickly slid his white linen shirt over his head, giving Brittany another brief glimpse of whipcord muscle and sinew along his arms and a taut, flat belly beneath his rib cage.

Her mouth went dry with some heretofore unknown sensation that made her uneasy.

He offered his arm. "Come, have you had your breakfast yet?"

She descended the last step and moved toward him but refused to take the proffered arm. "Aye, thank you. I wished to speak to you, my lord."

He raised an eyebrow that was black as a raven's wing. "Indeed. Well then, shall we?" He inclined his head to the door directly across from the entry hall.

He stepped back to allow her to go first, and, for the second time in less than twenty-four hours, Brittany found herself in the saloon. In an effort to collect herself, to rid herself of the alien feelings he was eliciting in her, she looked about the room, taking careful, deliberate note of the polished oak floor with its beautiful, tapestrylike Aubusson rugs; the carved and velvet-upholstered settees with matching chairs; the beautifully hewn marble mantel over the large fireplace. Brittany halted before an eglantine table, its marquetry top inlaid with boards for various games of cards and dice.

"Would you care for wine?"

She turned from her contemplation of the exquisite table and met his regard head-on. *"Merci, non."*

He nodded in acknowledgment and waited patiently for her to speak.

"I-I regret my sarcasm with your friend Master Stark last night, my rudeness to you, as well."

"You need not apologize, Brittany. You were owed an explanation, and I offered you none. Indeed, I should have asked if you wished to come to Wildwood before I carried you off."

She shook her head. "But I see now what you risked by saving me from Buckingham's advances. If he ever exacts retribution, I will forever feel responsible."

Tristan smiled and took a few steps toward her. "Any reprisals he may attempt will be a small price to pay for your safety."

Brittany frowned, confused. How could she gauge the sincerity of his words? More importantly, what manner of man was he? Either he was a man of noble ethics, or, more likely, she decided, his gallant words were merely a screen for some ulterior motive. She pushed aside this last conclusion.

He'd managed to move to within a few feet of her, and it was all Brittany could do to keep from retreating a step. His shirt clung to his still-damp chest, and she noticed, in spite of herself, the way his powerful upper torso moved gently with every breath. Although he'd tucked the stray locks of hair back into the thong that held the queue secure, he still looked warm and disheveled, with a light flush beneath the natural shade of his skin. He was utterly masculine—and Brittany's every instinct told her to run from him.

"I-I wished to tell you that I am grateful for your offer to find me a position. I was educated in the convent school of—" Almost too late, she stopped herself from revealing something that could possibly connect her with the school outside St. Malo. *"Eh bien,* I am qualified to be a governess. If you wish for me to demonstrate my skills, I would be happy to—"

"There is no need."

She arched her eyebrows questioningly. "No need?"

"Aye." He reached out as if to touch her, then evidently thought better of it. "I am offering you a position here at Wildwood."

Bewildered, she repeated inanely, "Here?"

"Indeed. You can run my household."

She sank onto a nearby chair. "But I've never run a household the size of this one, and—and how could you entrust such a thing to me when you don't even know me?"

"And how could I, in good faith, recommend you to anyone else before I've seen what you can do?"

"But Enis . . . what of Enis?"

"Enis was hired as my cook and took on the job of housekeeper of necessity when I could not take the time to find one. She will feel only relief, I assure you." He moved to another table where rested a decanter of ruby-red wine. He poured himself a glass and, after she gave him a hasty, negative shake of her head in response to his unspoken offer, he returned to stand before her. "I think you would be happy here, Brittany."

The words were low and soothing, dangerously dulcet, and a thought suddenly came to her with the force of a thunderbolt: *'Tis his way of keeping me here indefinitely. He never intended to let me go!*

She rose abruptly, ire darkening her eyes. "Happy here? I think you misjudge me, my lord! How much need can you have for a housekeeper? Your household seems well run, and although 'tis a lovely manor, 'tis nonetheless too small to require any great number of servants. Rather''— she narrowed her eyes shrewdly, ignoring the fine edge of panic shearing up her spine—''it appears you seek a wench to warm your bed.''

His lashes lowered, shielding the expression in his eyes. ''Were you anyone else, I would say you flatter yourself. In truth, however, there is no man in his right mind who wouldn't wish to make you his.''

His gaze met hers and he reached out slowly, as one would to a wild creature one is afraid of setting to flight, and put a finger under her chin. ''Nonetheless, whatever you may believe, I would never do anything you didn't wish me to.'' His knuckle feathered up the gentle curve of her jaw, sending involuntary tremors through her body.

She felt paralyzed, knowing somehow that he could be right, if his sorcerer's touch could wreak such unexpected havoc upon her senses.

She jerked her head to the side, giving Tristan an enchanting view of her profile, and his questing fingers found the bodkins that anchored her chignon. Before she could react, her hair spilled over her shoulders and down her back like liquid amber. A smile of undisguised admiration pulled up the corners of his mouth.

''*Dieu!*'' she raged in a tautly controlled undertone, not about to give him the satisfaction of hearing her shriek like an alehouse bawd. ''You already take outrageous liberties!''

He immediately withdrew his hand, his smile dimming. '' 'Tis small enough payment to ask in exchange for my hospitality . . . and your anonymity, *Brittany.*'' The slight emphasis on her anglicized name echoed softly through the room as he raised the wineglass to his lips and drank. ''If I recall, mistress, you said you were from Bretagne, and I suspect you fear desperately for your safety . . . not so much from George Villiers as from others.''

Ignoring his reference to ''others,'' Brittany homed in

on his outright declaration that his infinitely unwelcome advances were only his due for his hospitality.

"Obviously, I am indebted to you for tangling with Buckingham on my behalf. Now, however, I see that you expect me to allow you sexual liberties in exchange for shelter in your home." She drew in a ragged breath. "So I will ask you again to let me go at once, for I have no need to increase the debt I already owe you."

"You owe me naught," he said. "I begin to see that your low opinion of me is such that a touch on the cheek suggests to you that I would exact a heavy toll when, in truth, I expect nothing." He moved to within inches of her, his mesmerizing gaze delving into her. "Nothing that you are not willing to give," he added softly, and bent his head to brush her lips with infinite gentleness.

For an instant, Brittany was unable to move, oddly affected for the briefest of moments by his lips touching hers. And then the old revulsion rose up in her, chilling her, filling her with a sickness of the soul as long-repressed memories pelted her like stinging drops of rain in a driving storm. She pulled away and wiped her mouth with the back of her hand, too distraught to notice something akin to pain flicker in the depths of his fathomless blue eyes.

"After the kindness you showed me last night, I thought that perhaps I misjudged you . . . that perhaps you were different from other men—a man of honor and compassion, a man to trust possibly." She edged further away from him and swung toward the door, throwing over her shoulder as she moved away, "But you are no better than any of the others."

Tristan watched her leave, her bitter words hanging in the air, sensing he could not stop her except by force. And that, he knew, would only make matters worse.

Brittany deliberately closed the door behind her, for an idea born of desperation had come to her as her fingers touched the handle. Who would stop her if she just walked through the front entrance and made for the woods—for

Chelsea? She paused for a moment, listening for sounds of Tristan's pursuit from within the saloon, but all was quiet. She glanced furtively to her right and to her left, but the hall stood silent and empty.

It was a wild, reckless move, she told herself as she stepped quickly to the door leading outside, but what had she to lose? She grasped the latch and lifted it slowly, sending a silent prayer heavenward. Noiselessly, the door swung open and Brittany stepped through it into the warm, beckoning sunlight . . . and stopped.

There, not five paces from her, stood Ikuuk, tall and magnificent in his naked savagery. His long, black lock hung forward over his left shoulder, and the ridge of hair down the center of his head quivered slightly as he canted his head to one side. His face was clean of its painted markings, but his black eyes appeared even more frightening. He stood absolutely still and allowed his eyes to roam over her in a most thorough scrutiny.

Brittany backed up against the door, feeling overwhelming fear. She paused, gauging her chances of getting past him. Without warning, he signed something to her, and Brittany instantly recalled this man's lithe agility as he'd wrestled with Tristan. The idea that she could ever out-maneuver him was ludicrous.

She allowed her gaze to travel beyond him and, as if reading her thoughts, the Indian shook his head and took a menacing step toward her. With a quick, darting movement, she turned, fled up the few steps and through the door, neglecting to close it in her haste. She didn't stop until she'd reached the haven of her room.

Tristan stood gazing through the leaded windows, his half-emptied wineglass held negligently in his hand, and mulled over the scene that had taken place only moments before. Why had he offered her a position as housekeeper when, as Brittany had said, he had no need for one? While he hadn't exactly lied—for Enis hadn't been hired to be a housekeeper—neither had he told the truth. Despite her occasional grumbling, Enis seemed to enjoy her new status and the responsibilities that went with it.

A twinge of guilt passed through him as he considered his small deceit. It went totally against the grain. And her reaction . . . He raised the goblet to his lips and drained it without realizing what he was doing. Why would a common serving girl show such aversion to warming the bed of a man who could offer her so much?

Because she's not common, a voice reminded him.

A knock sounded on the door and Matthew Stark entered with Enis close behind him. "Are you ready for your morning draught and perhaps a bite to eat, m'lord?"

"You may serve any time, Enis," he answered. She nodded and went out, leaving the two men alone.

"She cannot abide the thought of being my housekeeper."

Matt helped himself to a glass of wine and joined Tristan at the window. "She's no fool, Tris . . . and neither am I."

Tristan threw him a sidelong glance.

"Both Brittany and I know you've no need of a housekeeper." He scratched his chin thoughtfully. " 'Tis not like you to be dishonest."

Tristan was silent a moment before he said, "I would gladly make a place for her here instead of sending her out where she would be fair game for Buckingham."

"You don't seriously think he'll not put two and two together and come searching for her?"

A frown crossed Tristan's brow. "I've already thought of taking her to Carlisle Hall. Even Buckingham wouldn't dare confront my grandfather."

Matt shrugged. "I would say your biggest problem at the moment is getting her to like you."

"Am I so unappealing to women?"

"You know better than that."

Tristan gazed down at his empty goblet. "She abhors my very touch, as you so generously pointed out last night."

"Ah, Pale Wolf, are you so accustomed to European women falling at your feet that you forget the customs of your grandmother's people? You must win her first, and I hardly call offering her a place in your home the proper means of doing it. Surely she saw through your ruse, or you would not be standing here brooding over it."

"Win her over?" he mused aloud. Then a sudden thought struck him. "You say she accepted your help with the other girl at the inn?"

"Aye, but I wasn't successful last night." At Tristan's raised eyebrow, he elucidated. "She accused me of being in collusion with you, said she'd misplaced her trust." His expression became troubled. "Indeed, now she has reason to doubt my word, for I told her you would not keep her here against her will."

"And I won't. I will just have to double my efforts to win her over." But the somber look in his eyes belied the tone of his words.

Matt shook his head. "It *is* strange that a peer of the realm must put forth such effort to win over a tavern wench, beautiful or no."

Tristan leaned against the window frame, hands thrust into the placket holes at his hips, and stared into the distance. "I believe I've finally divined the answer to that, my friend. It's taken me a devilish long time to see it, but my guess is that she's been abused—and badly—at the hands of some poor excuse of a man. She trusts neither you nor me, and is terrified of Ikuuk."

"Anyone in his right mind who'd never seen a war-painted Powhatan would be terrified at first glance."

"But last night she was awakened by a nightmare, sweat-soaked and trembling, and my efforts to calm her only served to reveal her fear and revulsion toward me . . . toward men in general, I hope, and not me in particular."

Matthew finished his wine and walked over to replace the glass. "It seems to me you've mayhap taken on more than you bargained for, what with Buckingham sure to take some action, and the very girl for whom you risked so much bearing emotional scars that may make it impossible for you ever to be friends.''

Tristan joined Matt as he walked to the door, his expression suddenly roguish. "But there's the challenge, Matt, and nothing in life is worthwhile without risk or challenge." After a moment he added, "Drake is coming tomorrow evening to discuss a few business matters."

"Good. I am eager to hear what he has to say." Matthew opened the door and turned to Tristan. "There is a solution to your problem, if you're willing to be open-minded about it." His face was solemn, but he could not hide the laughter lurking in his hazel eyes.

"And what is that?" Tristan asked.

"Ikuuk asked me if I thought you would trade her for a fine horse."

A tap on the door caused Brittany to swing around skittishly. Immediately she chided herself for being so jumpy. "Come in," she bade.

At Tristan's entrance, her greatest fear was realized. He'd come to continue to badger her or, worse, to take up where he'd left off with his physical assault on her person.

She opened her mouth, but Tristan spoke first. "I have come to escort you to dinner, Brittany."

"I wish to take my meal up here."

"Then, I will do the same."

Seeing her plan fail, she stared at him in disbelief. Then anger took over. "I do not wish to eat in your company."

Ignoring the insult, he sat down on the bed and lounged casually, as if there were nothing out of the ordinary in his actions. His expression was studiously relaxed, and Brittany sensed trouble. "Then you may watch me eat alone. But," he continued, unruffled, "I've also come to inform you that I withdraw my offer of the position of housekeeper."

For an insane instant Brittany allowed hope to flare within her breast. "You'll release me, then?"

He ceased his contemplation of the embroidered coverlet, and his eyes met hers. "Nay, sweet. I cannot allow you to go back, for your own safety. Did you ever consider what Buckingham would do were he to find you again at the Hunter's Run?"

"Eh bien, I'll find work elsewhere."

Something in his chest twisted at the eagerness in her voice, and he wondered again if, indeed, it was only himself she so diligently resisted. "I know you are hiding from something or someone in your past, 'tis plain as day, and therefore you cannot take a position of any consequence or means without leaving yourself open to discovery, even if you *could* obtain the necessary recommendation." He sprang lightly from his reclining position and stood before her, his eyes daring her to retreat like a frightened rabbit. She stood her ground.

"My past—and my future—are none of your concern," she said. "I do not wish to burden you any longer, nor subject you to further retribution should the duke find me here. Let me go, and I will find my own way. I will send you payment in coin for your trouble."

He shook his head. "You will be my guest here. You will remain here, or at another place of my choosing should Buckingham send his henchmen to search Wildwood, until this incident blows over."

"But—but that could take months . . . *years!*"

His silence told all.

"Nay!"

"Very well, our mysterious Brittany . . . or is it Geneviève?"

Her head snapped up in unguarded reaction. How could he have guessed? His perception was exceptional, uncanny, and only increased her wariness of him.

"I see by your reaction that your response to Matt's use of the name back at the inn in Chelsea was not coincidental."

"That tells you nothing!"

"It tells me much, Brittany Jennifer St. Germain. Now

I must discover your real name. Geneviève St. Germain?
I think not.''

Her eyes misted with tears of vexation, and her throat
tightened. "I see you delight in verbal—and physical—
abuse of women.''

His eyes darkened and he reached out to grip her firmly
by her upper arms. "I do *not* abuse women—either physically or verbally. Nor have I ever. If you do not wish to
remain under my protection, I would have a small price
from you for your release. 'Tis only fitting that I should
name my reward for earning the everlasting enmity of
George Villiers.'' His conscience writhed at the blatant
lie. What had he ever cared about Buckingham's feelings
toward him?

But Brittany had closed her eyes tightly against the intensity of his gaze, and a tear slipped from beneath her
lashes to slide down a pale cheek. "Name it,'' she whispered. "I had thought you much more honorable than that,
last night and then this morn, but, as I said earlier, I see
I would have done well to follow my original assumption.'' Her lashes lifted, revealing anger and pain and . . .
yes, he thought, fear. "Name it.''

His finger gently brushed away the tear, his voice equally
gentle. "If you spend one night with me, you may leave
Wildwood.''

Her eyes widened and a dull flush crept into her cheeks.
She swallowed back the bile that rose in her throat, all the
old dread and disgust resurfacing. "I surely should have
guessed.''

The quiet contempt, the loathing in her voice, lashed
him as effectively as the bite of a cat-o'-nine-tails. "I said
nothing about rape, Brittany. You must spend one night in
my bed, nothing more, and you may go free.''

"Nothing more,'' she whispered. "Nothing more.''

Realizing his error, deeply regretting his thoughtless
disregard for her obvious terror of the act of love with a
man, he made an attempt to rectify his monumental blunder. He pulled her closer, willing her to come into his

arms, feeling an odd, overwhelming need to soothe and comfort her. "I withdraw my offer, Brittany."

She turned despair-dulled eyes to him, silently acknowledging that anything would be better than captivity—that if she were forced to remain indefinitely at Wildwood, things would not be much different than they'd been back in St. Malo with Raymond. Yes, even sex with Tristan Savidge would be better than the alternative: remaining his prisoner.

Deliberately ignoring his retraction, she said, "If you have no honor, at least give a St. Germain credit for yet retaining some trace of that same noble ethic. If that is what you consider fair payment for your rescue and hospitality beneath your roof for these two days, then so be it." She turned toward the door, shaking her arm free of his grip. "I believe I will take my meal downstairs, in the company of others because, you see, tonight will be the only other time I will allow myself to be alone with the likes of you."

Chapter 7

Dinner went fairly smoothly, considering Brittany's renewed animosity toward Tristan Savidge and her dread of what must come if she were to gain her freedom. If she'd offended him by her disdainful dismissal—she, an alehouse wench, and he, a Knight of the Garter—he gave no sign of it at the table, and allowed Matthew to coax her into carrying on polite conversation with him.

To her astonishment and dismay, however, the Indian Ikuuk took his meal with them. He was dressed in a white shirt and buckskin breeches, although his feet were bare, and his knowledge of English table manners was surprisingly good.

At first Brittany sat stiffly, unable to function with his unnerving black eyes trained upon her. If he'd been capable of speaking, he might have seemed more human to her, but his silence, the eerie impassivity of his features, made him seem all the more frightening.

Tristan sought to put her at ease, but she pointedly ignored him and appeared to engross herself in Matt's every word. And so, when Tristan fell silent, Brittany chanced a quick look his way from behind the shield of her lashes and felt a perverse satisfaction at what seemed to be a vaguely troubled look in his eyes.

Good! she thought. Let him brood over the abominable proposition he'd put before her, for she fully intended to go through with her part of the "bargain." Let Tristan Savidge learn what poor recompense he would receive for daring to spirit her away from London and hold her against her will. Let him learn how well versed she was in giving nothing of herself while going through the motions of the deplorable act that some absurdly labeled "love."

That she had been treated as a guest, given every consideration, she could not deny. But everything within her rebelled. She wanted no part of Tristan Savidge or any other man. She wanted her freedom—freedom to be allowed to find other employment; to earn enough money at some anonymous toil, no matter how demeaning; to escape to the Colonies and make a new life. True, she hadn't yet felt the familiar ache of loneliness since her arrival at Wildwood, but she'd long ago accepted it as her lot—part of her punishment for killing Raymond Chauvelin. And, of course, the most upsetting thing about the entire episode was that her carefully hoarded earnings at the Hunter's Run were still up in her room, safely hidden, yet all but unobtainable now.

"—wishes to demonstrate his prowess with a bow and arrow," Matt was saying to her.

All eyes went to Brittany. Sensing her lingering reluctance and fear of having anything to do with Ikuuk, Tristan quietly interjected, "Only if you wish it, Brittany. He means well and will do you no harm. Indians are human beings, too. One must merely become accustomed to their ways." The tone of his voice, as one would use to calm a recalcitrant filly, was, indeed, unexpectedly soothing to her. "He seeks to make friends with the English woman with hair like the coat of a lynx."

Instead of looking at Ikuuk, however, Brittany found her gaze caught and held by the one who now represented to her all the inherent evils of the opposite sex. He seemed to communicate some silent message to her, but Brittany merely frowned, unwilling to put forth the effort to decipher it.

She pulled her gaze from his face and looked at Matthew Stark, then at the redman sitting at the table with them as if it were perfectly natural for a man who wore war paint and breechclout, who shaved one half of his head and allowed the other half of his hair to grow to a length as long as her own, to take his meal among civilized men.

The strangest urge to laugh aloud at the incongruity of the situation forced Brittany to bite her lip and lower her gaze to her half-empty plate. Were they all mad? Surely it was more like a scene out of Bedlam than what one would expect in the home of an English peer.

Then she remembered they were awaiting her answer and, savage or no, it would be discourteous to ignore his offer. With the greatest effort, she looked directly at Ikuuk, wondering how much English he understood, and said, "Thank you, no. I-I'm certain your skill with weapons is commendable, but I wish to retire to my room."

To her surprise, comprehension appeared in the intelligent black eyes and he nodded, seeming unoffended by her refusal.

Brittany pushed her chair away from the table and Matt, the closest to her, immediately moved to help her. Tristan stood and watched them with an unreadable look on his face.

Matt escorted her to the bottom of the stairs and Brittany ascended with all the dignity of a queen, giving Stark no time to engage her in further conversation.

As she reached for the handle of her door, something on the floor before the half-open portal caught her eye. Brittany bent to retrieve the object and held it up as she entered the room. It was a string of shells, delicately small and beautifully arranged. Instantly she guessed who'd placed it before her door, and wondered why. She knew nothing of Indian customs and could only guess that it was a token of tentative friendship from Ikuuk.

She fingered the exquisite shells, which tinkled softly in the silence and, in spite of herself, felt the tiniest bit of gratitude toward the man whom she believed sought her friendship. Until a sobering thought struck her. Could he, too, merely wish her to warm his bed? Could a man—an

Indian—ever have only platonic friendship in mind when he gave a woman a gift? Brittany remembered all too well the attempts to buy her favors during her two years at the Hunter's Run.

She stared at the necklace in her hand as if it were a snake, wondering if Matthew Stark would throw in his bid for her body as well. And then there was Georgie . . .

The beads slipped from her slack fingers to the bed, and Brittany slowly moved toward the door. She shot home the bolt and positioned a chair before the window. Sinking down onto the cushioned seat, she leaned her head against the high back and gazed blindly into the distance, never noticing when purple shadows began to ease across the land.

"Mistress Brittany!"

Brittany sat up with a start at the sound of Genna's voice.

"Mistress, please open the door. Are you ill?"

Brittany felt a niggling of guilt at the distress in the girl's voice and wondered how long she'd been at the door while Brittany had slept.

"*Je me regrette*, Genna," she answered as she threw the bolt and opened the door, still slightly groggy. "I fell asleep, nothing more."

Genna looked around the semidark room with a frown, then at Brittany. " 'Tis time for supper, mistress. Can I help you get ready?" she asked as she lit the taper beside the bed and bent to start a small fire in the hearth.

Unbidden, laughter bubbled up within Brittany and spilled softly from her lips. "Get ready? What is there to do, *chère?* I have no other clothing and my hair is still secure." She touched her hand to the severe chignon.

Genna quickly finished her task and stood up. "You have such beautiful hair, mistress. Would you like me to brush it into a more, er, becoming style before you go down to supper?" Her cheeks pinkened at her boldness. "I'm sorry, Mistress Brittany, but 'tis just that Enis says I need to practice dressing a lady's hair before I can become truly a lady's maid, for I've had no one until you came.''

Brittany smiled. "Of course you may dress my hair. Only I'm not hungry, so you may help me undress and brush out my hair for bed. Will that do?''

Genna's dark curls bounced beneath her white cap as she nodded. "*Oui*. But when you do not come down to supper, m'lord will wonder what ails you.''

"My lord will know exactly what ails me.''

At the petite French girl's look of puzzlement, however, Brittany did not elucidate, but gave herself up to Genna's ministrations.

Brittany was performing her nightly ablutions and Genna was turning back the coverlet when the maid discovered the small heap of shells still on the bed. "What a lovely necklace,'' she observed as she held it up for inspection and placed it on the table. "I've never seen the like.''

"Aye, 'tis very pretty,'' was all Brittany said. She looked at Genna as the maid straightened. "Genna, which room is Sir Tristan's?'' Despite her determination to be calm and rational, her face flamed, but she kept her eyes steadily on the other girl.

Obviously well trained by Enis, the girl registered little reaction save that of thoughtfulness. "Why, he's changed just recently because of some, er, renovations being done in the master bedroom. His room is to the other side of yours.'' She inclined her head slightly.

"Thank you.'' Brittany feigned interest in the lantern clock on the wall until she recovered her composure.

She glanced at the brush on the small, shapely table that served for writing and cardplaying, as well as the requirements of the toilette. She began to unpin the chignon when Genna took over and brushed out her hair until it draped over her shoulders and back like a shimmering amber cloak. Then the diminutive French girl took a small book from the drawer of the bedside table and placed it in Brittany's hands.

"M'lord asked me to give this to you, mistress. He said

even though you knew the story well, he thought you might enjoy reading it again before you retired.'' Brittany gazed down at the beautifully bound leather tome. The gold lettering proclaimed it simply as *Tristan*, and her breath caught in her throat.

''I was to give it to you when you returned to your room after supper, but I doubt he will mind since you are retiring early.'' She paused. ''Sir Tristan said to tell you to enjoy the story and sleep well in your bed until morning.''

Brittany nodded absently, her thoughts on the contradictions that made up the man. He would have her read one of the most romantic stories in folklore, attesting to the fact that he remembered what she'd said in the stable at the Hunter's Run. Was he the romantic he seemed in light of his gift? Had he really meant ''sleep well in your bed until morning''? *Her* bed?

Then he will never let you go.

''Will that be all, mistress?''

With an effort, Brittany brought her thoughts back to Genna, who stood waiting beside her. *''Oui,''* she whispered, her throat constricted with emotion.

The door closed softly behind Genna, but Brittany was in another world. A world of pure, unsullied love and eternal loyalty. ''Would that Tristan Savidge proved to be the smallest bit like the Tristan of the legend,'' she murmured to the quiet room. Through a blur of tears, she opened the book to read the simple inscription: *For Brittany, from Tristan.*

She hugged the tome to her breast and allowed the tears to come. Rocking back and forth in her pain, she allowed the dreaded loneliness to wash through her, leaving the familiar feeling of devastation, of despair, in its wake.

Sentimental fool! a voice chided, *this changes nothing! 'Tis but a cold bargain, in spite of the offered fripperies, and you still must sleep with him. Have done with useless tears and steel yourself to get through it.* But to no avail. Clutching the book as a drowning man clutches a buoyant object, she bent over and touched her warm brow to the cool, polished surface of the table.

Tristan walked up to Brittany's door and paused before continuing on to his own. He'd missed her at supper, and Matt and Ikuuk had both looked disappointed when Genna informed them that Brittany was not coming down to join them.

He knew exactly why she'd shunned them, yet he hoped that his gift to her and his instructions to Genna had set her straight about his proposed "bargain." What had he been thinking when he'd put such a proposition before her? He'd extinguished the gleam of tentative friendship and hope in those splendid green eyes because he couldn't keep his hands from her. Then he'd watched those same eyes blaze with fury at his insane proposal. God, he was a fool!

A small fire had been lit in the hearth, for even though it was the end of August, the nights of late had been cool. He glanced at the portable clock on the mantel. Almost ten. Surely she was sleeping peacefully in her bed—where she belonged.

He shed his shirt and tossed it onto a chair, his mind on things that had nothing to do with disrobing. Nay, he thought. She belongs in *my* bed, close beside me, safe and protected. She has only to discover that fact.

From the moment he'd looked into her eyes that first time last May at the Hunter's Run, he'd known she was an extraordinary woman, one who intrigued him while at the same time eliciting a response in him that prompted him to shield her from Buckingham. Her past did not matter to him, except possibly as a way to better understand her and help her become whole again, for he'd sensed that her quiet courage and dignity went much deeper, that there was another Brittany buried beneath layers of defenses, a woman of love and laughter. Finding that woman was worth the enmity of a score of Buckinghams.

Yet instead of helping to allay her fears, he'd only made matters worse.

He rubbed a hand over his face with a profound weariness. Thank God she'd taken his meaning and remained in her room.

Assuaging your conscience, Savidge?

He shook his head to clear it of the bothersome voice and proceeded to pull off his boots. If she should appear at his door, he thought, he would show her just how wrong she was about him . . . that he could win her over with tenderness rather than sex. As he stood to undo his hose and breeches, he was suddenly aware of another presence, and swung to see who'd entered so quietly.

Expecting Ikuuk, he was surprised to see Brittany standing just inside the door that he'd so carelessly left ajar, the volume of *Tristan* in one hand. He began to speak and then thought better of it. "Good evening, my lord," she greeted. "I wished to thank you for the loan of the book—"

" 'Twas a gift, Brittany, purchased weeks ago. Did you not see the inscription?"

She nodded and looked down at the volume in her hand. *"Ma mère* had a book—although not so handsome as this— that told the story of Tristan and Isolde. But I had to leave it behind when I came to England."

Tristan sat down on the bed, partly so as not to frighten her away and partly to steady himself, for he felt a curling heat within his loins at the mere sight of her. Without realizing it, she'd managed to look as beautifully seductive in Genna's short nightgown as Eve herself. The firelight reflected off her hair, burnishing it to a deep shade of old gold as she stepped further into the room and approached the foot of the bed.

Tristan sat absolutely still and drank in every detail until, realizing that he was staring, he lowered his lashes briefly, carefully schooling his expression to one of neutrality.

When he raised his gaze to hers, he was in control of

himself once more. "I am pleased you like it. But surely you haven't finished the story already?"

She shook her head, the movement causing her hair to slide over her shoulders like curling silk. "I wished to ask you if your gift was given only to further obligate me to you"—she paused—"or if 'tis a token of farewell . . . an indication of your good intentions where I am concerned."

Silence held sway for long moments, with only the spit and snap of the fire disturbing the quiet. "What do you think, Brittany?"

"I believe, as much as 'twould give me great joy to think otherwise, that you have no intention of letting me go if I do not surrender to your base male instincts and crawl into bed with you."

Taken aback at the brutal frankness of her words, stung by the realization that she was serious about deriving great joy from his sending her away from him, Tristan did not at first trust himself to speak. And his silence only served to incriminate him.

Her eyes grew dark as deep forest pools as she interpreted his failure to deny her words, and the book slipped from her fingers to the bed. "I will do anything you ask, do you hear me?" Her voice carried a hint of hysteria. "I will do anything to keep my end of your abominable bargain . . . I will have my freedom!"

"Come here," he directed softly, and patted the bed beside him.

Stiffly, woodenly, Brittany come around the bed to where he indicated and sat down, the fingers of her right hand clamped tightly around the left fist in her lap. He laid a hand over hers. "You wrongly assume so very much, love, when, in fact, you have no idea what I meant when I invited you to my bed."

She stared into the fire, her body rigid, her fingers icy. "I am not stupid, my lord. Just because I gave naught of my body to the drunken beasts at the Hunter's Run does not mean I am ignorant of coupling." The last word emerged as something infinitely foul, spat from her mouth in disgust. She turned slightly toward him, her fingers pulling from beneath his to automatically begin unlacing the satin ribbons at her throat.

He reached up to still her movements. "Nay. Leave them." He rose and strode over to pour a glass of wine. Pushing it purposefully into her hands, he bade her, "Drink."

"You prefer your wenches sotted?"

He smiled enigmatically. "Nay."

Brittany downed the wine without pausing and silently handed back the glass, deliberately avoiding his fingers. The vessel slipped and fell to the polished oaken floor, shattering with a high-pitched clatter that violated the stillness of the room.

Without a word, he knelt to pick up the pieces as if nothing were amiss, feeling her eyes upon him as he worked. When he stood, his handsome mouth twisted wryly. "I assure you, mistress, you need not avoid my touch for you'll find no vermin upon my person. The Powhatan are known for cleanliness, bathing every day, even during the winter." His eyes met hers, and Brittany, ashamed of her overreaction, looked away.

He disposed of the shards of glass and divested himself quickly of his breeches and hose. With a gesture of invitation, he motioned toward the pillows, and Brittany's response was to lie down, suspicion instead of resignation shading her eyes. He slid in beside her and propped himself up on one elbow to gaze down into her face, but Brittany stared sightlessly at the carved plaster ceiling above, deliberately ignoring the blue eyes that intently perused her tense countenance.

He drew a light blanket over both of them, then repositioned himself beside her without a word. Finally, he asked, "Who abused you so, sweet? Who did this to you?"

Green eyes clashed with blue. "You surely are puffed up with yourself to believe that anyone did aught to me merely because I do not desire you."

He shook his head with maddening slowness and fingered a lock of hair that fanned across the pillow like honeyed gossamer, his thoughts awhirl. He'd cavorted with Indian maidens, playful and uninhibited as kittens, and engaged in loveplay with sophisticated women at court. Yet in all his experience, he'd never encountered a woman such as this one. That a man could have instilled such terror in a woman—any woman—shamed him because he was also called man.

It also angered him.

"Perhaps I am puffed up, as you put it, but I would give much to discover who terrified you, for I suspect he is the reason you fled your homeland. I would see such a one drawn and quartered for his brutality."

Tears unexpectedly welled up in Brittany's eyes and traced their way down her temples into her hair. "It matters not," she whispered. "He is dead."

His lips grazed the side of her face, kissing away the salty wetness. Brittany started at the touch of his mouth. "What do you want of me?"

As he gathered her rigid body into his arms, she sensed the time was at hand and suddenly turned limp and unresisting. "Only to hold you in my arms, Brittany Jennifer St. Germain. Close to my heart."

He laid his head upon the pillow beside hers, cradling her protectively, his chin resting on her head. "There once was a proud and beautiful Indian maiden called Running Deer. Many years ago she harkened to the lure of adventure as eagerly as any Indian brave, and was chosen to accompany the princess Pocahontas to England."

He felt her begin to relax within his embrace, and reveled in the feel of her, the scent of her. Like the sweep of a moth's wing, his lips brushed her forehead with infinite gentleness. She'd haunted his every waking moment since his eyes first met hers in a crowded taproom, and now she was his to cherish, to nurture, to heal. His chest tightened with emotion, and Brittany turned her gaze to his, a touch of bemusement within the depths of her eyes.

"Surely you will derive no payment for rescuing me by regaling me with stories."

He smiled down at her. "I said only that you must spend one night in my bed. There were no other conditions. Now, lie still and let me finish my tale."

Unconvinced, Brittany nonetheless did as she was bid, allowing the effects of the hastily downed wine on an empty stomach to lull her into complacency. Tristan's voice came to her from close by and she allowed her eyes to close.

"—earl was much taken with her and they conceived a child."

"And did he wed her?" she asked, her cheeks taking on a hint of delicate color as she succumbed to Tristan's soothing, resonant voice.

"Nay, sweet. He already had a wife and a son—an heir. So he let her go, never to see her or his natural son again."

"So like a man," she murmured. "To take his pleasure without regard for the woman . . ."

His heart wrenched at her low opinion of men. "Aye, but he regretted it for all his days and, if he could have done it over again, things would have been different. Yet, in his old age, he managed to make amends with his grandson and contented himself with that."

"And what of Running Deer?"

"She took an Indian husband, who raised the child as his own, and she is still revered for having traveled across the great water and mated with a powerful white man." He stroked her hair from her brow, studying the alabaster eyelids that hid the jeweled orbs beneath, the dainty nostrils flaring gently with each exhalation, the sweetly molded lips that he longed to worship with his own.

"And what of their son?" The words were barely audible, her breathing deep and even.

Tristan released the pent-up breath he'd been holding for fear of disturbing her. "He wed an Englishwoman living in Virginia and took her name instead of his natural father's, to the earl's disappointment," he answered softly.

Brittany struggled to open suddenly sleep-weighted eyelids. Why did the story sound familiar? *Oh, what did it matter?* her sensible side asked. For once it was wonderful just to relax without fear in the shelter of strong, comforting arms.

She gave in to the overwhelming urge to slip into peaceful slumber.

"But the best part of all, *chère* Geneviève, is the ending. 'Tis a happy one," he assured her in a voice barely above a whisper, after watching her fall asleep, "for the son of Richard and Amanda Savidge found the other half of his soul, and vowed never to let her go."

Even as he murmured the words, the realization that he loved her . . . and that now he truly could never let her go . . . struck him with unexpected force.

As he'd intended, Brittany didn't hear the ending, for she continued to sleep as trustingly as a child.

Chapter 8

When Brittany awoke the next morning, she was alone and in her own bed. The room was dim, for the sky was overcast, but her spirits rose as she remembered falling asleep in Tristan Savidge's arms. Nothing had happened, she was certain. There was no tenderness between her thighs, or soreness anywhere else. Her experience with Raymond Chauvelin had taught her to search for marks and bruises in her mirror come morning, but she knew with certainty that she was unscathed. And, she reminded herself, she would have awakened immediately had he done anything the least untoward during the night. Rather, she marveled, she'd slept the dreamless sleep of a sheltered, well-loved, but exhausted child.

She rolled over and hugged the pillow, strangely at peace with herself. Was it, she wondered, because she'd discovered a man who was actually good? A man of strength, but also compassion? A man who had not taken advantage of her after all?

Brittany smiled, her thoughts turning to her imminent departure from Wildwood, and almost at once the smile began to fade. The desire for freedom had been so strong that she hadn't thought exactly what she would do once she obtained it. Common sense told her to stay far away from the Hunter's Run, yet she needed her small cache of earnings. Perhaps Janie could get that to her if Brittany sent a message . . . Janie. It seemed years since she'd left her friend up in their tiny room, unconscious.

She sat up, hugging her knees to her chest and resting her chin thereupon. As she mulled over her future, the glow she'd felt upon first awakening, that wondrous feeling of anticipation, dimmed . . . and Brittany suddenly knew why. She would disappear in teeming London, or somewhere else, and never see Tristan Savidge again, never get to know him . . . and that left her with an odd and unexpected sense of loss.

She shook her head in an attempt to negate her thoughts of entertaining any genuine interest in Tristan Savidge. He was handsome and, from what she could see, wealthy. She'd been lured by his sensuality, his gallantry, his beauty. Nay, let him find a woman to love and wed and give children. He deserved more than she was willing to share.

Yes, she could afford to be magnanimous in light of her newfound contentment. She'd upheld her part of the bargain—she'd spent one night in Tristan Savidge's bed. And now, despite the unsettling feelings underlying her elation, she would count herself fortunate and continue on, resuming her life.

Feeling more optimistic than she'd had in a long time, she threw back the light cover just as Genna's knock sounded at the door.

Genna informed her that Tristan was in his office, downstairs, just off the saloon. Soon afterward, with her rumbling stomach appeased, her spirits buoyant, Brittany sought him out.

Just as she brought her hand up to knock on the door, it opened and Matthew Stark almost collided with her. "Pardon, Mistress Brittany." He stepped aside to allow her to pass. "Have a care in there," he murmured conspiratorially, "for Pale Wolf is on the warpath."

At her puzzled frown, he enlightened her. " 'Tis his Indian name." He winked, bowed gallantly, sweeping his cavalier's hat before him, and sauntered away.

Brittany entered the office and closed the door behind her. The room was small compared to the saloon, but spacious nonetheless. The walls were lined with stepped bookcases, and the smell of parchment and old leather and sandalwood, Tristan's scent, assailed her senses and stirred in her an ineffable yearning. That the smell of books should excite her, Brittany understood, for she'd always loved to read. That the scent of sandalwood should act in an equally stimulating way disturbed her, but she brushed aside her vague uneasiness.

"My lord?"

He was seated on one corner of a great walnut desk before a large, cantilevered bay window, his arms crossed over his chest and one leg swinging idly, his frowning gaze on something outside. At the sound of her voice, he swung around, his regard fusing with hers. Her heartbeat skittered uncomfortably, and the unexpectedness of it stole her resolve. For a moment, Brittany was at a loss for words. Why did he look so stern?

Tristan came to her rescue, a smile softening his face as he took in her pink cheeks, her glowing eyes. "A good morrow to you, sweet. Did you sleep well last night?"

Her cheeks deepened in color. "Aye, my lord. I thank you for what you . . . did not do last night. I'm afraid I misjudged you."

He arched an eyebrow and lowered his gaze to a silver paperweight atop a neat stack of papers. "There is no way you can have accurately judged or misjudged me, Brittany. You have not walked in my moccasins."

She raised a silky, winged eyebrow.

" 'Tis an old Indian saying—that you must walk for three days in another man's moccasins before you can accurately pass judgment on him." He uncrossed his arms and gestured for her to take a seat.

She did so, not trusting her legs in light of the sensations sifting through her as his eyes sought hers once more. The immaculate white shirt, open at the neck, made his smooth, golden-bronze skin seem even darker in contrast, and for some inexplicable reason, Brittany found herself staring at his neck and throat. Even when she'd been courted by Raymond, she'd not experienced such strange and powerful feelings.

"I've decided to send Janie a message," she said, "asking her to meet me at another inn to give me the coin I left behind. You—you spoke truly when you said 'twould be dangerous to chance encountering the duke again."

"Just being seen in another inn could send up a hue and cry, for Buckingham's influence extends everywhere—even into France."

Her head jerked up from contemplating his lean fingers as they idly toyed with the paperweight. "France?"

"Indeed, sweet. Now, are you still so eager to leave here?"

Suspicion crept into her eyes. "I kept my part of the bargain, did I not?"

He slid off the desk and came around to sit on his heels before her. "Aye, that you did." He took her hands between his, and Brittany allowed him this small liberty. "Would you grant me one more concession before you walk out of my life forever?"

Something flickered within his eyes, but Brittany could not discern the emotion. She tried to withdraw her hands from his, but he wasn't ready to release her. "What is it?"

He stood and firmly drew her up with him. He stood very close, his warm breath sighing over her features and, like prey catching the scent of a predator, she tensed, her eyes widening, attempting to gauge his next move.

"Will you give me a kiss to remember you by, my sweet Brittany?"

His eyes were as guileless as a babe's and, clinging to her newfound trust, she steeled herself and nodded. What could it hurt? If his kiss was half as gentle as his other actions as she'd lain in his arms the night before, there could be no harm in it.

But a belated warning sounded in her brain as his breath mingled with hers before their lips touched.

Tristan Savidge was a man skilled at eliciting a response

in a woman, a man who abhorred brutality involving the opposite sex, a man who for many years had lived in the shadow of his sovereign and, in the best tradition of Charles Stuart, had learned to play a woman like a finely tuned instrument, needing only a practiced musician's touch to bring her to vibrant, pulsing life.

Tristan Savidge was a man who'd waited weeks . . . months, for the opportunity to kiss her.

The infinite gentleness of his lips touching hers caught Brittany off-guard and, instead of the familiar revulsion, she felt her insides begin to melt at the surprisingly tender onslaught. His arms went around her, and she leaned toward him while his tongue lightly traced the contours of her mouth, the warm wetness unexpectedly sending liquid desire shooting through her. Again, the warning echoed stridently in her mind as her rational self began to panic, but her body was turning unexpectedly, traitorously submissive.

She halfheartedly attempted to pull away, but Tristan's hand was on her head, exerting just enough pressure to keep her mouth to his without causing her to feel trapped.

When her lips parted beneath his, his tongue invaded the delights within, searching, stroking, gently plundering until, in answer, Brittany felt her knees give way. And, wonder of wonders, her own tongue responded, touching his briefly and then withdrawing, touching and parting in a luring love dance as old as man.

As Tristan's hold tightened to support her, the admonishing voice deep within her cried out again, and Brittany suddenly tore away from his embrace, sinking down into the chair behind her, the back of her hand against her mouth.

Tristan flinched inwardly at the accusation shining in the narrowed green eyes.

"Have you had enough, my lord?" she demanded. "Is that enough *concession* for you? Something to *remember* me by? I wonder how much more you will require before you will release me."

He remained standing over her, looking tall and forbiddingly masculine. His eyes were dark with emotion—an emotion that looked suspiciously like regret, she thought.

Then a sudden, sobering thought struck Brittany. *He has no intention of letting me go . . . So much for his honor! So much for his promise!*

Her mouth opened, but no words emerged.

Tristan shook his head, a mute answer to her unspoken question. "I'm afraid I cannot," he said in a low voice.

Something in her eyes died in that moment, and the regret he'd felt at having to nullify the very proposition he'd put before her turned to a dull ache within him.

"You never meant to, did you?" Naked pain darkened her eyes at his betrayal, and it affected Tristan more deeply than anything in his twenty-seven years.

"I should have known better. I should have guessed that last night was a ruse, a trick to win my trust, to pave the way for my cooperation. Now you have the temerity to ask me for some token before I walk out of your life forever?" She was past tears and hysteria. Her voice was deathly calm, her eyes as cold as newly cut gemstones. Tristan was not prepared for the tonelessness of her words, as if an inanimate puppet were talking and not the young woman before him.

"Before you came to my room, I had every intention of releasing you," he said, "although I must admit I'd pinned my hopes on the slim possibility that after we'd . . . after a night in my arms you'd not be so eager to leave." He crouched down before her again and tried to take her hands in his once more, but this time she didn't allow him even that small gesture of intimacy.

"How certain you are of your sexual prowess! And, indeed, how good of you to reveal your noble intentions. Yet somehow I suspect I would have fared better at Buckingham's hands. He may have abused me, but at least it would have been over and done with and I'd not be a prisoner afterward. Whatever you may think, Sir Tristan Savidge, I am not the one to give you the kind of recompense you obviously seek for what you term my 'rescue.' And''—her voice lowered dangerously—"I would look to my back if I were you. I took a man's life for less than this, and I just might be driven to such desperate measures again.''

His expression briefly revealed surprise before their gazes collided, fire and ice. Time stretched tautly between them, the air charged with tension.

Then, suddenly, the anger drained from her, to be swiftly replaced by distress as she realized her blunder. *Dieu!* What had she done? How could she have revealed the crime she'd kept locked in some dark corner of her mind since that long-ago, fateful night?

Tristan read the frightened realization in her eloquent eyes with keen perception and instantly sought to diffuse the situation. Without warning, he laughed softly, the sound shearing through the strained silence. "I suspected from the first that you had enough mettle for three. Now I know I was right.''

She frowned, bewildered at his ready acceptance of her confession. Heaven knew, she'd not meant to say it, but desperation did strange things.

He stood then, knuckled hands on his hips as he looked down at her, deliberately making light of her revelation in an attempt to win her trust. "A Powhatan woman would protect her own to the death—even if it meant taking another's life.''

"You are insufferable! I said naught about killing to protect you. Rather, 'tis your own safety you should guard, for your demise would see me gone in a trice.''

But the amusement in his eyes told her he'd known exactly what she'd meant and was not the least affected by the revelation. "If you raised your hand to me, 'twould undoubtedly be well worth the pain, for your punishment would be to tend me." Her mouth began to drop open at his audacity, but he continued as if nothing were amiss. "But don't worry, love. Your secret is safe with me.''

Brittany rose and sidestepped from between him and the

chair. She turned to face him, her fingers curled over the high back of the chair revealing her agitation. "You will regret this."

"I would regret it more if I were to allow you to expose yourself to Villiers by returning to London. Whatever you may think, your safety is of utmost importance to me and, if I have to spirit you away to the Colonies to keep you unharmed, I will do it gladly." He smiled wryly. " 'Tis no light offense, I can assure you, thwarting the duke. If the king takes his side, we may, both of us, find ourselves fugitives."

"If I become a fugitive, 'twill be your doing," she said through set teeth, then realized how absurd a statement it was. She'd been a fugitive for over two years now and he'd come uncomfortably close to guessing the truth. After what she'd revealed only moments ago, it wouldn't be long before he guessed exactly why she was in England.

How was it that Tristan Savidge had the irritating ability to anger her to the point that she would not only make such a ridiculous statement, but also reveal what she'd been so desperately trying to hide? The sooner she could get away from Wildwood and plunge herself into the haven of anonymity, the better.

"I think you know better than that," he said quietly. "Not only will you be safe here from Buckingham, but also from any inquiries from France."

Brittany moved around the chair and walked to the window behind the desk, gazing out at the brightening day as the clouds skimmed across the sky before a rising wind. "How can I be safe from the duke when you yourself implied he might come searching for me even here? Even if I agreed to stay—which I have no intention of doing—I would not necessarily be safe."

Tristan's answer came from close behind her, although he didn't touch her. "I will use every means available to keep you from harm, you can be sure of that. I am not without friends and influence."

Brittany turned misery-clouded eyes to his. "I do not

doubt you would do as you say. Rather 'tis your motives that mystify me.''

There was no amusement in his eyes, only an intensity that made her pulse race. ''If I told you, you would not believe me. But I can tell you this. Whatever you've had to deal with in the past, you will find naught of it while you are under my protection. I only ask that you trust me.''

She lowered her gaze. ''I cannot trust any man—especially one who does not keep his word.'' She swung away and moved past him.

After she'd gone, her condemning words resounded through his mind like birds entrapped within a tower, beating vainly against the enclosing walls. It went against the grain to lie or go back on his word, if not so much from his training among the English and French as among his Indian relatives. For fifteen years he'd mingled at will with the Powhatan, almost as one of them, and he'd learned the solid strength of truth. Yet now he'd lied to the woman with whom he most wished to be honest, and all to keep her at his side. Small wonder she could not trust him, she who'd trusted and been betrayed—brutally betrayed—in the past.

He'd been less than honest with her . . . had betrayed his own sense of honor, making his task of winning her over even more difficult.

But Tristan Andrew Savidge was patient, and no matter how long it took, he vowed he would have her in the end.

That evening at supper, Brittany pretended unusual interest in her breast of mutton, brawn, potatoes, bread, and cheese as she listened to Tristan and Matthew Stark discuss the lighter side of their business affairs with an agent named John Drake. A short, plump man with a tonsurelike fringe of hair and an appetite equal to that of Tristan and Matt combined, he was nonetheless shrewd in matters of business.

He was cordial to Brittany and unruffled by Ikuuk's

presence. From what she could gather, Drake had worked with them for as long as they'd been partners in a shipping enterprise between England and the Colonies. But Brittany was not so much interested in their business endeavors as in the fact that they would continue their discussion at greater length after dinner in Tristan's office, thus creating a diversion that could aid her in her plans to get away. Of a certainty Tristan would realize her determination to be free of him when he discovered her gone in the morning. If he had any nobility of character—any honor—at all, surely he would respect her decision in the face of such indisputable evidence of her wishes.

She slanted a look at Ikuuk and was startled into raising her lashes as those dark, depthless eyes studied her with silent eloquence. *He knows,* she thought. *He knows as surely as I am sitting here.*

She returned her gaze to her plate. *It does not matter. I will leave, and the Indian be damned!*

"—a game of chess, perhaps?"

Tristan's voice rolled over her like warm water in a deep, still pool, a soothing sound to her agitated senses. At first she was incapable of answering calmly in the unexpected rush of mixed emotions that went surging through her under his warm and tender perusal and, as once before, Brittany felt an inexplicable sense of impending loss.

"Are you well, sweet?"

"Aye . . . You asked me to play chess after supper?" At his nod, she hedged, "But what of your business matters?"

"Oh, we have the entire night," Matt answered for him. "Drake is staying over."

At this revelation, it was all Brittany could do not to show her jubilation. Her smiled acceptance of Tristan's invitation was due in no small part to her near-uncontainable exaltation at the way everything seemed to be falling neatly into place. Wouldn't he be less suspicious of her if she complied with his wishes rather than retiring early? Perhaps, too, it would throw the Indian off the scent.

If Tristan wondered at her easy capitulation, he didn't show it. "Then let us finish our repast and repair to the saloon." His words were for everyone, but his eyes never left Brittany's face, and a frisson of unease rippled through her. Did he truly believe she wished to remain in his company for a leisurely evening, or did he, too, see more than he let on?

Brittany pulled her gaze from his and helped herself to the delightful treat of grapes and muskmelon Enis had placed upon the table, something she'd not had since she'd left France. The increasingly popular coffee was served and it was all Brittany could do to hide her rising anticipation . . .

In her room later that evening, the time dragged and Brittany found herself glancing at the clock with unnecessary frequency. In spite of her plans, she'd fallen prey to the easy camaraderie of Tristan and Matt, and Drake's warm courtesy. It was only Ikuuk who'd made her uneasy as he sat cross-legged upon the floor and whittled some kind of primitive pipe.

Instead of chess, they'd decided to play ombre on the beautiful eglantine table. Since it was a three-handed game, Matt sat the first one out, with Tristan giving his place to Drake for the second game.

That had been Brittany's undoing. With his warm regard on her for the duration of the game, she'd been hard-pressed to maintain her concentration. Her cheeks became flushed from wine and self-consciousness and, in spite of a growing, reckless confidence in her escape plans, she knew that after her initial agreement to play cards, her chances of arousing Tristan's suspicions grew with each passing moment.

And so she'd politely declined a third round and excused herself.

Now, as time crawled with maddening slowness, Brittany exchanged Genna's nightgown for her own shift and skirt, and made up the bed to look as if she were still sleeping in it.

That this was a wild, rash scheme, she acknowledged readily, but it was also possibly the only chance she would get. With Tristan occupied with Matt and John Drake, and the rest of the household abed, she need only exercise caution and pray for a bit of luck to get out of the house. Once outside, she would flee toward Chelsea, with only the possibility of running into Ikuuk to foil her plan.

That worried her. Hadn't Tristan himself said that one never knew where the Indian was or what he was about at any given moment?

"I cannot allow that to unsettle me," she said aloud. "I need all my strength and faculties to succeed."

She gazed out into the clear, star-sprinkled night, grateful for a bright half moon to light her way to the woods. The light from the heavens could be either a help or a hindrance, but Brittany refused to allow her thoughts to turn pessimistic. "The Indian is undoubtedly fast asleep," she assured herself softly, "and the lack of clouds will make my task easier."

The clock struck eleven and Brittany's palms grew moist. Excitement shot through her, and she geared herself for her ordeal. Surely eleven of the clock was late enough to be certain that the servants were asleep, yet still early enough for the men to be occupied in Tristan's office.

She walked to the door, dismissing the fact that she had no money. She could walk to London and, if luck was with her, be at the Hunter's Run early tomorrow. She could take her earnings and leave . . . She halted her thoughts. *Concentrate on what you must do now.*

Slowly, she turned the handle and soundlessly opened the door. She stepped into the hall, just as quietly closing the portal behind her, and flattened herself against the wall. Only the low murmur of voices disturbed the stillness.

Brittany crept down the dark stairs, pausing in dread anticipation when one creaked with her weight. Once in the hall downstairs, the drone of men's voices became louder, but she repeated the silent opening and closing of the front door and let out a bottled-up breath of relief when she emerged from the house without incident.

Descending the few steps, she glanced first toward the stables and then toward the other side of the grounds, but all was quiet. As her foot touched the earth, Brittany drew in a deep, sustaining breath and sprinted across the grassy grounds toward the trees. The balmy night air upon her warm cheeks felt wonderfully refreshing, and as her legs worked, the blood pumped through her body, revitalizing her, until she felt as if she could fly from sheer exhilaration. With every step away from Wildwood, her feet grew lighter, and so did her heart. Her hopes soared at the prospect of imminent success . . . for, after all, hadn't she escaped the Chauvelins?

And then she was at the edge of the woods. Slowing to a walk, she rapidly drew the clean night air into her lungs and expelled it just as quickly in an effort to catch her breath. At a look over her shoulder, she was rewarded with the sight of a dark and quiet house, and not a soul to be seen anywhere on the grounds.

With a soft cry of triumph, she turned and plunged into the trees.

Chapter 9

Running across open ground was one thing, but trying to keep pace through a darkened wood was another. The moonlight couldn't penetrate the living, night-blackened awning overhead, and Brittany was unfamiliar with the forest and therefore constantly running into low-hanging boughs and stepping into unseen depressions. In immediate danger of wrenching or breaking an ankle, she slowed considerably, only to discover that she could still trip over exposed roots and other debris littering the ground.

Her breath was becoming raspy with exertion, her lungs burning as her earlier ebullience was replaced by the grim reality of muscles heavy with fatigue. A stitch pierced her side with irritating regularity as she moved as quickly as possible within the inky blackness of the sheltering trees. Her heavy hair had long since been torn free of the confining bodkins and now hampered her efforts as it whipped about her and snagged on protruding branches and low-slung vines.

She stopped to catch her breath, her alarm rising with the wind. I must get hold of myself, she thought. Stop long enough to collect my scattered wits and ease the burning in my arms and legs. What harm can a few moments do?

She squinted into the darkness and could make out only the solid boles of the trees surrounding her. The sky was hidden from view and the sight of Wildwood manor long ago obliterated. She suddenly realized that she had no idea

which way was north or south, east or west. The thought
that she could be moving in circles caused her inordinate
dismay.

In an effort to calm her ricocheting thoughts, Brittany
closed her eyes and just stood there, willing her breathing
to slow, her heart to cease its smashing against her ribs.
She was rewarded with a semblance of calm as she paused
in the embrace of the light breeze that sighed through the
leaves and whispered over her flushed face and bare arms,
the soft crackle of—

She stiffened instinctively. She'd heard the sounds of
nocturnal creatures scurrying about their business, the
scudding of dead leaves over the woodland floor in the ebb
and flow of the wind, the *swish* of the leaves that formed
a canopy above . . . But suddenly these sounds became
ominous. Tipping her head to the side, Brittany listened
intently. Nothing. The soft noises were no different from
those she'd been hearing all along. Rather it was a sense
of another presence that caught her attention, alerted all
her faculties.

Ikuuk. Surely if anyone could follow her through the
woods as silently as a phantom it was the Indian.

She turned to run and then hesitated, an idea worming
its way into her mind, an idea born of self-preservation,
dodging a myriad of jumbled, fright-induced thoughts.

She crouched to the earth, desperately feeling for a substantial weapon—a short branch, a rock. On the second
pass her right hand encountered a good-size stone and her
fingers wrapped around it, a sigh escaping her lips. She
moaned softly, but the sound was carried away by the
soughing breeze. She moaned again, this time more loudly,
then, holding her breath and watching, listened.

"Brittany?" A dark figure emerged from the trees, unnervingly close to her.

Tristan, not Ikuuk.

Her fingers tightened on the rock, every muscle poised.

"Brittany, are you hurt?" He came toward her and
squatted down beside her. "What is it?"

Concern sharpened his voice, but Brittany felt not the slightest compunction at her deception. Ikuuk or Tristan . . . it did not matter. She *must* get away.

" 'Tis my ankle—the right. I wrenched it."

Gentle hands probed beneath her skirt. "Can you stand?"

"I think so." She slowly straightened to give him better access, and his fingers lightly explored the 'injured' area.

"I feel nothing out of place, sweet . . ."

I took a man's life . . .

Her hand mechanically raised above his unprotected head.

I just might be driven to such desperate measures again.

Then, without warning, something within her balked, a silent scream of protest rising sharply to the level of awareness. But it was too late. The stone came crashing down on his skull, with substantially less force than she'd intended, but enough to send him sinking into oblivion.

She watched him crumple to the ground, a cry of denial caught in her throat. Then, as once before, the word *murderess!* rang through her mind like a clarion. The rock fell unheeded to the ground, and Brittany bent suddenly boneless knees to crouch beside him, images of Raymond Chauvelin's crushed skull flashing before her eyes as she stared down at the still form beside her. The urge to be violently ill surged over her in a wave and she turned away in reaction.

Suddenly she was shoved aside by a third person, landing with breath-snatching force against the earth. Looking up in shock, she instantly recognized the tall form looming over her. She stared in horror, knowing he might take her life for raising her hand to his blood brother.

He squatted down beside Tristan and put his fingers to a pulse point in his neck.

Brittany lurched to her knees. "Is he—is he . . . ?"

With a growl of contempt, the Indian roughly pushed her back to the ground. He gingerly raised Tristan's head, searching for the injury, while Brittany stubbornly got to her knees again, the discarded rock suddenly clamped in her hand once more. "Push me again, you painted savage, and I'll cleave your skull in two."

But Ikuuk was not Tristan—no gentle and loving protector, he. Before she could make good her threat, Brittany found herself flat on her back, the Indian kneeling over her, his powerful fingers at her windpipe. The soft, deadly sound that issued from his throat left no doubt as to his intention.

For a measureless time, they remained thusly, only the rasp of their breathing disturbing the stillness. Brittany stared into his face, noting the sinister cast of his features in the night shadows. His eyes burned blacker than the night itself, two holes in the expressionless mask that was his face. Yet for once he'd lost the power to frighten her, for all her thoughts were on the man lying unconscious on the forest floor beside them.

She began to pull at his fingers, struggling to free herself. "Let me go," she demanded in a choked whisper. But his grip only tightened. "I but meant to stop him from taking me back. I'll be no man's captive!" She wound desperate fingers around his wrists and pulled, even as spots began to appear before her eyes. "You do him no good—fighting with me when he should be taken to the house and tended."

Just when she thought she would faint, the pressure eased and Ikuuk stood in one lithe movement. Turning to bend over Tristan, he lifted him off the ground and slung him over one shoulder, staggering slightly under the weight.

Without a backward glance, he strode through the forest, leaving Brittany alone . . . and free to go.

For moments—or was it hours?—she knelt there on the earth, then sank onto her heels, the words *alone* and *free to go* reverberating in her mind in a beckoning chant. Yet above those echoes there rose a sudden realization, one that she'd heretofore been too caught up in her antagonism toward Tristan Savidge to acknowledge. Only once—and briefly—had she experienced the dreaded, soul-rending loneliness while under his aegis. Nor had she worried about discovery, if she were to be absolutely truthful with herself.

She tilted her warm face up to the cool caress of the wind, essaying to organize her chaotic thoughts. She was being foolish, sitting alone, doing nothing, when she could be halfway to Chelsea. But Tristan Savidge's face rose before her mind's eye, smiling at her with genuine warmth and laughter in his beautiful, beguiling eyes.

She would never know how badly he'd been hurt—or if he . . . Brittany shook her head to break the image into fragments before willing it to disappear. Surely if he'd been dead, the Indian would have killed her without a second thought.

That is not to say that he will not perish before the night is over. Or perhaps he will never fully recover, and you will be responsible. Is not one death on your conscience enough?

"But what good will my presence do him?" she whispered in an anguished voice.

Go back then, fool. Go back to the Hunter's Run . . . to Buckingham and possible exposure. Go back to a life of waiting tables and fighting off drunken beasts . . .

"Enough!" she cried softly, shaking her head. "I have no choice. My coin is there and I need it to survive." She staggered to her feet, tears rising in a torrent to blur her vision before splashing down her cheeks. "I will not stay here and be his whore!" she announced to the swaying trees and the low-keening wind.

No one said you had to stay, silly girl.

She stilled. Not stay? Why, of course. She would return to see how he fared, and perhaps remain until he was well. Then . . . A sobering thought struck her. Why would he ever allow her to leave if he hadn't done so before her flight?

Because you tried to kill him.

She raised her tear-ravaged face to the unseen sky above . . .

"My God, Ikuuk. What *happened* to him?" Matthew Stark raked his hands through his hair as he watched Enis minister to his unconscious friend.

Enis answered for him. "Well, beggin' yer pardon, Master Stark, ye'd have to be blind not to see he's been hit over the head!"

Ikuuk signed emphatically to Matt. "A rock? Sweet Jesus . . . she actually hit him over the head with a rock?"

Ikuuk signed again, his face dark with anger.

"She tricked him, he says, then tried to brain him."

"Faith!" Enis muttered. " 'Twould seem we've befriended her a mite too easily. She even fooled m'lord here."

A somber-faced Genna helped her bathe the cut. "Will you stitch it?"

Enis nodded. "Have to cut off some of his hair, though, in back here."

"Why would she ever have run away in the first place?" Matt questioned. "A tavern wench fleeing from a man who risked the duke of Buckingham's fury by snatching her from beneath his nose—and," he added darkly, "not without insult and injury to Villiers, either."

Enis threaded a needle. "You'd better hold him, one on either side. This will hurt—may even bring him to."

As the two men did as they were bid, Genna looked into Matt's eyes, her own imploring. "She wanted to leave, I know it. Surely Master Tristan knows that you cannot keep a wild bird caged."

Matt's features softened as his eyes met the girl's. "Wild indeed, Genna. The pity of it is that ofttimes the creature is too dumb to realize it's being contained for its own good. Or, in this case, until the danger was past."

As Genna moved to help Enis, Matt stared down at Tristan, a part of him grudgingly admitting that Tristan had had no right to detain the wench if she wanted to leave. It wasn't like Tris to do something harebrained like that.

He shook his head, clamping down harder on Tristan's shoulder as the latter wrenched upward in reaction to the needle spearing in and out of his scalp. He'd actually *liked* her at first. Unless he was a poor judge of character, she'd seemed to be genuinely grateful for his help with her friend at the inn. But then, where there should have been a sense of obligation to Tristan, there'd been only resentment, and they'd unknowingly given shelter to an asp, an ungrateful creature who'd turned on its protector.

Tristan strained once more against the hands that held him, his eyelids fluttering briefly, and then sank back to the mattress, just as Enis announced, "There, 'tis done."

"Where is she?" Matt asked Ikuuk as the women began to remove Tristan's clothing.

The Indian signed an answer with a swift, slashing motion, indicating his agitation. "Good. Let her go. Let her run back to her own kind." Matthew walked to the window and stared out into the night.

But Genna, ever the one to stand up for her country-woman, asked, "Master Stark, what made m'lord suspect that Mistress Brittany had fled Wildwood to begin with?"

Even before the words were out, Matt knew the reason for the question—the implications of the answer before it was given. He met her gaze. "I'm not certain," he said slowly, mentally chiding himself for being less than truthful.

"I think you've said quite enough, girl," Enis told her.

But the lively Genna would not remain quiet until she'd had her say. "Could it be that m'lord suspected her attempt to run away because he was the only one who knew he'd decided to keep her here . . . against her wishes?"

Enis's face flushed a dull red with anger. "You overstep your bounds, Frenchie. Watch your tongue before Master Tristan—"

"—tells you . . . that you're . . . absolutely right."

Four heads turned toward the figure on the bed.

Matt spoke first as he sat down beside his friend and put a hand over Tristan's. "Thank God you've come out of it." His lips twitched suddenly. "And with such perfect timing to defend your errant tavern girl."

Tristan tried to smile and winced. He closed his eyes in an attempt to dispel the wooziness. "No one . . . could remain out cold . . . with Enis ruthlessly needling his scalp."

He looked at Ikuuk, who was standing at the foot of the bed, arms crossed over his bare chest. "Thank you, my friend, for bringing me back . . . but where is she?"

Ikuuk's eyes narrowed as he made an abrupt gesture.

Tristan's eyes closed wearily.

"Well, what would you have had him do, Tris?" Matt said. "Bring her back so we all could have welcomed her with open arms?" A frown creased his brow. "Ikuuk's first concern was to bring you back here for us to tend to you, the girl be damned! If she seeks so desperately to flee, then why not let her go? Christ, she could have killed you—"

"—but she didn't," Tristan interrupted. "She's out there somewhere, frightened and confused and alone, and no one deserves that." His now lucid gaze went to his blood brother. "Will you find her . . . for me?"

The Indian stared long and hard at his friend, not a muscle moving except for the steady rise and fall of his bare chest. When the silence lay heavy upon them, Ikuuk gave his assent with a disgusted grunt that sliced through the air of expectancy. He swung away from the bed and froze, his expression turning ugly.

The abrupt cessation of movement caught Tristan's attention and, though Ikuuk blocked his view of the doorway, he needed no one to tell him who stood on the threshold.

Ikuuk turned back to Tristan, thus providing an obstructed view of Brittany. *She has come to see her handiwork,* he signed to Tristan, but Tristan's full attention was on the woman standing at the open doorway.

Her clothing was soiled and rent in several places. Her

hair hung about her shoulders in snarled magnificence, her face streaked with dirt and dried tears. But it was the wild look in her eyes that made something twist in Tristan's gut—a message communicating uncertainty and wariness, as well as regret, and something more, something that made Tristan ache to take her in his arms and comfort her. Somehow he knew she was no murderess, despite her past revelations, her recent actions.

Matt opened his mouth to speak and then obviously thought better of it. His expression, however, left no doubt as to his feelings.

"Come in, Brittany. I'm glad you've come back."

Brittany studied him through wary eyes, at first unable to believe he was sincere. But the tone of his voice, so guileless and free of deceit—not the fawning, unctuous inflection Raymond used as a prelude to abuse—was just one of many things about Tristan Savidge that was slowly setting him apart from other men.

She raised her chin and stepped into the room. "I do not believe I am welcome here, my lord, and descrvedly so. Nevertheless, I am relieved you are alive and well, and I have come to offer my services until you are up and about."

A slow smile spread across Tristan's features. She might not have apologized—and that it was glaringly apparent to all in the room he could sense—but she'd been concerned enough to return to Wildwood to see if she could somehow make amends. That realization caused him no small amount of happiness. "I shan't be abed for long, rest assured, but your concern is welcome, and any apology unnecessary."

Matt cleared his throat loudly, but Tristan ignored him. Ikuuk remained where he was, his eyes boring into Brittany, while Enis and Genna began to clean up. "Why don't you let Genna fetch water to wash in—or Ikuuk can help her bring up enough for a bath if you prefer—and then, when you are ready for bed, come back here. There is still a small matter we must discuss."

She nodded, her eyes still on Tristan. Then, with a soft "As you wish, my lord," she turned and left the room.

"I don't understand why Master Tristan would keep you here against your will," Genna began. At Brittany's startled look, she bit her tongue. "I'm sorry, mistress, for being so bold. Enis is always after me to guard my loose tongue and—"

"*Ce n'est rien, chère.*" Brittany managed a distracted smile as she stripped off her soiled clothing, glad to have an ally in Genna.

"Well, there can be only one reason he wishes to keep you here." She glanced slyly at Brittany, but the other young woman was rolling down her light woolen hose, her attention occupied. "I think he is in love with you."

Brittany's head jerked up. "In *love* with me?" She shook her head, her eyes narrowing, her expression suddenly hard. "You've been listening to too many romantic tales, Genna. There is no such thing as love in that sense. The most a woman can hope for is a husband who does not brutalize her." Bitterness edged her words.

At Genna's shocked look, Brittany quickly amended, "But perhaps you have found differently, *chère.* I only know of my own experience." Why disillusion the girl? She would discover the way of it sooner or later.

Genna went to brush the tangles from Brittany's hair, somewhat mollified. "I only know that Master Tristan would never keep you here out of sheer cruelty. Indian blood or nay, he is not a cruel man."

No, but he would use my body, as did Raymond. That is his so-called love. How many others had he housed at Wildwood for the same purpose? Wasn't it a man's need to have either a wife or a mistress to satisfy his lust?

Genna, who'd finished brushing Brittany's hair, had gone to a carved and paneled oak chest and brought out a sweet coffer, or dressing casket. She broke into Brittany's thoughts when she laid it upon the small table before her.

"What is this?" *Something, no doubt, to paint and perfume the women who'd stayed here, in this very room.*

"M'lord bade me give it to you earlier." She smoothed her hand over the carved ebony lid, then, as if reading Brittany's thoughts, she said, " 'Twas for Mistress Beth Ann."

"Beth Ann?"

"*Oui*. M'lord's sister. Enis said she was to visit him just before I was hired on at Wildwood, but she had an accident . . . was thrown from her horse and permanently bedridden."

As the words registered, Brittany felt suddenly monstrous for her thoughts regarding his "women." She opened the lid to view the contents, wondering what Tristan's sister was like. The inside of the lid was fitted with small Venetian glass mirrors, a treasure in themselves. Lined in black velvet, the coffer revealed cosmetics and perfumes, each article carefully wrapped in a wisp of toile. Brittany touched each item reverently, unable to comprehend that a man should give a serving girl—a virtual stranger—such a gift, and one that had been meant for an obviously well-loved sister.

How little she actually knew Tristan Savidge.

"I-I cannot use something meant for his sister." But even as she spoke, Brittany was carefully unwrapping a flask of violet perfume. She'd had several vials of her own while wed to Raymond, but had soon stopped using them because he'd told her how the scent of perfume on her skin bewitched him. Indeed, he'd proceeded to demonstrate exactly what effect it had on him.

But violets . . . the fresh, fragile fragrance that had been her mother's favorite, and then hers. She unstoppered the flask and breathed deeply of the scent, allowing it to waft upward and wrap her in its delicate essence. She closed her eyes, letting her thoughts drift back to a time when her mother had been alive, when she'd been happy and carefree . . . and loved.

Brittany opened her eyes to find Genna still beside her,

her frank gaze admiring the treasures within the small chest
before she stifled a yawn. "You must be tired, Genna, for
'tis well past midnight. Why don't you go to bed?"

When the girl had left, Brittany touched a finger to the
neck of the vial and tipped it. Applying it to just below
her ears and the hollow at the base of her throat, she suddenly felt beautiful and desirable and, yes, bewitching.

She stoppered the perfume and put it away. She was
mad for even thinking such things. After experiencing the
results of "bewitching" Raymond by the simple act of
wearing a fragrance, she surely was a fool to apply it before going to Tristan Savidge.

There is still a small matter we must discuss.

She swung toward the door, then paused, taking a quick
inventory of the room. What could she wear over the
nightgown?

*He's seen you twice before without a wrap. You've even
lain beside him in his bed wearing nothing more than this
same gown. What does it matter at this point?*

With a soft sigh, Brittany opened the door.

When she entered his room, his eyes were closed yet,
despite the whispered footfalls of her bare feet, his lashes
raised immediately upon her further entrance.

Brittany stood before the bed. A cup of what looked
and smelled like the same concoction he'd given her that
first night sat on the bedside table.

He glanced at the cup, then back to her again. "Ikuuk
takes very good care of me," he said solemnly, but levity
lit his eyes.

"How is your head?"

"Better, thanks to another remedy of Ikuuk's." He
frowned then, taking note of Brittany's tightly crossed
arms. "We must better see to your needs. You have only
the clothes you arrived in and a nightgown—obviously
borrowed from Genna." His gaze moved down to her exposed ankles and lower calves.

She drew up a chair and sat down, tucking her feet as

far beneath the chair as possible. "I will not be here long enough to need clothing from you, my lord. But thank you for your concern." Then, changing the subject, she asked, "What was the 'small matter' you wished to discuss with me?"

He reached out a hand toward her, then, as if knowing she would never take it of her own volition, he smoothed his fingers over the bedclothes. Brittany's gaze was drawn to the lean, long fingers that contrasted starkly with the pale coverlet. His chest was exposed to her gaze and she noticed a copper disk suspended from a slim leather thong around his neck, similar to the one the Indian wore. She also noted, once again, the absence of body hair on his upper torso.

"Your punishment."

Her thoughts scattered and her gaze flew to his, a question in her eyes.

"Do you not remember my words this morn? I said that if you ever raised a hand to me, your punishment would be to tend me."

Her breath left her lungs in a soft exhalation of relief. "Yes, I remember."

"Well then, Brittany Jennifer St. Germain, I'm chilled."

Brittany immediately stood and reached for the cup on the table, which was still warm. But when she offered it to him, he shook his head and, again, the movement directed Brittany's attention to the contrast of sable-dark hair against the pristine white of the pillow beneath him. "I need no sleeping potion."

"Shall I stoke the fire?" She replaced the cup and began to move away from the bed when his answer stopped her cold.

"The chill I feel is from within, undoubtedly the result of the shock from the blow." Her gaze met his, sudden suspicion shading her eyes. "Only a warm body beside mine will help."

Her mouth tightened at his boldness, and Tristan delighted in the ire that flashed in her eyes, momentarily, he suspected, purging her of any fear. "Then why not ask Genna?" she bit out. "Have you not humiliated me enough by expecting me to jump in and out of your bed on command—*without* benefit of any recompense from you?" *Like my promised freedom,* she accused silently.

"Ah, yes. Recompense. You seem to delight in throwing that word at me." His voice belied the sober look on his splendidly hewn features. "Now, I wonder, who owes recompense to whom? I snatched you out of harm's way and gave you shelter. You, on the other hand, repaid me by fleeing my protection and cracking me on the head with a rock." He ceased toying with the coverlet and turned his hand palm up. "Surely you cannot hold it against me that I simply could not allow you to return to London where Buckingham undoubtedly has his cronies scouring every inn and alehouse in the city—and beyond—to find you."

A riposte died on her lips for, in truth, she'd worried about the same thing. She glanced down at his hand, lying so still and so near to her.

"Take my hand, Brittany." It came to Tristan in that moment that it was now or never . . . that in the wake of her attempt to escape, he had to take this chance to make her his in every sense of the word, or he would surely lose her.

She refused to meet his gaze, fearing the effect of his probing perusal. Yet the sound of his voice, soothing and magical in its rich, warm timbre, drew her hand to his as effectively as a moth to a light, and Brittany was suddenly powerless to do anything but comply.

His fingers closed over hers, and she felt the faintest of tremors in his hand. Could he have told her the truth? Then how much more serious was the effect of the blow than his outward behavior would allow? She cast him a furtive look from beneath her lashes and took in the slight, uncharacteristic pallor of his face, missing completely the determination that lit his eyes.

Guilt assailed the citadel of her old fears and aversions.

His fingers massaged hers, his thumb gently kneading the area between her thumb and forefinger, and a sudden, unexpected excitement went singing up her arm and down into the center of her being. The old terror fought with, and lost to, a debilitating languor, and a familiar voice sounded an oft-repeated warning in the back of her mind.

Chapter 10

"Come sit beside me, love."

His fingers played over her slender wrist and the silky flesh of her lower arm, wreaking devastation wherever they touched. She shook her head halfheartedly, even as she sank to the bed beside him, every instinct protesting.

Leisurely he drew her relaxed fingers to his lips, his warm breath sighing over them, his mouth grazing the back of her hand. His eyes, dark as the night sky, drew hers, and Brittany gazed in wonder at the compassion, the tenderness . . . and the gleam of intense longing that seemed to draw her into his very soul.

Here was a man, she acknowledged with a slow, sweet awakening, who was as different from Raymond Chauvelin as night from day, sun from shadow, and she suspected that intimacy with him would be equally as different.

Yet when he murmured, "Come lie beside me, sweet," she hesitated.

His eyes promised, *I'll not harm you, little one. Trust me . . . trust me . . .* And Brittany obediently crept into bed beside him, stretching the length of her body to press against his and impart warmth.

They lay unmoving, unspeaking, for a time. Slowly, slowly she felt his all-but-imperceptible trembling subside, and joy filled her heart at this one small thing she could do for him to help ease her guilty conscience. As he had held her the night before, so did she hold him.

She raised her head from the pillow and met his regard. "Touch me, sweet Brittany. Touch me."

She stiffened, suddenly afraid of where such an exploration would lead. Warm, moist lips brushed hers, his tongue skimming over her softly parted mouth, moving back and forth, gently teasing, sweetly inviting. Reason went fleeing into the night. She pulled her mouth from his to watch a hand—was it her own?—tentatively touch the smooth expanse of his chest, gliding over the rippled muscle and sinew, the rounded ribs and taut abdomen. At his sharply indrawn breath, she hastily moved her hand upward again, her cheeks burning with something more than awkwardness.

She rested her head on his breast, lulled by the steady cadence of his heart. Tristan's hand rode up and down her spine, from neck to lower hip, sending delicious sensations rivering through her. Her lips parted and moved to take a male nipple, which lay beneath her cheek, into her mouth. It seemed so natural to do this, something she'd been forced to do on previous occasions, with no thought of her pleasure . . . only pain and degradation.

Tristan groaned softly and the pebblelike bud nestled between her teeth sprang to life. The touch of his hand on bare skin where the gown had ridden up over her thighs acted to send a burgeoning, liquid fire through her midsection, and her breasts hardened and throbbed against his chest. Lost in mindless sensation, Brittany made no demur when he eased the gown up her body and over her head. It fell with a sigh to the floor.

"Brittany," he murmured, and gently pulled her head from his chest to meet her lips with his. For the very first time, she gave herself to a man, offering her mouth, and so very much more, eagerly now. She pressed against him with an urgency born of the long-suppressed need to share her innermost self with a man, to give the most precious gift she possessed. Mouth to mouth, breast to breast, thigh to thigh, they drank of each other until they were breathless.

"Brittany, love," Tristan whispered over and over again between bouts of exquisite oral loveplay. Then his tongue reengaged hers in a clash and play, entwined and retreated, until one or the other needed a moment to draw in a revitalizing breath.

If I'm to die, came her prayer, unbidden, *let it be thusly, in this man's arms, with this heart beneath mine.*

He turned her onto her back, his eyes fusing with hers, a question in the cobalt depths.

She pulled him over her, wrapping her legs around his, her arms pulling him to her even more closely. *Here is your answer,* her eyes returned. *I trust you as I've never trusted before.*

He lifted himself slightly for better access to her and then slowly, with infinite tenderness, he stroked the silken flesh between her thighs. She shuddered and arched toward him in ancient invitation, and Tristan complied, holding an iron restraint over his own need. He entered her gently, with her name on his lips, a verbal caress, and the scent of violets enveloping them.

Brittany closed her eyes in sweet rapture, all memories of hurt fading as Tristan worshipped her body with his, as with his tender reverence he wiped her mind free of all thought of Raymond Chauvelin. Sheathing him eagerly, she aided him in establishing a rhythm of gentle thrust and withdrawal, the first time she'd ever done more than lie passively, a lip between her teeth until she tasted blood, a scream blocking her throat.

She strove for that heretofore undreamed of peak of fulfillment with this man who would teach her of his kind of love. She knew not what to expect, but she sought it with all the urgency her churning emotions could command. The rhythm quickened, a gathering tightness deep within her threatening to overcome all reason . . . And then they crescendoed, he with a groan and a shudder, and she with a wondrous sense of completeness, of oneness with this man . . . of surprise at the beauty and tenderness of an act she had previously associated only with hurt and debasement.

Tristan opened his eyes to find hers already upon him, studying him with newfound wonder. And immediately he knew he'd been the first . . . the first ever to share physical love with her. Nor, he realized in that moment, had he ever given of himself as he had with her.

He smiled into her eyes. "Such tending you give, wench. I've never had the like."

Her long, thick lashes lowered and a blush shaded cheeks already flushed with lovemaking. Rolling to the side, Tristan gathered her in his arms and pulled her close, cradling her lovingly.

"How—how is your head, my lord?" She gingerly touched the snow-white plaster that covered the stitched cut.

"Much better now." Soft laughter rumbled from deep within his chest. "You provided the perfect restorative, Brittany Jennifer St. Germain. Between Ikuuk's remedy and yours, I feel little pain now."

He nuzzled her cheek before planting a kiss thereupon. "And you?" A sudden frown creased his brow. "I didn't hurt you, did I?"

She turned toward him, her eyes suddenly filling. "Nay," she whispered. A tear spilled across her temple and Tristan kissed it away before it reached her hair. There seemed no point in keeping her secret from him now. "I—I had a husband in France."

"I suspected as much. And he abused you until, in self-defense, you stilled his black heart forever."

Her hands twisted in the coverlet, the fingers suddenly bloodless with the death grip she sustained. Tristan placed a hand over both of her smaller ones, kneading away the tension with his magical touch.

"I—I murdered him. I bludgeoned him to death. Surely you see now that you took a mad dog into your home . . . and your bed." Her words ended on an agonized whisper.

He put his lips to her forehead and pulled her even

closer. "I do not believe that for a moment, sweet. Tell me what happened."

She was silent for long moments, waging an internal battle.

"You do not have to tell me aught if it distresses you."

"Nay, I must. Yet there's not so much to tell." Her voice curdled with bitterness. "Raymond abused me from our wedding night on, through two years of marriage. He—he liked men even more than abusing me."

Tristan's arms tightened around her in reaction, his expression turning grim as he gazed into the orange-tinged embers of the fire.

"On the night I murdered him, he'd forced the stable-boy right out in the open." She shuddered and instinctively pressed her face against his chest. "When I think now of what he did, I know he was mad, but who would have taken my side? Certainly not *mon père*. Nor Raymond's family. They knew all along—they had to. Why else would they pay *mon père* to give me to Raymond in marriage—a commoner to a man of the aristocracy?"

Tristan stroked her hair, the gentle pressure of his hand at odds with the murderous urge that rose up in him at the thought of a man so treating a woman . . . especially this woman.

"That night, after he'd assaulted Garrard, he tried to do the—the same thing to me." Her voice suddenly drained of emotion. "When I refused, he took a knife to me and I hit him over the head with a candlestick. Then I fled to England and found work at the Hunter's Run." She turned lifeless eyes to him. "So, you see, you harbor a murderess beneath your roof."

He propped himself up on one elbow and gazed down at her. " 'Tis not murder to defend yourself."

Brittany rolled her head from side to side, fresh tears forming in her eyes. "But I *planned* to kill him someday. I *wanted* him dead, don't you see?"

"I only see that you rid the world of one more piece of offal. No matter how you wished him dead, wanted to kill him, you acted in self-defense, and 'tis a far cry from murder." He brushed back a glossy lock of her hair. "And your name is Geneviève St. Germain?"

"Geneviève Elise Renault Chauvelin. My mother's name was St. Germain."

He was silent for a moment. " 'Tis just the sort of thing Buckingham would relish using to his advantage if he found out. You say Raymond was of the nobility?"

"*Oui.* Of the Chauvelins of St. Malo."

"I've never heard of them, but that is not to say his relatives are not searching for you." He traced the sloping line of her jaw with a light finger, admiring anew the flawless, peach-toned skin. "It seems that you are safest here, for now, so you must promise you'll not attempt to, ah, demonstrate your prowess with a rock again."

Their eyes met, contrition shining in hers, laughter in his. He brushed his lips over hers, inhaling deeply of her femininity and the faintest trace of violets. "Now, go to sleep, green eyes. We can talk more in the morning."

Brittany closed her eyes and allowed his wizard's fingers to soothe away her worries until she fell fast asleep.

"Tristan!" Matt barged into the room without ceremony.

Tristan bolted upright in bed, the euphoria of sleep instantly banished from his brain. "What is it?"

Brittany stirred sleepily, her lids refusing to open and end a night that words could never describe. But as the sound of Matt's voice registered, she came awake, embarrassment at being discovered in Tristan's bed swiftly overcoming her contentment.

"A message from the king." Matt strode to the bed and handed the sealed letter to Tristan, giving Brittany no more than a cursory look. "You know 'tis urgent," he continued as Tristan broke the seal and opened the letter. "His majesty is never up this early without just cause. I sense trouble."

Brittany sat up, holding the coverlet to her breasts and

feeling self-conscious. How could she retrieve her discarded nightgown and leave the room with dignity?

As if sensing her dilemma, Tristan placed one hand on her leg, stilling her. "He says Buckingham is sending men to search Wildwood this morn."

Matt began to pace the room. "Why didn't Charles interfere on your behalf? He is friend to you—"

"—and to George Villiers, as well," Tristan replied. "This is between Buckingham and me. I wouldn't expect the king to choose between us. What of Drake?"

"He left for London an hour past." Matt plowed a hand through his hair in frustration just as Ikuuk appeared in the door. Brittany unconsciously compared Matt's visible agitation to Tristan's calm deliberation as the latter nodded in greeting to his blood brother. "You obviously do not see, my friend, that Charles does me a great favor by telling me of the duke's plans." He motioned toward his clothing lying across a chair nearby. "Would you hand me my breeches?"

Matt absently picked up the requested article and tossed it to Tristan. "Well," he said, stopping suddenly to stare pointedly at Brittany, "you might be able to hand her over to Buckingham and settle this whole thing."

Brittany mentally recoiled at the anger marring his features . . . the man who'd befriended her at the inn. Yet surely she deserved his enmity after what she'd done to his friend.

Tristan casually handed Brittany her nightgown and blocked her from Matt's view as she slipped it over her head. "I've put my little mishap out of my mind and I expect you will do so as well. No doubt she thinks you irascible enough already, Stark. You *have* been out of sorts these last few days . . . as testy as the earl."

Matt snorted. "If I've been testy, as you put it, 'tis because she has mistrusted us both—attributing our actions to the most dastardly motives." His eyes locked with Brittany's. "And after I showed her kindness at the inn

and then you saved, if not her life, at least her honor."
He looked as if he wanted to say more but held back.

Brittany said it for him. "Then I repaid your kindness
with accusations, and that of Sir Tristan by doing him
physical harm." Her gaze went to Tristan. "If I could
undo it, I would in a moment," she said with quiet sincerity.

He flashed that quick, easy smile that had so affected
her from the first. "Do I look any the worse for last
night?"

Color swept across her cheekbones. Although he re-
ferred to the blow to his head, his eyes spoke of other
things. "You are only a bit pale yet, my lord."

Ikuuk, who'd been standing at the foot of the bed taking
in Brittany's disheveled hair and hastily donned nightgown, signed to Tristan and pointed to his head.

"Much better, my brother. There is only a dull ache
now, much dissipated since I took your potion."

Brittany flung back the covers and made to leave the
bed. "Stay, sweet. I would have you hear my plans before
you depart from Wildwood."

Her eyes met his, questioning. Surely he was not sending her away?

*Only hours ago you would have killed him to be free
and now, after tasting of his love, you are dismayed at the
prospect of leaving?*

Tristan, however, had begun speaking to Matt without
waiting for an answer. He pulled his shirt over his head,
his voice muffled as he said, "I want you to take Brittany
to Carlisle Hall."

"Carlisle Hall?"

"Aye. 'Tis the safest place I can think of at the moment.
Even if Buckingham suspected that Brittany was hiding
there, he wouldn't dare search the manor of an earl."

"You want me to take her all the way to Surrey?"

" 'Tis less than fifty miles, Matt. You travel hundreds
every year across the Atlantic, yet you are dismayed by
the prospect of such a short trip?"

"Only with a woman who would have no qualms about braining me for some slight or imagined offense."

"*Enough.*"

The tone of Tristan's voice and the dark frown that furrowed his brow left no doubt that Matt had gone too far.

Matt blew out his breath in resignation and looked at Brittany. "Forgive me, mistress. I will gladly take you to Surrey." He glanced at Tristan before adding, "If you give me your word you'll take *my* side should we have the misfortune to be accosted."

Tristan's frown deepened until he caught the unexpected gleam of mirth in his friend's eyes. He looked at Brittany to see if she'd been offended, but her lips were already curving upward in answer to Matt's quip. "Ikuuk will make sure you are supplied with a sack of suitable stones," Tristan said with mock solemnity.

All three laughed—even Ikuuk's expression lost its grimness—and Tristan delighted in the animation that transformed Brittany's features. That she could display such easy humor warmed his heart and supported his belief that there was a very different woman buried beneath the layers of her defenses.

Tristan said something in Powhatan to Ikuuk and the Indian left the room. "We've little time to lose. Enis will bring breakfast up here and while we're waiting, go to your room and dress," he directed Brittany. "Take anything you wish along with you, sweet, for I know not when you will return."

Brittany obediently stood, a look of bemusement on her face. "But who resides at Carlisle Hall?"

With a gentle finger, he traced the straight line of her nose to its impertinent tip. "The earl of Weyrith . . . my grandfather. Matt can explain everything to him, although"—he smiled vaguely—"Grandfather is not one to ask unnecessary questions. When Buckingham's agents arrive at Wildwood, they'll find me, ah, indisposed." He glanced at Matt. "Brittany's tap on the head was well timed, for now the injury will serve my purposes."

He brushed his lips lightly across hers. "Go now, sweet. I will come to you by this eve—"

"Your head will never take the pounding of a ride so soon," Matt observed wryly.

"We shall see . . . the morrow at the latest," Tristan promised.

Tristan was not surprised when Buckingham, as well as the expected henchmen accompanying him, arrived at Wildwood not an hour after Matt and Brittany's departure. From his aerie on the second floor Tristan watched them dismount, unaided by servants from Wildwood, and then he slipped into bed.

When he entered Tristan's room, the duke wore a frown of suspicion that was not lost on the servants. Georgie was busily pretending to repair a section of railing at the head of the stairs so he would be near his master should the need arise. A pistol rested securely at his waist beneath his shirt. Jims, the boy who assisted him in the stables and with the tending of the grounds, was likewise occupied inside the house.

The three men entered Tristan's room to find him propped up against two pillows, pale-faced, his head swathed in bandages and a fully painted, fierce-looking Ikuuk sitting cross-legged beside the bed.

Buckingham strutted forward, the picture of sartorial splendor in short doublet with slashed sleeves revealing the silk shirt beneath, flounces of lace at wrists and throat, ribboned and bowed petticoat breeches, and great periwig. At the sight of the Indian he stopped in his tracks, the other two men already shocked into halting.

Tristan met Villiers's astounded gaze. "You've not heard of my blood brother Ikuuk, Villiers?"

"Nay, and I've never seen the like, Savidge . . . but then one can never expect the conventional from a breed." Without missing a beat, he added, "Rather, I am appalled at the lack of training of your servants upon the arrival of a guest. Although," he added, lifting a scented handkerchief to his nose, "one can expect no better from servants trained by an uncouth colonist."

"Do have a seat, George, before your growing insults weigh too heavily upon your impeccably dressed person."

Ikuuk rose in a fluid motion and placed a chair beside the bed. The duke motioned for his companions to wait in the hall and seated himself. The cold blue stare roamed over Tristan's face and head without the briefest flicker of sympathy or concern.

"To what do I owe the dubious pleasure of this visit?"

Buckingham leaned forward on an exquisitely carved silver and ebony walking stick, his regard ruthless and unrelenting. "You know damned well why I am here. I can have you stripped of all you possess for what you did to me."

Tristan's eyes narrowed. Refusing to deny anything, he merely said, "Your word against mine."

"I have witnesses who were in the taproom that night as you flaunted your tawdry prize to all and sundry. How arrogant of you, Savidge. I would have given you credit for more intelligence than that. You might even have gotten away with it had you been more discreet."

Tristan shrugged negligently, then feigned a wince with the movement. "She's not here, Villiers. I only took her to a friend's in the city until she awoke. As far as I know, the wench is still in London."

The duke's eyes narrowed ominously. "All the denials and all the bandages in England will avail you nothing. The ruse is good, but not good enough. Where *is* she?"

Tristan smiled without warmth. "I suspect if she's to be found at Wildwood, your men are equal to the task." He canted his head slightly, listening to the muffled noise of men searching the house. The servants had been instructed to let the men do what they would, as long as they inflicted no damage upon the manor or grounds. So far Buckingham did not seem to suspect the king's interference, which caused Tristan some small bit of relief. Not only would Charles's letter of warning go undiscovered, but also perhaps Buckingham would come to believe that Brittany was not under Tristan's protection. Perhaps. The man was uncannily shrewd.

"I'll find her if I have to tear apart this place plank by plank, stone by stone."

"Tsk, tsk. Such behavior over a common wench."

Buckingham's gaze raked contemptuously over Tristan. "I would not call your behavior the other night worthy of a peer of the realm." He put his handkerchief to his nose once again. "But then, you were not born to a title . . . rather you were given one by an overly generous king." He looked at Tristan through eyes heavy-lidded with indolence. "I don't wonder that such a bawd would appeal to you. After all, your illustrious grandfather coupled with a savage."

Tightly restrained emotions heightened the tension between them before Tristan spoke, ignoring a number of scalding retorts that rose to his lips. "You're very sure of yourself, Villiers . . . insulting my grandmother, who possessed more nobility of spirit than you can ever hope to attain with all your blue blood. If Ikuuk should decide to take offense—for he owes his life to my grandmother— I wouldn't lift a hand to stay him."

Buckingham raised the tip of his cane and pointed it meaningfully at Tristan. "If you or your painted friend so much as touched me, 'twould be the last move either of you would ever make. You'll not get away with injury to a duke before witnesses, Savidge."

Tristan closed his eyes in dismissal. "The woman is not here, I tell you, although why you should be so interested in her when you've already condemned my own interest is a mystery to me."

Buckingham rose and stood towering over the bed. " 'Tis none of your concern, Savidge, but his majesty is the one who has expressed an interest in her, not I. Especially since I've told him on several occasions since our bet last May that she is fairer than even Barbara."

Tristan said nothing for long moments, seeming to have fallen asleep. Buckingham's men reappeared at the door.

"Beggin' pardon, yer grace, but we found no wench anywhere, except for two female servants, both of 'em dark-haired."

The duke nodded, his eyes still on Tristan's placid features. "Before I leave, Savidge, I warn you that this is not over between us. Charles may take your side and protect you until his heart's content, but you overstepped your bounds when you raised your hand to me, and I'll not be satisfied until I see your stinking carcass rotting in Newgate . . . or hanging at Tyburn."

He strode to the door, then paused and faced the Virginian from across the room one last time, infuriated by Tristan's negligently opened eye beneath one cocked brow. "And you can tell your doxy that I have something very special in store for her, as well."

Matthew and Brittany reached Carlisle Hall without mishap. The evening shadows were lengthening as they made their way down a winding country lane and past a small church. Then suddenly across an expanse of lawn bordered by gigantic yew hedges stood the manor. As she and Matt reined in, Brittany drew a breath in reaction to the improbable vision before them, limned in gold by the sun setting over the woods directly behind it.

It spread out majestically, built of the mellowest red brick, gabled, pinnacled, and pepperpotted, its white stone quoins and charming gazebolike window dressings giving it the appearance of an enchanted palace. Long service wings with Dutch gables framed the central structure on either end.

"This—this is where my lord's grandfather lives?" Brittany asked in a reverent whisper.

Matt nodded, also awed by the beauty of Carlisle Hall. "I see now that the title Tristan may inherit is a matter of no small concern. He said nothing about the splendor of the seat of the Carlisles." He looked at Brittany. "But that is his way. He is not impressed by wealth or trappings. Come.'' He touched his heels to his horse's sides and they moved forward together.

Suddenly filled with trepidation, Brittany belatedly realized she'd thought of little but Tristan Savidge for the entire ride from Wildwood, to the exclusion of what lay at the end of their journey. She'd come to terms with the fact that he wished to protect her from Buckingham. She had also accepted, although with more difficulty, the fact that she had feelings for him, not the least of which was trust, something so astonishing to her that she still believed she must be dreaming. But that she was actually allowing Matthew Stark to take her to Carlisle Hall was proof of that trust.

She glanced up at the building before them, new doubts assailing her. What would the earl say when he saw the likes of her—a common wench astride a horse with her rough woolen skirts rucked up to permit ease of riding, arriving unheralded upon his doorstep? Was she mad to have docilely gone along with Tristan's proposal?

Surely I am undone, she thought in bemusement, under the spell of a blue-eyed *sorcier*. Whatever happened next, of one thing Brittany was certain. Tristan Savidge was now a part of her life, for however brief a time it might be, and she was glad of it.

The thought bolstered her determination and, with a hike of her chin and a squaring of her shoulders, she continued toward Carlisle Hall and her uncertain future.

Chapter 11

"So you're Stark, eh? Tristan's partner?" Richard Carlisle, the earl of Weyrith, studied Matt through shrewd eyes.

"Aye, your lordship."

They were in the earl's bedchamber, the old man sitting in a chair with one foot propped up on a padded stool. The soft glow of lighted candelabra held the evening shadows at bay.

"And my grandson told you to bring this young woman to Carlisle Hall."

"Yes. Tris is involved in an ongoing disagreement with George Villiers and—"

"Villiers?" Carlisle sputtered. "Why, that arrogant degenerate! Couldn't abide the man's father either—a bungler of foreign affairs who unnecessarily involved England in wars with France and Spain under the king's father. If he hadn't been assassinated—" He shook his head. " 'Sdeath! I'm rambling again." He eyed Stark, then his penetrating gaze moved to Brittany, who was standing quietly to one side.

"Come here, m'girl. Let's have a look at you." Brittany obediently moved forward and stopped beside Matt, her eyes meeting Carlisle's without wavering. After studying her from head to toe, he said, "You're a fine specimen of a female, and I'd wager this 'ongoing disagreement' with Villiers is more than likely over you—even if Buckingham prefers men, as his father before him."

"Sir Tristan saved me from physical assault by the duke, your lordship, at the inn where I was employed. I'm afraid he had to—to strike the duke to do it."

"Tristan raised his hand to Villiers?" The earl cackled with glee, genuine pleasure lighting his eyes. "Why, the young devil! I knew he had a mind of his own . . . a Carlisle through and through."

Matt smiled and added, "He knocked him out cold, your lordship, and, never one to hide aught, he walked right through the crowded taproom with Brittany in his arms. Otherwise, Buckingham could have proven nothing."

The earl threw back his head and laughed again. "So now he's got his hands full, eh? That'll teach him."

He reached for a glass of water on a small table, his eyes still on Brittany. "If he was a bit rash, I can easily see why. The prize was well worth the risk."

Brittany's gaze slid uneasily away at the unexpected compliment.

"Well, surely you are tired from your journey. You say Tristan will be coming before long?"

"Aye. He said either late tonight or on the morrow."

"Good. He's stayed away long enough. I regret we've become acquainted so late, and I would make up for lost time with him." He tapped his walking cane on the carpeted floor. "I'll say one thing for the boy, he's got good taste in his women, and that's a Carlisle trait as well."

Brittany's face grew warm under the earl's frank scrutiny.

"Well, have Burke give you something to eat and show you to your rooms. We'll talk more in the morning." He laid his snow-white head against the high back of the chair, his eyelids beginning to droop. "Good to have young people at Carlisle Hall again . . ."

Matt guided Brittany to the door, but before they could make an exit, the earl's voice came unexpectedly from across the room. "You may stay at Carlisle Hall as long as you like, child. Whatever else you're fleeing from cannot reach you here, under my protection.''

Brittany stiffened, wondering at his uncanny insight. Or was she so obvious? So terrified of discovery that she wore her fear like a visible garment?

"What is your name?" he pressed.

"Brittany . . . Brittany St. Germain."

His eyes closed again. "I expect when you're ready you'll tell me the truth."

When the door was closed behind them, Matt observed, "He's eerily astute."

"*Oui*. Yet I think he would respect one's privacy, that one's darkest secrets would be safe with him."

Matt nodded his agreement and steered her toward the stairs. "Are you hungry?"

"I could honestly say ravenous were I not so concerned about Sir Tristan."

Matt laughed softly as they descended the huge staircase in search of the ancient Burke. "You do not know Tristan well enough, mistress, if you fear for him. Even if he were unable to handle Buckingham alone, he has the fearless Ikuuk at his side, and the Indian would protect his blood brother to the death." He chuckled again at some private joke. "And if that weren't enough, Georgie is a crack shot with a pistol and Jims most adept with a pitchfork."

Brittany laughed softly, missing entirely the look of surprise that flitted across Matt's features at the sound. "Well, in that case, I will have a bite with you before going to bed."

Later that night Brittany slept the sleep of the dead, feeling safe within the walls of Carlisle Hall. Exhausted from the tension she'd been under since the night of Buckingham's assault at the Hunter's Run, she allowed her new-found trust in Tristan Savidge and now, strangely, in Richard Carlisle, to ease her doubts, her fears, her anxieties. Why not allow herself to be cared for and sheltered for the time being? She'd been on her own and under a tremendous burden since killing Raymond—had been under inordinate strain since the travesty that was her wedding night, with no one to whom to turn.

Yes, she would deal with each day as it dawned, would worry about nothing except getting through one day at a time until . . . She fell asleep without completing the thought, a smile curving her lips.

"Wake up, lazy wench," murmured a voice in her ear.

Brittany snuggled more deeply into the bedclothes, unwilling to leave her pleasant dreams . . . dreams of Tristan Savidge.

Warm lips nuzzled her neck and the delicate shell of her ear, sending delicious shivers through her and immediately bringing her fully awake.

"My lord!"

"At your service, mistress." Laughter shone in his eyes and Brittany tensed in unthinking anticipation of the familiar and dreaded panic.

"I've missed you, love," he told her, his mouth moving to gently take hers. Instead of the unwelcome repugnance, Brittany felt only increasingly pleasant sensations rippling through her.

I'm cured, she thought in wonderment. *As surely as the sun rising to greet the new day, he's healed me.*

Her lips parted gladly, eagerly, to receive his tongue, her arms disentangling from the sheets to wrap around his shoulders and hold him to her with unexpected fierceness.

When he finally pulled away to gaze down into her face, Brittany noticed the circles beneath his eyes, the whisps of loam-dark hair that had escaped his queue, and the dust that still clung to his face.

"Why, my lord, have you come fresh from your journey to my bed—without even washing the dirt from you?" Despite her words, she was secretly flattered that he had not been able to wait that long. He even smelled suspiciously like horses.

"Now you would have me smelling like a rose, combed

and perfumed, when I've ridden half the night to hold you in my arms?''

"*Dieu,* but I'm thoughtless. Forgive me, my lord, for—'' His lips silenced her apologies before he rose from the bed.

"My grandfather asks that we meet him downstairs in half an hour, sweet. I'll make myself presentable and then return for you. We must rescue Ikuuk, you see,'' he added, a corner of his full, sensual mouth quirking with humor.

"Ikuuk?'' She sat up in bed, modestly holding the sheet to her breast.

"Indeed. Grandfather insists he needs a haircut—told him he looks like a rooster robbed of a hen.''

Brittany's lips twitched in answer, and then, unable to contain her merriment, she burst into laughter, the sound reminding Tristan of a singing rill gaily tripping along its course. She was so very beautiful, he thought, with her unbound hair framing her face in curling disarray and laughter animating her features. *How I love you,* his heart whispered, his lips not daring to even hint of it yet.

She sobered then, caught and held by the intense look in his eyes, a look that said many things she could not yet decipher. A look that nonetheless sent joy singing through her blood.

As he left, a woman about Enis's age entered and introduced herself as Mildred. Starched and straight-faced from years of service in a great house, she was the model of efficiency and quickly drew a bath for Brittany, then laid out a jonquil-colored dress, explaining, "His lordship thought you might fit in the late countess's clothing, until your own arrives. My lord Tristan expressed a wish to show you Carlisle Hall after breakfast.'' After ascertaining that Brittany would not have further need of her services, she withdrew and closed the door behind her.

After her own clothes arrived? Brittany thought with some bewilderment. A sense of despair invaded her newfound happiness. Surely this was all a dream. Here she was, an escaped killer, with decent antecedents only on her mother's side to her credit, and ensconced within the ancestral home of an earl . . . Her eyes alighted on the elaborate chest of drawers upon which sat the coffer that had been in her bedroom at Wildwood.

Emotion filled her throat. It hadn't been there when she'd retired the night before. She reached up to take it down and the back of her hand touched something else—a book. She picked up the leather-bound tome. *Tristan.*

Tears threatened, but she blinked them away. Surely she was becoming too emotional. What was happening to her? Just because she'd shared one night of love with Tristan Savidge, she was acting like a sentimental schoolgirl, touched by a book and a chest of cosmetics.

No, a voice disagreed. *Touched by the fact that he was thoughtful enough to bring them across two counties to place them in your care once more . . .*

She shook her head to clear it of the taunting voice. She would not allow herself to become overly emotional. That Tristan Savidge had claimed her body was not enough reason—not nearly enough—to cause any change in her plans to leave England as soon as she had enough money. She would be no man's harlot, no matter what he gave her in return . . .

Replacing the book, Brittany walked to the dressing room. The mohair, rose-dyed wall-hangings were stamped to resemble watered silk, as they were in the bedchamber itself. The tub sat in the middle of the small room, steam collecting in clouds above the water in invitation, and beyond that was the closet with its velvet-padded close-stool just visible from where she stood. She marveled at such luxury as the morning sun streamed through one window, reflecting the soft, dusky pink of the walls.

Quickly, she divested herself of the nightgown that had been laid out the night before—another borrowed nightgown, she'd thought wryly as she'd donned it—and stepped into the tub. Ignoring her colliding thoughts, Brittany determined to think only of the fact that she was safe from Buckingham. Safe even from her past demons, for hadn't the earl said nothing could reach her here, under his protection? It felt wonderful to relinquish herself to the care of others, to let slip the cloak of her woes for even a short time. For now she would think only of how vitally alive she felt, how valuable and treasured Tristan Savidge made her feel.

She began to bathe, ignoring an instinct that warned her to beware of the potent tonic of Tristan Savidge's attentions.

"You can stay as long as you like, m'girl," the earl was saying.

"Thank you, your lordship."

They had broken the fast in Carlisle's room, and now only Tristan and Brittany remained with the old man. Brittany sat in the chair beside the bed, and Tristan gazed out on the grounds of the manor, his profile etched by the bright light from outside.

Brittany found her gaze straying again and again to the magnificent bed that dwarfed everything and everyone in the room. Made of carved walnut, the paneled headboard reached some eight feet above the floor to protect the sleeper from draughts, with massive, intricately carved posts at the foot. The headpiece and posts supported the huge wooden canopy extending over the entire bed, a short red velvet valance the only fabric adorning the entire structure.

"—seems to me you've landed yourself in an unenviable situation, child, and none of it your fault."

As the earl's words registered, distress darkened Brittany's eyes. *Oh, why did Tristan have to tell him?* she thought miserably. How much more difficult to keep the secret of her identity with each person added to the number who knew of it.

At the shadow that crossed her features, however, Carlisle quickly added, "Oh, I know the Chauvelins—rather I know *of* 'em—and madness runs in the family. No matter what you've convinced yourself you've done, 'twas not

murder.'' He eyed her more closely. ''My Evelyn's dress
fits well enough, although you're thinner than she was.
Imagine 'tis out of fashion but, unless you plan to attend
some social affair in London—''

''You need not worry about that, Grandfather,'' Tristan
interrupted as he swung away from the window. ''Brittany
has no intention of returning there.'' His eyes met hers,
and her irritation at his supposition disappeared with
alarming ease as his gaze caressed her face.

For the first time, the earl commented on the small plaster on the back of his grandson's head. ''What happened
to your head, boy?''

For a moment Tristan was caught off-guard, and Brittany's heart froze in mid-beat. Quickly recovering himself,
however, he explained with a casualness that Brittany envied, ''Brittany thought I was Ikuuk the other night in the
woods and tried to protect herself.''

A servant knocked on the door and entered to clear
away the remains of their breakfast. The earl, however,
was not to be diverted. His sharp eyes caught the glance
that passed between the two people.

''I see you've a regular penchant for braining men,'' he
stated bluntly, his eyes narrowing.

Embarrassment stained Brittany's cheeks, proclaiming
her guilt.

'' 'Twas an accident,'' Tristan said.

But Brittany had already glimpsed the love the earl har-
bored for his grandson—a sentiment far stronger than any
inclination to protect her—and she saw a thinly veiled
warning in those unnervingly perceptive eyes. Explana-
tions would avail her nothing.

''There is only one problem with your having brought
her to Carlisle Hall,'' the old man added. At Tristan's
raised eyebrow, he explained, ''Your cousin John is ever
eager to curry Buckingham's favor. If he should mention
Brittany to the duke—for he pops in and out of here on a
regular basis, especially when he needs more funds to pay
his gambling debts—the secret will be out.''

Tristan's brows met in a frown. "Buckingham wouldn't dare do anything while Brittany is here."

"Nay, of course not. But if he does discover she is here, he will watch and wait with the patience of a hungry wolf. I suggest you marry her if you seriously wish to keep her safe from Villiers."

Tristan regarded Brittany with an indefinable look in his eyes, but Brittany's bemused gaze flew to Carlisle. Stunned disbelief flickered across her exquisite features before she shook her head. "That is out of the question, your lordship." Why would she ever wish to become any man's chattel again? And why on God's green earth would the grandson of an earl ever wish to have her for a wife? A woman of questionable background . . . a woman who'd killed her husband?

"—mother was a St. Germain, so Tristan tells me. 'Tis an old and esteemed name in France. And, of course," he added emphatically, "my grandson cares naught for wealth or titles."

But Brittany was having none of it and, in the wake of the old, familiar panic, she shook her head again before Tristan came to her rescue. "Perhaps 'twould be better if I took her to the Colonies," he suggested.

Hope surged through her, only to be ruthlessly crushed with the earl's next words. "You cannot leave England when I need you here to assume your responsibilities as my heir."

Tristan stood before the bed, one hand clasped tightly around an ornately carved post, the only outward sign of his agitation. "John is your heir . . . or did you not speak truly when you said I would inherit only upon his demise?"

"Ye gods, you're a stubborn one. What if I deem John unfit? The continuation of the Carlisle line and the preservation of the earldom and its holdings are more important than your misplaced loyalty to a fledgling colony across the sea." The conviction in his voice suggested to Brittany that Tristan was up against more than just a simple clash of wills. If Richard Carlisle, earl of Weyrith, wanted Tristan Savidge as his heir, it would come to pass, despite Tristan's ties to Virginia or his wishes to have it otherwise.

"We can discuss it another time," Tristan said with an obvious effort to keep his voice calm, and Brittany guessed at the iron control he exercised, evident only in the muscle that twitched faintly in his cheek and the bloodlessness of the fingers still wrapped around the bedpost. "If you'll excuse us, Grandfather, I would like to take Brittany around the manor."

Carlisle nodded. "As you wish. Show her the grounds as well and, if she wishes, take her riding—the horses grow fat and lazy in the stables. I'll see you both at dinner."

They stood in one of the long galleries before a full-length portrait of Richard Carlisle at Tristan's age. The earl's eyes were exactly the same stunning deep blue as his grandson's.

Brittany shivered as she stared up at the commanding figure, remembering how she'd felt the first time she'd looked into Tristan's eyes. His arm immediately went around her shoulders. "Are you cold in this draughty gallery?"

She pulled her gaze from the painting and looked up at him. "Nay, my lord, only under the spell of the Carlisle eyes."

"Tristan," he corrected. At her faint frown, he elucidated, "I am Tristan to you, love, not my lord. My father would scorn the title." He guided her away from the painting.

"His majesty must think highly of you to have awarded you knighthood."

Tristan shrugged, his thumb absently massaging her upper arm. "My loyalty is not given with the hope of earning wealth or titles, nor is my behavior dictated by the same."

Brittany reached up tentatively to touch the fingers at

her shoulder, as if to make certain he was real. The contact threatened her very reason as warmth splayed through her body. "And just what did you do for the king to merit such appreciation?"

Tristan looked down into her eyes and desire shot through him with all the force of a cannon volley. His gaze moved to her slightly parted mouth, and it was all he could do to answer her question. "I traveled between the Continent and England while he was in exile, making contact with Royalists still living here and searching for a way to restore him to power."

He stopped before another full-length portrait, but Brittany's attention was still on him. "You risked your life for him."

He smiled down into her eyes, dismissing her sober words. "As I would gladly for you, if you would but let me, *chère* Geneviève."

The sound of her given name in his flawless French sent a frisson of excitement through her, but his other words gave her pause. Her lovely eyes with their generous, umber lashes narrowed in a bemused frown. "There is no need for such a thing," she said in a low voice. "You hardly know me."

He lifted her chin to meet his probing gaze. "I've known you forever, my love." With one arm still around her shoulders, he gently pulled her to him, his other hand riding up her back and reaching beneath the heavy spill of her hair to caress the velvety skin at the nape of her neck.

His mouth descended with agonizing slowness, and Brittany's eyes left his to fasten upon his mouth in delicious anticipation.

The joining was leisurely at first, with Tristan's mouth working over hers with deliberate thoroughness. As their tongues met, he brought his hands up to cradle her face, holding her as a willing captive while his lips and tongue played havoc with her senses.

"Geneviève . . . Geneviève," he whispered, dragging his mouth from hers to kiss her cheeks, her eyes, the fragile skin at her temples. And Brittany suddenly leaned into him, the building languor so debilitating that her legs refused to hold her weight. He left off his worship of her face to sweep her up into his arms, his eyes dark with desire.

"Would you like to see the grounds?" he murmured. At her look of dismay, he laughed softly. "I should think you'd be weary of saloons and withdrawing rooms and great halls and . . . bedchambers."

Brittany laid her head against his shoulder, a long, shuddering sigh escaping her lips. "You are cruel to tease me so."

Barely forty-eight hours ago you avoided my very touch, he thought with a sense of elation, but he merely said, "However cruel you may think me, my grandfather would require me, at the least, to treat you with respect while under his roof, instead of taking you here on the gallery floor as I long to do."

Shyly, Brittany raised her head enough to touch her lips to the smooth column of his throat. "I would do anything you commanded me, for I have no will of my own when I am in your arms."

He released her legs and deliberately allowed her body to slide down the length of his before her feet touched the marble-tiled floor. "I would never command you to do aught, sweet. Now, will you accompany me outdoors, or would you rather we continue to entertain Ikuuk?"

Brittany's head jerked around. "He's here? In the gallery?"

"Indeed." He inclined his head toward a long shadow beside a pedestal bearing the bust of some Carlisle ancestor. "He does not trust you to be alone with me."

Her eyes met his in guilty acknowledgment, but the absence of concern in his expression acted to soften his words. "Well, then, I will have to put his fears to rest concerning my intentions toward you, won't I?" She swung toward the shadow. "Ikuuk, would you like to accompany us outdoors?"

The Indian silently materialized from his hiding place and came to stand before them, seeming not the least embarrassed at being discovered. His dark eyes studied Brittany before he nodded and signed something to Tristan.

"What did he say?"

Tristan was silent for a moment, as if hesitant to interpret Ikuuk's message. "He said he'd much rather be a witness to our making love than war."

Color flagged her cheeks, but for the first time since she'd met him, Ikuuk smiled—rather lasciviously, but a smile all the same.

"Come." Tristan took her hand and led her toward the far end of the long hall.

"Have you decided to return to Virginia this trip?" Tristan studied Matt from across the room as the latter examined a book he'd taken from one of the cases in the earl's office.

Matt looked up at his friend, snapping the tome closed. "Nay. I'm entrusting everything to Simms. He knows as much as I do about sailing and, with the cargo completed, it only remains for me to make one final check before the *Virginia* sails off." He paused. "I'll be leaving in the morning. I want that ship safely back in London before winter sets in. Simms can do it with a bit of luck and good weather."

"If they are quick to catch favorable winds at Dover, they'll have the needed edge." Tristan smiled. "Genna has naught to do with your decision?"

Matt shrugged, an answering gleam of humor in his hazel eyes. "I never said that." He sobered. "Buckingham and your safety have even more to do with it."

Tristan moved to stand before Matt. Gripping his friend's shoulder, he said, "And since when am I unable to take care of myself?" He glanced meaningfully at Ikuuk, who sat astride a wooden chair, notching feathers to a new arrow. "Even as we speak my bodyguard is increasing the weapons in his arsenal for my protection."

Ikuuk looked up and frowned.

" 'Tis no laughing matter, Tris. Even the Indian for once disapproves of your careless levity. You mark my words—more will come of this rift with Buckingham than you ever dreamed, I feel it. Although you have the earl behind you, Buckingham's influence extends everywhere, and he has tremendous wealth to back it." He looked Tristan straight in the eye. "My advice, which I know you'll not heed, would be to let her go. A cat always lands on its feet, and she did well enough before you came along."

Tristan's hand fell to his side, his expression suddenly free of humor. "In other words, just throw her to the wolves."

Matt sighed in resignation. "She seems to have done well enough until Buckingham entered her life. Even after your rescue, she had only accusatory words for both of us." He replaced the book and turned to face Tristan. "But the final straw, I should think, would have been her attempt on your life."

Tristan unstoppered a glass decanter and poured half a goblet of crystal-clear sack. He motioned toward Matt, but the latter declined with a shake of his head. "You are not usually so easily offended by the actions of the fairer sex."

"And you consider her cracking your skull an inoffensive action? She could have killed you—"

"—as you've already pointed out."

Matt closed his eyes in surrender. "All right, so you've forgiven her. Yet I remember a time when your head was not so easily turned by a comely face. Half the women at court are mad for you because of your unusual background—the challenge of a handsome buck with Indian blood running through his veins still has them all panting, including Barbara, Lady Castlemaine—"

"Brittany is much more than a comely face to me, Matt."

"—a time when you were so fiercely Powhatan in your ways that your mother begged your father to send you to Europe to civilize you. Ikuuk is right, you're getting soft since—'' He stopped in midsentence as Tristan's words registered. His eyes widened in sudden comprehension. ''Well, I'll be damned . . . You love her.''

''You're to be congratulated on your fine perception, even if 'tis a bit dulled.'' One side of Tristan's mouth quirked.

In a trice, Matt was upon him, slapping him soundly on the back, causing some of the wine in the goblet to slosh over the rim and onto the floor. ''Well, if it's love, you won't be the same until you've recovered.'' He rolled his eyes.

I never intend to recover. ''You'll stop in at Wildwood occasionally then?''

''Aye. There's more to lure me back there than Enis's sharp tongue.'' Matt sobered suddenly. ''But surely the king will summon you back to court?''

''As far as he knows, I'll be getting to know my grandfather and helping him execute certain business matters. I doubt Buckingham will say anything more to him, and he's even less likely to come here in search of Brittany.''

''Let's hope so. Once arrangements for the *Virginia* are completed, I'll give you a full report.''

Tristan nodded. ''Come, let's toss the dice with Ikuuk. He's notched enough arrows to supply the entire Powhatan confederacy.''

Amidst the ensuing laughter, the three men positioned themselves cross-legged on the floor to try their luck at dice in easy camaraderie.

Chapter 12

The last few days of August were an idyllic interlude for Brittany. Basking in the glow of Tristan's affection, she began to blossom, slowly fulfilling the potential of the young woman she was before her marriage to Raymond. Now there was no bitter father, André Renault, to constantly remind her that she was to blame for her mother's decline and death. No once beloved father turning indifferent and packing her off to the small convent school to keep her out of his sight.

Despite the earl's disapproval of what she'd done to Tristan the night she'd attempted to flee Wildwood, he accepted her readily. Although no further mention was made of marriage, Brittany had the distinct impression that the wily Carlisle hadn't discarded the idea, that he was merely biding his time until her defenses were leveled beneath his grandson's gently persistent onslaught.

And what an onslaught it was! If Tristan had planned his strategy for years, it couldn't have been more successful, couldn't have assaulted her protective barriers with greater effect, breaking down her remaining reservations one by one.

She often wondered if perhaps she was, after all, a woman of easy virtue to allow herself to be lured into the bed of a virtual stranger that night before she'd left Wildwood. And in light of her aversion to men, why had she given in so easily? He'd not made love to her since, but she knew without a doubt that all he had to do was take her in his arms and pull her down to a bed, a grassy knoll, or even a fern-strewn glade, and she would be lost, for he was the magician and she his willing subject. Yet the question remained, teasing her at the most unexpected moments.

When the answer came, she and Tristan were taking a leisurely ride about the Carlisle lands on the last day of the month, he on Gorvenal, she on a spritely chestnut mare. The day was drenched in sunshine, and the wild-flowers in the woods and fields through which they rode were redolent with fragrance, as if indulging in one last burst of glory before the nip of coming autumn sent them into slumber.

A hare darted into their path without warning, startling the horses and causing her mare to rear. Brittany was skilled enough to keep her seat, but Tristan immediately edged Gorvenal up beside her mount and took hold of the animal's bridle, his look intense with concern.

The expression triggered a memory from the spring before, the night she'd first encountered him at the inn. His eyes had met hers for one brief eternity, and she must have sensed it even then—sensed that the intensity of his gaze signaled only sincerity and genuine concern, nothing less. Then, in the stable a fortnight later, those same eyes had invited her to become his friend, a friend she'd needed badly. They'd also invited her to trust him, and now, as she assured him that nothing was amiss with a smile that animated her features from the sheer joy of being with him, Brittany knew why she'd willingly joined with him at Wildwood. She'd needed to know that there, indeed, existed a man who lived up to her girlhood ideal—the man her mother had so earnestly assured her would gather her under his protection and care for her. A man who could free her of the specter of Raymond Chauvelin. The streak of romanticism within her, the spirit that had been battered but not quite extinguished by her husband's perversity, cried out for another chance to discover love, in spite of her experiences.

You must always remember the verse, petit chou, her

mother had told her. *The verse from the legend . . . It is
so very simple, yet says all.* The verse that would always
represent her beloved mother, weak-willed dreamer that
she was, and her belief in the promise of eternal love.

> A man, a woman; a woman a man:
> Tristan, Isolde; Isolde, Tristan.

I wanted to trust you, to believe in you, and could do
no less than give in to your desires . . . and mine, she
silently told the man before her.

"If you're not shaken, why do you not answer, love?"
The voice was light but the eyes remained unconvinced.
She hastened to dispel her errant thoughts and put him at
ease. "I am unscathed, I assure you. Surely I am heartier
than you give me credit for."

But so fragile inside yet, he thought. "Aye, that you
are." His expression revealed how very aware he was of
her physically—that she was many other things besides
hearty—and Brittany felt giddy with the promise in his
eyes.

They continued onward in contented silence, emerging
finally from a copse to come upon the brook that ran across
the rear of the manor grounds. Ikuuk stood bent in the
middle of the stream, stock-still and gazing intently into
the water. Only a slight upward cant of his head in their
direction acknowledged their presence.

"What is he doing?" Brittany whispered.

"Watch, you'll see."

They sat their horses, as unmoving as the Indian until,
without warning, one of his raised hands shot downward
into the clear, cold water and emerged just as quickly,
fingers clamped around a wriggling fish.

Ikuuk straightened and proudly displayed his prize to
Brittany.

"Oh, Tristan, tell him to let it go!"

Tristan slanted a look at her, his expression one of

feigned disapproval. "Surely you jest, woman. To what purpose?"

"We've so much to eat, what need have we of another fish?"

Tristan rolled his eyes and pinched the bridge of his nose with thumb and forefinger. "You'll insult his abilities when he but seeks your approval." He let his hand fall and dismounted, and Brittany was struck by the fact that although he might dress in the latest mode, although he might be as intelligent and cultured as any of the blue-bloods she'd seen at the Hunter's Run, he was without the incisive wit or stinging sarcasm of the true courtier. As he reached up to help her down, he pleaded with mock humility, "I pray you, beautiful lady, soothe the savage or he'll be after that lynxlike hair he so admires."

Brittany's gaze instantly left Ikuuk to meet Tristan's, distress marring her brow. "You're not serious?"

He shrugged and lifted her down. "One can never tell with Ikuuk. He's been away from home for several years and finds much solace in his Indian ways. Just flash him your devastating smile and the only penalty for being slow to appreciate his skill will be having to eat trout every day for the next week." He inclined his head toward a small hill of flapping fish on the bank.

Sudden deviltry lit her spring-green eyes. "Surely you can do as well as Ikuuk?"

He raised an eyebrow warily. "I? There was a time when I could do as well as he . . .''

But Ikuuk had caught Brittany's question and was signing emphatically to Tristan. The latter glanced at the Indian and shook his head. "Now see what you've done, sly wench. He'll not be satisfied until he bests me." He was already lowering himself to the ground to remove his boots.

"Eh bien, I think you should put him in his place once and for all . . . if you can."

Tristan squinted up at her. The sun high overhead cast her features in light shadow, yet made a golden halo of

her hair. Mildred had been dressing her tresses in curls
and ringlets pulled back from her temples to tumble down
her back, and the result was extremely becoming. How
exceedingly lovely she was, he thought, with her cheeks
flushed from riding, her eyes dancing with mirth, her expression relaxed and happy. What a difference between the
young woman he'd taken to Wildwood and the woman who
stood before him now. He would do anything to keep that
look intact, even if it meant making a fool of himself trying to catch fish barehanded.

And so it was that Sir Tristan Savidge, in stockinged feet,
waded into the water to take up the challenge. He tried several times, and each time Ikuuk shook his head in mute
disdain, while Brittany stifled her laughter with her hand.
Tristan, however, merely smiled good-humoredly and positioned himself for yet another try.

Just when it seemed as if he surely must give up, his
arm flashed through the water and emerged triumphantly,
squirming fish in hand. He looked over at Brittany expectantly.

"Bravo, Pale Wolf!"

But when he glanced at Ikuuk, the Indian merely
shrugged in obvious dismissal of Tristan's lone catch.
"Why, my haughty friend, I should hope you have a few
more than I. You've undoubtedly been at it since sunrise."

He took a step toward the bank. Before Brittany could
warn him, Ikuuk catapulted himself through the air and
caught Tristan behind the knees. The trout went flying and
so did Tristan—face first into the stream. Both men came
up struggling and sputtering, the battle joined.

As they thrashed about, first one attacking and then
the other, Brittany unobtrusively made her way to Ikuuk's
mound of fish. Carefully choosing only those still wriggling or gasping, she tossed them back into the stream
one by one and watched them dart away, a smile of satisfaction curving her lips. She walked back to the mare
and continued to observe the horseplay as if nothing were
amiss.

With a cry of victory that sounded suspiciously like a war whoop, Tristan dragged the Indian to his feet, one arm pinned behind him. "So, you think to put me to shame before the lady with your sneaky tactics, do you?" he panted in Ikuuk's ear.

The Indian stood unmoving, his face expressionless.

"He cannot answer you with his arm pinned behind him, Tristan."

Tristan looked up at Brittany, water runneling down his face from his hair. "I didn't intend for him to answer . . . only to listen."

Ikuuk gave an uncooperative grunt with a jerk of his head, and Brittany hid a smile behind her hand as the water-logged ridge of hair bisecting Ikuuk's scalp wilted even further from the move.

Tristan forced his blood brother toward the bank where Brittany stood. "I may be getting soft in the ways of the Powhatan, but I am not considered so in the ways of the English. Shall we see how you do against my sword, my smug brother, or against a pistol?" He emphasized his words by repeating them in Algonquian as the two men emerged from the stream.

But Ikuuk seemed not the least affected by Tristan's half-serious banter. Instead, as his glance came to rest upon the much depleted pile of fish remaining on the bank, his dark eyes widened slightly, then narrowed as they settled on Brittany.

She flushed guiltily before her chin climbed to a lofty angle in unspoken defiance. "They—they were dying slowly . . . suffering needlessly. If you had killed them first, I wouldn't have touched a one."

Tristan chuckled. " 'Twould seem the joke is on you, after all, brother. Will you give me the battle?"

Ikuuk nodded and was immediately released. "The lady obviously does not like to see any creature suffer," said Tristan. "I suggest you find another way to try and diminish my worth in her eyes."

With a snort of disgust, Ikuuk bent to scoop the remaining catch into a nearby pouch.

"I fear we've both spoiled his sport."

Tristan raked his hair back from his face with both hands. "He knows the consequences of losing a scuffle with me. If he hadn't been so eager to make me look the fool before you, he wouldn't have lost face . . . or half his catch." He grabbed the reins of Gorvenal and the mare and led them to the edge of the water to drink. "No doubt he will only move upstream and replenish his supply," he said as he watched Ikuuk's retreating back. He called something to the Indian in Algonquian, before Ikuuk was out of earshot, but he received no answering acknowledgment.

Tristan came up to her then and took her hand. "Come."

"Where are we going?" she asked as he led her in the opposite direction.

"For a swim."

A protest bubbled to her lips, but she knew that he would brush it aside.

"I know what you're thinking, but 'tis the Indian custom to bathe every day." He guided her to where the trees grew almost to the edge of the stream, providing more seclusion, and shed his shirt. "The water is deeper here." He stopped and looked at her expectantly. "Do you swim?"

"A-a little."

He took her in his arms and kissed her gently until her frown of uncertainty vanished. Then he deftly began unfastening the back of her dress.

"My lord!" she demurred halfheartedly. "What would your grandfather say?"

"I suspect not a word, but he need not know," he murmured into the hair at her temple.

"But—"

"Hush, love." And before she realized it, Brittany stood clad only in Evelyn Carlisle's chemise and drawers. The trees whispered above them, beams of sunlight spearing through the boughs to create a trellised pattern of light and shade over their bodies. He pulled her against him once more, the contact of her breasts through the thin linen garment against his bare chest sending hot desire raging through her. She'd hungered unashamedly for him since she'd first tasted of his lovemaking, her desire for him ever since that blissful night simmering just below the surface. Now it sprang to life with a throbbing urgency that left her weak for want of him—she, who'd abhorred a man's touch until he'd wooed her body with gentle hands, her heart with tender words, her soul with his magnificent eyes.

Her knees buckled and he lifted her in his arms, his mouth never separating from hers, and carried her into the water. The hot sun burned into them, adding to the flame of her need, while the water eddied around them, its coolness a sharp contrast.

Tristan set her on her feet and, taking her hands in his, pulled her down with him until they were up to their chins in the water, their eyes locked in tense anticipation. His eyes narrowed against the glare of the sun, the dense tangle of his ebony lashes scoring the brilliant blue behind them. Never had she seen such stunning blue eyes, and his male beauty unexpectedly struck her with the force of a physical blow.

Dieu au ciel . . . What is happening to me?

"Do I please you, sweet Brittany?" His husky voice broke into her thoughts.

"You do more than please me . . . you take my breath away with your splendor. Surely you aren't real, *sorcier* . . . "

He pulled her to him and rose to stand with her, waist deep, in the laughing brook. "I assure you I am very real, and with a very real need for you." He took her hand and guided it to the rock-hard evidence of his arousal.

For an instant, Brittany felt a familiar flash of panic as she touched him, her eyes widening slightly. But it disappeared just as quickly as he whispered her name, his breath mingling with hers while his lips and tongue teased her half-parted mouth.

He swept her up into his arms again, dripping wet, and strode through the water to the sylvan bank. Dropping to his knees, he laid her down upon an emerald patch of grass beneath a sheltering oak and pressed his lips to hers once more. A flash of excitement flared through her abdomen as he invited her fingers to stroke and explore him—to unfasten his breeches and gain access, flesh to flesh.

His palm came up under her hair to caress the velvety skin at the nape of her neck, his other arm tightening around her waist, lifting her and bringing her up against him more firmly. Their hips undulated with growing urgency, until Brittany broke away from his kiss to drop her head back in utter abandon. Tristan's tongue glided up and down the arch of her throat, and Brittany felt as if she would die from the intense pleasure that was singing through her body, racing along her veins as the most potent wine.

"Make me yours, Tristan . . . make me yours!" she begged softly, the words seeming to come from someone else, far away. She opened her eyes to gaze beseechingly into his.

His eyes caressed her face. If he'd thought he might be moving too fast for her, the notion disappeared as her eyes darkened to the deep green of the forest around them, desire and invitation clearly apparent therein.

He fit her to him with maddening deliberation, allowing her to sheathe him slowly, sweetly, rejoicing in the trust he read in her eyes. He rested within her for a while, still and content, relishing the moment.

Brittany's fine, silky brows drew slightly together. "Why do you wait, *mon coeur?*"

The endearment caused a rush of exaltation within him as nothing physical could have done, and he began to respond to her body beneath his. "My impatient little wanton," he chided softly, matching her movements stroke for stroke. The pleasure built to an exquisite pitch and, of their own volition, the words slipped out before he could stop them. "I love you, *chère* Geneviève . . . God, how I love you!" and his rhythm increased in intensity until she was exploding, utterly consumed, into myriad shards of exhilaration, her soft cry of release captured by his mouth so that only the sounds of the birds and the breeze and the water lapping along the banks ruffled the stillness.

She lay within the shelter of his embrace, a contented sigh escaping her as the warm air caressed her passion-flushed flesh. She stretched languorously and opened her eyes to meet Tristan's amused countenance above her. "Such a greedy wench you are," he said in a dulcet tone that belied his words. His hand cupped a breast, the thumb circling the aureole, bringing the coral bud of her nipple springing to life anew.

"Oh, Tristan . . . did I not pleasure you?" She worried her lower lip with even, pearly teeth, even as she fought the sensations his thumb was creating.

"You please me in all ways, at all times, my love."

Pretty words, she thought, but how could she know if she'd been the only one to reach the pinnacle of sexual gratification? Tristan, however, seemed unconcerned. "I sought to please you, and I succeeded. That is enough." His marauding thumb left off its stimulating play and his hand moved to trace the sweet slope of her jaw, the fine lines of her mouth, the delicate arch of her brows.

Changing the subject, he informed her, "I must go to London, sweet."

Brittany went absolutely still. "London?" Sudden dread washed over her, an inexplicable feeling of impending loss. Her expression turned nonplussed.

"Only for a while. The king wishes my presence at Whitehall. His messenger came late last night."

Aye, and you will jump to his tune. Why shouldn't you? You'll never leave England, will you? With your duty to your king and now your grandfather . . . But she fought to keep her distress to herself, and drew her pride about

her like a protective cloak, feeling some of her newly realized trust in him begin to crumble. "Then you must
go."

Tristan kissed the tip of her nose and nuzzled the silken
flesh below one ear. "I don't want to leave you." His
voice was soft, muffled, and she didn't hear the urgency
underlying the words.

"When?"

He raised his head, his gaze delving into hers. "On the
morrow . . . Brittany, I love you."

She nodded. *Words to help ease your conscience.* But
she merely said, "There is no such thing as love . . . only
lust."

He frowned. "What you feel for me is only lust?"

Evading his question, she said, "Love—and trust—
merely cause pain."

His eyes darkened. "Don't deny me, Brittany."

Her throat closed with emotion at the stark hurt in his
eyes. Oh, why did she suddenly feel so possessive of him—
as if he were betraying her simply by going to London?

"Nothing has changed . . . nothing," he said. "I will
return as soon as I can get away. I can't think what could
be so urgent." His lips brushed hers. "I've been away
longer than ten days before and he's never summoned me
like this." His eyes came to rest upon a stray lock of her
hair that lay across her neck. He picked it up between his
fingers and watched it slip strand by strand to the grass
beneath her head. "I must make him understand that while
I gave him my loyalty, I owe him naught else. I will return
to my home one day."

"But what of the earldom and the title you stand to
inherit?"

A pleat of concern furrowed his noble brow, his features
taking on a look of dark intensity. Brittany unthinkingly
reached up to smooth it away. Without waiting for an answer, she slid her fingers around his neck and pulled his
mouth to hers, needing to wipe the bleak expression from
his face. "Forgive me," she whispered against his

mouth. "I will be waiting for you, my lord . . . most eagerly."

The kiss deepened before Tristan pulled away and smiled down at her. "After all, you'll have the earl for company . . . and Ikuuk."

She laughed softly, her eyes brightening to the lush green he loved so well. "Where do you think he is?" She raised up on her elbows and scanned the forest.

Tristan pushed her back down, laughter playing about his mouth. " 'Tis a bit too late, I would say, to worry about his whereabouts. If he wished to watch us make love, he undoubtedly has seen his fill." He didn't tell her that he'd instructed the Indian to stay upstream.

"Oh, Tristan . . ."

He silenced her with yet another kiss, and this time, his excitement growing apace with hers, Tristan matched her urgency. As the birds caroled in the trees, as the light, somnolent wind tickled over them, as the brook sang over its course, her body told him what her lips would not, her actions promising all that she was with him . . . and only him.

When they returned to the manor house, a carriage stood in the brick-paved front courtyard and servants moved to and fro carrying gaily decorated boxes through the great front doors. A groom ran forward to take their horses and Tristan caught Brittany around the waist and helped her down, a mysterious half smile on his mouth.

"Only Didier would have the gall to bring his creations in through the front entrance," he said.

Didier? Where had she heard that name before?

Tristan led Brittany straight up to her room and through the open door. As she realized the packages were being deposited in her bedchamber, she suddenly recognized the name Didier—a famous dressmaker in London. Her gaze flew to Tristan questioningly.

"All for you, sweet," he answered her silent query.

"They would have arrived sooner had we remained at Wildwood."

Brittany pulled her eyes from his, allowing them to rest with a mixture of longing and reluctance upon the boxes, from which Mildred was already taking colorful garments fit for a queen. Rich-looking dresses with gloves and shoes to match, lace-trimmed undergarments in fine linen and silk, hats, several riding habits . . .

"But—but what need have I of these beautiful clothes?" she asked as Tristan led her to the testered bed where Mildred was unpacking. "I cannot go to London, and surely you would never think of allowing me to appear at any function held here at Carlisle Hall."

He cocked a sable eyebrow. "And why not? There is no reason in the world for you to hide in this room should Grandfather decide to entertain. I suspect he would enjoy doing so now that you and I are here."

Brittany turned troubled eyes to him. "But to have spent so much money on me! And—and Buckingham—"

"Buckingham be damned. Undoubtedly he already suspects you are here, but there isn't a thing he can do about it. I didn't defy him in the first place only to keep you hidden away like a nun in a convent." He took a length of emerald silk from Mildred's hands and held it up to Brittany, admiration lighting his eyes. "Someday, love, you will take London by storm."

Brittany sighed and gazed down at the garment, then turned misery-filled eyes to his. "You forget, my lord, why you found me at the inn in the first place."

The last of the crates was brought in and Tristan dismissed Mildred with a smiled thank-you before responding. "I am sending one of the earl's most trusted agents to investigate exactly how sought after you are by the authorities and the Chauvelin family in France. Perhaps Grandfather's money can buy their cooperation. Surely the authorities in St. Malo knew of your husband's malady . . . and that the likelihood of your coming to blows with Chauvelin was a real possibility."

"No!" She whirled away from him, her hands balled into fists. "You cannot jeopardize my anonymity. Don't you see? The Chauvelins are wealthy in their own right. There is nothing they wouldn't do to discover where I am and haul me back to St. Malo to be hanged for murder!" She shivered with terror, hugging herself in her agitation.

Tristan took her stiff body in his arms and held her close, one hand riding up and down her back in a comforting motion. "Do you think I would ever let anything happen to you? How little faith you have in me. Even if my grandfather's influence could not protect you, I would find a means to whisk you away to the Colonies."

She shook her head against his chest. "I would never expect you to do such a thing for me—to jeopardize your position as possible heir, to anger your king by leaving England. I would never have you leave England because of me." *Nor will I cling to you like a helpless female and watch your affection turn to resentment.*

She raised her head from his shoulder, her eyes dulled with stoic despair. "Please—I beg you! Do not become involved in my sordid affairs." Clutching his shirt in both hands, she touched her forehead to his chest. "What am I to do?" she whispered. "What am I to do?"

Tristan crushed her to him, his lips in her hair, the scent of violets drifting up to his senses. *This is because of me. Because of my interference, she's come to Buckingham's attention—and possibly the king's as well—and all because of my self-serving heroics.*

"Very well, my love. I shall not interfere. We will leave things exactly as they are." He held her away from him, his heart twisting at the anguish in her eyes. "For now, however," he began lightly, "I would have you dress in one of those splendid gowns for dinner. I bought them for a selfish reason, if the truth be known. I wished to feast my eyes on you in finery that suits you—not in a tavern wench's garb."

Her lips quivered as she attempted a smile, but did not quite succeed.

"And," he promised as he cupped her face in his hands, his thumbs grazing her porcelainelike cheeks, "I shall take every delight in personally undressing you—button by button, bodkin by bodkin—before we retire . . . together."

Chapter 13

Every moment Tristan was gone seemed like an hour—each day, a week. The last night they shared together was indelibly engraved upon Brittany's heart and soul, as the most beautifully memorable interlude of her life. Never had she dreamed a man could be so ardent in his love-making, yet so infinitely tender. As his hands had caressed her body, his lips had wooed with the poetry of a lover, a soothing mélange of French and Powhatan and English.

He'd left her in the early morning hours while she'd slept on, sated and replete, her dreams of him—a man equal to the legend in every way—and the memory of his promises of a swift return filling her mind like a gentle benediction.

When she'd finally awakened, the euphoria remained with her, for now she trusted. If he said he would hurry home to her, Brittany believed him without question.

The only thing to disturb her sense of peace and well-being was a second unexpected gift—a pair of beautifully beaded doeskin moccasins setting outside her door, discovered as she'd prepared to leave the room that morning. She'd bent to retrieve the gift, marveling at the velvet-soft fur and the exquisite craftsmanship obvious in the colorful, intricately beaded patterns. Only one person could have been responsible for the gift, and while she no longer feared Ikuuk, the thought that he might be attempting to lure her affections away from Tristan was disconcerting. Yet she also guessed that the Indian's loyalty to his blood brother was too strong for him to do anything to under-

179

mine their relationship. Perhaps she was making too much of it. Perhaps it was just a peace offering after her encounter with Ikuuk in the forest behind Wildwood.

When she did thank him, all she received was his rare, enigmatic smile. And so, considering her duty done, she put the incident out of her mind.

Brittany purposefully set out to relax and enjoy the unlikely combination of an aging, irascible earl and a virile, full-blooded Powhatan for company. It was soon apparent that the two got along well, a certain unspoken bond springing up between them that, for some reason, did not surprise her. She suspected that the bond had something to do with Running Deer, the woman whom the earl had loved, and also to whom Ikuuk owed his life.

The day after Tristan's departure, the three of them were near the edge of the woods behind Carlisle Hall, enjoying the balmy September day.

"I haven't felt this good in years, by God," Carlisle declared.

Brittany glanced over at him from where Ikuuk was showing her how to string a bow. A smile danced across her lips. "You look wonderful, as well, your lordship."

He leaned his head against the chair one of the servants had set out for him—despite Burke's unspoken disapproval—and closed his eyes. " 'Tis pure pleasure to smell the earth, to taste the wind, to feel the sun penetrate these old bones."

Ikuuk's hands over hers paused, and Brittany glanced up into his hawklike features to find him studying Tristan's grandfather. Something about his expression, an intelligence, a certain intensity, unexpectedly reminded her of Tristan. Yet, although his features were more craggy than the patrician lines of his blood brother, his countenance was nonetheless noble and fine.

With uncanny swiftness, his dark eyes met hers briefly before he handed over his bow, which he'd temporarily modified for her.

" 'Tis your doing that he's out here in the sunshine,

Ikuuk, with a smile on his face and healthy color in his cheeks,'' she told him quietly.

The Indian's mouth quirked, whether in humor or some other emotion, Brittany could not tell.

"The next thing you know, he'll be asking to have a horse saddled—"

"What d'you say to going ariding on the morrow, Brittany, m'girl? The gout's been better the last day or two, and I've a mind to feel a good piece of horseflesh beneath me again.'' He trained one eye on the two young people only yards from him. "I miss my grandson, and the busier I keep myself, the faster the time will pass, eh?"

Brittany's gaze went to Ikuuk, but the Indian was already making a vigorously negative sign to the old man.

"No, you say? Humph. No balls, boy," Carlisle opined as he shook his head in disgust. "Treat me like a helpless babe and I'll surely pass on before I ever see my grandson again.''

Brittany came to the rescue, the bow momentarily forgotten. "Mayhap we can try it, your lordship.'' She looked askance at Ikuuk, her eyes asking him to humor her. "Let's see how you feel, first. Then, if the weather holds, perhaps we can all take a leisurely ride.''

The earl met her gaze head-on. "Ah, Brittany the peacemaker. Who are you attempting to mollify—the Indian or myself?" But the twinkle in his eyes belied the gruffness of his tone.

Later, after Brittany had her first lesson in archery, Ikuuk sat cross-legged at the earl's feet while she removed a picnic dinner from the wicker hamper and set it on a pristine white tablecloth spread over the ground. They ate in companionable silence, enjoying the cold roast beef and cheese and bread, with a jug of fresh cider from one of the earl's orchards. The somnolent wind sighed softly through the trees, and the dulcet whisper of the grass and wildflowers bordering the woods lulled them comfortingly.

Just when Brittany thought the earl had fallen asleep, an

unfinished piece of bread in the hand resting in his lap, his unexpected words dropped heavily into the silence.

"I've never said a word to anyone—not a soul—but mayhap 'tis time." He roused himself and stared at the majestic manor across from them, resplendent beneath the sun's glow. "I had no wish to send Tristan fleeing to the Colonies by revealing my suspicions—suspicions that have become almost a certainty in my mind—concerning his cousin John. I wanted to give him time to become accustomed to the possibility of being named my heir should anything happen to John. Yet now, even though I can prove nothing, more than ever I want to disinherit the scoundrel and name Tristan as the next earl of Weyrith."

Brittany lowered her lashes to shield the dismay she knew would be apparent in her eyes. Disinherit John Carlisle? Then there would be no question that Tristan must live out his life in England. Profound disappointment, followed by shame, washed over her. How selfish she was.

"—most likely is a bastard. His mother spread her legs for anything in breeches, 'twas well known, but my profligate son William cared little. He was too busy committing his own transgressions to be concerned." His expression turned briefly pained and he blinked away what looked suspiciously to Brittany like tears. "A vile streak runs through the Carlisles, and I would give anything to see it purged by an infusion of new blood." His eyes locked with Brittany's. "Even Indian blood . . . and French."

Brittany raised her gaze to meet his. "I'll not be a party to your machinations, your lordship. Even if I had any influence over Tristan, nothing I could say or do would ever sway him toward something he was set against."

"Odds fish, girl! Can you not see he's head over tail in love with you?" At her look of skepticism, he added, "He would need only your consent to marry him and the knowledge of your wish to remain in England." He glanced around him, his gaze encompassing all that was within his vision, like a king contemplating his realm.

Brittany threw a look at Ikuuk from beneath her lashes, but the Indian remained impassive, staring into the trees. "All this—and much, much more—I could offer him. Enough wealth and prestige to make him forget about that godforsaken wilderness across the ocean." His eyes returned to lock with hers, a fierce determination deepening the faded blue.

Brittany, however, refused to be moved. "I appreciate your intentions toward your grandson, but the situation is such that I cannot remain in England, whether Tristan would wish it or no." A delicate pink creeped across her cheeks, in spite of her effort to remain unaffected.

Carlisle narrowed his eyes shrewdly. "Very well, young woman. I'll say no more for now . . . except that John Carlisle has returned from France and is back from his dirty dealings with his unsavory cronies at Louis's court—bloodsucking leeches, I call 'em." He smothered a yawn and closed his eyes once more, letting his head fall back against the chair. "I can only hope he gets himself killed before he antagonizes Tristan. How naturally things would fall into place, then." His last few words were a mumble.

Ikuuk rose and approached him. " 'Sdeath, boy!" the earl exclaimed. "Not only are you the sneakiest thing to ever walk these grounds, but your needless fussing over me is irritating—just like a mother hen!" He raised an eyelid in warning. "Except for that comb of yours. Now, when I'm ready to go inside, I'll walk. You'll not carry me like an infant again!"

In spite of her concern over the earl's words regarding John Carlisle, Brittany bit her lip to keep from smiling at the picture they made—a standoff, with Ikuuk looming over the earl, arms crossed uncompromisingly over his chest, and Carlisle glaring up at him, clearly at a physical disadvantage.

"Ikuuk," she interjected, "why don't you teach me your sign language, so that I can interpret for his lordship?"

Ikuuk, however, remained where he was, apparently not convinced that the earl shouldn't be returned to his bed.

Carlisle's expression softened to one of mere annoyance. "Aye." He motioned at the Indian with one bird-like, fluttering hand. "Go away. Teach 'er the signs, boy. Then mayhap the next time you drop a damned week's worth of salmon at my feet, you'll save me a fit of aploplexy from thinking 'twas poachers."

The royal yacht gracefully rode the river, its sails snapping smartly in the breeze. Originally the *Surprise,* it had spirited the fugitive Charles Stuart away from England after the battle of Worcester. Rechristened *Royal Escape,* it was fitted up as a yacht after the Restoration and painted, at the king's request, by Willem Van de Velde.

Tristan leaned into the wind at the rail, catching the sights of London as they passed in smart procession, like a line of toy soldiers. Ignoring the bloated carcass of a cat that bobbed past, he inhaled deeply.

But while the air skimming across his upturned face was invigorating, it lacked the fresh, clean smell of the James that ran past his home in Virginia. And the Chesapeake, with its crisp, salty tang, and the azure skies arching over it, gulls dipping and wheeling . . .

"—launching of William Petty's *The Experiment.*" Charles pointed toward an unwieldy-looking craft moored across the way.

Tristan narrowed his eyes against the sun's glare. "A double bottom?"

"Indeed. We are to launch it in a sennight or so. Awkward as it looks, Sir William has offered to lay odds for it against any of our best boats." Charles flashed an enigmatic smile meant to conceal his deeper melancholy. "Odd-looking as 'tis, I am not fool enough to lay the bet." His smile deepened. "But I'll not let up the teasing."

The corners of Tristan's mouth curved upward in response. "The outcome would have been interesting."

Barbara Palmer's husky, feminine laughter drifted over from the other rail, reminding Tristan that the queen was not on board. He glanced at the king's mistress and her companions, one of whom was Lady Diana Hartland, with whom he'd flirted on occasion at court. "Her majesty chose not to sail?" he asked.

Charles sobered and brushed a long lock of his dark, curling hair out of his eye. *"Le mal de mer.* She prefers the land."

"I see."

The Experiment fell behind as they continued on their way, passing the Parliament House and Westminster Hall, with the majestic, buttressed and spired Westminster Abbey towering behind. Unexpectedly, the passing sights reminded Tristan of another trip through London, at night and in a hackney, with Brittany in his arms.

He turned to Charles and said without ceremony, "Might I ask why you've summoned me here, majesty?"

The king ran one hand back and forth over the polished rail before him. "There was a time, and not so long ago, when you would not have questioned my actions, when you would not have removed yourself from court with such ease and frequency."

Tristan caught sight of the lovely Barbara strolling along the deck toward them and, hoping she would not have a mind to interrupt their discussion in the manner of the pampered mistress, he deliberately turned his face toward the water, presenting his profile to Charles. "The first time, my grandfather summoned me to Carlisle Hall," Tristan explained. "Now, he but wishes to continue our acquaintance—I suppose to make up, in what way he can, for his failures where my father was concerned."

Charles nodded. "Can it be that he is grooming you to be the next earl of Weyrith?" He studied his friend through hooded, perceptive eyes. "That would make me very happy."

Tristan shrugged and leaned his elbows negligently upon the rail, unwilling to reveal his inner unease at the direction the conversation was taking. "John Carlisle would be a fool to allow anything to get in the way of inheriting the earldom. Reckless and dissolute he may be, but he is not stupid.''

"Oh, but he is. Why else would Richard Carlisle be so eager to prepare you to take his place?''

Tristan's eyes met his king's. "He is doing little but getting to know me better, sire.''

Charles nodded and smiled a greeting to Barbara as she passed by with Diana and several other ladies. "Then it must be Isolde.''

"Your majesty?''

"The mysterious lady you so boldly—and recklessly, I might add—spirited away from the Hunter's Run . . . and George.'' He paused meaningfully and Tristan followed his gaze to Diana. "Tsk, tsk, Tristan. I would have thought your tastes ran to someone more like Diana Hartland, the daughter of a duke, with a sumptuous dowry to go along with her fine looks and high spirit.''

Diana waved gaily when she saw she had their attention, her pale blond hair blowing in the wind.

At Tristan's silence, the king added, "How is your head, by the way?''

"Still resting easily on my shoulders.''

Charles snorted. "George was nearly apoplectic, you know. He's not accustomed to being thwarted.''

Tristan's eyes darkened with annoyance. "I would no sooner subject her—or any other woman—to his perversion than throw a lamb to a hungry wolf.'' He ignored an inner voice reminding him that his next words were less than truthful. "The lady made her choice.''

For a long moment, the silence between them was punctuated only by the wind rushing by, the water churning against the sides of the boat, and snatches of feminine chatter. Then the king said, "Not even if this 'lamb' attempted to kill her husband? Attempted to kill him, left him for dead, and fled France?''

Tristan went absolutely still, his jaw tightening. "Who spreads such vicious lies?''

Charles slowly shook his head. "If they are lies, I would

be relieved for your sake, my friend. Yet John Carlisle returned from France only days ago. He closets himself with George Villiers for hours and—''

''Villiers and Carlisle? Why, Buckingham can't abide him!''

''Oh, I've confronted George, and he swears he is merely conducting a business deal through Carlisle for friends in France—''

And you can tell your doxy that I have something very special in store for her, as well.

''—but as far as I can guess, without showing an unseemly interest or calling him a liar, especially in light of *our* friendship, their scheming involves you and this mysterious lady of yours.''

Tristan's hands tightened around the rail. He had to get back to Carlisle Hall . . .

Charles sighed. ''The lady Diana pines for you, my friend. Why don't you have done with this tavern girl and let it all blow over? Diana Hartland would make you a fine wife.''

Tristan turned his suddenly cold gaze to the king. ''I have no interest in Diana Hartland.''

The king studied his friend through heavy-lidded eyes, and then, with a sigh, steered the conversation to safer ground as Tristan mentally determined to politely take his leave the moment the *Royal Escape* docked.

For the next few days, the earl seemed revitalized, getting around unaided except for a walking stick, even riding on one particularly good day. The three of them—Carlisle, Ikuuk, and Brittany—walked their mounts at a leisurely pace around the grounds and through the stretch of forest between the back of the hall and the stream.

On the fourth day after Tristan's departure, Brittany received a short but tender missive from him that brought roses to her cheeks and a song to her heart. At last he was going to pin down Charles regarding the latter's reason for calling him to London. He expected to return within the next day or two.

The day after she received the letter was chill and dismal. Rain sheeted from leaden skies, with no sign of letting up, and the three of them were forced to remain inside near a warm fire that chased the dampness from the air.

Shortly before the supper hour, Brittany stood before a costly, silvered Venetian glass in her room, adorned in doeskin skirt, finely dressed and fringed skin mantle, and moccasins. Ikuuk's beaded necklace hung around her throat.

Only weeks ago the thought of an Indian, male or female, would have sent fear shimmying through her. Yet here she was, in full Powhatan attire except for body paint and the dressing of her hair, and all at the behest of the earl, whom, for some reason, she wished to please in all things. "Indulge an old man," he'd said. "They belonged to Running Deer."

She pirouetted slowly before the glass, admiring the colored birds and animals that decorated the mantle. For modesty's sake, she still wore her chemise beneath the cape, and color rose in her face at the thought that Powhatan women obviously wore nothing above the waist in warm weather. Still more disconcerting, however, was the thought that Tristan had seen many bare-breasted women during the time spent with his grandmother's people. For the first time in her life, Brittany knew irrational jealousy.

"*Bête!*" she thought. *Fool, to even think such things.* And she gathered her nerve, leaving the room to seek out the earl and Ikuuk.

As soundlessly as she entered the saloon in her new footwear, Ikuuk looked up immediately. His eyes lit with obvious—and unexpected—pleasure at the sight of her. He stood and approached her, catching the old man's attention.

Brittany paused shyly just inside the great double doors and, with surprising gallantry, Ikuuk took her hand and led her before the earl. To cover her self-consciousness, Brittany raised her chin.

"Turn around, girl," Richard Carlisle ordered.

She complied, the turn swifter than the one executed before her mirror, causing the skirt to sway gently above her slim calves, the mantle to swirl gracefully around her hips.

"Magnificent," murmured the earl.

But it was the look in the Indian's eyes that both warmed her and made her heart suddenly ache for him. As his hand moved toward her throat to finger the beads, Brittany said gently, "You miss your people, don't you?"

He lowered his lashes and shrugged, his fingers falling away from the necklet. The longing she'd glimpsed in his expression vanished. He reached into the pouch he wore belted at the right side of his waist and pulled out a bone pipe.

"Mayhap, if the rain stops by the morrow and Tristan returns, I can demonstrate my dubious prowess with a bow," she ventured in an attempt to change the direction of Ikuuk's thoughts.

The earl chortled loudly, drawing her attention away from the Indian. "Next thing you know, you'll be setting up a wigwam in the courtyard and displaying the scalps of your admirers."

Ikuuk grunted and signed to Brittany.

"What's he flappin' his hands about for now?" the earl demanded.

Brittany pursed her lips at Ikuuk and shook her head emphatically. "I believe he's just offered to teach me how to take scalps." She shuddered.

"And why not?" asked a voice from the doorway. "You look every bit the savage in those stinking rags."

All three heads turned simultaneously toward the sound. A man who could have been approximately Tristan's age, with dark hair and pale eyes, leaned leisurely against the door frame, contempt smeared across his dissipation-ravaged features.

The earl was the first to react. "As usual, you've not the common courtesy to be announced."

The man pushed away from the jamb and entered the room with an arrogant saunter. The hair on the back of Brittany's neck prickled, and she couldn't help but notice that Ikuuk tensed in response.

Brittany stepped into the uncomfortable silence, wary not only of the challenge on the interloper's face, but even more of the sword that rested menacingly at his side. "Rest easy . . . he means no harm," she assured the Indian, and moved nearer to him. As she laid a restraining hand upon his forearm, he quickly disengaged it and stepped in front of her, putting his body between Brittany and the stranger.

"How very amusing," observed the newcomer as Brittany determinedly stepped from behind her would-be protector. He turned toward the earl. "Do you not find it so, Grandfather? Whose protectiveness is stronger, I wonder—the savage's or the whore's?"

The earl's eyes narrowed in warning. "You'll keep a civil tongue in your head or leave the premises. How dare you come into my home and insult my guests."

John Carlisle shrugged in dismissal of his grandfather's words. "Tsk, tsk, your lordship. Such a nasty greeting for your prodigal grandson. Do you deny this woman is Tristan Savidge's doxy?"

"I will not grace that question with an answer," the earl returned with a smack of his walking stick against the floor. "Now, for the last time, I ask you to mind your manners and conduct yourself as befits your station."

A travesty of a smile spread across John Carlisle's lips. "And just what station is that? The miserly pittance you grant me is not nearly enough to encourage anything but the meanest behavior—forcing me to obtain funds from any source available."

"And I do not doubt that you stoop to the lowest."

John shook his head in feigned regret. "I do not remember your being quite so . . . insulting, Grandfather, before your acquaintance with your bastard's son."

He turned toward Brittany, who now held one of Ikuuk's powerful upper arms in both hands, as if she could stop him from doing anything rash. Ignoring Ikuuk with insulting ease, he continued, "Allow me to introduce myself, in my grandfather's failure to, er, act as befits his station." His gray eyes raked over her once, then again, coming to rest insolently on her exposed calves and ankles and then where the ends of her mantle gaped slightly to expose the chemise beneath. "I am John Carlisle, and I already know who *you* are."

Brittany's heart began to churn sickeningly within her chest, and, as the world threatened to recede, she clutched Ikuuk's arm in a death grip, desperately essaying to maintain her composure.

"And who might that be?" snapped the earl, calling his bluff.

John Carlisle studied Brittany's face, as if seeking a rift in the armor of her equanimity. "Why, the mysterious tavern wench whose allure drove the king's most esteemed lackey to do bodily injury to George Villiers."

He grinned nastily and walked over to a crystal decanter of port sitting upon one of the tables scattered about the magnificent red and gold appointed room. As he poured himself a draught, Brittany relinquished her hold upon Ikuuk and sat down on a scarlet velvet settee, her bottom lip caught between her teeth in agitation. She had the distinct impression he was toying with her—with them all— as a predator will sometimes spar ritualistically with its victim when there is no real contest. What did he really know? she wondered as she watched Ikuuk retreat to the shadows behind the earl. Although the Indian positioned himself at the periphery of the room, she sensed the move did not signal a retreat.

As John turned to face them once more, a softly taunting melody from the Indian's pipe permeated the room in unspoken defiance of the younger Carlisle's obvious scorn for all things Indian. His expression turned to one of derision. "Must we be subjected to such barbaric accompaniment?'' He gestured with his glass to the paintings that adorned the walls, slowly pivoting on his heel as he made a visual tour of the room, his sword clinking conspicuously at his side, a grim reminder that he'd come to his grandfather's home armed. ''Amidst all this blue-blooded heritage, amidst all these illustrious antecedents, we are required to listen to that primitive screeching?''

The earl said nothing and the melody continued, softly jeering.

''You are getting even more senile,'' he said to the old man, ''when you allow such a thing in the splendor of our ancestral seat.''

''Mine, but not necessarily yours.''

Brittany glanced quickly to the earl, then to the younger man, fearful of the effect the revelation of Richard Carlisle's secret suspicion might have upon his grandson. But John only grinned unpleasantly and shrugged. ''Of course,'' he said with exaggerated patience, and inclined his head with infuriating nonchalance. ''Whatever you say, Grandfather.''

As Brittany studied his features, she had the presence of mind to notice that he was not only boldly attempting to discredit anything the earl might say or do, but also that he bore no resemblance to the earl—or Tristan, or any of the portraits she remembered gazing upon in the gallery. True, he could have taken after his mother but, in general, those that made up the higher echelon of the aristocracy were fine-featured. And his eyes . . .

Of a sudden Brittany found herself impaled by those translucent gray orbs, and she was unexpectedly, repulsively, reminded of Raymond Chauvelin. The old, infinitely unwelcome nausea hit her with the force of a physical blow, a nausea of the body as well as of the spirit, a nausea capable of insidiously siphoning away the beginnings of true happiness, created by the man who was not present to defend her.

''—most certainly unfortunate that I missed my half

cousin," John was saying, "for I have an interesting bit
of information for him."

His gaze held hers, like a cobra and its charmer, and
Brittany's mouth went dry.

"And what can you possibly have to say to Tristan,
eh?" barked the earl. "He told me himself you avoid each
other like the plague."

John drained the last of his port and poured himself
another. "And so we do." When he turned back to Brittany, the light in his eyes revealed a triumph that no amount
of distracting pipe-playing could diminish. "While I was
in France I learned a few things."

The music ceased and Ikuuk emerged to stand behind
Brittany, one hand dropping to the knife sheathed at his
waist. Brittany knew only a growing dread, a sinking feeling in the pit of her stomach and the thundering of her
heartbeat in her ears that threatened to drown out John
Carlisle's next words.

"—you possibly have learned in France that would be
of any interest to Tristan?" the earl was demanding in a
voice that sounded thready and leagues away to the distraught young woman.

"You look a bit pale, *Geneviève*," John Carlisle said.
"But despite your pallor, you fit the description exactly of
Geneviève Elise Chauvelin—the description that your
brother-in-law Julienne Chauvelin gave, if not that of his
spiteful mother, Charlotte." He took a step toward her
and then checked, obviously not unaffected by Ikuuk's
presence so close behind her. " 'Hair the color of old gold
in sunlight, and darkest honey in shadow . . . eyes like
the emerald fields of Bretagne . . .' " He paused meaningfully. "Quite the poet, Julienne. I believe the boy is
half in love with you himself, but . . ."

Brittany came slowly to her feet.

"Of what interest can any of this nonsense be to you?"
the earl interjected icily. "Do you now derive pleasure
from spreading malicious gossip?"

"Dinner is served," Burke announced, his words

sounding stentorian in the strained silence. No one moved, no one acknowledged him, and he discreetly withdrew.

"Not usually." John Carlisle's eyes bored into Brittany's, to the exclusion of everyone else in the room. "I merely wished to apprise my cousin that you truly belong in France, not England."

Her nails digging sharply into the flesh of her palms, Brittany answered through stiff lips, "Why? To be hanged for the crime of self-defense?"

His brows climbed upward to an exaggerated peak over his eyes. "Hanged? Whatever gave you that idea, m'dear?" He unbuckled his sword and threw himself down on a nearby chair, steepling his fingers against his lips. His gaze went first to the earl, then to Ikuuk, and back to the young woman standing rigidly before the settee.

"Nay. There is no reason to hang you, Geneviève Elise Chauvelin. Only to see that you are returned to St. Malo. And to your husband, Raymond."

Her face turned ashen. "Ray-Raymond is alive?" she whispered disbelievingly.

Carlisle flashed her a twisted smile. "That he is. Tsk, tsk, Geneviève. Leave it to a woman to botch the job." He lowered his gaze with exaggerated—and utterly false—sympathy. When he raised it to hers once more, it was to home in with brutal impact. " 'Twould seem your blow to his head wasn't quite enough to gain you your freedom, for he is very much alive—in a manner of speaking—and awaits you, as does his devoted mother, in St. Malo."

Tristan

Chapter 14

December 1662

The night sky was a kaleidoscope of light and shadow, a frigid wind sending the ghostly galleon of the moon slicing through the cloudy seas on high. Below, waves raced toward the base of the craggy bluff and hurled themselves against solid granite cliffs, thundering their frustration and spitting foam in their fury at the unyielding rock.

A solitary figure stood on the ramparts surrounding the rocky promontory upon which perched the city of St. Malo. A hooded cloak provided little protection against the fierce elements, the hem of the garment flapping and swirling in accompaniment to nature's raging cacophony. Suddenly the hood fell away in a reverse gust of air to reveal a woman's long, unbound hair.

She lifted her face into the keening wind, seemingly unmindful of the cold, and turned her head slightly to the north, her eyes narrowed, as if to see across the Gulf of St. Malo, across the English Channel . . . to England. For long moments she stood thus, the wind lashing her slim body. There, across the water, lay love and life. Here, in the city that had always been home, lay despair and death.

At last, her lashes lowered in defeat, and a tear slipped from beneath them to lay winking upon her cheek in the erratic flashes of moonlight. She turned from the ocean below, her beautiful face a study in anguish, and huddled against what protection the cold, unrelenting rock could give, in an attitude of utter defeat.

Geneviève slowly straightened from lowering Raymond into a chair. One hand went to the aching small of her back, the other brushing across her perspiration-beaded brow. As her arm dropped to her side, fingers closed over her wrist, gripping with clawlike tenacity.

Her gaze flew to the man sitting in the chair before her. The only movement of which he was capable was with his right hand and arm. Yet his motions were uncoordinated and spasmodic, as if nature were playing some last, macabre jest on Raymond Chauvelin.

Geneviève searched his pale, blank gaze for some sign of emotion or recognition, but the cold blue eyes remained fixed on the wall across from them.

"Laissez-moi, Raymond." She began to pry his fingers off, but as soon as she loosened one digit, it tightened again when she moved to the next. She glanced up at the face that now haunted her waking as well as her sleeping hours. His left temple and cheek were sunken, partly from loss of weight, but more from the blow she'd given him almost three years ago.

It was a miracle that he still lived . . . and an abomination.

Her throat tightened in frustration—oh, how easily she was reduced to tears of late! she thought as she struggled with his hand upon her arm. "Let me go, Raymond," she grated, and began to claw at his fingers with rising panic.

Was it her imagination or was one corner of his mouth quirked ever so slightly?

She suddenly ceased her struggles and stared down at her reddened wrist before allowing her gaze to move once more to the grotesque mask that was his face. "Why do you not go for my throat instead, Raymond?" she taunted softly. "Why do you not just put an end to it?"

But she knew that no matter how low her spirits, no

matter how great her exhaustion, she was not ready to die. And so she began to pull at his fingers again.

"Geneviève?" called a masculine voice from downstairs.

"Up here, Julienne. Help me."

In an instant a young man appeared at the bedroom door, recognizable as Raymond's brother by his height and build, his chiseled features, and his blue eyes. But the resemblance stopped there. His hair was light brown, not blond, and his expression one of warmth and concern, something unheard of in her two years of marriage to Raymond.

"Dieu!" He reached her side and helped her pry his brother's fingers from her wrist. "Are you all right, *chère* Geneviève?"

She paused in rubbing her aching arm, her heart twisting within her. How many times had Tristan Savidge called her the same? And always with unerring concern and tenderness—

She shook her head and moved away from both men to change the soiled bedclothes. "I am unharmed, Julienne, and most relieved that you were here to help me." She threw him a halfhearted smile and bent to strip the bed.

There was a long silence, then he exclaimed, "Why do you do this to yourself?"

She paused, her head coming up momentarily before she continued with her task. "Do what to myself, Julienne?" She moved to the other side of the bed, affording the man standing across the room from her a view of her somber features.

"Look at you!" His blue eyes narrowed as he shook his head in puzzlement, a shock of hair falling over his forehead with the motion.

Geneviève plumped the pillow and straightened, looking at him with a profound weariness. "The mirror is in the other room."

At her reply, Julienne turned impatiently away from her, and Geneviève was briefly reminded of Raymond when she'd first met him. The light from the unshuttered window emphasized Julienne's fine young profile. She fought the distaste that rose in her whenever something—or someone—reminded her of her husband.

"I do nothing to myself, Julienne," she said softly. "Rather, 'tis Charlotte who plays the tune I must dance to. She can have me prosecuted for attempted murder."

He swung away from the window. "Ah, *oui* . . . always Maman." He furrowed the fingers of one hand through his tawny hair, then glanced at his older brother. "Why do you not just come away with me?" He crossed the room and met her at the foot of the bed. "I adore you . . ."

Geneviève was moved by the earnest entreaty in his eyes. "And what would we do, Julienne?" she asked gently. "We would both be fugitives from your mother's wrath. You are betrothed to Françoise and I am wed to Raymond. It would be pointless to hurt your betrothed and anger Charlotte." She looked over his shoulder at Raymond sitting in the chair near the window. "And I cannot desert him. He is my husband."

Julienne took her hands in his and squeezed them. "You make light of my declaration, Geneviève. I am only a few years younger than you, much as you may try to make me look the child, and I care not what Françoise or Maman may say or do. I do not love Françoise—"

"What does love have to do with it? 'Twas arranged long ago, Julienne, a most advantageous alliance. And if you anger your mother, she will cut off your funds. What would you do for money then?" His jaw tightened and, in an effort to divert him, she said, "Come and help me get him back into bed."

"Very well, but you have not heard the last of this. I will not allow him to sap your strength and energy until you are as useless as he is."

" 'Tis not so bad as you think. I have Jacques."

Julienne wheeled Raymond's chair to the side of the bed and took the brunt of his weight as they transferred him.

"And where is he, pray tell? No doubt sitting in some common room, drinking himself senseless."

Geneviève positioned the pillows behind Raymond's back and shoulders. "I know where to find him if I need him."

"Oui, but what good is he? My brother is dead weight—much too heavy for a woman to be hefting about. And rest assured that I know Jacques is employed by Maman not so much to help you as to watch you."

"Then she is wasting good coin, for I am not going anywhere." She walked to the door, brushing a loosened tendril of hair from her cheek. "Come, have a glass of wine with me."

He followed her down the stairs to the small kitchen. As she procured two cups and a bottle of burgundy from a carved wooden cupboard, he drove home one more point—a declaration that served to endear him further to her. "I know you did not try to murder Raymond, whatever anyone else may think . . . especially Maman. I know that, however much you may refrain from defending yourself, you struck him in self-defense." He took the wine from her, his gaze locking with hers. "No one knew Raymond better than I—his perversion, his penchant for brutality—and never will I believe ill of you for attempting to protect yourself."

For the first time since he'd come, Geneviève smiled genuinely at his staunch defense of her. *"Merci, mon ami."*

"I want to be more than a friend." He brushed his lips across her forehead, and she could not take offense. "I suspect you will hold up only so long. Your emotional strength will ebb even as your physical energy. And then I will take you from here, even if I have to carry you bodily . . . Maman be damned."

When he had gone, Geneviève prepared Raymond's supper and took it up to him. She absently spooned sopped broth into his mouth, dabbing the excess liquid that dribbled down his chin.

Utterly bored with the day-by-day, unchanging regimen, she allowed her thoughts to wander. Julienne had told her that Raymond's father had been cared for here in St. Malo before he died. He'd been prone to violence and seizures. Charlotte Chauvelin had had him confined to this dingy town house at the end of the particularly narrow Rue Maclou in the mazelike layout of St. Malo. While the rest of the family spent their time in the grand house in the country, Edouard Chauvelin had languished within these walls, hopelessly insane.

And now she, Geneviève, languished within the same confines—with the man who'd made her life a hell on earth.

"What a master your mother is at dealing with those who cross her," she told the silent invalid. "But at least now you are not capable of aught but clutching my arm. Living with you while you were in good health was worse than any torture Charlotte could devise."

She put aside the empty bowl and reached beneath the bed for a pan she used to assist him with his bodily functions. But as she eased it between his thighs, she realized the folly of telling him exactly how she felt. Behind those blank, staring eyes was enough comprehension to exact the only kind of revenge of which he was still capable. His gown and the newly changed bedding were wet.

She drew back her hands in disgust. "So you do not like to hear the truth, Raymond?" She stood over him, her eyes dark with ire. "Well, you have only made it worse for yourself, for now you may lie in your own waste till morning!"

She replaced the pan with a *thunk* and blew out the bedside taper. Picking up the empty bowl and towel, she moved through the darkness toward the door and snapped it shut behind her, her anger temporarily purging her of fatigue and despondency.

It was her best—and only—weapon.

Geneviève glanced around the kitchen to make certain everything was in order, then wandered into the parlor and did the same. Charlotte Chauvelin had an unnerving habit of paying visits at the most unexpected times, and she was a stern taskmaster. She expected Geneviève not only to tend Raymond, but also to maintain a spotless household. That, too, was part of her plan of vengeance—her invidious scheme to wear down her daughter-in-law's spirit and stamina. Her visits were most unpleasant, and something Geneviève had come to dread.

Of a certainty, Charlotte wished her slow death as punishment for what she'd done to the woman's favorite son. Nothing less would satisfy Raymond's mother. It was only a matter of time . . .

She moved to the door and checked the bolt, then laughed softly with irony. Who would have the slightest inclination to enter a home where a madman had been kept? The house stood at the end of a narrow, winding street that descended a gentle incline toward the sea. It was only a short walk to the ramparts on the northwest corner of the granite isle upon which the old city was built. It was a quiet street for the most part. And the neighbors avoided Geneviève.

She went to close the shutters over the square-paned windows. Isolated and tethered to the husk of a man that was her husband as securely as if with iron fetters, Geneviève wondered how long it would be before she went mad.

She paused, her hands just reaching for the wooden shutters. There, in the shadowed doorway across the street, stood the tall, caped figure of a man. He shifted slightly, and in the feeble light from the starlit sky, Geneviève caught the movement. Only part of the figure was visible now . . . and had she not seen the hem of his cape flare in the brisk December wind, she would have dismissed it as her imagination.

She stared into the darkness, straining to make out the form, then thought of Charlotte. No doubt the woman used Jacques as a decoy, his unreliability and erratic appearances a smokescreen for the man Charlotte had evidently hired to keep watch in earnest. How like the woman to go to such lengths to lull Geneviève into thinking it would be like taking candy from a babe to slip away from Raymond and St. Malo.

And then perhaps it was only a smuggler—the city was full of privateers and corsairs and slave-traders. A shiver rode up her spine. Why would a smuggler hide in the shadows of a city known for its questionable activities? Perhaps it was someone who posed a greater threat than a smuggler—a thief, or a murderer . . .

She closed the shutters abruptly and dropped the bar in place with a *thud*.

Up in her room, for the first time in weeks Geneviève paused in her ablutions and took a good look at herself in the small, steel plate mirror. Julienne was right—she looked ghastly. Mauve smudges rested above her cheekbones, and her cheeks themselves were drawn—almost as sunken as Raymond's, she mutely acknowledged. She raised a hairbrush and, absently stroking her unbound hair, noted how the bones in her wrist protruded. Just like a scarecrow, she thought.

She swung away with a frown. What did it matter? For whom must she look fetching? The bristles dug deeply into her scalp as a familiar agitation gripped her. A voice she'd fought valiantly to silence answered, *Tristan Savidge.*

Without warning, laughing blue eyes appeared in her mind's eye. *I love you, chère Geneviève. God, how I love you!*

Her arm dropped, the brush falling to the floor, unheeded. She turned back toward the mirror, and his face was before her as clearly as if it were really his reflection she gazed upon.

"You are so beautiful," she whispered to the image. But he could not hear her, and changing expressions flitted across his face, reminding Geneviève of the different facets of his personality. Stern and sober, as when she'd first seen him at the Hunter's Run . . . jovial and full of humor, with laughter teasing the corners of his handsome mouth and sparkling eyes as he wrestled with Ikuuk or sparred verbally with his grandfather . . . intense yet tender when he made love to her, whether with his words or his body . . .

The image suddenly dimmed and disappeared, and Geneviève felt such an overwhelming sense of loss that she started to reach toward the mirror in supplication before she realized what she was about.

She spun away and crawled into bed. *'Twas only your imagination, fool! He is in England and you are here . . . you must forget him.*

She lay dry-eyed, staring into the darkness, and allowed herself the heartrending luxury of thinking about him. Splendid of looks he was, yes, but his was more than a surface beauty. Raymond had been good-looking as well, but he'd been as rotted as corroded metal inside, as she'd quickly discovered. But Tristan . . . ah, Tristan, who'd drawn her to him as a flame draws a moth; yet instead of death, she'd found life, instead of destruction, she'd found renewal.

You healed me with the balm of your love, she silently told the night shadows. *Oh, my love, I will never see you again. Aye, my love, for I know, now that 'tis too late! that I love you . . .*

She lay wide-eyed, staring into the darkness and thinking of Tristan Savidge until exhaustion finally claimed her.

"How dare you leave my son lying in his own urine?" demanded a voice in her ear.

Rudely wrenched from the soothing depths of sleep, Geneviève bolted upright to a bright-flamed candle held uncomfortably close to her face. The day had not yet dawned, she judged from the dimness of the room, and here stood Charlotte Chauvelin, her eyes narrowed with venom.

"I-I cannot watch over him every moment . . ." she

began, guilt at the thought of what she'd done in a moment of temper acting to banish the last vestiges of sleep.

"And why not? You are his wife—his caretaker. There is no reason why you cannot sleep in the same room at night." A malicious satisfaction curved her mouth. "Nor is there any reason why you cannot sleep in the same *bed* with him, and therefore be aware of his every need during the night."

Rebellion kindled in Geneviève's eyes. "That is absurd! I need not sleep with—"

Pain blurred her vision as Charlotte's palm cracked across her soft cheek. "Mind your tongue, slut! You spread your legs easily enough for a filthy heathen savage after you left my Raymond for dead. Now you dare tell me 'tis absurd to sleep with your own disabled husband? The embers in the hearth are cold and his skin is like ice." Her pale eyes glittered with unsuppressed fury.

But Geneviève's thoughts suddenly took another turn. How did Charlotte know so much about Tristan? And what could that mean in terms of his safety? The tentacles of the Chauvelin influence reached far—even into England. *Dear God,* she thought in rising alarm, *what could Charlotte do to Tristan?*

Charlotte began to laugh. "You're as readable as a babe, Geneviève, did you know that? Your concern for your Indian is scrawled across your face as plainly as if with quill and ink." Her humorless smile faded. "But you need not worry. As long as you conduct yourself to my satisfaction, your paramour is safe." She stood back from the bed. "Get up and see to my son."

Geneviève's chin lifted. "As soon as you allow me some privacy to dress."

Charlotte's expression turned ugly. "Do not push me too far. I can have you tried for attempted murder, at the least—you, the daughter of a lowborn farmer. Do not take advantage of my magnanimity, else you will wish your lover dead rather than to suffer what we have in mind for him."

Green eyes clashed with frigid blue for a long, tautly strung moment. Then, with trembling hands, Geneviève flung back the covers and slipped out of bed.

George Villiers, second duke of Buckingham, sent the befuddled tavern girl tumbling out of bed and leveled his most chilling gaze at the man before him. "You think to threaten *me* after your part in separating Tristan Savidge from his ladylove?" He arose from the bed and stood to his full height, buck naked.

John Carlisle eyed him brazenly from head to toe, the light of unnatural interest in his eyes. "Perhaps we can strike a bargain of some sort?" he asked smoothly.

Buckingham's features twisted with contempt as he strode across the room to retrieve his shirt and breeches. "I do not sleep with scum."

Carlisle's head snapped up. "Yet here you are, having just spent the night in a tavern known for its disreputable clientele, and in the company of a common whore."

The duke's eyes narrowed. "Guard your tongue, Carlisle, before you lose it to my dagger blade."

"And you have a care as well, Villiers, for you insult the next earl of Weyrith," he shot back with foolhardy audacity. "Besides," he added, "I have need of additional funds to repay a—a gambling debt, not for sexual gratification."

A knock sounded at the door. At Buckingham's growled "Aye?" the same comely serving girl reentered the room with a tray bearing the duke's breakfast. He broke off a chunk of bread without bothering to offer the same to Carlisle. "So 'tis blackmail, is it?" He poured a draught of ale and took a sip, eyeing Carlisle over the rim of the cup. "I would advise you to take your threats and leave here while you still can. You see, my dear earl-to-be, I've assured the king that my hands are clean where Tristan Savidge is concerned, and that 'twas solely your doing that his doxy returned to her husband in France. He has no idea that I sent you a directive to investigate this 'Brittany'—that circumstances played right into my hands and provided me with the means to wreak havoc in Savidge's life.'' He paused, letting Carlisle assimilate this information. "Therefore, although I refuse to stoop to your puny attempts at blackmail, I would be most . . . unhappy to discover you told Charles otherwise.''

Carlisle's mouth stretched into a sneer. "So you seek to blacken my name, Villiers? If you had been a little more circumspect, you wouldn't have had to go to such lengths to remain free of suspicion." His sneer deepened. "If you do not pay up, I'll march straightaway to Whitehall and obtain a private audience with the king.''

"Take your threats and get out.''

John Carlisle held the duke's gaze for a long moment and then sighed with exaggerated resignation. He pushed away from the window and moved leisurely toward the door. "Very well. You've made your choice,'' he drawled. "A most unwise choice, but a choice all the same. Good day, *your grace.*''

But outside the tavern, Carlisle silently cursed that his stratagem hadn't worked. Not that he necessarily thought it would, but it had been worth the try. What *would* Buckingham do if he told Charles how the duke had contacted him by messenger while he was still in France? Of Buckingham's unrelenting pursuit of the truth concerning Tristan Savidge's Brittany? Well, he thought sourly, no matter. I'll get nothing from him.

He hurried down a set of stone stairs to the river in the rain-soaked morning. Dropping a coin into a waiting bargeman's hand, he stepped onto the barge, his thoughts on the debt he owed one of London's most notorious highwaymen and moneylenders—The Crow, a name the criminal had acquired for his reputation of "picking" his victims clean when they'd borrowed over their heads and couldn't repay the debt and accompanying exorbitant interest. As they moved upstream, John planned how he would stall for more time to raise the money, silently cursing his tight-fisted, senile grandfather. If the old man didn't drop off soon, he might have to hasten things along, if only to support his own style of living.

The ride seemed interminable, the chill December dampness from the Thames rising around them and penetrating his clothing to his very bones. Water lapped against the barge and the sounds of an awakening London echoed along the river. He was shivering by the time they glided to a halt before another stairway. Disembarking, he swiftly strode up the steps and made his way through the gardens of the old Carmelite monastery to the narrow Ram Alley in Whitefriars, a part of the district that gave sanctuary to criminals and debtors.

John hurried up the street, past numerous taverns and run-down houses, failing in his haste to notice two shadowy figures emerge from an alley and follow at an inconspicuous distance. A dog barked and a woman's shrieks filtered from a room above one of the taverns. An eerie sensation skittered through him.

"Goin' ta pay The Crow a visit, are ye?" rasped a voice in his ear. "He's missed ye, Johnny boy."

John turned sharply. "A pox on you, you bloody footpad. If you don't disappear as quickly as you managed to gain my side, I'll run you through."

On the instant, a second interloper appeared on his other side. "Ye got a gripe with Jake here, Carlisle? Tsk, tsk," he clucked. "And him only askin' ye if ye was goin' ta see The Crow . . ."

Panic made John clumsy as he attempted to draw his sword. A beefy hand closed over his like a vise. "I wouldn't if I was ye. Why don't yc show us what ye brought The Crow and we'll leave ye be. Fair enough, Johnny boy?"

"Take your hands off me, you slimy pricklouse!"

But the fingers increased their pressure over the bones of his hand until he felt a sickening crunch. "Are ye bringin' 'im some gold, Johnny boy? 'Tis long overdue, ye know . . . and so's the interest. Why don't ye show us and we'll let ye be."

"I'll show you nothing! My reason for coming to see
The Crow is between him and me. Now get yourselves
gone before I—"

With dizzying speed he was slammed against the stone
wall of a house, flattened and pinned by his burly assail-
ants. Hands ran over his person with ruthless efficiency,
and fear made his mouth go dry. The crotch of his breeches
was suddenly wet. Oh, God, why had he come alone?

One of the men stood back, arms folded across his massive chest, and shook his head sadly. "Ye've naught that
would interest The Crow . . . except fer yer weapons . . ."
He reached to unbuckle John's swordbelt, and Carlisle
struck out at him with his booted foot. His head crashed
back against the wall, and lights exploded inside his brain.
"Ye've got a real bad attitude, Johnny boy." The gravel-
toned voice was in his ear again, an unbearable pressure
against his windpipe. "And now ye'll have to be punished
. . . first, fer comin' empty-handed, and second, fer tryin'
ta unman poor Red here."

The pressure increased, until he could do nothing but
whimper pitifully for mercy. But no mercy was forthcom-
ing. As the blackness of oblivion closed over him, his last
thought was that now he would never live to be an earl.

Chapter 15

Silence held sway in the town house at the end of Rue
Maclou. A log in the hearth of Raymond Chauvelin's bedroom crashed and disintegrated with a soft *whoosh*, sending sparks and flame shooting up the flue.

Jacques Marquet finished off his bottle of wine and sat
staring, bleary-eyed, into the fire, the light thrown by the
red-gold flames bringing out the silver in his dark hair. He
could have been a corsair, with his weather-scarred countenance and perpetually fierce frown. From somewhere far
off came the sound of Christmas revelry, and he roused
himself from his chair to throw another log onto the fire.

He sat back down and watched as the licking flames
greedily surrounded and began to devour the wood. There
was no hint of holiday celebration within this bleak household, he mused. No greens decorating the rooms, no yule
log burning in any of the hearths. Chauvelin's beautiful
wife had no cause to celebrate, he acknowledged, and
rightfully so. He glanced over at Raymond, but the latter's
eyes were closed in sleep. Jacques slouched into a more
comfortable position and propped his feet onto a low stool.
She would be back, he thought, as the potent red wine
began to take effect. The fire seemed to swim before his
eyes and wondered briefly if perhaps he shouldn't have
imbibed so much.

As his lids slowly descended, he decided it didn't matter. There was nothing better to do tonight. He did not
doubt for a moment that Geneviève Chauvelin would re-

turn to her onerous duties, for she was too noble-hearted to desert her invalid husband, much as she obviously hated him. Lady Charlotte would never have agreed with Jacques, but what did she know? "Eaten up with hatred," he muttered under his breath.

Well, it was easy coin, this job he'd taken, and if he'd had a conscience, his spying on the beautiful Geneviève would have bothered him—but Jacques Marquet had no scruples. As soon as spring came, he would sign on with one of the numerous privateering ships that sailed in and out of the harbor. Who knew, anyway? Maybe Chauvelin would slip away some night and free both Jacques and his lovely wife.

He lifted leaden eyelids and cast one last look over his shoulder. Chauvelin's pale eyes were staring blankly at the wall. Jacques made a halfhearted gesture that could have been a shrug. What did it matter if the poor devil was awake? There was nothing he could do, trapped within his prison of mindless flesh . . .

Jacques's eyes closed and, moments later, he slept the sleep of the dead.

The shadows deepened. Stillness blanketed the room, with only Jacques's snores and the cough and cackle of the fire disturbing the quiet. A single candle sent its small, guttering flame pluming upward, causing shifting patterns to dance across the motionless, linen-draped form of Raymond Chauvelin. It threw into relief the still-handsome right side of his profile, his blond hair, and rendered the weak blue of his eyes almost colorless as they remained fixed upon the wall.

In a sudden, spastic move, his right arm swept outward in a horizontal arc, sending the candle and holder on the bedside table toppling onto the neat stack of bed linens and toweling. The flame was not extinguished by the fall, but burned on to ignite a linen sheet. It smoldered insidiously for long moments, then produced a new flame which consumed the top layer before firing the material beneath it . . .

And Jacques Marquet slept the sleep of the dead.

* * *

The sun was setting as Geneviève walked the ramparts, market basket over her arm. Coral and teal striations spilled across the horizon to the west, while the bay below glowed golden from the sun's muted rays. White-capped waves struck the rock formations that jutted from the ocean floor and geysered upward, spewing foam into the air.

She loved the sound of the sea surging into the bay, battering the isle that contained the old walled city. Connected to the mainland only by the old causeway, Le Sillon, St. Malo flourished as a center not only for privateering, but also for shipbuilding, deep-sea fishing, slave trading, and foreign trade. The city derived its name from the sixth-century Welsh monk Maclou, who had fled there and later became a bishop. Its history was colorful and fascinating, and Geneviève knew she would never forget this place where she was born, in spite of all the heartache since her mother's death.

There is no reason to think you will ever leave here. Raymond could outlive you.

Despair pierced her soul. It was little comfort, indeed, to remain in St. Malo while shackled to Raymond Chauvelin, enduring Charlotte's endless demands and harping.

She turned her face into the wind, toward England, ignoring ominous clouds scudding out of the west. It seemed that each time she faced north, seeking emotional and spiritual comfort in the knowledge that Tristan Savidge was somewhere across the water, truly not so far away, the effect was a little more diluted—as if her melancholia were slowly eating away at her natural ability to put aside her misery. Aside from her walks along the old city walls, the occasional visit from Julienne Chauvelin was the only other bright spot in the endless drudgery of her life.

Self-pity will not avail you, she told herself sharply, and swung away from the panorama before her. The blush of twilight was fast becoming the deep shadow of dusk as Geneviève headed toward one of the great gates in the ancient walls. The wind chased through the narrow, winding streets, hitting her with unexpected force as she turned a corner, buffeting the basket that hung from her arm and flinging back her hood. For once she would welcome the warmth of the dismal town house.

With one hand holding the hood of her mantle in place, she leaned into the wind and rounded the corner of Rue Maclou. She lifted the latch to open the door, but the wind snatched the wooden portal and sent it crashing back against the stone wall. Unease sifted through her at the intensity of the storm brewing off the sea.

She managed to close the door, but her unease deepened. What was that odor? Even as she mentally asked the question, she knew the answer. Alarm tingled along her nerves. Dropping the basket, she hurried up the stairs, the smell of smoke intensifying until it surrounded her at the upstairs landing in a billowing, choking cloud.

"Jacques!" she called as she entered Raymond's bedroom, holding one corner of her cape over her mouth.

Through the haze she could make out the still form of Jacques Marquet, slumped in the chair by the hearth. *Dieu!* She started for him, then realized that Raymond was in more immediate danger, flames shooting upward from the stack of clean bedclothes, eating up the table beside the bed, scorching the joists above and threatening to ignite the bedding.

"Jacques!" she cried. "Help me!" She threw herself at the man sleeping in the chair, praying he hadn't succumbed to smoke. "Jacques, wake up. Help me get Raymond to safety!" She shook him with desperate, bonewrenching force, slapping his cheek in rising hysteria. *"Réveillez-vous!"*

His head lolled frustratingly and she gave him another stinging slap. He jerked upward. Through the smoky pall, she could make out the confusion clouding his eyes.

"Get up, Jacques! Fire! Help me with Raymond!"

The acrid odor of smoke penetrated his befuddled senses and he shook his head as if to clear it, then wrenched

himself from the chair. "Fire? Get out of here, woman!"
He stood swaying for a moment, then shoved her toward
the door, the sight of the growing conflagration whipping
his thoughts into focus.

"Raymond! We must get him out of here—"

"Forget him!" He lunged through the doorway, giving
the end of the bed a wide berth and dragging her with
him. "Leave him. Why save his useless carcass?" he
shouted, dead sober now.

Geneviève shook her head, her eyes and nostrils smarting. She pulled her arm from his grip and ripped her cape
from about her shoulders. "Help me!" she cried, beating
out the flames that had caught the edges of the blanket.
"Help—" She spared a glance at the door, but Jacques
had disappeared.

The room felt like a furnace, the heat and smoke suf-
focating, the roar of fire like thunder in her ears. She tore
back the covers and bent to wrap her arms around Raymond's emaciated chest. As she strained to pull him to a
sitting position, her gaze went to the ceiling and she froze
in mid-motion, horrified. The ancient joists above were
disintegrating like kindling.

She tugged with renewed vigor, knowing she had to
drag him off the bed and out of the room before the beam
directly overhead crashed down upon them both.

A burning missile glanced off her shoulder, singeing the
skin through her clothing and caused her to relinquish her
hold and straighten to slap at her smoking garment.
"Non!" she cried, and tears began to stream down her
face. She gasped for a breath of clean air.

The joist overhead cracked ominously and, before she
could bend to take hold of Raymond again, the fingers of
his right hand closed over her wrist, shackling her. For
one fleeting moment, her eyes went to his questioningly,
but that eerie stare never wavered from the almost obscured wall at right angles to the door.

So this is how it is to end, she thought. *We will die
together, you and I.* She stared into his expressionless face,

defeat washing over her. Her eyes went to his fingers, as if she could will them to relax their hold.

Burning wood suddenly showered over them from above, and Raymond, prone beneath the rapidly deteriorating support overhead, was all but buried in flames. Galvanized into action, Geneviève struggled to pry his fingers from her aching arm, sparks striking her face and hair, the edge of her skirt beginning to smolder.

"Non!" she screamed with a choked sob. *"Non!"* But the grip held with inhuman strength as the sickening stench of burning flesh invaded her nostrils. Her hem burst into flame and she desperately batted it with her free hand. The heat of the fire that was consuming the bed scorched the skin of her face and neck, her hands . . .

And then there was a sudden, unexpected movement, a flash of metal, and she was free, the fingers of Raymond's arms falling slack as the bloodied stump of his arm dropped back to the burning pyre. The sword disappeared with a repeated flash, this time of silver flecked with crimson, and the newcomer flung away the disembodied appendage.

She raised her gaze to the black-caped figure towering over her just as her knees began to crumble, the light of the growing inferno reflected in the blue blaze of his eyes, more intense than the holocaust raging around them.

Tristan! She mouthed the word, but her parched lips and sore throat were incapable of articulate sound.

He swept her up into his powerful embrace, high against his chest, and spun away from the bed just as the beam crashed downward, crushing what remained of Raymond Chauvelin. Too late . . . The flame-eaten support lay like a barrier of fire rivering across the floor, between them and the door.

"Hold on," Tristan said in her ear and, tightening his grip, he backed up a step. She felt every muscle in his body tense, and then he was surging forward, his cape flaring behind him, leaping the barrier and delivering her from certain death as the fire from the hearth met its blazing twin and the entire room went up with a roar.

It was pouring outside, great gusts of wind sending the rain sheeting across the cobblestone street. Beneath the camouflage of thunder, wind, and rain, no one had yet noticed the fire. The house adjoining theirs was deserted.

"Tristan, we must warn the others," Brittany began as soon as they'd rounded the side of the town house.

He set her down, pulling her close as he leaned against the wall of the building, hungrily searching her face. He wrapped her in the folds of his heavy, damp cape, sharing his body warmth. "The stone walls will contain what the rain doesn't extinguish, sweet."

And then his lips were slanting across hers, branding her with an urgency, a desperation, that were foreign to her. Never had his kiss tasted sweeter, been more infinitely welcome. Tristan, whom she'd thought never to see again . . . Tristan, her champion, her love. She eagerly responded, the elements still shrieking around them, forgotten. His mouth burned a path of sweet fire across her cheeks and up to her temples, to rest against her forehead; his body molded to hers, as if he would never let her go.

"I will not ask why you left me for him, because I already know," he murmured against her brow.

"Tristan . . . Tristan," she said breathlessly, "how did you get here? When did you come?"

A hundred questions rose to her lips, but his own silenced them, sending liquid heat curling through her body with an intensity that made her impervious to the vicious December wind. When he pulled slightly away, it was to answer, "I've been here for nigh on a month, watching you, my love." He frowned, his eyes burning with a ferocity that took her aback. "Did you think I would ever let you go? I would have snuffed out his miserable life myself before I'd ever have given you up!" She tilted her head back, staring up at him, her eyes brimming with love.

" 'Twas you the other night, then . . . standing in the shadows across the way?''

"Aye."

"Oh, Tristan . . . you risked so much by coming here. Charlotte Chauvelin can—"

"—do nothing. I am taking you back to England with me, where you belong. You are free now.'' His arms tightened around her with little of his characteristic gentleness, until she thought surely her ribs would snap.

Too full of joy to care, she laid her head against his chest and listened to the steady beat of his heart beneath her ear.

They stood in the relative shelter of the wall until they heard shouting voices. "We must leave here," he said against her hair.

"But—but I cannot leave now—"

"You must! The circumstances are too incriminating for you to remain. Come, *chère* Geneviève, before they see us."

Her head snapped up, and she pushed clear of his embrace so she could look into his eyes. "Please . . . don't ever call me that again! I am Brittany now . . . and forever."

He smiled tenderly into her eyes. "You can be whomever you please, love, so long as you consent to be my wife." And before she could assimilate his words, he was leading her away from the Rue Maclou and down toward the ships in the bay.

Muted light spilled from the brass lamps attached to the wall of the cabin and pooled along the polished wooden floorboards. A bunk with a storage chest at its foot, a desk and chair, a metal brazier, and a tiny table with a smaller chair, furnished the miniscule room. A captain's log, sextant, compass, maps, and quill and ink lay strewn haphazardly over the mahogany desktop.

In the middle of the cabin was a slatted wooden tub, which took up most of the remaining space. Brittany allowed the gentle rocking of the ship to lull her as she sat in the warm bath on board the *Virginia*. Her eyelids drooped, and she fought fatigue, for she was safe on board a ship that would take her away from St. Malo once and for all . . . with Tristan Savidge.

The door opened and closed without a sound, and unexpectedly a warm, wet cloth was gently applied to her face. She smiled and her lashes lifted, her gaze encountering eyes of deepest sapphire.

"The burns will leave no scars, sweet—"

"Such beautiful eyes . . . I conjured them up in my mind many times in the past months." Her lips curved in a languorous smile. "And your lashes—tsk, tsk!—are so very long . . ."

Tristan raised a black brow. "Indeed. A man does not have beautiful eyes, my befuddled wench."

"You do."

He soaped the cloth and moved down to her neck and upper chest, noting that her lids were drooping once more. "The fire left you addled," he teased softly.

Her eyes flew open, and at her look of sudden distress, where before there had been only relaxed contentment, he mentally berated himself for the thoughtless reminder.

"Tristan . . . why can we not sail tonight? I know 'tis more difficult during a storm, but the wind seems to be letting up and—"

He silenced her rush of words with a tender brush of his lips across hers. "Hush, now. No one saw us leave the town house, let alone head for the harbor. And who is to say that even if someone had, they would have recognized you? I think you overestimate the interest of your neighbors. In a city with a reputation like St. Malo, much is deliberately overlooked."

"But Jacques—"

"—is no fool. He'll make up some tale to cover his negligence or, more likely, he'll disappear. Why should he wish to be confronted by the Chauvelins? Now," he said with a firmness that indicated the subject was closed, "let's wash the soot from your hair and get you to bed."

Brittany sighed and allowed him to wet and soap her heavy blond-brown mane. He expertly massaged her scalp until she began to fall asleep in the tub.

Rinse water poured over her roused her with a sputter, however, and before she could protest, he pulled her to her feet, wrapped her in thick toweling, and lifted her from the tub. Like a devoted servant, he dried her from head to toe; like a lover, he lingered over her thighs and breasts. "You are much too thin, Brittany love. We'll have to ask Ikuuk for something to fatten you up."

At the mention of the Indian, she smiled wistfully. "I missed him—and the earl."

Tristan sat on a chair before the small brazier, holding her between his thighs, and began toweling her wet hair. " 'Twas all I could do to convince Ikuuk that he would only draw attention with his warrior's crest and lock."

Brittany laughed softly, stimulated by Tristan's vigorous motion.

Tristan saw the haunted look in her eyes disappear as a smile transformed her lovely face, and his heart caught at the beauty in the exquisite lines of her features, the lush green of her eyes. His mouth tightened at the thought of Chauvelin's mother and how she'd used Brittany's natural goodness to lure her back to France, back to the detested invalid who had been her husband.

"Why do you frown, my lord? You have a willing woman in your arms . . ." A hint of delicate color flared in her cheeks. "One who desires to please you in all ways." The words were low, seductive, and hit him with the force of a blow after four endless months without her.

He rested the towel around her shoulders and began brushing the tangles from the damp, honey-blond tresses. "You do please me already, baggage. Now I would only ask that you sit still so that I can—"

But Brittany was already turning in his arms and taking the initiative with an enchanting mixture of boldness and

shyness. She loosened the lacings at the throat of his shirt
and pressed her hands against his sculptured chest. The
brush dropped to the floor, and he caught her with one
arm around her shoulders and lifted her chin between his
thumb and forefinger to receive the honeyed delights of
her mouth.

"Shameless wanton," he chided against her lips, "to
attempt to arouse me when I but wish to see you safely to
bed." But her hand wandered down from between their
chests to the turgid evidence of his desire, which seared
her hand through his breeches, and he drew in his breath
sharply at her touch.

"See what you've done, scheming seductress . . ." But
laughter underlied the urgency in his deep voice.

"Now you'll have to put me to bed, my lord . . . and
join me so that I do not catch a chill."

He stood with her in his arms and gazed deeply into her
eyes, his own so dark with desire that they looked black.
"Will you marry me, Brittany Jennifer St. Germain?"

Uncertainty flickered in her eloquent eyes, and then she
closed them, leaning her head against his chest. "I do not
want to be wed again . . . to anyone." *Nor to remain in
England,* she silently added.

He strode to the bed and deposited her. "Then I will
have to persuade you otherwise, for I'll not be satisfied
until you are mine in name, as well."

He stood and began to disrobe with maddening deliberation, while Brittany lay sprawled wantonly across his
bed, wanting him with every fiber of her being. Oh, how
far she'd come since she'd first allowed him to kiss her!
Her eyes devoured the magnificent form being slowly revealed to her—long, well-shaped legs, taut belly and slender flanks, splendid upper torso and iron-thewed arms.

Desire roared through her with all the devastation of a
flash flood—she, who'd abhorred a man's touch only a few
months ago. She held out her arms to him, desire rippling
through her.

Tristan tossed aside his shirt and stepped quickly out of

the breeches. He moved toward the bed, his eyes fusing with hers, and stretched out beside her, drawing a blanket over them.

"You are not sleepy now, I see," he observed.

"Indeed not." Brittany leaned upon one elbow, determined to take the initiative in a half-acknowledged desire to repay him for rescuing her. Her hair cocooned around them, an amber curtain, binding them together in intimacy. Her finger's lovingly traced his straight, dark brows, feathered over the black tangle of his lashes, then down his straight nose to his firm, warm lips. "I didn't thank you for rescuing me earlier this eve, my lord."

"There's no need," he said simply, and took her finger into his mouth to gently suckle its dainty tip. When she drew back, he added, "I'll always be there, Brittany, whenever you need me."

Her eyes glistened with emotion and slowly, with the slightest of tremors, she brought the same finger to her own lips in a suggestive gesture that caused a tightening of his loins. She slid a bent knee over his legs, a heartbeat away from his arousal, and pressed her breasts against his smooth, rock-hard chest, causing his grip to tighten in response. Only his infinite patience and iron restraint kept him from turning her onto her back and uniting with her.

"Tell me," she murmured, "why you have no hair on your chest . . . nor does Ikuuk."

He raised a brow. "You wish to talk *now?*"

She smiled like a contented cat. "We have all night, do we not?"

"All our lives."

A ghost of a frown chased across the smooth, peach-tinted skin of her brow and then was gone.

"Indians do not have body hair like the white man. If they do, 'tis very fine and they pluck it out with clam shells, for they think it unsightly."

"But you are only part Indian."

"Aye." He tucked in his chin to see what he could of

his chest. "Look, there are several . . . if you would but open those jeweled orbs that can stop a man in his tracks."

"Ah, Tristan, the gilded-tongued courtier," she commented softly, and obligingly followed his glance. Sure enough, there around his nipples were several dark, wiry hairs. Seizing the opportunity to continue her playful exploration, she laved a warm, wet circle around one pap before taking the bud into her mouth and nipping it gently with her teeth.

His groin contracted with incendiary heat, and his entire body tensed. "Have you done with your questions and experimenting, wench? Mayhap I should inform Charles of the scientific bent of your mind. He is forever muddling in his new laboratory."

Brittany knew that in spite of his obvious needs, his gruffness was feigned, and he was allowing her to do as she would, in her own good time, without a sign of irritation at her questions. She marveled at his self-control.

"I've no desire to do any experimenting except with you." She glided one hand downward between their bodies. If he had little chest hair, nature's arrow from his navel down to his manhood was very much in evidence—silky, straight, and true. She neared the downy nest wherein lay the essence of his masculinity, and paused, continuing to gaze into his eyes. How much could he take? she wondered naughtily.

But he lay still, except for his burgeoning arousal, which he could not control.

"You do not give in to torture, I see," she observed.

"Indians are known for their stoicism."

She levered her body over his, parting her thighs to receive him. Slowly, she impaled herself upon the silk and steel shaft of his desire, her eyes never leaving his. "Stoic, umm?" she murmured huskily, beginning an intoxicating tempo of love as the sheathing was completed. Her eyes told him what she was yet unwilling to admit with words, love and adoration shining in their depths.

Suddenly his hands were at her hips, his own thrusting

and retreating in an answering rhythm. ''But Indians are not necessarily stoic in matters of love,'' he murmured. And they worshipped each other with straining bodies, whispered words, and eloquent gazes . . . until their souls were united.

Chapter 16

The next morning when they sailed out of the harbor, the storm had given way to blue skies and billowy clouds. The wind, however, was still gusting, and spume-crested waves dashed against the great sides of the *Virginia*.

Wrapped securely in one of Tristan's capes, Brittany gloried in the cold, salty air that nipped her cheeks and blew loosened strands of hair into her face. Tristan stood behind her at the rail, one arm on either side of her.

As St. Malo receded, her spirits soared, for she'd already said goodbye to the place of her birth. Again, the enormity of what Tristan had risked for her struck Brittany—that he'd come for her and waited patiently for the chance to snatch her from beneath Charlotte Chauvelin's nose. Raymond was dead, St. Malo receded with every league they traveled, and she had Tristan's promise of shelter and protection . . . and love.

She leaned back to gaze up into his eyes. The blue seemed even deeper—a rich indigo now—against the brightness of the day, and her heart skipped erratically as he bent his head to touch his warm mouth to hers.

"You are a man of many talents, my lord . . . to captain such a magnificent ship."

He threw back his head, and his laughter was caught and swept away by the wind. "I am no captain, sweetheart. I am only co-owner." He looked away, then back again, an eyebrow raising conspiratorially. "Here comes the captain now."

Brittany followed his gaze to see Matthew Stark striding toward them.

"Matt? Of course . . ."

"Good morrow," Matt greeted them.

"Good morrow," Brittany answered hesitantly. Was there disapproval in his eyes?

"Since I've not had the privilege of being apprised of what happened last eve, and the lady is safely on board, I trust all went well?"

His sarcasm was not lost upon Brittany. Did he resent the danger to which Tristan had subjected himself and the ship which had crossed the unpredictable waters of the Channel for her sake alone?

"All went smoothly," Tristan assured him. His eyes met Brittany's. "Matt is merely upset because I forbade him to accompany me on the rescue mission." He glanced at Stark again, and Brittany couldn't see his expression, but concluded that it must have held some kind of warning, because Matt's annoyance eased somewhat.

"How do you like the *Virginia?*" he asked.

Brittany gazed up at the unfurled sails. " 'Tis impressive. I used to go into St. Malo with my parents before my mother died, and while Father conducted his business, Mother and I would wander close enough to the docks to watch the ships enter and leave the harbor, the loading and unloading of them." She smiled tentatively at Matt. "The *Virginia* compares to the best of them."

His face lit up at the compliment and his attitude changed. No longer did he seem to force himself to be pleasant as he picked up on Brittany's interest in his ship. "Actually, Tris deserves credit for the acquisition of this vessel. It was a Dutch Indiaman at one time. While Tris was on the continent with the king, he won it in a card game with a wealthy Dutch nobleman."

Brittany's eyes widened with interest and she turned in Tristan's arms to face him. "Tell her the story," Matt urged his friend.

Tristan shrugged and gazed out to sea, his eyes narrowing against the sun's glare upon the water. "He insulted Charles . . . accused him of cheating. Actually, de Graaff was in his cups and accused us both of being light-handed." He grinned rakishly at Brittany. "What was I to do—allow him to insult our very honor?"

"Never!" supplied Matt.

"Well, what did you do?"

"I challenged him to another game and said that if I lost, I would overlook the insult. If I won, I would take any one of his possessions of my choosing."

"But what about the king?"

Matt answered for him. "Ever the peacemaker, Charles said that he could not take offense with a man who was foxed, and gracefully backed out of the game."

"As you can guess, unlike Charles, I had no qualms about taking a ship from a drunken boor of a Dutchman, noble or nay."

Matt leaned his back against the rail and crossed his arms, his gaze moving about the ship with pride. "Tris was younger then, you see, and considerably more rash."

"I do not remember you showing any hesitation to enter into a partnership with me."

Brittany allowed her gaze to climb the mainmast directly behind them. It seemed to spear the cottony clouds above, its upper sails rumbling in the gusty wind. Her lips parted in awe at the yards of canvas stretching above them.

As if reading her mind, Matt said, "Thirteen thousand square feet of canvas, from the spritsail to the lateen mizzen. Of course"—he nodded toward the mainmast—"they're not all set now, only the upper top, t'gallant and royal . . . the wind's too strong. But we need every inch of sail on a calm day to move fourteen hundred tons of ship."

His voice rang with pride, and even Tristan's gaze reverently roved from polished wooden decks to graceful spars and billowing sails. "This is the ship that will take us back to Virginia."

"But your grandfather—" Brittany began.

"—will have to accept the fact that I am not his rightful heir."

But he suspects that John Carlisle is not his legal grandson.

"And scum like the younger Carlisle always seem to land on their feet," Matt added. "No doubt, despite his deplorable lifestyle, he will prevail."

"Now who's side are you on, Stark? Would you see me stuck in England as a stuffy earl?"

"Of course not." Matt's look turned contemplative. "Why don't you challenge him to a duel? Heaven knows you have reason enough after what he did to Brittany."

Brittany touched Tristan's arm. "No, you cannot do such a thing! If John Carlisle hadn't done so, then Buckingham would have revealed my whereabouts to the Chauvelins. You said you suspected he played a part in discovering that Raymond was alive."

"Ah, yes . . . Buckingham." The soft menace in his voice frightened Brittany. "But he swears to Charles that he had naught to do with it—that 'twas solely John's doing."

"Bah! I don't believe that for a moment. But it wouldn't hurt to confront Carlisle. Perhaps if you use the proper, er, inducement, he will confirm your suspicions," Matt said. "I do not remember him being particularly loyal to anyone. Perhaps if you grease his palm with enough gold, he will forget any pledge of cooperation he may have made to Villiers."

"Perhaps. I will ferret out the truth of the matter and then—"

"Cap'n!" came a shout from one of the crew across the deck.

With an abbreviated bow to Brittany, Matt excused himself and went to answer the seaman's summons.

"Oh, what does it matter?" Brittany asked, her look full of trepidation. "What's done is done. I have no liking for John Carlisle . . ." In spite of the warmth of the cape and Tristan's nearness, she shivered at the memory of the younger Carlisle's face—the cruel light in his eyes, the air of unconcern about anyone except himself, the utter lack of compassion or principles.

Tristan gently cradled her face between his hands, his thumbs grazing the velvet smoothness of her cheeks, his gaze resting first on her parted lips and then seeking her eyes. "Do not trouble yourself over my intentions. Will you go to the Colonies with me?"

His expression was sober, earnest, and she could not doubt the sincerity of his intentions.

"*Oui,*" she whispered.

"We'll leave in the spring. I've missed my home so very much." His expression changed to one of boyish enthusiasm. "You'll meet my family. My mother and father will love you, as I do, and Beth Ann . . ." His eyes clouded briefly.

"Your sister?"

"Aye." His expression cleared. "She will love you especially, for I sense that you are kindred spirits." He tilted her face lovingly up to his. "You will be my wife, sweet Brittany . . . my wife." And his mouth silenced any protest she might have raised.

He took her to Wildwood, the place she loved best, because it was the place where he'd wooed and won her with his gentleness, where he'd forgiven her without hesitation for almost killing him, where he'd defended her to everyone and given her the beautiful volume of *Tristan*.

Genna and Enis gave her a hearty welcome, Enis's first comment being, "My heavens, mistress, but we must put some meat on those bones!"

And Ikuuk appeared, as silently as a wraith. He stood in the doorway of the saloon, his arms crossed over his buckskin-shirted chest, his dark eyes trained unwaveringly on Brittany.

She stopped before him, uncertain of his acceptance after she'd seemingly deserted Tristan. Unexpectedly tears welled up in her eyes, for his approval had become important to her.

"Ikuuk," she whispered, giving him a watery smile. "You beautiful savage."

His lips curved crookedly and Brittany followed her instincts and stepped into his open arms. He hugged her with rib-crunching force before releasing her and signing to her that she was too thin. Brittany laughed, the sweet strains of her delight echoing through the room.

"Ah, Ikuuk, you are as subtle as always, I see."

She spun around and noticed the greenery decorating the room, the giant yule log in the hearth. The saloon looked and smelled like Christmas. This was a home, not a dingy, lifeless house where dwelt only bitterness and—

"My lord said to decorate for Christmas, for he promised to have you home by then," Genna volunteered.

Brittany's eyes met Tristan's across the room. "You are every bit as rash and overconfident as when you took that poor Dutchman's ship from him, Tristan Savidge. However could you have known?"

"I knew."

Something in the tone of his rich-timbred voice warmed her heart until tears threatened once again. "And—and what of the earl?" she asked, turning the subject to safer ground.

"Oh, Master Tristan," Enis interrupted, "we received a letter from him this very morn—the third in as many days!"

She left the room and quickly returned to hand Tristan the three letters sealed with the Carlisle shield. He glanced down at them before purposefully laying them aside. "Let us sup first, Enis. Then I will see what is so damnably important that he sends three missives in three days when he knows I've been in France for the past month."

Supper was relaxed, with both Tristan and Ikuuk passing the platters of food frequently to Brittany. "I cannot regain all my lost weight in one meal!" she protested laughingly when the roast beef came around for the fifth time.

When the meal ended, Tristan drew her into his office and closed the door. He walked over to the desk and pulled open a drawer, his movements slow and his expression mysterious. He withdrew a small package and came to stand before her. "I know 'tis a few days early, but I see no reason to wait. Please, open it now." She looked down at the beautifully wrapped package, a question in her eyes. "Open it, sweet."

She began to unwrap the gift. Inside was a miniscule wooden box, and nestled within the satin lining was a ring. Of gold filigree, it was set with an emerald and a sapphire in the very center, surrounded by a score of tiny, winking diamonds. Her breath caught in her throat, for the sapphire was the exact shade of his eyes as he stood watching her in the candlelight, and the emerald . . .

"The emerald matches your eyes." He took the ring from the satin folds and placed it on the third finger of her left hand. "A token of my love, Brittany Jennifer St. Germain. If you care for me at all, you'll never remove it."

" 'Tis beautiful, my lord, but I do not deserve such a—"

He pulled her into his arms and silenced her with a kiss so tender and intense that it left them both breathless and shaken.

He withdrew his mouth from hers and ran a gentle finger over her trembling lower lip. "Say you will be mine, that you will never leave me! Say you will bear my name and my children, that you will grow old with me and delight in our grandchildren, that someday you will lie beside me in a peaceful churchyard in Virginia for all eternity . . . Please, say it."

Tears of emotion glistened in his beautiful eyes and tugged at her heart. "Aye, I will, my love." The box dropped to the floor, forgotten, as she ran her fingers through his silky, sable hair, then pulled his mouth down to hers. "I will, my love," she whispered as their breath mingled, their lips touched. *I can do no less,* she thought when their tongues met and the familiar fire raced through her body, *for I am surely lost.*

Brittany slowly emerged from the soothing realm of sleep. She reached out automatically and curled her arm around Tristan's waist. "So you're wanting more after last night, wicked wench?" an amused voice murmured in her ear.

She smiled and purred deep within her throat, her hand moving down to caress his slender hip and flank.

Tristan propped himself up on one elbow and gazed down at her, his finger tracing the sweet slope of her jaw up to a dainty ear, then down her satin-smooth neck. His breath ruffled the downy hair at her temple as he leaned over to plant a kiss on the tip of her nose. "The morn is almost gone, so long did we sleep because of your insatiable appetite throughout the night . . ."

Brittany smiled languidly at him. "I do not recall any complaints."

He smoothed back the silken strands of her hair that had fallen across one cheek. "I'm too much the gentleman to ever—"

The clatter of horses' hooves in the yard below resounded in the morning stillness and, with a flick of the covers, Tristan rolled off the bed and strode to the window, naked. Brittany feasted her eyes on his awesome form bathed in the late morning sun, desire sending the last vestiges of drowsiness scattering like smoke before a brisk breeze.

"Good God! 'Tis he!"

Alarm made her sit up instantly. "Who?" she asked, thinking he meant Buckingham or someone equally unwelcome.

"Grandfather—in a coach and four. By the Mass, I'd like to know how he did it."

Drawing a sheet around her, Brittany slid from the bed to join him. Sure enough, there stood a shiny black coach with the Carlisle shield magnificently emblazoned across the door, a red cross upon a silver background, with a fleur-de-lis at either end.

Richard Carlisle was already hobbling up the walk, aided by his footman. He paused to look up at someone just out of sight, and suddenly shook his head emphatically, waving his cane in the air for emphasis.

Ikuuk came to view and effortlessly lifted the frail old man into his arms. The cane dropped to the ground and Brittany smiled at the look of outrage that darkened the earl's features. "I can just imagine what he's saying to poor Ikuuk," she told Tristan.

He returned her smile, the light of unmistakable humor dancing in his dark blue eyes. "Indeed. I'd better go down and rescue my blood brother, don't you think?" He kissed her lingeringly, then began to dress with the economy of emotion that she so admired. He went through his ablutions in less than half the time it would have taken Brittany and said over his shoulder as he opened the door, "Please join us as soon as you can, love. I may need rescuing myself."

When Brittany entered the saloon sometime later, Genna was serving a late breakfast for Tristan and his guests. The earl sat in a chair with his foot propped up, a jaundiced eye upon Ikuuk. "And just when I've learned to get about without assistance, *he*—" he poked his cane in the Indian's direction—"takes it upon himself to *mother* me." He took a mug of ale Genna offered and continued. "A rooster wears a crest, Indian, not a damned mothering hen."

When he saw he'd lost Ikuuk's attention, he followed the Indian's dark gaze to Brittany standing just inside the door. His face lit up. "Ah, little one, you're back safely. He did well, my grandson, didn't he?" His shrewd perusal examined her from head to foot. "Come closer and let me look at you."

Brittany obligingly came forward. "Your lordship, how are you?" She knelt before him and held his hand to her cheek. He rested the other on the top of her head. "You're thin as a stick, girl. We'll have to anchor you down in the next high wind.''

She met his gaze, her eyes shimmering. "Not for long. Enis and Ikuuk will soon see to it that I'm as stout as a barrel.''

He held up her hand to examine the ring on her finger. "I'd say my grandson wishes to make you his wife . . . and soon." His eyes met hers. "Are you free now?''

"Oui," she answered softly with a lift of her chin.

Genna discreetly withdrew, and Ikuuk rose in one fluid motion, preparing to do the same.

"Stay," Tristan told the Indian. "There is nothing between my grandfather and me that you cannot hear.''

The earl studied first Tristan and then Brittany, still on her knees before him. "He's stubborn, ye know. After you left he wouldn't listen to me about waiting until things took their natural course." He fingered the exquisite ring. "He said I'd waited so long to go after Running Deer that, in the end, I never went at all. And he was right. 'Twas the biggest mistake of my life.''

Brittany sat back on her heels, giving his words her full attention. "Why don't we let Brittany have her morning draught and bite of breakfast before—''

"I sired a legitimate heir who was worthless . . . so worthless that he cared little about his obligations to produce an heir of his own . . . so irresponsible and dissolute that he ignored his own wife and never even knew that the son she bore was not his.''

Across the room, Tristan stiffened.

"But, in spite of my blundering, everything will turn out for the best, for 'twould seem Tristan had exquisite timing when he went after you.''

Brittany glanced at Tristan in perplexity.

Richard Carlisle, seventh earl of Weyrith, unexpectedly rose from his chair and drew Brittany to her feet with all the grace of a man thirty years younger, his eyes flashing with triumph. "You will make a splendid countess, m'girl.''

Tristan's eyes narrowed, his fingers tightening around his cup of ale. "You cannot ignore the fact that, despite your suspicions, you can prove nothing—that, much as you may wish it otherwise, John Carlisle is alive and well and, to all the world, your legal heir."

"Not anymore." The words dropped into the sudden silence like pebbles plopping into a placid pond. "He was found just days ago, floating facedown in the Thames." Brittany fought to absorb this stunning information without outwardly revealing her dismay. Her eyes went to Tristan and she found him watching her, a silent question in his expression.

"I should think there would be little need to ever return to that savage wilderness across the ocean now," the earl continued. "You'll have your hands full with learning all that I must teach you, and then, of course, assuming the title upon my death."

Brittany pulled her hand from his and turned away, struggling to hide her bitter disappointment from the man standing across the room, the man who'd come to mean everything to her, the man who now could never be her husband. Ever since her return from St. Malo, her determination to escape to the Colonies had taken precedence over everything else. How could she marry a man who could not provide protection from the Chauvelins? Protection that only leaving England could guarantee?

Tristan crossed the room and took her hands in his, turning her to face him. "This changes nothing," he said in a low, agitated voice. "Do you hear me? You'll be my wife. What matter that it be in England or Virginia? Raymond is dead, Brittany—dead! Your ties with the Chauvelins are forever severed."

She nodded, not wishing to expose all her misgivings, her terror at the thought of living out her life with only the narrow English Channel separating her from the Chauvelins and their influence. She couldn't shake the feeling that she'd not heard the last from Charlotte. And then there was the threat from Buckingham, if he chose to punish both her and Tristan further . . . She had to get out of England.

Tristan dragged his gaze away from hers to face Carlisle, his fingers still imprisoning hers. "Are you certain 'twas John? My God, 'tis sometimes nigh on impossible to identify a body bloated from—" He left off suddenly at the look on Brittany's pale face. She averted her gaze.

"Of course I'm certain!" Weyrith barked. "Do you think I'd be careless about so important a matter?" He glanced at Ikuuk, who was studiously polishing off a portion of baked fish on a plate between his crossed legs; then his gaze went to Tristan, who was looking at Brittany as she stared blindly out the window.

" 'Sdeath, but I've never seen such a bunch of long faces at such good news! No one here stands to do aught but gain from this death."

Tristan reluctantly released Brittany's hands and approached his grandfather. "When I agreed I would allow you to name me your heir in the event of John's demise, I never dreamed he'd get himself killed! He had the reputation of squandering his money—of keeping questionable company, aye—but to end up murdered? The heir to the earl of Weyrith?" He leaned toward Carlisle, his eyes burning with suspicion. "If I didn't think you above such shady dealings, my lord earl, I would readily suspect your part in removing John Carlisle as an obstacle to your—"

Carlisle's hand came up with surprising swiftness and struck Tristan's cheek with a sharp crack.

Tristan saw it coming but, out of deference to the old man, allowed him to avenge the insult without more than a slight, reflexive jerk.

"You whelp! How dare you accuse me of such treachery?" He stood staring at Tristan, blue eyes clashing with blue, a standoff of Carlisle against Carlisle . . . And then the fight seeped out of the earl with alarming speed. His taut features went flaccid, the fire in his eyes died, and he fell back into the chair with a gusty sigh.

"Grandfather?" Tristan queried anxiously.

"I'm all right," came the tired answer. "How would *you* feel after altering an overgrown path to accommodate a coach and four? Add a few decades to your age for good measure before you answer that."

Tristan's expression turned baffled. "How *did* you come here?"

Carlisle opened one eye and trained it on his grandson. "Certainly not the way you would have done. But, as you seem to have forgotten, I was born and raised in this country. I know London and its environs like the back of my hand, you inflated young jackass." As Tristan looked to Ikuuk, the earl reached for his cup of ale and downed it to the dregs. The Indian shrugged to indicate his ignorance of the route the earl had taken.

"I cannot force you to do something you don't wish to," the old man continued, "but both of you"—he looked meaningfully at Brittany—"stand only to gain. I am not so dull-witted as to be ignorant of Brittany's reason for wanting to leave England. But the Chauvelins can do nothing to you if you marry my grandson."

She turned slowly to face him, her head held regally, but her eyes were clouded with pain and doubt, and Tristan was reminded of the young woman he'd first brought to Wildwood. He turned toward her, and then halted at Carlisle's next words. "As for Buckingham, he's not totally unredeemable. But you must take the offensive in your war with him. If I were you, I would take Brittany to London, show her off, introduce her as your wife—or your betrothed. Show him you've done with hiding, for he loves nothing more than bullying. Confront him face to face if it must come to that, but cease these hit or miss tactics and bring it all out into the open." He paused and looked from one to the other. "England can be home to you both—you have only to face your demons and dispel them."

There was a long silence before Brittany spoke. "Your lordship, you do Tristan a great disservice when you accuse him of hiding. He's as brave and gallant a man as you'll ever know, and the only thing he hides is *me*." She looked down at her hands interlocked before her waist, the knuckles white in her agitation. "I would never be the cause of his throwing away an earldom. He loves and is well loved by the king—he's important to Charles. He is also important to you, and now he has obligations that compel him to remain in England where, as you've said, he belongs. But *I* must leave. Since I first thought I killed Raymond Chauvelin, my wish has been to make a new life for myself in the Colonies." Her voice was still calm, her words evenly uttered. Her eyes, however, fused with Tristan's. "There is nothing more important to me now."

Chapter 17

"So you've taken it upon yourself to tell me, before all and sundry, that I belong in England."

Brittany sat next to her bedroon window, staring out into the yard where Tristan and Ikuuk had once cavorted in adolescent abandon. Now, all was in darkness, the slate-gray winter sky having given way to the gloom of night. The room was in shadow, except for the feeble light of twin tapers set in a brass and marble candleholder beside the bed, and the orange-gold flames in the fireplace unfurling upward like incandescent fingers. At Tristan's quiet words, she raised her head from her contemplative attitude and flung back the heavy tresses that had obscured her downcast face.

She pushed herself to a sitting position and regarded him with a sad smile. "You are all that a courtier should be—and more. You would give your life for your king—have nearly done so, by your own admission—and now stand to inherit all that your grandfather and his antecedents have acquired and fought to maintain for centuries." She tucked her knees beneath her chin and rested her cheek thereupon, her gaze touching his shadowed face. "Indeed, my lord, who belongs here more than you?"

He moved slowly toward her, his expression difficult to read in the dimness. At the edge of the bed he paused, as if changing his mind, and sat down. Gazing into the flame of one taper, he spoke. "Do you ever think of St. Malo? Surely the fact that you took the name of the province where you were born tells me how much you loved your native France." His lashes lowered and he stared down at his hand on one bent knee, a sculpture of living flesh and blood, magnificently wrought, splendidly beautiful as the faint light from the candles threw the planes of his face into softened relief and shadow. "Do you ever feel a lancing pain in your heart when you think of the happy times in France? Of your childhood . . . your loved ones . . . the beauty of the land that has long since become a part of your soul?" A frown drew his black brows together. "Do you ever wish so feverently for your homeland that you feel you will die of it?" He looked up at her, and she was taken aback by the stark longing in his eyes.

"My grandfather and my king may say I belong here, and even you may mouth the words, but that cannot alter the fact that my heart and soul will be forever in Virginia."

She went to sit beside him. Their fingers entwined, tightening, clinging, each deriving strength from the other in this moment of introspection. "Forgive me, my love," she murmured. "I knew not what I said."

He relaxed his grip on her hand and touched her cheek with one gentle finger. "I do not ask you for aught more than to remain here with me for a while." She raised her gaze from their clasped hands. "I know 'tis selfish of me, but we were apart for an eternity—" His eyes kindled with an intensity that made her feel weak all over. "Pray do not leave me yet—you are my anchor. Pray continue to be the one solid thing within my suddenly uncertain future. I will do everything in my power to smooth things over with Buckingham. I will apologize—" His mouth tightened, and before he could continue, the image of this proud man humbling himself to the despotic Buckingham rose up before her.

"*Non!*"

One corner of his mouth curved upward at her vehement denial. "Then at least let me try to set you at ease. While I draw breath, you will suffer no harm from the Chauvelins, you can believe me." He leaned forward and touched his lips to hers, his hand caressing the nape of her neck and urging her to lean into the kiss as it deepened and sent her wits scattering as swiftly as a flock of pigeons before a hawk.

How can he do this to me? she wondered. *How?*

He drew away to whisper, *"You* are the only thing that can keep me here right now . . . no one, nothing else."

Guilt flooded through her and distress welled up inside her in the wake of his admission—an admission that placed the burden of his decision to remain in England on her. Only her presence could make him continue to cleave unto his king and hold on to an earldom.

"How can you do this to me?" came her ragged whisper. "How can you hang such an albatross of responsibility about my neck?"

"You said you would never leave me. You wear the token of that pledge."

The ring seemed to grow heavy on her finger, a filigreed fetter, shackling her to him and England.

"That was when I believed we were to go to Virginia." She looked down at the shining stones on her finger and, in a last bid to make him change his mind, asked, "What of Ikuuk? What of your Indian heritage?"

His gaze slid away from hers, and he drew in a long, shuddering breath. "Stay at least until spring. April . . . even March. Then, if you still feel the same, you can sail with Matt on the *Virginia.*" Their eyes met again, and Brittany knew what it cost him to ignore her question. "Just until spring, Brittany. I need you, my only love . . . I need you."

His uncharacteristic vulnerability tore at her heart until she ached for him. How could she ever deny him? What difference would two or three months make?

All the difference, whispered a faint voice she could not ignore. *He will have you so enslaved because of your love for him that you will do anything he wishes . . . anything.*

But was that so very bad?

Her green eyes dull with her own hurt and confusion, she gave an all but imperceptible nod. He pulled her into his arms, his breath sighing over her cheek as he murmured, ''Brittany, Brittany . . . you know I would follow you even into hell itself were it not for this damnable situation. When I sought you out in St. Malo, I swore I would not leave the city without you. And now I must deal with losing you because you do not trust me to protect you against all harm? To love you and keep you safely at my side?'' He buried his face in her hair, his chest pressed against her breast until she could feel the strong, urgent tempo of his heart as it beat in steady harmony with her own.

Brittany struggled with her fears, her love for him, and the burning wildfire that sped through her, threatening to obliterate reason itself. ''When does the *Virginia* sail?'' she queried, a quiver in her voice.

He tensed. ''The first of March.''

''Very well, my lord. I will remain with you until then. I owe you at least that much.''

He held her away from him, his eyes black with some emotion that took her breath away, even as it frightened her. ''You owe me nothing! There is no price for my love, for my rescuing you from Villiers, from Chauvelin . . . You may leave on the morrow, if that is what you believe, for I would more willingly see you leave because you feel no debt owed to me.''

She averted her face and sat unmoving, steeped in her own misery, until he gently pushed her down onto the bed. ''Forgive my harsh words, sweet. For now, just let me love you. I have you for two months . . .'' His fingers slid from her waist to tenderly cup a breast. ''I have just over sixty days . . . and nights,'' he added huskily. ''And I can be very persuasive.'' His fingers expertly opened the lacings of her bodice until her nipples strained against the delicate linen of her chemise. His hot breath burned through the thin cloth as he nipped the aroused bud with growing ardor. ''Mayhap''—he lifted his dark head to look into her eyes, a gleam of determination sparking within the mesmerizing gaze—"I can win you over to my cause."

For the next few weeks Brittany basked in the soothing warmth of Tristan's love, thrived on it. The shadows under her eyes, the pinched look about her mouth, disappeared with the radiance of happiness.

If she found herself fretting about leaving in March, she purposefully pushed the disturbing thoughts aside, reasoning that what was to be, would be. She refused to allow the coming parting to intrude upon her bliss. If, when the time came, she found that she couldn't leave, then perhaps it was not so important to her happiness and peace of mind as she'd once thought.

The earl remained with them for a week, enjoying the rustic charm of a smaller country home, surrounded by the three people closest to him. Brittany secretly suspected he was allowing Tristan some time before he took up the burden of learning what the assumption of the title and role of an earl entailed.

At Carlisle's urging, Tristan informed Charles by messenger that he'd returned to Wildwood. He did not reveal, however, just where he'd been for the month of December, although he suspected the king had already guessed.

Ugly rumors regarding John Carlisle's death were certain to be rife at Whitehall, but the inhabitants of Wildwood avoided the subject, and only once did Tristan question the earl about the burial. "He was interred beside my son, only to avoid further scandal," was the answer. "He deserved nothing more than a potter's field."

The day before the earl was to leave, Matthew Stark emerged from the path in the woods, riding hard for the house in the chill January air, clouds of vapor streaming from horse and rider alike. Ikuuk was teaching Brittany sign language while Tristan listened to the earl speak of his trusted agent in London.

At the distant thunder of hoofbeats, Brittany and the Indian turned toward the mullioned window in unison.

Tristan glanced their way as he, too, caught the muffled sound.

" 'Tis Matt," Brittany said.

Within minutes, Stark was striding into the room, holding aloft a letter. He handed his cape to Genna, who appeared as if by magic, and smiled down into her eyes, the others momentarily forgotten. As color splashed over the girl's cheeks, Matt seemed to remember himself and turned away.

"I see the lady at Wildwood comes second only to the lady docked on the Thames," Tristan observed wryly.

Matt bowed to Brittany with agile gallantry, ignoring Tristan's comment, and bid them all a good afternoon.

"You are missed at Whitehall, Tris," he told his friend as the latter moved to pour him a glass of wine.

"And you, I see, are enjoying yourself enough for both of us." Tristan handed him the wine and motioned toward a settee.

Matt shook his head. "You know I've not much interest in all that. But the king misses your company and sought to wheedle every last detail from me concerning your mysterious absence from court. And," he added, sobering, "he is most anxious to offer his condolences upon the unfortunate demise of John Carlisle." He looked at the earl. "As am I, your lordship."

The older man nodded in acknowledgment. "No doubt the king's missive to that effect lies waiting in my office at Carlisle Hall."

"Dare I ask what they are saying?" Tristan said with deceptive casualness.

Matthew's eyes narrowed thoughtfully. "Carlisle evidently owed a vast sum of money to John Oliver, The Crow. The king sent several men to investigate, but all they could discover was that the last time Carlisle was seen alive, he was leaving Dagger Tavern. A bargeman told them he'd taken a well-dressed man fitting Carlisle's description to the old Carmelite monastery in Alsatia."

"Alsatia," the earl repeated, using the other term for

the Whitefriars district in London. "Don't surprise me
. . . I've known he kept poor company for years. He was
destined to come to a bad end." There was no trace of
grief in his voice.

Tristan went to stand before a painting depicting a scene
of lush woodlands in spring, his gaze taking in the lifelike
representation. "Aye, and as he's indicated he would be
in the past, Charles is without a doubt delighted that now
I have something to bind me to England." His gaze
clashed with his grandfather's.

No one spoke for long moments, and the scrape of
Ikuuk's knife against a small piece of wood sounded loud
in the quiet room.

Matt threw the letter he'd been holding onto a table and
sat back, crossing an ankle over his knee. "Here is your
excuse to make an appearance at Whitehall and tell Buckingham to go to hell."

Tristan picked up the missive bearing the royal seal and
tore it open. His eyes scanned the contents before he
looked up, thoughtfully silent. Although he finally spoke
to Matt, he looked at Brittany, sitting quietly, her hands
clasped in her lap. "I would like nothing better than to
best Buckingham," he said softly. "But now I can do it
without uttering a single word."

"That's m'boy!" cried the earl. "He's directly responsible for destroying Brittany's anonymity, I'd stake my title
on it."

"But he freed me from the specter of murder," Brittany
pointed out.

Carlisle snorted. "You damn near perished."

"You can believe me when I say the self-serving George
Villiers freed you very unintentionally." said Matt. "His
purpose was to get at Tristan through Carlisle and you. I
wouldn't be surprised if Buckingham put those cutthroats
up to murdering John. Villiers's incredible wealth buys
him whatever he fancies."

Tristan glanced down at the letter once again, then at
Brittany. "It depends on how you feel," he told her. "Are

you willing to attend a masked ball at court in a fort-night?''

She didn't answer immediately, the memory of Buckingham's assault flashing through her mind. She stared unseeingly at her hands in her lap, trying to deal with the ambivalent feelings that rose within her.

"I'll not ask this of you if you will be uncomfortable . . . or afraid."

Inadvertently, the word *afraid* struck a nerve. Afraid. She'd been living with fear for almost five years.

She met Tristan's gaze. *I will do everything in my power to smooth things over with Buckingham. I will apologize . . .* The recollection of Tristan's selfless offer caused a spark of rebellion to flare within her breast. Why should he even have to consider humbling himself to Villiers? Tristan may have struck the duke, but it was in her defense, with no real harm done. Yet Buckingham had wielded his influence against them . . .

What had she to fear with Tristan at her side? Even the thought of a meeting with the king suddenly held no unpleasantness for her. She would like nothing better, she abruptly realized, than for Tristan to have his day with Buckingham, to successfully defy him while revealing that all the duke's scheming had been for naught.

Her blood heated at the challenge, her eyes lit with excitement, and her lips curved upward in acceptance of his bold proposition. "And why not, my lord?" she answered. "But of course"—she tapped a finger against pursed lips—"we must attend as a Powhatan brave and his woman, since his grace the duke has such an aversion to Indians."

Tristan's face broke into a grin. "A most enterprising—and devious—idea, coming from the sweet and shy Mistress Brittany Jennifer St. Germain." He glanced over at Matt. "Wouldn't you agree, Master Stark?"

Matt let out a whoop that made even Ikuuk grin. "My kind of wench," he said, laughing. "Fascinating, fearless . . . and French." He glanced at the door and caught the swirl of Genna's skirt as she moved past. "Come here, Genna, sweetheart."

She peeked inside the half-open door. "*Oui*, Monsieur Stark?"

"How would you like to attend a ball at Whitehall with us?"

Her dark eyes grew round. "Me?"

"Aye. Wouldn't you relish the opportunity of seeing George Villiers and his cronies again?"

Her eyes slitted, as if at an unpleasant memory. "I would relish the chance to kick his grace in the shins a time or two as we dance, *n'est-ce pas?*"

"And damned if I've not a mind to observe the whole thing firsthand!" interjected Carlisle, thwacking his walking stick against the floor for emphasis. "Were I not supposedly in mourning," he added darkly.

Tristan retrieved the decanter of wine and held it high. "Then another libation for everyone—to toast our venture."

Their voices rose in enthusiastic assent and their laughter rang through the air.

The earl left for Carlisle Hall, after extracting a promise from Tristan to join him there a day or two after the ball. Matt stayed on at Wildwood.

While Matt wooed Genna with sweet words and adoration, Tristan conducted his own campaign to wear down Brittany's resolve to leave England. If he'd been tender before in his lovemaking, he now sought to win her with an urgency that swept her breath away. He spent every free moment with her and spoiled her shamelessly, insisting upon doing everything for her until she laughingly protested.

"You'll have Ikuuk jealous, my lord," she'd teased one day as they stood in the kitchen.

"Jealous? How so?"

"Well, I hardly see him anymore—and he's already presented me with a beautiful shell necklace and a pair of beaded moccasins. Just yestermorn I discovered a bow and quiver of arrows outside the door that were exquisitely crafted for a woman of my size and strength, clearly designed for a woman with a love of archery.''

He raised an eyebrow. ''Indeed. And did you thank him for his thoughtful gifts?''

''Aye, but he will not admit to aught, silly man.''

He came up behind her as she was putting the finishing touches on a pie she'd made for Genna, to free the girl of her duties so she could be with Matt. Tristan's arms encircled Brittany's waist, and his lips leisurely trailed from her ear to the edge of her dress, just above her shoulder.

''Tristan—'' she protested softly, the pie balanced precariously in one hand.

His warm breath misted her cheek as he whispered in her ear, ''Did you never suspect that *I* might have given you those gifts?'' Her knees felt boneless as his mouth worked its havoc upon her senses, and she managed to set the pie down on the table.

''You?''

''Aye, love. A Powhatan warrior places fine gifts before the tepee of the woman he wishes to take for his wife.''

How romantic, she thought with a pang. And all along she'd thought it was Ikuuk . . . ever since she'd first come to Wildwood. She turned in his arms. ''It was you from the very first?''

''Even then.''

The pie forgotten, her lips met his, her determination to fight the sweet snare of his spell weakening a little more.

The day before the masquerade, Matt announced at supper that Genna had agreed to become his wife and would sail with him to the Colonies in March.

After everyone expressed their felicitations, Tristan said to Brittany, ''It seems my need of another housekeeper is in earnest now.''

"Surely you will sell Wildwood, anyway? Your home will be Carlisle Hall."

He shook his head, fingering the stem of his goblet as he studied her. "I will never give up Wildwood."

He knows how much I love Wildwood, she thought. *Beautiful as Carlisle Hall is, I prefer the simpler life here . . .*

Was this another of his attempts to woo her into staying in England?

But in an attempt to keep things light she only said, "Why would I ever wish to be housekeeper when I've been offered—"

Too late, she realized her error.

"You can have it all, Brittany, as my wife," Tristan said softly.

There was absolute silence at the table. Matt stared at his plate, while Ikuuk studiously scraped his clean. Genna, in an attempt to cover the awkwardness, rose quickly to her feet and began clearing away the dishes. "I must get back to my work," she began. "Why don't you—"

"Enis can clear the table this once," Matt said. "Come . . . toast our good news, Tris."

Tristan wrenched his gaze from Brittany's flushed countenance and cleared his throat. "Forgive my poor manners, my friend." He signaled for Enis to bring more wine, then, after their glasses were refilled, proceeded with his toast. "To Matt and Genna—may their union be gloriously happy . . . and fruitful."

But Brittany found that she could barely swallow, so great was her distress. Nor could she meet the intense eyes solemnly watching her from across the table. *Dieu,* she thought miserably. *How can I hurt him like this after all that's happened?*

Brittany couldn't take her eyes from him. He'd pulled his shoulder-length hair to the left side of his head, anchored it in a knot, and decorated it with a bird's wing, the feathers of which were tied with small rattles that clicked softly with each movement of his head.

Rather than wearing a mask, he'd elected to paint his face, until he looked so fierce and unrecognizable that Brittany kept glancing into his eyes to make certain he was, indeed, her beloved Tristan.

"Don't look so frightened, love," he told her as he put the finishing touches on his body paint. "You remind me too heart-wrenchingly of the fearful young woman I first brought to Wildwood."

Brittany mustered a smile and stood, smoothing down the doeskin skirt that had been Running Deer's. "You'll catch your death without a shirt, Pale Wolf."

He grinned, his expression at odds with his facepaint. "I'll wear one of Ikuuk's shirts until we arrive at White-hall. The banquet hall will be stifling with so many in attendance and I'll be envied my unclothed chest."

"And you've been to many such gatherings, I would imagine." An unreasonable jealousy gripped her at the thought of Tristan and the court beauties he surely must have—

"Enough." He turned to her, hands on hips, and Brittany took in the splendid breadth of his shoulders, the way his upper torso tapered down to slim hips beneath buck-skin breeches. From the waistcord around his taut middle hung a skin bag ornamented with a leather fringe at the bottom.

"And what might you carry in your pouch?" she asked in an effort to divert her sensual thoughts.

"Come see for yourself."

She reached her hand into the pouch. The heat of his body seemed to sear her hand through the skin. She withdrew a knife, a pipe, and a flaker. Replacing the first two items, she glanced up at him questioningly, the stone tool resting in her palm.

"Just in case I need to notch an arrowhead for Buck-ingham's black heart," he explained with a twitch of his lips. He took the stone and drew her into his embrace. As he nuzzled her temple, he pressed her hand between their bodies. "See what you've done, sweet. Now we'll be late for the ball."

Brittany thrilled at the evidence of his desire, awed that she possessed such power over his emotions. She touched his lips with hers, then drew away, sighing. "We mustn't spoil your paint or—"

"Promise me something," he said, his voice taking on a huskiness that had nothing to do with arousal.

She regarded him questioningly.

"That you will stay away from the king." At her frown of bemusement, he elucidated. "Charles is much taken by a beautiful face . . . and you are possessed of so much more than lovely features."

Her fine brows arched in exaggeration and her eyes lit with deviltry. "You do not trust me?"

"Nay, sweet. 'Tis Charles I do not trust."

Something within her wrenched painfully at his uncharacteristic doubt, at the troubled look in his eyes. Tristan, who'd been so confident and capable since the first time she'd met him. Tristan, who now stood robbed of some of that self-assurance because of her refusal to commit herself to him. Her conscience threatened to throw all caution aside, urged her to say the words he needed to hear, but the tether of lingering uncertainty held her back.

She attempted to distract him with levity. "I can always shave the front and sides of my head, like an unmarried Powhatan maiden. Surely Charles would be disenchanted with me then?"

Tristan laughed. "Ikuuk has done his work well, I see." He stroked the thick braid that hung down her back. "Nay, not a hair shall you remove from this fair head."

She rested her cheek against his chest, listening to the steady beat of his heart.

"Promise me," he entreated softly.

"I promise."

He let out a soft exhalation that sounded disconcertingly like relief. Brittany had little time to feel responsible for it, however, for his hands crept up under her cloak to caress her cool, naked skin. "No chemise for you, eh?" he murmured. "How accommodating. How very accommodating . . ."

Chapter 18

They approached Whitehall Palace in a hackney. Circumventing the complex, unattractive cluster of buildings until they came to the Banqueting Hall where the masquerade was being held, the foursome alighted to join the milling guests who laughed and chattered on their way to the impressive entrance.

Designed by England's first professional architect, Inigo Jones, the Banqueting Hall of Whitehall Palace was a building of pure Roman classicism. Beautiful in its simplicity, it was considered one of his finest works. Brittany gazed up in admiration at the rusticated masonry, the tall, square-paned first-floor windows between Ionic columns with their alternate round and triangular pediments.

"Come along, love, before we're trampled," Tristan urged in her ear.

With Matt and an awed Genna behind them, they entered the building, where they encountered even larger crowds.

'Twill be easy to avoid not only the king, but any others in this mass of humanity, Brittany thought.

Musicians played in the gallery at one end of the hall, while liveried servants replenished tables of refreshments, saw to the comfort of the guests and, in general, supervised the affair with capable thoroughness.

Beneath the ceiling depicting the Restoration in allegory, Charles and Catherine were seated on a raised dais.

Chatting with several courtiers, the royal couple also observed the goings-on with interested pleasure.

"We are not the only Indians present, I see," commented Tristan as he led Brittany to a table of wines, ales, and various other libations.

She followed the direction of his gaze and stifled her laughter at the sight of the unrealistic costumes of several overly creative masqueraders. Her green eyes sparkled through her demi-mask. "Ikuuk would be appalled."

"It looks to *me* as if some of these, er, *ladies* have used the excuse of wearing a costume to flaunt their charms," Genna commented for Brittany's ears alone.

Indeed, even as Genna spoke, a tall woman with beautiful Titian tresses threw back her head and laughed at some remark made by her companion, accenting the long, white line of her throat and the mounds of her generous breasts that threatened to pop free of her low-cut tavern girl's blouse.

" 'Tis Castlemaine," Matt informed them, and Brittany's attention was immediately riveted to the king's beautiful mistress. "And Lady Diana Hartland, if I'm not mistaken," he added ruefully. The woman Matt identified as Diana Hartland was lovely as well, from what Brittany could see, clad in a scandalously revealing mermaid's costume that molded to her luscious curves like a second skin.

Beneath her fingers, Brittany felt a slight tensing of Tristan's forearm, and she realized it was not because of either of the ladies just mentioned. She followed his gaze and encountered the icy blue stare of the duke of Buckingham, recognizable to her—and obviously to Tristan, as well—in spite of the mask he wore. His height and build, his deceptively casual stance beneath his black devil's costume and cape, the arrogant angle of his chin—all gave him away as readily as a trumpeted proclamation.

Matt, dressed as a Puritan, led the primly attired Genna toward the guests who'd already begun to dance, and Brittany's grip tightened on Tristan's arm. "Shouldn't we all stay together?"

Tristan dragged his gaze from Villiers and smiled down at her. "There is strength in numbers, you mean, my Powhatan maiden? Tsk, tsk—such a lack of faith in the warrior who has sworn to protect you. Let our Puritan husband and wife watch the dancers and perhaps try their hand at it."

"But—" She glanced over to where Buckingham had been standing and found he'd disappeared with unnerving ease among a group of bacchanalian revelers in Roman dress.

"We've driven home our point, I do believe. He has no power to frighten us," he drawled with soft virulence as he, too, noted the duke's disappearance. "Would you care for some Rhenish?"

Distracted, Brittany accepted a proffered goblet and took several long draughts to steady herself. As she felt the wine immediately warm her, she finished the drink and glanced around while Tristan spoke to a man dressed as a Viking, complete with rounded shield and battle-ax, leather jerkin, skin leggings, and drinking horn.

He turned to Brittany. "Sweet, this is Sir Geoffrey—"

"Tristan Savidge, you rogue!" interrupted a husky feminine voice, and all three people turned toward Barbara Palmer, countess of Castlemaine, whose violet eyes regarded them through her mask with keen interest, first taking in Tristan from head to toe, then Brittany. Brittany immediately recognized the woman in a mermaid's garb beside Barbara, and felt jealousy claw through her as the diminutive Diana, her unbound golden hair falling in rippling waves halfway down her back, boldly stared up at Tristan. Her breathing seemed unnaturally labored, and Brittany stared in unwilling fascination at the creamy expanse of her breasts above the strapless costume. The only thing hidden was her nipples, and belatedly Brittany realized that the exaggerated rise and fall of her chest was intended to accentuate her bosom.

Brittany instantly sensed that Tristan and Diana were more than mere acquaintances, and she had to ball her hands into fists beneath her cape to quell the urge to strangle the woman.

Tristan bowed gallantly and performed the necessary introductions. Ignoring Brittany, both women oohed and ahhed over his fierce facepaint and nude chest. "Ye gods, Sir Tristan," exclaimed Diana, a delicate hand going dramatically to her breast, "you're enough to give a lady a fright."

"Or make her wish she were the one to share your pallet tonight," Barbara added slyly.

Tristan reached for Brittany's hand and smiled politely. "I thank you for the compliments, ladies. A warrior is supposed to look fierce and—" he glanced down at Brittany, laughter at some private joke between them lighting his eyes—"virile."

Diana boldly ran a finger around the rippled lines of his chest. "Faith, but I do hate hairy brutes, Tristan." She smiled into his eyes with audacious familiarity. "You are no such thing, are you, my lord?" She touched the gleaming copper amulet. "What an interesting medallion . . . so *pagan!*"

" 'Twas a gift from my grandmother," he answered.

Sir Geoffrey cleared his throat, as if to remind them he was still present. "Might I have this dance, Mistress Brittany?"

A vague frown furrowed Tristan's brow, but before he could speak, Diana chimed in, "Oh, aye, Sir Geoffrey, and then Sir Tristan can dance a set or two with me."

Barbara was already reluctantly turning away as her husband, Roger Palmer, caught her attention. There was nothing to be done without seeming rude to Geoffrey or Diana, so Tristan nodded and they began to make their way to the space cleared for dancing, Diana hanging on his arm. He glanced back at Brittany, but she seemed content, already in easy conversation with her new acquaintance.

The stately strains of the pavane, a series of curtsies, advances and retreats set in two-quarter time, rang through the spacious hall. With Sir Geoffrey's hand beneath hers, Brittany struck the appropriate poses in this dignified and aloof dance she'd studied at school. Other women with trains as part of their costumes swept them about in the manner of a peacock parading his tail, for which the dance was named. Although the pavane was more popular in Italy, Spain, and her native France, Brittany noted with interest that the English did the dance justice.

She caught sight of Tristan several times, and in spite of her high pique over Diana Hartland's bold overtures, she admired his lithe grace, incongruous though he looked in his barbaric attire and bright body coloring. As her eyes read the steady assurances in his gaze, she gave no thought as to how she herself must appear dancing with a fierce-looking Viking.

King Charles himself led the next dance, the branle, with Catherine. Brittany moved easily into it with her partner, noticing that Tristan and the lady Diana were lost from view as more and more guests joined the dancing. A vague uneasiness sifted through her, but Sir Geoffrey was so gallant, his smile so genuine, that Brittany laughingly gave herself up to the dance. Never in the past five years had she dreamed she could enjoy herself so much, and at court no less, moving to the music with a natural rhythm and grace that made her feet seem to skim over the floor.

And then, to her dismay, the devil in black was bowing before her, and Sir Geoffrey courteously gave her up to the duke of Buckingham. She performed the rest of the dance in a fog.

"You are just as bewitching in the garb of a savage as in that of an alehouse bawd. Small wonder Savidge managed to retrieve you from the arms of your lawful husband."

She looked up at him, refusing to allow her fear to show. "To what purpose have you usurped Sir Geoffrey's place as my partner?"

"Only to tell you that Charlotte Chauvelin now accuses you of murder. You have not heard the last of her."

The growing conviction that she would be safe beside

Tristan Savidge, even in England, shriveled like a singed strand of hair, and a knot of dread formed in the pit of her stomach.

As they neared the royal couple, Brittany searched desperately for a sign of Tristan or Matt, but in the sea of masked faces there was no one who looked even remotely familiar.

Promise me that you will stay away from the king.

The branle ended, and Buckingham was suddenly leading her directly toward Charles and Catherine. Brittany dug in her heels and pulled him to a halt as unobtrusively as possible, not wishing to call attention to herself. "What are you doing?" she demanded through set teeth.

"Only taking you to meet Charles, sweetheart. The way I see it, my little grudge against your breed lover will be considerably reduced by your introduction to Charles."

Promise me . . .

She would not have found a meeting with the king objectionable were it not at Buckingham's behest, and in direct conflict with her promise to Tristan.

Villiers pulled her forward once more, their silent struggle going undetected among the raucous crowd. And then she stood face to face with Charles Stuart.

"Your majesty," Buckingham began, "I bring you the most beautiful green eyes in London."

Catherine's attention was engaged by a knight errant and his squire, and her back was to them. No help from that quarter, Brittany thought with a sinking sensation as she heard the queen laugh delightedly at something the knight was saying.

Dressed as Nero in toga, mantle, and sandals, Charles looked regal, his curling dark hair flowing over his shoulders, his height impressive in any crowd. He bowed elegantly, his dark eyes meeting Brittany's appreciatively. "And who might you be?" he asked in a voice that was both dulcet and commanding.

What could she say? Should she tell him the truth? she

wondered in a panic. *"Je—je m'appelle* Geneviève," she answered, reverting to French in her confusion.

He smiled, revealing even white teeth. *"Enchanté, Geneviève . . . enchanté."* He took her hand from Buckingham. "You have done well, George," he told him. "But has she no escort?"

"He is, er, occupied elsewhere, majesty."

Charles smiled again, his heavy-lidded dark eyes shining with good humor and heightened interest. *"Eh bien, chère* Geneviève, let us dance, shall we?" He signaled a nearby page. "A courante," he told the boy. "Tell the musicians we would like a courante."

When Catherine went to turn back toward the king and Brittany, the knight immediately requested she dance the set with him. She threw a sweet-humored but apologetic smile at both Brittany and Charles before complying. There was, it seemed, no way to avoid being partnered by the king. Brittany allowed him to lead her into the vigorous dance, even as she silently prayed Tristan would not glimpse them and think she'd betrayed her promise.

Despite the lively retreats and advances, the pas glissés, or gliding steps, Brittany was able to observe firsthand just what gossips related as the king's physical attributes. He was uncommonly tall for a man, slightly taller than Tristan, with fine legs and an impressive torso. His mouth was sensual, mobile, and he looked more foreign than English—for he was one-quarter each Scots, Danish, French, and Italian. His swarthy complexion, the legacy of his Italian ancestors, the Medici dukes of Tuscany, was complemented by his dark, expressive eyes, so full of humor and melancholy and mystery. To his sexual prowess, she could not attest, but that he was charming and magnetic, she could not deny. Against her will, she was fascinated . . .

Diana Hartland insisted Tristan remain with her through the second dance, prettily pleading her case by accusing him of staying away from court of late.

With a speculative lift of an eyebrow, he asked her, "And how, indeed, can you dance anything more lively than the pavane in the guise of a mermaid, Diana?" He glanced down at her tail. "Where exactly *are* your feet?"

She burst out laughing at his gentle gibe. "Oh, come now, Tristan, you know perfectly well they're beneath the costume." She thrust one daintily slippered foot from beneath the tail and waggled it.

With a sigh of good-natured resignation, he allowed her to coerce him into the branle. Though Diana flirted outrageously with him, even falling against his chest once so that he was forced to grip her bare upper arms to steady her, Tristan gave her only half his attention. His eyes scanned the crowd, searching for Brittany and Sir Geoffrey, but the dancers were legion now, and when the music for the courante began, he finally begged off, determined to search for them in earnest.

Escorting a disappointed Diana to the edge of the dancers, he excused himself and began skirting the crowd, a frown of unease making him look savage beneath his paint. He found Matt and Genna, but neither of them had seen Brittany since they'd parted company. When he spotted Buckingham standing to the side talking to his cousin Barbara, sudden suspicion swept over him, for at the same moment he noticed that all the women in the hall were standing, an indication that the king himself was dancing.

He pushed through the dancers to the middle of the huge floor. And then he saw her, the light from a thousand candles burnishing the thick braid of her hair to richest old gold, her cheeks flushed, her lips curved in laughter . . . and her eyes locked with those of the king of England.

Tristan went absolutely still, his body suddenly rigid as he watched his sovereign and the woman he loved pay court through the movements of the dance, advancing and retreating, teasing, taunting, sliding gracefully first this way and then that. And the look in Charles's eyes . . . He knew that expression well, the expression of a man hot on the scent of a desirable woman—a man who held absolute power and, with that power, a knowledge of his own potent charm and irresistible attraction.

With a conscious effort, Tristan thrust aside his jealousy and doubt. He would let them finish the dance—he did not dare interrupt the king—and then he would introduce Brittany to Charles as . . . as what? *As your betrothed, fool, and be damned!*

Aye, he thought, renewed determination purging him of his momentary uncertainty. As the betrothed of Charles's friend, Brittany would be safe from any dishonorable intentions the king might harbor. The sooner her identity was revealed, the better . . .

" 'Tis an honor any woman would seek, to sleep with the king," said a voice in his ear.

He tore his gaze from the couple in the middle of the crowd and spun to face George Villiers. Forcing himself to smile with seeming indulgence—a smile that did not quite reach his eyes—he replied, "He will do naught when I reveal who she is."

The duke's eyes widened skeptically. "Your waterfront doxy? The woman you stole from her husband? Before she murdered him, that is . . ." His pause conveyed deliberate insolence. "We shall see, Savidge . . . we shall see."

Tristan did not rise to the bait. "You have something in mind, then? 'Twould seem you are not quick to learn your lesson, Villiers," he drawled in foppish imitation of the duke. "Do not think for one moment that I would refrain from raising a hand to you again, justifiably or even unjustifiably if I lose my patience with your asininity." And he looked pointedly at Buckingham's devil's tail drooping onto the floor.

The duke's eyes slitted behind his mask in anger, but Tristan turned away in careless dismissal, seeking Brittany and Charles as the dance came to an end. Charles took her hand and held it to his lips, turning only to acknowledge something said by a passing servant.

As Tristan moved forward, Charles called for the country dances to begin, crying, "Cuckolds All Awry, if you please, and we will lead it!"

An avid sportsman, Charles was in excellent physical condition from playing tennis, swimming, hunting, riding, and a host of other less strenuous activities. That he should participate in several different dances—and consecutively, no less—was not unusual. And so, as Cuckold's All Awry, a dance of old England, began, Tristan was not surprised that Charles led it with Brittany.

A servant passed with a tray of filled wine goblets, and Tristan helped himself, deciding that even though he'd have a devil of a headache in the morning, a bit more wine might aid him in his cause—a thing so uncharacteristic for him that he paused in bringing the goblet to his lips.

"Ah, there you are, Sir Tristan." Sir Geoffrey Peckinpaugh gained his side, perspiration runneling down his temples and into his thick, fake beard. "Too strenuous for me," he added. "Especially with all this paraphernalia." He removed his horned helmet and brushed an arm across his forehead.

"Here, drink this." Tristan extended the untouched wine.

"My thanks." Peckinpaugh gratefully downed the chilled beverage in a few swallows.

"I see you lost your partner to the king," Tristan commented.

Sir Geoffrey frowned slightly. "I *am* sorry, but"—he strained to see through the moving dancers to better observe Charles and Brittany—"actually 'twas Buckingham who cut in during the branle and gave her over to his majesty."

Tristan's lips tightened and one hand moved to finger the knife through the skin of the pouch at this side. "Somehow that doesn't come as a surprise," he said, more to himself than to Sir Geoffrey. "But I will beat him at his own game."

The dance ended and, excusing himself, Tristan moved purposefully toward the center of the dance floor.

A leg shot out of nowhere and caused him to stumble. "Pardon me, guvnor," mumbled an unapologetic voice. Tristan whirled to face the miscreant and took a solid fist to his jaw, causing him to stagger backward.

"Ye sure are unsteady on yer feet fer a redman, ain't ye?" chortled another voice beside him, but Tristan caught the cultured tones beneath the rough speech.

A hand clamped onto his upper arm in a death grip, and a burly-looking sailor came up on his other side. Like lightning the thought flashed through his mind that Buckingham was behind this altercation—Buckingham, who was intent upon keeping him from Brittany while she held the king's interest. No explanation was requested, no excuse made, as Tristan bent at the waist, wrenching his arm free of the first thug, and caught the sailor in his midsection with the top of his head.

A sharp exhalation sounded as the air left his assailant's lungs and he doubled over in pain. Several milling bystanders backed away to give them room.

"Why you—"

The other man seized Tristan's arm again, but this time he was ready. He snaked an ankle around the man's lower leg, knocking him off balance, and neatly threw him over his hip. The attacker landed heavily on the floor.

"I may be unsteady on my feet, but I excel at wrestling. Beware the next time you think to attack an unarmed Powhatan."

"Need any help?" Matt asked.

Tristan faced his friend and noted a red-faced Sir Geoffrey behind him, swinging his battle-ax threateningly at the man recovering from the blow. A grin split Tristan's face as he wiped blood from the corner of his mouth with the back of one hand. "Not now, Stark. Where the hell were you a few moments ago?" He glanced down at the man sitting up on the floor. "You can make certain they don't forget their lesson while I retrieve Brittany from an obviously besotted Charles."

Genna came up behind Matt just in time to hear Tristan's last words. Both people looked past Tristan to Brittany and the king. *"Dieu nous sauve* . . . she danced with the king himself," she breathed, awestruck.

"Aye. Would like to meet his majesty, Genna?" At her look of uncertainty, Tristan added, "If you change your mind, you have only to tell me." He swung away, throwing over his shoulder, "Wait here, and we'll all dance the next one."

Brittany saw him first, for she'd been looking for a way out of yet another dance with the king, fearing not only to hurt Tristan with her broken promise, but also to offend the queen. She needn't have worried, however, as several men and a woman came up to Charles and claimed his attention. His hand over hers loosened and Brittany pulled away, almost running to meet Tristan.

"Tristan, I—" The distress that darkened her eyes made him catch her hand and draw her to him.

"I know, sweet . . . I know." He smoothed back a gossamer wisp of hair that coiled sweetly over her cheek. The love and forgiveness in his eyes touched her deeply. He understood, this gentle, accepting man.

"What happened to your mouth?" She gently touched the cut at one side of his cleanly molded lips.

"A foxed sailor who has an aversion for redmen." He shrugged just as Charles and Catherine came up behind them.

"If you point him out, I'll have him arrested," Charles offered, his eyes grave.

Tristan shook his head and turned to bow first to Charles and then to Catherine. "Your majesties."

"Tristan," Catherine exclaimed in her accented English, her rich brown eyes glowing with pleasure. "How good to see you again. We've missed you."

"Indeed we have," Charles added.

Tristan acknowledged the compliment with an inclination of his head. "Majesty, I fear my disguise is not as foolproof as I'd thought, since you recognize me so easily," he told Catherine.

"The ladies would know you anywhere, my friend, and especially in your feathers and paint," Charles observed wryly.

"And who is your graceful partner?" Catherine inquired.

"Allow me to present Brittany Jennifer St. Germain, late of France." He paused and looked at Brittany, hesitant now to actually name her his betrothed, as his brief bout with uncertainty had long since vanished. His glance moved to the king, whose perusal of Brittany was warm and interested.

"So this is Isolde."

Tristan's eyes met and held the king's as he immediately took the monarch's meaning. "It is."

"Well, Brittany or Geneviève—whichever it is—we are delighted to have made your acquaintance." He bowed gallantly to Brittany and took Catherine's hand as the music for another country dance commenced. "Please honor us with your presence at Whitehall more often . . . with Tristan or without." He nodded to Tristan. "I tender you my condolences upon the untimely death of your half cousin, John." But the eloquent dark eyes registered more satisfaction than sympathy.

"Thank you, majesty."

"And, pray, do tell me later what transpired during your long—and rather mysterious—absence from court." He raised a dark eyebrow, ignoring the dancers around them as they began to move to the music.

"Indeed, one day I shall, majesty. But for now, you would do well to ask Villiers."

Charles frowned, but anything he might have said was interrupted by a new voice. "Your majesties?" called a stout shepherdess as she headed for their small group, the staff she brandished effectively clearing her a path.

Charles shrugged apologetically as the woman sailed into their midst, obviously desirous of attracting the undivided attention of Charles and Catherine. "You will excuse us?" he reluctantly offered to Tristan and Brittany.

Tristan bowed once more and took Brittany's hand. "Indeed we shall, for we are to meet Matthew Stark and his Genna for this dance."

The hackney lumbered through the city toward Chelsea. By the soft radiance of the single lantern, Brittany watched Genna fall asleep, her head resting trustingly on Matt's shoulder. Matt's cheek touched the top of her dark head and he, too, appeared to doze. They made a handsome couple, Brittany thought, and she suddenly envied them their total absorption in each other—their happiness, their coming marriage.

And why can't you have the same? a voice asked. *He loves you—wants you to be his wife.*

Her heart somersaulted at the beauty of Tristan's chiseled profile, and at the heady thought of lovemaking that would follow their return to Wildwood. He taught me of love and trust, of true happiness and contentment . . . and he pledged to protect me . . .

You have only to face your demons and dispel them, the earl had said.

What could the Chauvelins really do to her now, especially once she became the legal wife of an earl? Tristan himself witnessed her attempt to save Raymond from death and the near loss of her own life. And Buckingham with his threats . . . She pushed the thought aside, trusting Tristan to handle things.

What had she to lose by marrying Tristan, when she had everything to gain?

She made a decision then, and sudden, unadulterated joy rose in her breast, sparkled in her eyes. She tilted her face up toward his, her pulse leaping with excitement as she realized what she must do.

Tristan turned from his contemplation of the sights beyond the window.

"Have I ever told you how very much I love you?" she whispered.

His face registered his surprise at her words, then his

delight. His lips took hers in a kiss that stirred her soul, chased away every thought save of him and their life together.

"Why did you not introduce me as your betrothed, Pale Wolf?" she murmured against his mouth.

"I could never lie at your expense."

"Then make it so. Ask me again."

He drew away, his eyes searching her face. "You're certain?"

With a peek at the undisturbed Matt and Genna, she wound her arms around his neck and pulled his mouth down to hers once again. "Very."

Chapter 19

The blissful interlude at Wildwood was over far too soon for Brittany. Tristan was called to Carlisle Hall for consultations with Richard Carlisle. Now that she'd consented to wed Tristan and remain with him in England, she expected to travel to Surrey with him in preparation for her own role as countess.

Tristan, however, thought it wiser for her to remain at Wildwood and learn from Enis and Genna before attempting to tackle Carlisle Hall. "You'll have Matt and Ikuuk to keep happy," he teased her. "At least until Matt and Genna leave for the Colonies." At her frown, he added, "And I know how fond you are of Genna. Why not stay at least until they leave?"

"If I didn't know better, Tristan Andrew Savidge, I'd believe you were eager to be rid of me."

"But you do know better, love. I promise I'll return regularly—'tis only for a few weeks, you know."

And so she made no further demur for, indeed, March was just around the corner.

The day—and night—before he left were stamped indelibly upon her memory, a day that began with the sun breaking through the cloudy February sky to chase away the chill. They rode Gorvenal over the leaf-carpeted forest paths, laughing and planning their future as only lovers do. His alabaster mane and tail fluttering in the gentle breeze, his magnificent golden-brown body shining like satin in the shafts of sunlight that speared through the bare

268

branches overhead, Gorvenal took their combined weight easily, his powerful muscles rippling beneath his coat, his surefooted steps carrying them swiftly or leisurely, at their whim, about the woodlands and grounds.

But the night . . . It began with a bath together that ended in lovemaking before they even left the tub. Replete, they lay in each other's embrace until the cooling water forced them to leave their wet bower. Tristan rubbed her dry with a length of toweling as they stood before the fire, both absorbing the heat of the flames, until desire began to seep into them anew.

He carried her to the bed, where they renewed their vows of love in hushed tones. They sought and discovered the secret delights that come with growing familiarity and leisurely exploration, thrilled to the contrast of male and female, firm and soft. They reveled in the way their bodies perfectly complimented each other to bring increasing pleasure, and finally a bright and burning ecstasy that sent them soaring to that sublime splendor, lifting them above the realm of mere mortals, beyond all prejudice, all distinctions, all concerns.

After Tristan departed, Brittany set herself to helping Enis and Genna with the young woman's wedding finery, listening patiently to Genna's doubts about the reception she'd receive from Matt's family. "Imagine," she confided one day to Brittany, "him bringing home a servant as his wife!"

"Matt's opinion is the only one that counts, *chère,*" Brittany told her, "and his father is a merchant, not an earl or a duke."

"But a wealthy one, by all accounts."

"Class distinctions are not so rigid in the Colonies, Genna. You will be fine. You must have confidence in yourself and in your love for Matt." As must I in Tristan, she added to herself, for although she was a minor aristocrat through her mother, to marry an heir to an earldom was daunting.

"Eh bien," Genna concluded, "Sir Tristan is part Indian and *he's* going to be an earl one day!"

They laughed in feminine camaraderie, shaking their
heads over the complicated system of class distinctions
men had created, when both knew it was not really important.

Three days after Tristan's departure for Carlisle Hall,
Matt left for London to help supervise the loading of cargo
onto the *Virginia.* Later that morning, a rider approached
Wildwood bearing news for Brittany. After one look at
Ikuuk, he insisted on speaking to her alone, and Brittany
obliged him by leading him into the saloon and closing
the door.

"Mistress, Maude Dobbs sent me to tell ye that Janie
Neggers is sorely ill."

Suspicion chased across her fine brow and shadowed
her eyes. "Janie?"

"Aye." He shifted nervously from one foot to another
and slicked his bottom lip with his tongue. "She asks for
ye, and although the doctor feels there is naught anyone
can do, Mistress Dobbs said ye might be inclined to come
and be with the girl in . . . in her last hours."

Ambivalent feelings raced through her, but in spite of
her distraction, Brittany had enough presence of mind to
offer him refreshment. The ale seemed to put him at ease,
which did much to legitimize his errand in her eyes.

However, the fact that Maude knew exactly where to
find her after all these months did not sit well, yet how
could she take a gamble and ignore the summons when
Janie might, in truth, be grievously ill? It was possible
that this news was merely a ruse to get her to London,
and alone, but mustn't she take that chance if Janie was
involved? And, of necessity, she must go alone. She had
no wish to endanger any of the others.

"I don't remember you from the inn," she told the youth
bluntly.

"I been hired to help Willie an' run errands fer Master
Dobbs."

Mention of the stableboy's name lent further credence to his story and, her decision suddenly made, she sent the boy on his way after telling him she would be along shortly.

It wasn't going to be easy to leave Wildwood, she realized when she encountered Ikuuk sitting cross-legged in the hall outside the saloon. "You were eavesdropping!" she accused.

Her offensive tactic didn't work. He stood to his full height and stared down at her, his dark eyes somber, a stubborn light in their onyx depths. He signed to her with quiet emphasis, and she shook her head angrily. "I must go. There is no other choice. She's my friend." Her words were low-spoken, but irritation gave them an edge.

She moved toward the stairs when his hand on her arm stopped her. She looked up at him, glad for once that he could not speak. "I promise I'll send word as soon as I arrive at the inn."

At the agitated sound of Brittany's voice in the otherwise silent house, Enis came into the hall with Genna at her heels. Brittany was conscious of Ikuuk's hand still gripping her arm and of how it must look. There would be no secrets from anyone now, she thought grimly.

"I must go to London," she informed the two women as she pulled her arm free of the Indian's grasp.

Enis frowned and Genna's eyes widened questioningly.

Drawing in a sustaining breath, Brittany said, "I cannot see how I must account for my actions to the servants if I am to be mistress of Wildwood." Her gaze clashed with Ikuuk's. "Nor my lord's bodyguard. Indeed, you are not mine."

Ikuuk's expression did not alter, nor did Enis's, but Genna looked hurt.

Ignoring her squirming conscience—she, the daughter of a man of the soil, a former tavern wench—Brittany went on, her expression unyielding. "I was just telling Ikuuk that I will send a message immediately upon my safe arrival at Hunter's Run. Should you not hear from me by this eve, you may send word to Carlisle Hall.''

Her gaze moved from Enis to Genna to Ikuuk, determination hardening her features. ''I will need the mare saddled immediately.''

Tristan and the earl were enjoying a cup of ale in the earl's study, before retiring. After a full day of going over complicated business matters Tristan's head was spinning.

''You'll have agents to do the work for you, boy,'' Carlisle assured him.

Tristan clasped his neck and threw his head back as he stood before his grandfather. ''I should hope so. I've no mind to go blind from poring over ledgers and the like.'' He sat on the edge of the earl's massive desk, one leg swinging idly. ''And I'll spend half my time in Virginia, you know.'' His gaze met the older man's. ''I want to raise my children in the lush forest and meadows of the New World, where the air is clean and a man can make his fortune, no matter what his origins.''

The earl grunted. '' 'Tis the Indian in you—craving open spaces and primeval forests.'' He sat back in his chair, studying his grandson. I've a mind to go there myself, ye know . . . before I die.'' He tossed down the rest of his ale. ''I wonder what your father would say.''

Tristan met his regard head-on, but he said nothing.

'' 'Twould be most appropriate, don't you think, for me to go to him and make amends for my mistakes?''

The corner of Tristan's mouth twitched. ''Why, Grandfather, I do believe you have mellowed since first I came to Carlisle Hall.''

The earl set down his tankard with a thud. ''Don't mean everything will be set to rights, ye know. But—'' He turned toward the window and stared out into the clear night, the stars pricking the black velvet of the heavens with cold, diamondlike brilliance. ''What have I to lose?''

They sat in companionable silence for long moments,

the earl musing over the feasibility of visiting the Colonies, Tristan's thoughts turning naturally to Brittany.

The clatter of horses' hooves on the cobblestoned courtyard intruded upon their reveries.

"Who the devil can be traveling to Carlisle Hall so damned late?" the earl asked. " 'Tis well after midnight."

"And certainly past your bedtime."

Carlisle scowled. "Watch your tongue, boy. I haven't felt this good in years."

Tristan stood and stretched. "I'm glad of that—but 'tis past my bedtime, as well. I will leave you to your mysterious visitor—"

"Your lordship!" The portal burst open and Ikuuk filled the doorway. An indignant Burke stood behind him, trying unsuccessfully to get past the Indian with as much dignity as he could salvage, to make a formal announcement.

But the sight of his blood brother deprived the scene of all semblance of farce for Tristan, for Ikuuk's presence could mean only one thing.

His blood suddenly ran cold.

She's gone to the big city, Ikuuk signed.

"What's he saying?" demanded the earl.

"When?"

Late this morning. A messenger came—said her friend was sick. She was to have sent word of her arrival at the inn—

"Hunter's Run?" But he already knew the answer.

Ikuuk nodded. *We heard nothing until I left Wildwood, just before the sun began to set.*

"By the Mass, what the devil is going on here?" the earl demanded.

"I'll kill him!"

"Who? What is it? Will someone *tell* me?"

Tristan spun to face his grandfather, his mouth a hard line, the light in his eyes quelling. The old man stared, slack-jawed, at the murderous look on this grandson's face.

"Buckingham has Brittany."

"Buckingham? But how—?"

"He lured her back to the Hunter's Run with a message that someone is ill." He turned toward the door.

"But are you certain? You can't just hie yourself off to London to confront him unless you—"

"Didn't you once tell me that I must face my demons and dispel them? Well, I am taking your advice, and duke or no, I swear before God he'll wish he'd never dared lay a hand on her."

"For the love of God, be sensible. He has the king's ear—"

"And I have not?"

"Since they were children, Tristan—children! All I ask is that you have a care. 'Tis not like you to be rash and impulsive."

A black frown formed like a thundercloud over Tristan's eyes. "Rash? Impulsive?" He stalked back to the desk and slammed down his fist. "By God, I ask you, how much must I take? I've been more tolerant of him than any sensible man would have been. And now he's made the most fatal of blunders, for he holds my betrothed, the next countess of Weyrith."

"But what if Buckingham had naught to do with this? What if the summons was legitimate?"

"Then there is no cause for concern, is there?" But the soft menace that infused his words was more ominous than an explosion of thunder.

He swung around abruptly, his movements uncharacteristically stiff, and strode to the door. "I will have satisfaction if I have to go to Charles himself—or call the bastard out."

Dressed in a riding habit of dove gray with black braiding, Brittany stabled the mare in Chelsea and hired a hackney to London. As she traveled the short distance to the city, she ruminated on the possibility that the message was a ruse, a ploy to get her away from Wildwood and into Buckingham's clutches. Visions of him at the masquerade haunted her, his threat regarding Charlotte Chauvelin mocked her. What had he said? *You have not heard the last of her.* A delicate frisson shuddered through her before she pushed the echoing words from her mind. The Chauvelins could not touch her now . . . Hadn't Tristan assured her of that?

Yet why would Villiers ever say such a thing after informing her that his grudge against Tristan would be lessened by her introduction to the king?

To keep you frightened, fool . . . to keep you quaking with terror, as a man of his nature is wont to do.

She drew in a steadying breath and gazed down at the ring on her left hand. "I have had enough of fear and hiding," she vowed. "If this is a ruse, Buckingham will find me not so meek and inclined to shrink from him this time." The thought of Tristan coming to London should things turn out for the worst added to her resolve, and she fingered his token of love with a smile.

The coach rolled to a halt, and Brittany alighted in the yard of the Hunter's Run. Old memories rushed at her as she stood looking around, remembering the time she'd spent there.

With a lift of her shoulders, she entered the back door of the inn and went directly to the kitchen. Maude Dobbs looked up from the roast duck she was basting and started. She straightened immediately, shoving the pan back into the great oven and turning to face her visitor.

"Good day, Maude."

Maude recovered and bobbed her head, taking in Brittany's appearance, from her black leather shoes to her small black hat with bobbing plume. "G'day to ye, too, Brittany." She wiped her hands upon her apron. "Ye seem to have fared well enough since ye left without so much as a word."

Brittany arched a fine brow questioningly. "Sir Tristan said you were paid well enough for the inconvenience of losing one of your serving wenches, Maude."

Maude had the grace to flush. "So 'e did." She paused, her expression softening. "How ye been, girl?"

Brittany smiled a little, remembering how Maude had always taken her side against her husband, Jack. Surely Maude would not allow herself to be involved in any underhanded scheme. "Well, Maude . . . thank you."

The older woman cleared her throat uncomfortably. "Well, if ye've come to see Janie, ye're not a mite too soon, so bad is she." She frowned, and Brittany's heart constricted at the thought of Janie so ill. "Can't keep anythin' down. The doctor don't know what more to do, an' a pretty penny it's costin' me—"

"Then I must go to her." Brittany swung toward the door without another word. Up the back steps she hurried, for two flights, to the door of the tiny attic room under the eaves that she'd shared with Janie, her concern for the young woman overshadowing her earlier suspicions. She lifted the latch and pushed open the door.

The room was dim, the gray February skies providing little light through the single window. "Janie?" she queried softly, moving toward the form huddled on the bed.

The door slammed shut behind her and she whirled, startled. Before she could make a move, a man's form came at her and a reeking rag was clamped over her nose and mouth. The fumes from the solution saturating the material sent her senses reeling, all coherent thought scattering into nothingness as her strength deserted her.

Brittany struggled upward from the depths of unconsciousness, her eyelids weighted as if with stone, her mouth dry, her head spinning. She was lying on a bed. Her hands and feet were bound, but she could feel the rough sheets beneath her cheek as she lay on her side. Her lashes fluttered and she fought the last vestiges of grogginess until she succeeded in raising her lids. At first everything was hazy, a gray mist clouding her vision, and then, gradually, it cleared.

It was early evening, and from the noises coming from

the street below, she surmised she was in a town house somewhere in London. It also sounded as if, possibly, she was not far from the Hunter's Run. She could hear the varied voices of the river, water slapping against the sides of docked ships, the rushing wakes of smaller vessels and barges hurtling toward the banks. Crates thudded and scraped as vessels were loaded with cargo, accompanied by the rough shouts of seamen. The cries of prostitutes selling their favors further strengthened her suspicions.

She struggled to sit up—no easy task, trussed up as she was—but when she finally succeeded, she was wide awake. Breathing heavily from her exertions, fighting the urge to retch from the rag stuffed into her mouth and held in place by a strip of cloth around her face and head, Brittany leaned against the wall behind the narrow bed, essaying to catch her breath.

Her gaze swept the sparsely furnished room. The spartan decor, with nary a distinguishing feature to reveal her captor's taste or financial position, provided no clue as to the owner's identity. The narrow bed upon which she reclined, the table and chair by the partially shuttered window that overlooked the street, the wooden chest against one wall and chamber pot against the other, all told her nothing.

It made no difference, however. Despite the fact that she hadn't recognized her assailant, she was certain she knew who was behind her abduction.

She worked at the rope holding her wrists together, inadvertently scraping her delicate skin on the taut, rough hemp. If only she could free herself . . . She tried to loosen the cords around her ankles, but was equally unsuccessful. The gag was stifling and, in mounting anger and frustration, she studied her surroundings once more. If she could find a sharp object—a projecting nail perhaps—she could hop across the floor. She'd not come so far from tragedy and despair only to be foiled by a crudely implemented plan of intimidation and revenge.

But the sound of the door downstairs opening and slamming, and footsteps ascending the stairs, put to flight all thoughts of escape. She lifted her gaze to the door and mentally braced herself. The footfalls reached the upper landing, crossed it in several strides, then stopped before the door. The latch lifted, and the panel swung open.

George Villiers, second duke of Buckingham, stepped into the room and closed the door behind him. He leaned back against it with a negligence that bespoke the true courtier.

"So Savidge's lady has awakened—the defiant bitch who had the temerity to return from France, in spite of my most skillful machinations to get her there." He pushed away from the door and moved to untie the cloth that held the gag in place.

She spat it out and raised her eyes to his. "What do you want from me?" she demanded through stiff, dry lips.

He raised his fair eyebrows in feigned bemusement. "Want from you? Why, nothing that you shan't be honored to give, my fairest lady."

Ire flashed in her eyes and she lifted her chin. "You can dispense with your facile-tongued answers when a word or two will serve. What is it you want?"

"Why, only what *you* want, lovely Brittany." He brought the chair to the side of the bed, his movements slow and purposeful as he placed his well-shod foot upon a rung and leaned one arm across his knee.

She met his smug perusal unwaveringly. "You told me your grudge against Tristan would be considerably reduced by my introduction to the king. Your deplorable actions tell me you lied."

A frown formed over his prominent nose. "And you, a harlot, dare to call me a liar?" His eyes bored into her before his expression smoothed and he seemed to relax, his features taking on the look of a cat before a cornered mouse, knowing victory was but a paw's swipe away. "But you have, however unwittingly, stumbled upon the crux of the matter—the king."

Her look turned wary.

"He was quite taken with you, you know . . . as I guessed he would be when I first saw you at the Hunter's Run. In fact, I haven't seen him so beguiled by a woman since he met my cousin Barbara—and with the queen so close at hand. Tsk, tsk, acting like a besotted schoolboy before his loving and devoted wife."

Suspicion crept into Brittany's thoughts and narrowed her eyes.

"I am not the villain Savidge would make me, you see. I merely took offense at the way he foiled my game, when I acted solely on behalf of Charles. What mattered a hundred pounds to me when I am one of the wealthiest men in England?"

She waited, now certain what he wanted from her, yet silently vowing to thwart him even before he said the words.

"One night, sweetheart . . . one night with the king, and you—and your breed lover— shall be free of all obligation to me. I shall at last get back at Savidge for making me look the fool that night before Charles."

"You delude yourself, Villiers, if you consider us under any obligation to you."

In the blink of an eye he dropped his foot from the chair and was beside her on the bed. *"Your grace,* to you, you *Indian* lover." His fingers gripped her chin until she felt the sting of tears. "Ah, now I get a reaction from you, do I? I see I must exert force to make your beautiful eyes glisten with tears, your unmarred face go white with pain."

He abruptly released her. "But I suspect you'll not be so unwilling to receive the royal rod between your thighs. You see, I noticed how taken you were with Charles." His knuckles rode up one cheek, over her forehead, and down the other cheek, but she refused to give him the satisfaction of twisting away. "I saw the fire of excitement burning in your cheeks, like a bitch in heat. You may be hot for Savidge, but I'd wager my title that you'd welcome a chance to couple with the king. Which brings us back to the point."

"How little you know of me, if that is what you think in your sick imaginings."

His gently exploring fingers fisted and drove into her chin, sending her head slamming back against the wall. Lights exploded inside her head, and for the space of a heartbeat, Brittany thought she would faint.

"Now, I suggest you do two things," he continued. "First, guard your insolent tongue, and second, agree to my proposition."

"Never, I say to both!"

He sat back and scrutinized her as if she were mad. "Come, come. I, as a lover of men as well as women, admit that Charles is not as perfect of feature as Savidge, but he is well endowed below the waist, and he *is* a monarch. While Savidge is pretty, Charles is commanding, and I've never met a woman who wouldn't jump at the chance to spend a night in his majesty's bed."

"*Eh bien*, I refuse, thus giving your statement the lie."

He sighed heavily and stood looking down at her. "I was so hoping I wouldn't have to use my, ah, *persuasion*. I do so hate such dirty tactics, but 'twould seem I have no choice." He assumed a resigned air that was so counterfeit as to be ludicrous. "You're quite certain?"

Her silence effectively conveyed her meaning.

"You leave me no choice," he said, shaking his head. He reached inside his doublet, withdrew an object, and tossed it onto the bed beside her.

It was the amulet Tristan always wore round his neck. Of beaten copper, the disk bore the likeness of a wolf's head in relief. The thong from which it was suspended was broken.

Brittany stared at it for long moments, the meaning of its being separated from Tristan dawning on her with slow horror. She looked up at Buckingham, her concern for Tristan surfacing in her widened eyes. "I don't believe it!" she denied, even as she knew her denial was futile.

Buckingham crossed his hands behind his back and rocked on his heels, a thoughtful frown on his face as he, too, stared at the amulet with its broken leather thong. "You can well believe it, wench, for my men were waiting for him within a few miles of Carlisle Hall, knowing he would come arunning when his savage friend informed him of your departure for London."

"Where is he?"

"Why, where else would be the man who tried to kill a duke? In Newgate, of course, awaiting my decree that he be put to death."

Newgate? Put to death? Numbness spread through her, blocking the very processes of her mind. When at last she was capable of coherent thought, she realized how little she knew of English law. Could Tristan be put to death for supposedly trying to kill Buckingham? Dear God, what if it were so?

"You know he struck with no intent to kill," she cried.

" 'Tis his word against mine," Buckingham answered with a chilling smile.

"Matt—Matthew Stark was present—"

"That small matter can easily be seen to, as well."

Confusion rose in her eyes, spread across her features, revealing just how vulnerable she was to his threats. And then a sudden thought struck her.

"The king," she breathed. "He would never allow Tristan to be put to death, especially not on your word alone."

"Why, sweetheart, he hasn't a clue that Savidge is in Newgate. You don't think my men neglected to rough him up and disguise him properly before committing him, do you? The gaoler was so staggered by the amount of money he was paid that he swore that even if the king's agents search the place for the scurrilous character, they will never find him." He threw back his head in laughter. "Don't you find that amusing, Brittany? The gaoler doesn't even suspect that the madman ranting that he is Tristan Savidge is actually someone of importance to Charles himself."

"*You* are mad, Buckingham," she accused, the lash of contempt in her shaking voice.

He threw up his hands in a gesture of appeasement, as if in the face of imminent success he could be magnanimous. "Now, let us come to terms, shall we? You spend one night with the king, and I will release you—and Savidge." He sank onto the bed once more, his face close to hers. "If, however, you utter one word about what I've just revealed to you, not only will I deny it, but I will also make certain that Tristan Savidge dies. Do you hear me?"

In a last, desperate attempt to find a weakness in his devious scheme, she insisted, "Charles will never touch me after learning that I am Tristan's betrothed."

"Are you, indeed? Well, you obviously weren't introduced as such, and the king believes what I told him . . . that you are like a cat, playing fast and loose as you please but always landing on your feet, that Savidge is so bewitched by you he cannot see straight." With one finger he traced the slope of her jaw, skirting the slight discoloration beneath her chin. "Charles has always hoped Tristan would wed Lady Diana Hartland, and so, should Tristan change his mind where you are concerned, his majesty would undoubtedly be delighted."

She wanted to strike out at him, to spit in his face, but he held all the cards in his corrupt and unyielding hands. In her utter frustration, she could only stare at him with venom sparking in her eyes.

He untied the bonds that held her and produced a cheap, polished metal mirror and a hairbrush from the chest nearby.

"Come now, sweetheart, make your repairs. The king of England awaits you."

Chapter 20

The night was black, oppressive. Clouds hung low in the sky, blotting out any sign of the moon or stars that might have shed their soft illumination upon the city. The barge slipped silently thorough the gently heaving Thames toward Whitehall, and with every movement of the bargeman's pole, Brittany's anxiety rose.

"Remember," Buckingham said softly in her ear, causing her to jump, "not a word of anything that has transpired this day or your lover's life will be forfeit."

Not deigning to answer, she turned from him to stare unseeingly at the vague, dark shapes of the buildings that lined the bank.

"It will be to your advantage to play the eager harlot . . . if you wish to see Savidge again."

His breath fanning over her ear irritated and repulsed her, and she pulled her shoulder away and crooked her head, conveying acute distaste. But Buckingham was already speaking to the bargeman.

How securely George Villiers held her within his grasp! she thought with stinging rancor. Certainly he must guess how much she cared about Tristan Savidge. Surely he must divine that she would do anything to spare Tristan's life, to ensure his safety, even if it meant paving the way for his marriage to Diana Hartland by demonstrating to the king that she would be willingly untrue to her beloved.

Yes, she loved Tristan that much and more . . . and nothing was more important than that he live. Nothing.

The barge slowed and came to a halt before what Brittany guessed to be the privy stairs. She caught the muffled clink of coins, and then the duke took her firmly by the elbow and helped her alight. He guided her into the palace and toward the king's apartments. It was late, and as they moved through the corridors, they passed only a few people still up and about, receiving no more than a cursory glance or greeting for Buckingham.

A man in the king's livery appeared as if by magic at the door of what Brittany presumed to be the royal apartments, and Villiers gave her into his care. "Progers, I entrust the lady to you," was all he said before turning and striding back the way they'd come.

Edward Progers, page of the backstairs, led her to the king's bedchamber and discreetly withdrew, closing the door behind him.

Charles was in shirt and breeches only, sitting beside the hearth, immersed in a book. At her entrance, he looked up and smiled. The book snapped closed and he came slowly to his feet.

"Mistress Brittany?" He approached her with his long, sure stride. "Ah, my dear, 'tis, indeed, you. George needn't have reminded me of your beauty . . . I would know those eyes anywhere!" He took her icy hands in his and led her further into the room, but Brittany found herself tongue-tied.

Charles motioned to a young page standing in the shadows, whom she'd failed to notice in her agitation, and the youth hurried to pour two goblets of wine.

Charles removed her cloak and drew her toward the fireplace, and Brittany forced her thoughts away from what was to come. She must engage him in conversation, for if he told Buckingham she'd stood as dumbly as a sheep waiting for slaughter, she did not doubt that the duke would make good his threat.

"The—the room is beautiful, your majesty," she said, her gaze taking in the black and white marble paving and matching mantelpiece.

Charles handed her the wine, amusement shining in the dark depths of his eyes. "I would be heartbroken if I'd thought you'd come here only to compliment the decor of the room. George said you were as taken with me as I with you."

Here was the heart of the matter, she thought. If only she'd not been so mesmerized by his good looks and grace, his charismatic presence, the undeniable mystery—and invitation—in his eyes . . . Color crept into her cheeks at the memory. She made herself sip the wine, welcoming the burning sensation that slid down her throat and into her empty stomach. Forcing a smile, she replied, "You are a most wonderful dancer, your majesty."

He set down his goblet and ran his fingers through the honey-gold tresses that cascaded down her back. His hand returned to the nape of her neck and drew her face toward his. As he bent to kiss her, Brittany fought a wave of panic and responded with all the ardor she could muster, Buckingham's words ringing in her ears like clarions. *It will be to your advantage to play the eager harlot . . . if you wish to see Savidge again.*

As it was, she was not repulsed but, rather, flustered by his kiss, which sent hectic color splashing across her cheekbones. Her lips parted beneath his questing tongue, and to her agitation was added the unwelcome yet undeniable sensation of arousal.

In self-disgust, she pulled away, her cheeks flaming, the soft curves of her mouth full and moist from his kiss.

"What is it?" he murmured, obviously interpreting her high color for passion.

She gazed into his dark eyes and suddenly imagined Ikuuk's eyes—black and full of censure. Frantically she fought for control as she sought words to ease his concern, a bemusement that could possibly lead to suspicion if she didn't apply herself. Dear God, if she had forced herself to respond to Raymond, surely she could do as much for the king of England. It was an honor to be bedded by the king. Many a woman, married or not, would give anything for the royal attentions.

" 'Tis—'tis only that I am cold, majesty," she lied.

"Then finish your wine and to bed with us." He pushed her goblet to her lips and made her empty it. Handing it to the page, he dismissed the youth.

And then they were alone.

He took her hand and led her toward the bed alcove with its heavy curtains. A spaniel puppy scooted from beneath the bed, sniffing curiously at Brittany's feet as she sat down. Charles divested himself of his shirt and pushed her onto her back, his fingers working deftly over the laces of her bodice. Pushing the garment off her shoulders, he pulled her chemise up and over her head, so eager for her that he buried his face between her breasts while she lay there, half undressed.

"So lovely," he murmured. "You've haunted me since the night of the ball." He took her hand and led it to his arousal, hard and hot. "George said you wanted me, as well," he said against her breast. "Come, show me how much, beautiful Brittany." And his lips and teeth suckled and caressed her with consummate skill . . . and fatal results.

Lust rose within her, unexpectedly potent, dismayingly powerful, even as it sickened her. Directing every last bit of her willpower to concentrate on pleasing Charles, ignoring the stabbing guilt over her betrayal of the man she loved above all others, she told herself again and again in the scrambled melée of her thoughts that she was doing this to save Tristan's life, not to betray him. She could give Charles Stuart her body without offering anything of herself.

With a sigh of surrender, she wrapped her arms around his neck and met his questing lips in a despairing capitulation. *Forgive me, my only love,* her heart cried, and a tear escaped from beneath a trembling eyelid to lay winking upon her thick, long lashes, the only outward sign of her anguish.

* * *

Quiet as a mountain cat, Tristan emerged from an adjacent hallway and approached Buckingham from behind. In a few swift strides he was upon him, grasping the duke's arm and roughly spinning him around. He shoved him up against a wall in the deserted corridor and took little satisfaction from the look of surprise that crossed Buckingham's features before he could gain control.

"Where is she?" Softly spoken, the question had all the menacing portent of distant, muted thunder.

"Who?"

Tristan's forearm banded across Buckingham's larynx with increasing pressure as the point of his dagger came up against the duke's ribs. " 'Twould give me the greatest satisfaction to kill you, Villiers, so do not play games. Where is she?"

"Where do you think? You're not blind . . . you saw them dancing together."

Tristan's eyes slitted.

"Take your filthy hands from me, Savidge, before I sound the hue and cry and the king's guard arrests you."

Tristan's answer was to increase the pressure across Buckingham's throat.

"My status has been raised since last I lifted a hand to you, Villiers . . . or have you not heard? And I have Stark as my witness to the incident last spring should the subject ever arise before the king. If anything, you would be the one arrested if I chose to bring the entire affair before Charles. Now, for the last time, where is she?"

"There is only one person at Whitehall who would summon her at this hour. How obtuse you are, Savidge, if you refuse to see what is before you."

In the quiet of the deserted passageway the tension between them was a palpable thing.

"You lie." It was a low rasp, a husk of sound.

Buckingham's head moved slightly from side to side in denial, his lips curving in a grim travesty of a smile. "I took only what was my due, in reparation for your chicanery last May.'' His shoulders moved in what could have been a shrug. ''She is undoubtedly enjoying herself. Remember, if you will, their mutual attraction at the ball.''

With an oath, Tristan released him and stepped back.

With maddening slowness, Buckingham straightened his shirt and jacket and readjusted his wig. ''Would you like me to accompany you to the royal bedchamber?''

''Get out.''

With a sly, satisfied smile, the duke continued down the corridor and into the night.

Tristan stood unmoving for a long moment, his thoughts a mad jumble.

'Tis an honor any woman would seek, to sleep with the king.

He shook his head to clear it. This was ridiculous. Brittany would never betray him with Charles—or anyone else.

With sudden purpose, he swung around, sheathing his knife as he turned. With an uncharacteristic frown of fury, he strode down the hall, his long, booted strides quickly covering the distance to the royal apartments. A tall, forbidding figure with his cape flaring behind him, his sword clinking faintly against his side, the ring of his heels resounding in the quiet as a warning to any who would stop him, Tristan pressed on, determined to put an end to Buckingham's eternal manipulations once and for all.

Say you will be mine, that you will never leave me! Say you will bear my name and my children, that you will grow old with me and delight in our grandchildren, that someday you will lie beside me in a peaceful churchyard in Virginia for all eternity . . .

Brittany tried to pull her mouth away from Charles's, guilt and self-flagellation ripping through her with sobering effect.

Tristan's life hangs in the balance, a voice whispered.

They were both completely undressed now. Charles lay sprawled across her body, his kisses moving again to her breasts, the pulsing evidence of his desire pressing into her thigh. He ran his lightly abrading tongue along the sleek indentation of her waist, across her taut, flat stomach, and lower still . . .

He was a masterful lover, his gentleness and expertise weaving a spell over her, holding in check the revulsion she'd experienced with Raymond.

In sudden panic over that very success, she gripped his hair, seeking to still his ravaging mouth, but her fingers were weak and ineffectual in the struggle between her self-reproach and her fear for Tristan. The king took it as a sign of burgeoning ardor and renewed his efforts, pressing heated kisses along the sleek length of first one thigh and then the other.

Tears spilled from her eyes and threaded across her temples into her hair as she waged a monumental battle with her conscience, the turbulence of her emotions paralyzing her. *Help me,* she pleaded in silent despair. *Dear God, help me!*

There was an unexpected commotion in the antechamber on the other side of the door, but Charles was too caught up in the heat of the moment to heed it. The sound of movement and muffled voices, however, registered in Brittany's tortured mind.

Before she could think to react, however, to remove her protesting hands from Charles's hair or disentangle herself from him, the door swung open.

She turned toward the sound and stiffened in horror at the sight of Tristan standing in the doorway, bemusement and then disbelief flashing across his features.

She struggled in earnest now as shame flooded through her. A shame that pushed aside the cool breath of relief triggered by the sight of Tristan, hale and hearty. Charles jerked his head up with a grunt of pain, then followed her gaze, his swarthy features shadowed with passion.

"Tristan!" she breathed.

He made no move beyond bringing up one hand to touch his forehead, his lashes lowering briefly as he collected himself. When he opened his eyes again, for one, fleeting moment, he looked shattered. Then his features cleared and a slow flush of anger rose beneath the bronze of his skin.

"By God, I'll have an explanation for this, Savidge!" Charles cried. "How dare you barge into my bedchamber unannounced. How dare you interrupt me when I am occupied with a wench."

"Forgive me, sire, for interrupting you at such a . . . *tender* moment. I did not mean to unsettle you by my unexpected appearance."

Brittany went to rise from the bed, but the king gripped her arm and held her back. "Were you not my friend, I would have you clapped in Newgate for your insolence."

Tristan laughed bitterly. "You make a mockery of the very concept, for as my *friend* you would not have bedded my betrothed."

"Then the mockery is of betrothal rather than friend, for she acted not the woman plighted."

"Tristan, 'tis not as it appears—" Brittany began, realizing she now had everything to gain by revealing to both men exactly what Buckingham had threatened.

"Silence!" Charles commanded. " 'Tis every bit as it appears, for she came to me willingly, with nary a protest at my fondling."

Tristan's eyes met hers, a silent question in them.

"I only . . . affected my responses, for I thought—"

This time Charles threw back his head in laughter. "If her responses were contrived, then she is the finest actress in London—nay, in all of England." He sobered, his perusal going to Tristan and then to Brittany. "I believe George was right when he called your Isolde a cat who always lands on her feet." He toyed with a lock of her loose hair, and a muscle jumped along Tristan's jawline. "She plays fast and loose, I see, first going along with my lovemaking, then prettily appealing to you as the wronged woman." He ran a finger down her bare arm, a beguiling smile crossing his face. "Tsk, tsk, my friend." He shook his dark head. "She would keep you happy in the bedchamber as your wife, but you would be forced to call out every man who came under her spell. And what could she possibly give you in the way of wealth or holdings? Would you have a tavern girl of questionable repute as the next countess of Weyrith?''

To Brittany's mortification, color crept into her face at the king's frank appraisal of her worth. Yet, even more, the shame that brightened her cheeks was caused by the knowledge that she had, indeed, betrayed Tristan. Although she had not actually coupled with the king, she was guilty of a very real betrayal of the body, of the senses.

Sitting beneath Tristan's penetrating blue gaze, she felt dirty, tainted . . .

She moved to pull a sheet to her breasts, her gaze sliding guiltily away from Tristan's, misery etching her features.

''Let her go.''

Charles leveled the royal regard at Tristan. ''Did I hear correctly? *You* just ordered *me* to let her go? Surely you are besotted to lunacy by this woman to speak so to your king.'' His mouth thinned into a hard line. ''Take your leave now, while you still may, and be grateful.''

''I am not leaving without her.'' The words carried the razor edge of menace.

Charles flushed a dull red, his dark eyes kindling with anger as they met and clashed with those of the man across the room. ''Call the guard,'' he directed a servant hovering behind Tristan. ''You will discover that you take too much for granted, Savidge. Any woman, married, betrothed, or unspoken for, is to be honored by my attentions, and her husband, champion, or lover discreetly looks the other way. You have much to learn about the role of king and subject.''

Two of the king's guards shouldered past Tristan and stood on either side of him, awaiting orders from Charles.

''And you have much to learn of love and loyalty,'' said Tristan. ''Of decency and honor among all men, noble or peasant. You will punish me for wishing to retrieve the woman who is pledged to me, while you conspire and scheme with the likes of George Villiers merely because you've known him since childhood?'' He looked at Brittany as the two guards moved in to take him by the arms, regret flickering in his eyes before he turned again to Charles. ''You have much to learn yourself, but most especially of friendship.''

Silence gathered in the room until the rasp of Charles's heavy breathing sounded unnaturally loud.

''I will have you hanged for this!'' he raged. And then, to the guards, ''Throw him in Newgate!''

Tristan's pain was like a knife thrust into Brittany's chest. His eyes dark with it—and an underlying, frustrated rage—his gaze delved into her soul, willing her to deny the evidence before him.

But her remorse over her wanton response to Charles kept her silent, and her gaze dropped before the burning intensity of his before he was hauled from the room.

Charles rolled away from her and off the bed. He took up a velvet dressing gown and slipped into it, his face tight with fury. With shaking hands he poured a glass of wine, anger evident in every movement.

Brittany sat very still, afraid to goad him further by reminding him of her presence. Charles Stuart was known for his admirable lack of temper, but he'd been unusually provoked tonight. She closed her eyes, feeling a profound weariness. Pride was involved here, she suspected, not so much the question of a betrayal of friendship.

If there was anything she could do to obtain Tristan's release, she would willingly oblige—even if it now meant appeasing the king, soothing his ruffled feathers, sleeping with him. What did it matter? She was already soiled, unclean. And this time Tristan really was in Newgate by the king's own orders. This time she had a valid reason for sacrificing what was left of her honor.

When he spoke, it was softly, his words weighted with regret. ''He risked his life for my cause more than once.'' He half turned toward her, so that she caught his strong profile. ''And he is wrong when he implies I place more importance on George Villiers's friendship. I love Tristan only too well."

He turned to face her, his expression free of ire. "But he can do better than to wed you, and I—we—thought perhaps to prove it to him." He shrugged, an apologetic smile pulling up one corner of his mouth. "You see, I thought to anchor him to me, to England, more securely by encouraging him to wed a woman of the aristocracy, with lands and wealth of her own."

Brittany nodded in understanding. Of course. Charles loved Tristan and didn't want to see him return to Virginia. She'd suspected that since she'd first met Tristan, but only now did she realize the extent of Tristan's inner struggle. Not until recently had she discovered how very much he loved Virginia.

But she had to speak her piece, to explain that she'd had no wish to be unfaithful to Tristan.

"Your Majesty, I would not vilify his grace, the duke of Buckingham, but he lured me to London and took me by force to a town house." Charles's eyes widened slightly. "I find you most attractive, but 'twas not my wish to come to Whitehall."

He set down the empty goblet and returned to the bed. Pulling the sheet from her fingers, he allowed his appreciative gaze to rove over her naked body, causing her to blush down to her toes. "If that is true, then I think they have evened the score, don't you? George and Tristan?"

Her eyes brightened with annoyance as his gaze met hers.

"No?" He smiled a little. "Ah, well, I admit George has some nasty habits, some unlikable qualities, but I cannot change his nature. He is spoiled and haughty where Tristan is unspoiled and good-natured. They are like night and day, yet each is of value to me." He lightly ran a finger over the graceful turn of her hip and down the length of one leg.

"I remember when first I met him," he mused aloud, more to himself than to her. " 'Twas in France when he was but seventeen and I two and twenty. He was barely civilized and there was something refreshingly untamed about him, something that still makes women swoon and men willing to lay down their lives for him. I saw in him an integrity, a rare valor, a sense of right and wrong, of honor and infamy . . .'' He frowned thoughtfully. "Mayhap our Tristan is truly out of his element here in England." His voice had lowered to a whisper, his expression troubled.

Then, with a shake of his head as if to clear it of such maudlin musings, he concluded, "Yet, much as I admire Tristan for all those traits and more, he must be taught a lesson." He bent to worship with his lips where his fingertips had skimmed a path, and Brittany started at the contact. "So, let us begin where we left off, shall we?"

He opened his robe and pulled her down to lie prone beside him. But this time, although it might have meant Tristan's release, she could not bring herself to respond. She'd had enough of guilt and remorse, of empty lust and pretense.

She lay passively, submitting to his attentions.

After a while he sat up and flipped the sheet over her. "I believe my ardor, as well as yours, has cooled considerably." He stared into her eyes, seemingly fascinated by them. "You've the finest eyes I've ever seen and a form that any female would covet." He sighed ruefully. "But the face of the man we both love comes between us now, until neither of us can do justice to the passion of which we are both, I sense, capable."

Brittany sat up, keeping a tight rein on the feelings of relief and hope that he might allow her leave. "May—may I . . .'' Her words trailed off, so fearful was she of refusal.

He leaned over the side of the bed and scooped up the puppy still ambling about the room, lifting the small bundle until he and the dog were nose to nose. A tiny pink tongue flicked the royal nose, causing Charles to chuckle.

When he turned back to Brittany, however, the smile

faded as he took the meaning of her half-formed question. "Nay, my fair Brittany, you may not leave. You will remain here with me until morn, so that no one suspects what has transpired—or rather has not transpired—this night."

Comprehension dawned and distress gave her eyes an arrested look.

He nodded. "You begin to understand, do you not? Tristan is not to be apprised of the truth, either. His punishment while he cools his heels in gaol, is to believe that you were mine tonight in every way."

He replaced the pup and slid beneath the covers across from her, lying on his back, hands clasped behind his head, his frowning gaze on the canopy above. "I have a reputation to keep, and so I will have your promise to say naught of this night." He was quiet a moment. "Well?"

Fighting the overwhelming urge to protest, knowing it would be futile—and would anger a king whose pride was already smarting—Brittany nodded, unable to speak past the constriction in her throat. Then she realized he was still staring upward.

"You have it," she answered quietly, and closed her eyes against the image of Tristan's shocked expression, the disbelief and denial in his eyes less than an hour before.

"You may be surprised at his reaction, *chérie*, for he is tolerant and forgiving."

She turned on her side, away from him, a tear falling to her cheek. How could any man, she wondered dully, even Tristan, be genuinely forgiving of such a transgression. If the tables were turned, she doubted she could be so generous. Although such a dalliance might be accepted among the nobility at Charles's court, and although marriages of convenience were intended to stabilize fortunes in an England still recovering from civil war, Brittany wondered how Tristan, who loved her and wanted to wed her solely because of that love, could ever accept such a betrayal.

Chapter 21

Originally a gatehouse, part and parcel of the city fortifications, Newgate Gaol had long received more care and attention to its external condition than that of its internal. The stone exterior was imposing by daylight, but what went on inside the prison represented the basest of human behavior.

Tristan had heard of the horrors of Newgate, but he'd never had occasion to experience them firsthand. From the moment he ascended the steps to enter the infamous prison, he knew the worst stories were true . . .

He was forced to surrender to the gaoler his cloak, his sword and dagger, and what money he had on his person. In exchange, he was given a paltry sum of shillings to pay for the quarters on the master side of the prison as opposed to the dreaded common side. His hands were shackled together with a thick, heavy length of chain.

Accompanied by an obese, snaggle-toothed turnkey along the candle- and burner-lit passageways, he was hit by the staggering, ever-present stench of the centuries-old gaol, little alleviated by the ventilator on the top of the prison. Fetid and foul, the overpowering odor made him force back the urge to retch as his stomach churned in violent reaction.

The moans of the sick and dying, the mad, and the condemned, echoed in his ears. Heavy chains grated and scraped along slick, filth-strewn floors, and he had to force himself to keep his eyes straight ahead while he questioned the strength of Charles's anger, an anger that had driven the king to send him here.

A stick-thin figure clad in tattered clothes came loping toward them along the hallway. He did a queer little about-face and fell into step beside Tristan, a pathetic figure in his rags. He peered into Tristan's shadowed face, his eyes glazed with madness. "Ye got yer shillin's, fancy man?"

Tristan threw him a sidelong glance, pity washing over him as he noted the bluish cast of the man's lips, the outline of prominent facial bones beneath shrunken skin.

"If ye don't, ye won't be able ta pay the garnish." His eyes narrowed shrewdly, a gleam of lucidity piercing the shadow of lunacy in the pale orbs. "Nor the cellermen should ye need a candle. Buy their spirits with the profits, they do." He winked. "Oliver Wendall Chalmers, at yer service."

"This one's fer t'other side, Ollie," grumbled the turn-key. "Git on to bed wi' ye."

Ollie's mouth made an O at this revelation. "Shoulda known, wi' them fancy rags. Can ye spare a shillin' for old Ollie, master? Lord mayor didn't see fit to provide our water t'day and Ollie's thirsty."

Tristan glanced at the man again, his eyes going to the parched and cracked lips, surely adequate evidence that not only did this poor wretch eat little, but that he had not had water this day—and God knew how many others.

Even as Tristan made this mental observation, the bailiff was heaving around, his beefy arm swinging to catch Ollie across the jaw. Tristan's hand on his arm stopped him in mid-motion, and dark, squinting eyes met those of burning blue. "Let him be."

Tristan delved into the small purse he'd been allowed to keep for his shillings and handed several coins to Ollie. The metallic *ping* acted like an alarm bell, and several other prisoners in the cells immediately around them moved to the bars to investigate.

"Whatcha got there, Ollie?" one man cried, and be-seechingly shoved his shackled hands through the bars.

"Give ol' Johnnie some coin, eh?" But Ollie was staring at Tristan through the tangled hair that spilled across his cheeks, an odd look on his face as he fingered the shillings in his hand.

Suddenly, another pair of arms poked through the bars directly behind Ollie and one wrist clamped around his thin neck. "How 'bout givin' *me* them coins, Ollie boy?"

Ollie's eyes bulged as the iron manacle dug into his larynx and the precious coins dropped to the floor. As Ollie attempted to pry the man's arm from its choking hold, other hands reached for the coins, and without warning the bailiff's club descended to crack against bone as he exerted his authority. "Go back ta bed, ye miserable curs, afore yer arses taste the kiss o' the lash fer makin' trouble." The club thudded against the elbow of Ollie's assailant and, with a grunt of pain, the man released his victim.

Tristan bent to retrieve the coins and place them in Ollie's hand. "Go and get your water, Ollie," he said tersely, deliberately keeping his look neutral. It would do Ollie no good, he suspected, to be singled out as a favorite of a newcomer.

They proceeded toward the other side of the gaol, with Ollie eventually dropping behind and disappearing.

At last they reached a section of the prison where the cells were somewhat larger and, from what Tristan could see in the perpetual gloom of the lightless, airless building, less crowded. The turnkey stopped and inserted an iron key from among those hanging from his belt. The barred door swung open with a loud screech and he shoved Tristan into the enclosure.

"I wouldn' waste my time wi' the likes o' Ollie, pretty face," he warned. "And"—he closed the door with a clank and locked it again—"I wouldn' interfere wi' my— or any other's—duty concernin' another inmate, neither." He shook his massive head, his small eyes resting pointedly on Tristan's codpiece. "Ye could lose yer manhood to my club. Then ye'd be no more'n a struttin' popinjay

. . . wi'out a rod to please the wenches.'' He threw his head back in coarse laughter before turning and lumbering back the way they'd come.

Tristan turned slowly to face the two other occupants of the cell. One was snoring loudly on a crude top bunk against the far wall, but the other was propped up on an elbow on the pallet below, watching him with the wariness of a cornered snake.

Although Tristan was in the master ward of the gaol, any cutthroat who could pay the extortionate fees was able to buy the same privilege. This had been magnanimously pointed out to him by the gaoler, obviously as a warning, but also as a broad hint that it would behoove Tristan to obtain funds from connections in the outside world.

He walked over to an empty pallet and, deciding that the filthy cot would be better than the mired and mildewed floor, he sat down, his back against the wall, one bent knee supporting his arm. He laid his head back, ignoring visions of vermin crawling within the straw of the pallet, the sounds of Newgate at night, and the unnerving stare of the man across from him.

Sleep eluded him for hours as the image of Brittany and Charles, entwined in intimacy, invaded his mind again and again with scarifying pain. He relived each moment, each movement, each spoken word, a hundred times, and always, always, the misery of telling shame in Brittany's eyes, the poorly concealed guilt in the king's, returned with unrelenting clarity.

Tristan could forgive Brittany anything if he thought she'd been coerced, but the memory of her fingers threaded urgently though Charles's dark hair, her eyes closed in sensual bliss . . . crushed his hopes that she'd been an unwilling victim. Even if there was the slightest chance that by some miracle she had been forced, the fact remained that she continued to warm Charles's bed this night . . .

It appeared, he thought bitterly, that he'd taught her the ways of love all too well. He buried his face in his hands, fiercely repressing the tears that threatened until his head ached.

It was the longest night of his life.

The scrape of a chain nearby brought him instantly awake. Before he could anticipate the attack, a fist crashed into his face, knocking his head against the stone wall with a sickening thud. Momentarily stunned, Tristan opened his eyes to penetrate the dimness as fingers closed around his neck and pinned him to the wall.

"Bein' the newcomer an' all, ye owe Charlie an' me garnish, Master High-an'-Mighty." The man's fingers squeezed with surprising strength for one so thin and unhealthy looking. "Pay up, or we'll take every last shillin' in that fancy purse o' yours."

With lightning speed, Tristan brought up his fettered hands and knocked away the man's arm with brutal force. The miscreant lost his balance and stumbled backward.

"And I recommend that you keep your filthy hands to yourself if you value your wretched existence." He swung his legs over the side of the pallet, his eyes narrowed first at his attacker and then at Charlie, who'd started to come to his comrade's defense.

" 'Tis our right . . . the rule," Charlie told him. "Ye don't pay us garnish, Jock an' me'll make sure ye don't git yer rations, guvnor." His lip curled in a sneer. "An' don't think we can't make good our threat."

They stood across from Tristan, glaring defiance, not quite ready to tangle with him, but their predatory stances, the hungry looks in their eyes, were enough to warn Tristan that it wouldn't be long before they'd catch him unawares and either rob him of his money and clothing or dispatch him in his sleep for his pitifully few shillings.

"How much?"

"Three shillin's each," Jock answered.

Tristan eyed them for a long, assessing moment. "I'll give you two apiece and no more."

Charlie opened his mouth to protest, but Tristan cut him

off. "Two shillings or I'll strangle you both while you sleep."

Jock canted his head to the side as he considered Tristan, allowing his gaze to rove slowly from the elegant, if slightly askew, lace ruffle at his throat to the tips of his boots.

"Two apiece it is, then," he mumbled at last, and stretched out a grimy hand.

Tristan removed the coins from the purse and dropped them onto the floor. Jock bent warily and snatched them up. As he turned to his cellmate, a voice called from the corridor, "Master . . . master, ye done good!"

It was Ollie.

"Two apiece is coin aplenty."

Tristan moved toward the door. "What are you doing here, Ollie?" he asked in a low voice, noting the angry bruise across the man's throat. "The turnkeys . . . they'll punish you if you get in their way." He threw a glance over his shoulder at his two cellmates, but their heads were together as they examined the coins.

Ollie stared up at Tristan through the tangle of his hair, squinting to see him better. "Don't ye know that madmen are given the run o' the prison?" For a moment his gray eyes cleared, and Tristan had the distinct impression that Ollie was conveying an unspoken message. "I wanted ta thank ye fer payin' fer my water last eve." He made a face. " 'Tis no better'n piss from the privy, but at least 'tis wet." He cackled at his words and Tristan noticed that his teeth were still relatively white—which meant that Ollie was probably still a young man.

"What's yer name, master?"

"Savidge."

"Ah, Master Savage." He pursed his lips thoughtfully. "Ye don't look savage ta me, but I'd not wish ta put it ta the test." He chortled, then stood on tiptoe to see Tristan's cellmates. "I'd watch them two," he warned softly. "They're not ta be trusted . . ." His voice lowered to a whisper. "They murdered the last one ta be locked up with 'em.'' Again his eyes cleared, shining with a lucidity, an intelligence, that convinced Tristan Ollie was no lunatic.

Tristan's new friend glanced down the passageway. "They're comin' with the mornin' rations. If I don't get back ta my cell, I'll get none.''

Tristan nodded. "Tell me first, Ollie, why you're in here.''

Ollie's gaze dropped, his thin fingers gripping the bars until the knuckles shone white. "I stole some fish from a vendor ta feed my daughter. Her mother was adyin' an' . . .'' His voice trailed off as the sounds of rations being doled out came closer. He brightened once again, all trace of anguish gone from his expression. "Got ta go, master. You guard yer coin, for ye'll need it. Blankets are one shillin' an' candles from the cellarmen are two,'' he said in a singsong voice, and loped away, his tattered rags flappping about him.

Tristan could not bring himself to eat the prison fare. On forays with the Powhatan, he'd been reduced to living on wild berries, dried meat, and corncakes in the forest, but that now seemed a sumptuous feast compared to the swill served the inmates of Newgate. His stomach turned at the sight of the gray gruel afloat with suspicious-looking brown specks. And the water . . . Ollie had been right. It was rancid and rank, and Tristan forced himself to ignore his suppositions as to where it came from as he took a tentative sip and spat it out in disgust. He'd fasted before; he could go without food and drink again.

When the bedmaker came along, Tristan purchased two thin and filthy blankets, for the cold dampness of the dank building penetrated to the bone, and he couldn't seem to get warm.

One of the men across from him had paid for the services of a prostitute. Tristan was outraged to see the prisoner and his harlot panting and grappling within sight of everyone—including the wife and four children of the man in the next cell. Tristan guessed that, at a loss without her husband, possibly turned out of their home, the woman had brought her family to come to stay with their father. Tristan was sickened by the sight of the four dirty but cherubic faces. The parents tried to turn them away from the lewd scene enacted to the accompaniment of the man's cellmates' bawdy encouragement.

Tristan looked away, repulsed, and sat silently, cursing his luck. And his temper. *What were you supposed to do?* a goading voice demanded. *Tell the king to go ahead and bed her with your blessing?*

Well, he'd be damned if he'd send any appeal to Charles Stuart. He supposed Brittany would eventually reveal his whereabouts to Matt or his grandfather, but he doubted she would have the courage to come to Newgate—not that he blamed her—let alone face him after what had happened.

Therefore, as he heard catcalls and other crude noises sounding along the length of the passageway, he tried to tune out the din, thinking that the news of what was going on across the way had spread like wildfire, a temporary diversion from the misery and boredom within the prison.

Turnkeys stalked up and down the corridor, thumping their clubs against the iron bars and shouting at the prisoners until the noise level lowered appreciably.

"Got a visitor, pretty face," called the bailiff who'd escorted Tristan to his cell the night before.

"Well, lookee here," said Charlie from his pallet.

Tristan glanced up, and there stood the reason for the uproar . . . Brittany.

Like a shot, Jock was up and off the lower bunk and approaching the bars, the leer spreading across his features acting to galvanize Tristan.

"Come ta give ol' Jock a fine piece o'—"

Charlie called out a warning, but it was too late. Tristan came up on Jock's side and, raising his manacled hands to shoulder level, elbowed him viciously in the side of his jaw, the crunch of bone and cartilage soft but distinct.

"Get away from her."

Jock staggered backward with a wail of pain, his hands clutching his dislocated jaw. Eyes dark with malevolence, he glanced first at Brittany and then at Tristan. "Ye'll not live the night, I promise ye, Master High-an'-Mighty," he slurred through his broken jaw. "Bid yer ladylove farewell." He limped slowly back to his pallet.

"Tristan." Her voice was a whisper of sound, the look of distress on her beautiful face so acute that he had the strongest urge to take her in his arms and kiss away her unhappiness, mold his mouth to the sweetness of hers and cleave unto her . . .

"What are you doing here?" he asked without ceremony.

Brittany noted the bruise on his cheekbone and longed to reach out and touch it, but the bleakness in his eyes chilled her, dissuaded her. She clutched the bars, searching for words to wipe his features clean of the anguish she knew was in his heart.

"This is no place for a woman," he said harshly. "Go home."

"What—what can I do to help you get out of here?" she asked in a low, strained voice.

A grimace distorted one side of his handsome face. "Perhaps another night with the king will secure my release." Even as he said the words, he hated himself, loathed the sound of the jealous suitor, the wronged lover.

The pride he'd first observed at the Hunter's Run rose in her eyes, and with a lift of her chin Brittany met his gaze squarely. "Before God, I did not willingly go to Whitehall! Surely you know of Buckingham's ruse to get me to London."

"Aye, and I would like to know exactly when you decided to make the most of your visit to the king. Did you consider such a thing the night of the ball?"

Ire flashed in her eyes and, in the midst of his emotional battle, Tristan thought she'd never looked more magnificent. "Tell me that you've never felt passion for another,"

she said. "Tell me that a skilled lover cannot arouse lust
within even a person deeply in love with someone else!
And then tell me, Tristan, how you won me over at first
if not by your expertise in the art of lovemaking."

He looked away, a tic working in his cheek as he struggled to concede the truth of her words. The realization
didn't alleviate the pain of betrayal that still clutched his
heart.

"Tristan, listen to me! Buckingham showed me an amulet exactly like the one Running Deer gave you. And—
and he told me that you were in Newgate unbeknownst to
anyone."

His eyes delved into hers, searching for truth among the
shattered remnants of pride and pain and love. "He tricked
you. My amulet is still around my neck."

She frowned, realizing that she had, indeed, been
duped. "He said that if I did not act the willing lover with
the king, he would make certain that you never returned
alive." The frown faded and her eyes pleaded with him
for understanding.

He ran a light finger over hers, which were clasped
tightly around the bars, her face disturbingly close to his.
"That, perhaps . . . but you remained with Charles the
night?"

The quiet despair, the utter lack of hope in his voice,
sent her heart tumbling to her feet, for she could not deny
that she had—nor tell him the whole truth.

"*Oui.*"

"I see." He pulled away his hand and dropped it to his
side with a clink of the irons. "Charles does not force
himself on an unwilling woman, no matter how much he
may desire her. The fact that you remained with him till
morning tells me all I need to know."

Color bathed her cheeks and she dropped her gaze, a
sense of helplessness lurching through her.

"I might have been persuaded to forget what I saw because of my understanding of Buckingham's character, but
there can have been no reason on God's green earth for

you to stay with the king other than the fact that you wanted him as much as he wanted you.''

She shook her head in denial. ''I only want you,'' she whispered, her eyes murky with misery as they met his once again.

He studied her with a detachment that chilled her. ''Being intimate with another man is hardly the way to lend credence to such a declaration.''

''Tristan—''

''Why don't ye invite the little lady in, guvnor?'' called a voice from the adjoining cell.

''Aye,'' added another inmate. ''We could use a bit more sport like that goin' on across the way . . .''

Raucous laughter pealed with ear-splitting discordance through the hall and surrounding cells, and Tristan's expression turned grim. ''Leave here, Brittany. 'Tis no place for a woman. Bailiff!''

''Do not send me away like this,'' she exhorted. ''You must tell me what I can do!''

''You can get out of this pest-ridden hole. Go back to Wildwood and wait until his royal majesty sees fit to release me.'' His mouth turned down at the corners. ''It shouldn't be long, for Charles is of a conciliatory nature. I suspect his conscience will trouble him soon enough.'' His voice dropped so low that Brittany had to strain to catch the words. ''I would think he'd guess that bedding you would be punishment enough.'' The words bore the soft but stringent tones of sarcasm, and Brittany glimpsed once again the pain that made him so bitter and cynical.

''Whatcha need, pretty face?'' called the turnkey as he strode up to the cell, his appreciative gaze on Brittany. ''Want fer me ta let 'er in?'' His eyes kindled with anticipation.

Tristan's eyes narrowed, his gaze hardening. ''Take her away . . . now.''

His voice carried the ring of authority and, with a sigh of disappointment, the turnkey took Brittany's arm. She jerked away, a mutinous look on her lovely face.

"I'll not leave you!"

"You don't understand, do you? I don't want you here—not now, not ever." He turned away in dismissal, leaving her staring at him in frustrated dismay.

"Newgate?"

Brittany nodded, her throat tightening with emotion as she remembered the bruise on Tristan's face, the filth in which he was forced to exist, and the cunning, desperate looks of his cellmates. "Charles had him incarcerated because he burst into the royal bedchamber and . . . demanded the king release me."

Richard Carlisle's eyes bored into her. "You'd best tell me the whole story. What happened after Tristan bolted out of here for London?"

She obliged willingly, leaving out nothing except the promise Charles had extracted from her.

"And did ye sleep with him after my grandson was taken away?"

The bluntness of Carlisle's question took her by surprise, but instead of lying to the earl, she told him, "I remained in his bed till morning."

He studied her shrewdly, noting the hectic color in her face, the spark of defiance in her eyes. "That doesn't answer my question."

"It will have to do."

He laid his head against the chair back, his eyes closing. They were in his office, where a fire burned in the hearth and the weak rays of the February sun shone through the windows overlooking the grounds.

He remained motionless for so long that Brittany moved toward him from her position before the hearth. "Your lordship?"

"I'm thinking, m'girl. Naught else." He reached for the bell pull behind him. "Perhaps some ale will revive both of us, umm?"

She doubted anything could banish the chill from her heart, but she nodded in answer. "The king told me later that he and Buckingham had thought to prove that I was unworthy of Tristan, that the lady Diana Hartland would make him a far better match than a faithless tavern wench.''

''You told him nothing of your background, your connection with the St. Germains?''

''To what purpose? The fact remains that I cannot, in truth, offer anything to the heir of an earldom.''

''The royal opinion be damned! No one knows who can better serve or please a man than he who has requested a woman's hand. You need bring no wealth or holdings or titles to this marriage. You are young and beautiful and possessed of enough mettle for three.'' He leaned forward over his desk to emphasize his words. ''And Tristan loves you, not Diana Hartland.''

Burke knocked and entered with a tray bearing a bottle and two mugs.

''Well, you did the right thing, child.'' The earl accepted the ale Brittany poured for him and took a long draught. ''I'll go to Whitehall this very day. I cannot abide the thought of my grandson languishing in that plague-ridden gaol.'' He grasped the arms of his chair and stood. ''There are a few other things that need clarification as well.''

At Brittany's questioning look he elucidated. ''This enmity of Buckingham's has got to end. I'm certain Charles knows little of what actually happened—and even less of George's relentless pursuit of vengeance.'' He moved toward the door, his steps steady and purposeful. ''I'll get to the bottom of it, Brittany girl. Meanwhile, you stay put until I return.''

Brittany followed him out the door, not convinced he was doing the right thing. ''But—but do you think the king will listen to you? That he will allow himself to be persuaded that Buckingham is at fault rather than Tristan?''

He paused and turned toward her, the light of determination in his eyes, an air of confidence about him, making the years drop away suddenly. ''Aye, he'll listen. I supported his father until his execution, I fought with Charles himself at Worcester and remained loyal throughout his exile.'' He put a reassuring hand on her shoulder. ''Don't look so doubtful, child. I'll secure Tristan's release before the sun rises on the morrow, mark my words.''

Chapter 22

The day dragged endlessly for Tristan, and the night, which was hardly distinguishable from day because of the perpetual darkness, was neverending. His poignant and painful ruminations regarding Brittany, and his constant vigil against an assault from the two miscreants with whom he shared the cell occupied all his attention.

And his burning thirst . . . That was worse than the hunger, for a man could go for days without food if he had water. Ollie had informed him that ale could be bought if one could afford it, but Tristan hadn't made the right connection that day and now must wait until the following morning. He did not doubt that Jock or Charlie could have apprised him of the procedure, but after what he'd done to Jock, it was inconceivable that either one would shed any light on the question.

With only time on his hands, Tristan came to a few conclusions and made a few decisions, not the least of which was that he could not live without Brittany, no matter what she'd done. Despite all the hurt and anguish of her betrayal, he still loved her. What would eventually become of them, he did not know for, in truth, he suspected it would be a long time before he could trust her again. The question now was, could he wed her and overcome his distrust? One could love, he discovered with painful clarity, and withhold trust at the same time. Yet, oh what a tortured existence that would be, to be suspicious of the very one to whom he was committed, heart and soul.

A chain clanked nearby and Tristan stiffened, his gaze piercing the gloom of the cell in the pitiful light of the cheap tallow candle he'd purchased earlier in the day. But the sound was only Charlie shifting in his sleep. Jock lay on his back on the lower bunk, unable to put any weight on the side of his face. Occasionally a groan escaped him when he inadvertently turned in his sleep, but otherwise the cell was relatively quiet.

With the dawn came the stirring of the inmates. The man two cells over was dying from gaol fever and kept crying out for water. Though Tristan's niggardly hoard of coins was dwindling fast, he gave a bailiff a shilling and asked him to purchase an extra ration of water for the poor wretch.

After rations were doled out, Ollie came sidling down the corridor, his face alight with excitement.

Tristan grinned in spite of himself. "Come for my breakfast, have you, Ollie?"

Ollie's look turned sheepish. "Only if ye don't want it again, master." He cocked his head like a curious rook. "Looks like ye got a visitor," he said conspiratorially.

Tristan frowned. "Did you see who it was?"

Ollie shook his shaggy head, his eyes narrowing. "Nay, but—"

A turnkey came sauntering down the hall toward them, but there was no one with him.

Ollie looked dismayed. "Yer goin' ta be released, I'll wager."

Released? Tristan eyed the burly bailiff, who shoved Ollie aside. "Get away, fool. Pretty face here's gettin' out." He shoved the key into the lock. "An' watcha gonna do now, Ollie boy, without yer guardian angel?" He swung open the door. "Come wi' me."

As Tristan left the cell, he removed the small purse at his waist and handed it to Ollie. There were only nine shillings left, but they would serve his friend well for a few days at least.

The bailiff slammed and locked the cell door, then turned away.

Tristan looked at Ollie, at a momentary loss for words, and was surprised to see tears misting the gray eyes, as lucid now as any sane man's.

"Ye been kinder ta me than anyone since I was brought here a year past, master. Take care o' yerself . . ." He turned away, as if he couldn't bear to see Tristan leave, his thin shoulders slumped in misery.

"Ollie—"

"Come along now, afore I tell yer deliverer yer already dead an' buried," ordered the bailiff over his shoulder.

"Go to hell," Tristan told him and put his hand on Ollie's shoulder. But the latter turned to him suddenly, the purse clutched to his middle and a wild look in his eyes.

"Best begone wi' ye," he crooned in his singsong voice. "Begone from here afore they get ye . . ." He let out a high-pitched shriek of laughter and scampered away.

"Are ye comin' or nay?"

Tristan stared after Ollie, a host of conflicting urges vying for supremacy within him. He wanted to go after him and comfort him . . . he wanted to slam his fist into the bailiff's porcine face . . . he wanted to . . . Oh, God, not the least of his urges was to leave this place with its hellish memories forever.

The gaoler returned his cloak, sword, and dagger—but not his money. It mattered little to him. All he could think was that he was walking out of Newgate and into the smoky, stale air of London, which seemed as sweet and pure as a spring day in the country.

Despite the gray mist that seemed to fall from the overcast skies, enveloping everything, Tristan had to squint against the bright daylight. He made out the impressive Carlisle coat-of-arms on the door of the waiting coach.

"Grandfather," he murmured in relief. If it had been

the royal coat-of-arms, he would have balked, for he was
not yet ready to deal with Charles Stuart.

A liveried footman opened the door, and Tristan set his
foot to the single step and sprang nimbly inside. The earl
sat on the far side, his head turning at the sound of Tristan's entry. He quickly took stock of his grandson's appearance.

"Somebody didn't like you—or did you sass the turnkey?"

Tristan grinned ruefully. "One of my cellmates attacked
me the first night."

Weyrith cackled as the coach wheels started rolling.
"And what'd you do to him?"

"Dislocated his jaw."

The earl thumped his walking stick on the coach floor.
"Dammee!" His smile faded. "Aside from the black eye,
you look fit enough, although you stink worse than a cess-
pit." He held a handkerchief to his nose.

Tristan laughed, feeling suddenly lighthearted. "Thank
you for coming to my rescue, Grandfather."

Weyrith eyed him speculatively. "Don't thank me,
m'boy. 'Twas Brittany who told me everything."

There was a moment of silence before Tristan repeated,
"Everything?"

"Aye, and you'd be a fool to let anything come between
you . . . even this."

Tristan stared out the window, his expression bleak.
"I'm surprised the king pardoned me."

"Didn't say he did. He's still piqued with you, but . . ."
He shrugged. "I reminded him of what you've done for
him."

A slow smile lifted the corners of Tristan's mouth. "By
God, you've got guts. I reminded him of the same thing—
indirectly, of course—and he clapped me in gaol."

"Takes the Carlisle charm, boy. But you'll learn that in
time."

Tristan threw back his head and laughed at the old man's
temerity. Their blue eyes met again and Carlisle said,

"Seems things haven't changed much since I was in there."

Tristan sobered. "*You* were in Newgate . . . the earl of Weyrith?"

"Wasn't an earl then. I was only the heir—younger than you. My cronies got me so foxed I couldn't see straight. Next thing I knew, I was in Newgate—only for the night, of course." He looked back at Tristan as the carriage came to a halt. "But even though 'twas a prank, I'll never forget it . . . and neither should you." He pointed an arthritic finger at Tristan. "Nor what you did to end up there."

The footman opened the door and stood at attention.

"Where are we?" Tristan asked.

"My town house. I knew you'd need a bath, and something substantial to eat . . . and a good night's sleep before we return to Carlisle Hall." His eyes narrowed as he leaned forward, his hands braced on the carved head of his cane. "Ye gods, ye can't go home to Brittany looking and smelling like *that*."

The elegant coach and four pulled into the cobblestoned yard in front of Carlisle Hall. Before it came to a stop, Brittany flung open one of the great double doors. But as Tristan emerged from the coach she paused, uncertain. For a brief eternity their eyes met and held, and then he was turning to help the earl alight.

She watched with mixed emotions as grandfather and grandson ascended the stairs.

"I told you I'd bring him back," Carlisle said to Brittany, poking the air with his stick for emphasis. "And looking a mite better than when I got him out, I might add."

Indeed, he looked wonderful, she thought. Tall and broad-shouldered, he appeared every bit the proud Royalist with his sword at his side, wearing his fine black cape and cavalier's hat, the plume dipping saucily as he bowed with the perfect elegance and grace of the courtier. Only the discoloration beneath one eye hinted at the ordeal he'd endured for forty-eight hours.

"Welcome home, my lord," she said shyly, her hungry gaze only for him.

He returned the smile, but the warmth and adoration she'd always read in his eyes was missing. Her stomach knotted even as she struggled to remain calm, her own smile turning artificially bright.

The earl moved through the doors mumbling something about the unenthusiastic greeting an old man was forced to accept when in the company of a younger buck.

Tristan and Brittany remained at the top of the stone stairs, at a loss for words. Tristan sought to push away memories of her in the king's bed and allowed his gaze to take in her attire. She looked lovely in the pale yellow silk gown with its straight neckline and broad band of creamy lace edging resting slightly off her slender shoulders. It revealed only a hint of the enticing curves of her breasts, but her hair—the pale rays of the sun turned the honey-brown tresses to molten gold.

She had defied convention and allowed her hair to fall freely in the manner he loved. Oh, God, how he wanted to take her into his arms and bury his face in that fragrant fall, forget his pain as the sweet scent of violets soothed away all awkwardness, all hesitation. But he could not. Instead, he said simply, "The color becomes you."

"Thank you, my lord." Her hopes were dashed upon the shoals of his aloofness. *Oh, Tristan, can you not say how good it is to see me? How you missed me?*

But she knew exactly why he did not say those words and, although she tried to understand, her heart cried out against the unfairness of it. *If you loved me above all things, you could forgive me,* she told him silently.

He stood there for an awkward moment until she dropped her chin in confusion and swung away to follow the earl into the manor, a blush streaking her cheekbones. "Supper will be served soon," she murmured and, picking up her skirts, hurried ahead of him through the door.

''What are you doing here?'' the earl asked gruffly as Brittany almost bowled him over in her haste before her eyes adjusted to the dimmer light inside.

She shook her head miserably as Tristan's footfalls sounded behind them. ''I-I must see to dinner.''

''What's wrong with the help?'' he began, but Brittany was already moving down the hallway toward the back of the manor.

The earl impaled his grandson with his hawk-eyed stare. ''You didn't give her much of a greeting,'' he commented.

Tristan handed his hat and cape to the silent Burke. ''I wasn't aware that you were watching.''

Carlisle glared at him. ''Don't change the subject!''

A troubled frown between his eyes, Tristan softly blew out his breath as he watched Brittany turn a corner and disappear from sight. ''Nay . . . 'twasn't much of a greeting at all.''

At dinner Carlisle made up for the two younger people's lack of scintillating conversation. ''I think I'll give you a break from learning your duties and responsibilities, boy,'' he told Tristan. ''And you''—he leveled his gaze at Brittany—''can remain here for as long as you like. You both need time to yourselves.'' He cleared his throat. ''You need to think about the wedding.''

Both of them looked at him rather than at each other. After a moment, Brittany said, ''There will be no wedding.''

He raised an iron-gray eyebrow and met her gaze. ''Of course there will be a wedding. You're just unsettled because of this nonsense with Buckingham and the king. Time will take care of that, I guarantee it.'' He looked at Tristan. ''And what have you to say, umm? Are you going to let her back out of it just like that?''

''Nay,'' he answered softly.

The intensity in his gaze—something that had been missing since his return—was back in full force, a fervor that made her pulses leap with joy.

"You will become my wife as planned."

At the businesslike phrasing of his statement, her excitement just as suddenly died. The kindling of emotion in his eyes was nothing more than determination to carry out his pledge to her—the only choice open to a man of honor.

She dabbed her mouth with a snowy linen napkin and pushed back her chair. Tristan stood to help her, but she stopped him with a wave of her hand. "I'm tired." She looked at the earl. "If you'll excuse me?" And she left the room with a graceful dignity that belied the misery that swamped her.

"You're a fool, boy. You chase her away and you'll never find another like her." Carlisle sat frowning at his grandson. "A love like yours comes only once in a lifetime . . . if you're lucky."

Tristan pushed away his untouched wine and sat back in his chair, studying his half-empty plate. "I have no intention of letting her go unless she wishes it. My feelings for her haven't changed. I just need time."

"Then tell her that."

Tristan looked up, his expression cold. "I need no advice from you. I don't imagine you ever found the woman you worshipped in the arms of another man."

"You know perfectly well that was Buckingham's doing. You can't hold that against either one of them." As Tristan's eyes narrowed in anger, the earl continued. "The king can't be blamed for wanting her if he thought she was willing. She's a beautiful woman and he was much taken with her."

Tristan shoved back his chair in a rare show of fury, his fists clenched at his sides. The chair tipped precariously backward before it righted with a soft thump. "Let's get to the heart of the matter, shall we, Grandfather?" He strode to the hearth and braced an arm on the mantel, gazing at the flames. Drawing a deep, calming breath, he said in a low voice, "She elected to remain with him the said in a low voice, "She elected to remain with him the night. That is hardly what I call the behavior of a woman in love with another."

"How do you know this? The king could have forced her—"

"Because I know Charles. He would never force an un-willing woman. He prides himself on the fact that few women ever show reluctance to be bedded by him." He leaned his forehead upon his outstretched arm, his eyes closing against the painful images that tore through his mind's eye with the force of pistol shots.

The earl rose and came to Tristan. "What ever happened to your self-confidence? Your natural self-esteem? Have you not taken a good look at yourself in the mirror? And even if you haven't, when has a woman—any woman—refused you?" He put his hand on Tristan's shoulder. "You are every bit the man Charles Stuart is . . . and more."

Tristan's arm dropped and he turned to face his grand-father, a sad smile softening his expression. "But I am not a king."

For the next week, Tristan's outward attitude changed slowly, and the distance he kept between them began to close almost imperceptibly. He and Brittany spent all their time together, as Brittany suspected the earl had intended. The old man locked himself in his office for hours, refus-ing to be disturbed, which left Brittany and Tristan free to amuse themselves at their leisure.

Some of Brittany's belongings had been sent from Wild-wood at the behest of the earl, and although she voiced her concern that she wouldn't be able to say goodbye to Matt and Genna before the *Virginia* sailed, Tristan assured her he would take her to Wildwood for their wedding.

They went riding every day, unless it rained, and Tristan tutored her further in the sport of shooting a bow and arrow. His smiles returned with increasing frequency, and although they weren't as spontaneous as before the fiasco preoccupation lessened with each passing day. He and Brittany practiced Indian sign language so she could surprise Ikuuk with her expertise, and once they went to London to shop for a wedding gift for Matt and Genna. They made a day of it, and at suppertime, Tristan took her to an ordinary, where they could dine. They ordered a bottle of Rhenish to go with a huge, steaming bowl of mussels, and finished the meal with the new, exotic brew, coffee. As evening fell, Tristan took her to spend the night in the earl's London town house.

That evening, before banking the fire and dousing the tapers, he kissed her chastely on the forehead and remained on his side of the bed, so heartachingly close, yet leagues away. She lay in the dark, cursing the fates and the damnable pride of Tristan Savidge and Charles Stuart. Perhaps, for Tristan's sake, she should leave England after all. Perhaps Charles had been right to believe that a woman of the aristocracy like Diana Hartland would be a more fitting wife for Tristan. As the daughter of the duke of Dansworth, Diana certainly had more to offer than did Brittany.

Hard on the heels of that thought came another, one more depressing and possessing the power to push her more firmly toward the decision to leave England. Tristan might love her still, but ever since he'd first taken it upon himself to defend her against Buckingham, he'd been the object of the enmity of one of the wealthiest and most powerful men in England. That the duke exerted more influence over the king than friendship merited was beside the point. Again and again Tristan had been her champion, successfully thwarting Buckingham . . . until this last time.

Perhaps it would be best to leave Tristan and England. Not only did she believe that things would never be the same between them, but by removing herself from his life, she would allow him to make amends with the king, to learn his role as future earl, and live his life as he was destined, without the daughter of a man of humble origins to hold him back.

With these troubled thoughts, with the feeling of loss they created, overshadowing the sense of fairness to Tristan, she fell into a fitful sleep.

The fire was all around her, shooting flames searing her skin and licking at her clothing. But she couldn't escape, for she was shackled by a skeletal hand that gripped her wrist with bone-snapping strength, pinning her to the burning pyre that held the charred remains of Raymond Chauvelin.

She screamed, but the roar of the blaze drowned out the pitifully inadequate sound. "Help me! *Au secours!*" she cried as the ceiling crashed down around her. She threw up her free arm to ward off the burning brands raining down, but it was too late. Smoke and heat scalded her throat and took her very breath away.

"Brittany! Brittany, wake up."

Her eyes flew open, but at first she couldn't make out anything in the dark.

"Brittany love, you were dreaming." Tristan's voice soothed her like cool water lapping over her heated body. He brushed back the tangled mass of her hair and touched his lips to hers. "I'm here, sweet. 'Twas only a dream."

Relief swept through her and she wrapped her arms around his neck and clung to him.

He held her tenderly, whispering assurances in her ear, stroking her hair.

"Raymond . . . the fire! I was trapped and—" She drew in a shuddering breath. "Oh, will it never end?"

His lips were suddenly at her temple, her eyelids, the corners of her mouth. "Hush, sweet. No one can harm you now."

As she slowly calmed, his stroking fingers moved to her neck and arms, then to her shoulders until, when at last she lay still beneath his gentle ministrations, he kissed her deeply, his mouth trembling with need and the exquisite pitch of his desire. His tongue traced the sweet contours of her lips before delving inside to explore the moist softness within. Their tongues met and twined, an unspoken apology, a joyous welcome. He pulled his mouth from hers and traced the sleek column of her throat, sending wildfire racing though her.

She arched toward him, all fear, all doubt gone. "Love me, *mon coeur* . . . love me."

"I will, my precious love . . . I do." And as he obliged, her heart soared, and she sent a silent prayer of thanksgiving to God for returning him to her.

They arrived back at Carlisle Hall the next evening. As they walked into the earl's study, hand in hand, Carlisle looked up and grinned.

"You shouldn't be working so late, Grandfather," Tristan greeted him.

"And why not? I feel better than I have in years, boy."

Tristan looked down at Brittany. "Either he belongs on-stage in the theater, or he's made a miraculous recovery. Do you remember how he did everything from his bed when first you came here?"

"Aye, but you have taken a great burden from him. Not only has his lordship met his grandson, but he's also obtained a competent and most eligible heir to his title. I would think that would be enough to make any man feel younger."

Carlisle scowled. "Enough of this talking as if I'm not even in the room." He tugged the bell pull. "Have you had your supper?"

"We ate at an inn only a few hours ago," Tristan answered.

The old man nodded and gestured to a chair. "Sit, girl. I have something to tell you both."

Burke entered, bearing a tray with three goblets, a bottle of sack, and another of ale. "Ah, how efficient he is." The earl nodded his thanks to the servant, who withdrew. "He anticipates my needs even before I communicate them." He gestured to the tray. "Pour us all a drink, grandson.'' He sat back, watching Tristan with a hooded gaze.

When Tristan had obliged, the earl raised his glass. "A toast. I propose a toast to your triumphant return to London."

Brittany glanced at Tristan, a question in her eyes, as the earl tossed down his ale with a flourish.

Tristan smiled reassuringly. "What return to London?" he asked, his glass raised halfway to his lips.

"Drink up, boy, drink up. You can't toast properly without drinking."

Something about his manner struck unease in Tristan as he sipped the wine. His expression turned wary as he eyed the earl over the rim of his goblet.

"I neglected to tell you this earlier, but the king promised to look into this affair concerning George Villiers." He held up a letter with a broken seal. "Here's proof that he has." He leaned forward. "Buckingham has been banished from court for six months, and the king has invited you to attend another ball at Whitehall!"

Chapter 23

For several moments, no one spoke. Then Brittany looked over at Tristan and said quietly, "Now, perhaps, without the king's support, Buckingham will cease his crusade for revenge."

But Tristan's gaze held Carlisle's, the silence gathering once more. He struggled with mixed emotions in the wake of Brittany's hopeful words, but anger won out and his expression of affability turned cold.

"What madness is this? He thinks to placate me by ousting Villiers from favor and inviting me back to court?" He set the glass down on the desk and swung away to cross the room with his long, lithe strides.

"He seeks to make amends in the only way he can and still save face."

Tristan turned back to his grandfather. "Aye . . . by expecting me to apologize for his outrageous behavior."

The earl's gaze lowered thoughtfully to the letter still in his hand. "Forgive my bluntness, but you said yourself that Charles would not force an unwilling woman."

Brittany's startled gaze went to the earl, who had not uttered one word of condemnation to her since her return to Carlisle Hall from Newgate. But he was obviously bent on pursuing his strategy, even in the face of the anger that brought Tristan to a halt before him. "You cannot blame a virile man for accepting the favors of a beautiful and willing woman," Carlisle persisted.

Brittany bit her lower lip, shame and angry frustration

washing through her. Oh, how she wished she could speak out! How easy it was for them to condemn her. A curse on Charles Stuart, she thought acidly. A curse on all men.

"I don't need you to point out what has been haunting my every waking moment since I discovered them together," Tristan said.

Brittany sharply sucked in her breath, and then realized as she drew the attention of both men that the question of whether or not she had been willing was moot. The important thing was that Tristan make amends with his friend and king, Charles Stuart. She would have to prove she was deserving of Tristan's trust, even though it galled her because of her very innocence. But she did not doubt that she could demonstrate the strength of her love and fidelity again and again . . . nay, a thousand times.

Her voice soft, she said, "I see no danger of being . . . seduced again. You may both think what you will, but I did not throw myself into Charles Stuart's arms."

Tristan's eyes narrowed a fraction, but she went on. "It seems to me, however, that the important thing is for Tristan to accept the king's unspoken offer of conciliation. Remember, you will be an earl one day, and you must regain your good standing." Her eyes darkened with the intensity of her words. "You have loved each other long and well, and whatever differences may have come between you, you must put them aside, swallow your pride, and accept his olive branch."

"I couldn't agree more," said the earl.

But Tristan's silent regard continued, as if he were carefully weighing her words, searching her face for some guarantee of sincerity. His eyes seemed to ask, *Are you actually eager to return to court and the king, or are you truly concerned about my damaged friendship with Charles Stuart?*

The shadow of suspicion in his eyes brought her to her feet. She put her hand to his cheek. "I love you and only you," she whispered, her lips trembling.

Oh, what have they done to you, my love? her heart

asked him silently. Indeed, what had they all done to him—this infinitely gentle and compassionate man, a man so tolerant and forgiving, once so self-assured? What had Buckingham and Charles Stuart and the earl, who had crushed Tristan's dream of living out his life in Virginia, done to him? Sweet heaven, how had they changed him? And what had she contributed? Had she not been directly responsible for the erosion of his self-confidence? First by leaving him without a word to return to France, then with her refusal to become his wife because of her nebulous fears, and finally by holding to her twice-damned promise to the king?

She let her hand fall away, but he caught it and pressed it to his lips. "We shall go to Whitehall," he said, and his expression seemed to lighten with his decision. He turned to the earl. "We shall, indeed, go to Whitehall, if his majesty wishes to make amends. But if Charles does not approach me, nothing will change. I agree to make the first move by accepting his invitation, but the rest is up to him."

"Sounds fair enough to me," said Carlisle.

"Good." He took Brittany into the loose circle of his arms and smiled down into her eyes, his earlier anger gone. "But first we've a wedding to attend in Chelsea two days hence."

They spent the night before the wedding at Wildwood, catching up on all the happy news from Matt and Genna. After supper, Matt, Ikuuk, and Tristan went into the saloon to talk and play cribbage, while Genna, breathless with excitement, took Brittany upstairs to see her newly finished wedding dress.

Enis came into the room just as Brittany was admiring the fine workmanship. "Aye, mistress," she said. "Genna's mother was a dressmaker, she was, an' ye can see the talent's rubbed off."

Brittany smiled her agreement.

"Eh bien, Matt said that perhaps I could open a shop

in the Colonies or work out of our home if I wish.'' She sighed. "I don't know how his family will accept such a thing, but he said it doesn't matter, that they will love me! Can you imagine?"

Brittany laughed. "I don't see how they can help it." Her expression sobered. "I wish to apologize to you both for my rudeness before I went to London. I-I had no right to speak to—"

"Ah, don't fret yerself over so little a thing, mistress," Enis hurried to assure her. "You couldn't 'ave done anything else, what with two mother hens and a rooster bent on protectin' their chick."

Genna giggled and Brittany joined in the merriment over Enis's calling the proud Ikuuk a rooster. "He doesn't seem to harbor any resentment, either, but I'll speak to him."

Later, they all went downstairs, Enis returning to the kitchen to finish cleaning up while Brittany and Genna joined the men in the saloon.

Brittany knelt beside Ikuuk, who was restringing his bow with a length of dried stag's gut. "Are you angry with me?" she asked softly.

His dark eyes met hers, a rich warmth burning within their depths. *I took no offense,* he signed to her.

She smiled and touched his knee, grateful for his affection and friendship—she, who'd once been terrified of him.

What is this sadness I sense within my blood brother? he signed.

Her gaze fell beneath his scrutiny and she stared at the bow lying across his lap.

"What are you two conspiring about now?" Tristan asked from across the room.

Brittany looked up and smiled. " 'Tis self-defeating to conspire and tell," she teased.

Before Tristan could answer, Matt leaned over and waved his hand before his face. "Pay attention, Savidge. I'm the one getting married on the morrow, not you." He rolled his eyes. "That's a point for me on the pegboard, if you can concentrate that long."

"Oh, I can do it for Sir Tristan," Genna said, and leaned over to place a peg on Matt's side of the board.

Tristan obligingly returned his attention to the card game.

There is sorrow in his heart. Why? Ikuuk persisted.

Her cheeks pink, Brittany signed back, *He believes I betrayed him with the king—and there is something I am sworn to keep from him.*

The king made you give your word?

She nodded.

"Ah, Savidge, two out of three—tsk, tsk . . ." Matt shook his head at his opponent. "Your mind is somewhere else this eve. Or are you, too, in need of wedding vows to straighten out your thoughts and restore your peace of mind?"

Tristan flung down his cards and sat back in his chair, one arm draped over the high, carved back. "It would behoove you to be at your charming best this night. Your wedding gift hangs in the balance."

Genna's eyes widened with surprise and pleasure. "A wedding gift?"

"Of course, Genna sweetheart," Matt said patiently. "One does receive gifts from one's friends and relatives when one ties the knot." He pulled her onto his lap to soften the irony of his words.

As Genna began to push against Matt in embarrassment, Tristan slid back his chair and stood. "Come, Ikuuk, help me. Brittany chose the heaviest object in all of London."

The Indian obediently followed Tristan from the room. Despite Matt's wheedling, Brittany would not divulge a single clue as to what the gift might be and, to her relief, the other two men returned forthwith with the large crate.

"Perhaps we shouldn't unpack it now," Genna said. "Would it not be easier to wait until we are—"

"A hammer and a few nails will reseal it, love," Matt assured her, "and we can send it on ahead then."

When the lid was pried open, Genna gasped softly at the treasure that rested within the straw packing.

"Ye gods, Tris, you've outdone yourself this time," said Matt.

Nestled within the straw was a full length, silvered Venetian glass mirror. Edged in olive wood, it boasted an outer frame of lively Stuart embroidery in colorful silks and wools.

" 'Twas Brittany who did the choosing." Tristan held out his arm in invitation, and she stepped to his side.

Genna looked up at them, wonderment in her sparkling dark eyes. *"Merci . . . merci bien,"* she breathed.

After the betrothed couple expressed thanks and admiration for the mirror, Tristan proposed a toast on the eve of their marriage, and finally, after much merrymaking, they packed away the mirror to be shipped to London, and all retired early.

The day dawned overcast but bright. Brittany helped Genna dress and fixed her hair. The men packed the remainder of Matt and Genna's things to be forwarded to London, for they'd decided to spend the last few days before the *Virginia* sailed on board the vessel. "Genna can't wait to get me to herself and lock us in my cabin," Matt explained with a roguish grin.

" 'Tis rather that I want to see some of London before we leave," she corrected tartly, a fiery blush belying her words.

The wedding was small and quiet, the ceremony performed in the tiny chapel of a larger church in Chelsea.

Tristan stood up for Matt, and Brittany was Genna's matron of honor. As they stood across from each other and listened to the words joining the couple after they'd exchanged their vows, Brittany felt heat rise in her cheeks and a sudden excitement race along her veins at the thought of becoming Tristan's wife, to be one with him in name as well as heart and soul.

During the Mass she'd had time to think back to their

first meeting, to her dreadful fear of men and how Tristan Savidge had slowly, gently, and with infinite patience banished her fears and won her trust and finally her love.

They congratulated the newlyweds with hearty hugs and laughing kisses, and waved them away in the bright sunlight that broke through the clouds just as they emerged from the church.

They walked hand in hand to a nearby inn for a light dinner.

"We must set our own date, love," Tristan said as Brittany lifted a hand to right the hood of her cloak, which the chill breeze had snatched from her head.

He smoothed back the sun-gilded strands of her hair, settling the garment back in place. He hugged her shoulders with one arm as they walked in the fresh air. "Well?"

His beautiful smile made her heart turn over with love. But there was the slightest shading of . . . was it the shadow of his lashes or the dark reflection of uncertainty?

The pain at that hint of doubt twisted in her chest until the tightness actually ached. She reached over and took his free hand in both of hers, squeezing tightly. "As soon as it can be done properly, *mon cher amour*," she answered, her eyes brimming with adoration. "We'll speak to your grandfather when we return from London, for he'll surely want everything to be done as befits his heir."

At the mention of London and the reminder of the coming ball, Tristan's smile faded. "Ah, yes. One more obstacle to be overcome. One more trial by endurance and then, if I succeed to his majesty's satisfaction, the royal grace will be reinstated—at least until the next trespass upon my friendship." Bitter irony weighted his words.

They neared the inn and Brittany turned to him, her face tilted earnestly up to his. "Tristan, if you are so against it, we need not go."

He gazed down into her upturned visage. Her expression was so concerned that Tristan instantly regretted his sarcasm. He cupped her cheek and lowered his lips to hers. "Forgive me," he murmured as his mouth briefly brushed hers, as lightly as the stroke of a butterfly's wing. "I'll not speak of it again."

Although not with words, he did speak of it again that night, and the next three that followed. He made love to her with a driven urgency, a fatalistic desperation . . . as if to claim his possession of her.

And, most heart-wrenchingly, as if to convince himself that she was, indeed, his alone.

For the three days until the ball they'd decided to remain at Wildwood with only Ikuuk and the servants for company. True to his word, Tristan did not mention the ball, or the king, or his apprehension, but Ikuuk watched his blood brother like a hawk, with that all-knowing yet implacable expression. The Indian seemed intent upon banishing Tristan's preoccupation and proceeded to challenge him to wrestling, racing, hunting, and throwing the dice. Brittany was poignantly reminded of her first days at Wildwood.

With the help of Georgie and Jims and several men Tristan hired from Chelsea, they also worked to widen the overgrown path leading through the woods to Wildwood. Tristan told Brittany it would be ludicrous to make the trip to Chelsea on horseback dressed in their finery, and that work on the path was long overdue.

Ikuuk's efforts to lighten Tristan's mood seemed to succeed, for Brittany frequently heard his laughter or caught him smiling at some practical joke instigated by the Indian. Meanwhile, she doubled her efforts to remain carefree and loving, although she, too, dreaded the coming trip to Whitehall. It helped to remind herself that Charles was known for his good nature and fairness, and that since the earl had spoken to him, the king had seen the necessity of punishing Buckingham.

If only she could tell Tristan the truth . . .

The day of the ball arrived. After an early dinner, Brittany took a leisurely bath, hoping the warm, scented water would help calm her increasing jitters. Enis helped her dry and style her hair, and between the two of them, they managed to coax the heavy tresses into ringlets. When the curls had set, Enis carefully parted the hair down the middle and pulled it back from the side, anchoring it with bodkins.

"Lovely," Tristan commented from the doorway.

"Oh, m'lord!" Enis exclaimed, flustered at Tristan's presence with Brittany clad only in chemise, corset, and drawers.

"Have you finished with her hair?" he asked, coming into the room and waving one hand in dismissal of the servant's discomfiture.

"Aye, m'lord."

"Then I'll help her dress, Enis."

After a quick exchange of glances, Brittany nodded at Enis, and the woman quit the room.

"This is most unusual," Brittany said, a shy smile curving her mouth.

"A task in which I will delight even after we are wed." He carefully picked up her dress from where it lay spread out on the bed, a confection of spring green, and approached her chair. "Careful now . . ." He lifted it over her head, avoiding the newly arranged curls falling down her back.

The satin gown glided over her body with a sigh, and as Tristan stooped to smooth the skirt over her legs, his lips touched one silk-clad knee.

"Are you trying to dress me or seduce me, my lord?"

Demons danced in his eyes as he straightened. "Why, dress you, of course, wench. 'Tis later that I intend to ravish you most thoroughly."

Giddiness washed over her at the thought.

"That shade of green becomes you," he observed. " 'Tis not so dark as emeralds, yet not too pale."

Brittany smiled at the compliment and turned toward the polished mirror. She arranged the slightly dipping neckline with its broad band of white lace until it rested just off her shoulders. Although the neckline was almost horizontal, it was low enough so that the corset's support and constriction of her breasts allowed their smooth swelling to be just visible.

Tristan began to fasten the back of the stiff, boned bodice while Brittany critically eyed the stomacher, of paler green material with a row of spring-green bows. The sides of the overskirt were pulled back and anchored with larger bows to expose the pale silk underskirt. Flouncing and ruching decorated the latter, and ruffles edged the sleeves, which ended just above her elbow.

"You will dazzle them," he murmured in her ear, and before she could reply, he was placing a choker of diamonds and emeralds around her neck. She glanced up to see his expression, but his lowered lashes screened his eyes.

" 'Tis lovely," she said.

" 'Twas the earl's wife's," he said, "but there is more." He fastened matching earrings to her dainty earlobes.

She turned to face him and he stepped back to admire his work. The pleasure in his eyes sent a tingle along her nerves, and she wished the ball were over and they were already returned to Wildwood.

"I'll leave you to finish up while I dress," he told her, and with a light kiss, he departed.

Enis returned just as Brittany was attempting to weave a slim green length of ribbon through her ringlets. "Here, mistress, let me."

She gave herself up to Enis's pampering, allowing her thoughts to return to Tristan. It seemed he was doing an admirable job of overcoming whatever trepidation he might have—and especially by presenting her with jewels that could only enhance her appearance. She had briefly wondered if he would deliberately encourage her to look less than her best, and now felt a guilty pang at such ignoble thoughts.

Possibly, she thought, the evening would go well.

For the finishing touches, Brittany applied a light dusting of rouge to her cheeks, a bit of lip pomade, and a tiny, heart-shaped patch to one corner of her mouth. Lastly, she touched the moist stopper of her violet perfume to the pulse points below her ears, at the hollow of her throat, and at her wrists and elbows.

She met Tristan outside her room and together they descended the stairs to the hall. In his high-heeled, silver-buckled shoes, Tristan seemed exceptionally tall beside her. The fine hose he wore beneath his petticoat breeches emphasized the excellent turn of his leg. It occurred to her that, despite the garment's feminine name and its resemblance to a woman's short petticoat, the full, knee-length apparel looked anything but feminine on Tristan. He took her cloak from her arm and fastened it around her shoulders, then did likewise with his own and led her outside to the waiting coach and four.

Lantern light danced across Tristan's sculpted features as the coach rolled through the forest toward Chelsea. "This is all so familiar," he said. "Only a few short weeks ago we traveled this very route with Matt and Genna."

"Oui, but you were a fierce-looking Powhatan warrior then. Now you are an elegant English courtier."

He grinned rakishly. "Which do you prefer, my lady? I am yours to command."

"I love you both more than I can say."

He sobered. "I once thought never to hear you say such words."

She leaned forward and touched his hand. "But you are a patient man, are you not? *Tout vient à point à qui sait attendre.*"

"Everything comes to him who waits? Ah, a philosopher now."

"But 'tis true—and most especially in this case, is it not?"

"Would you like me to sit beside you and receive some further tender reward for my patience?"

"You'll crush my dress . . . and besides, I like you sitting across from me so I can look at you." She paused, noting the glow of pleasure in his eyes. "You are most fortunate, you know."

He raised his dark brows.

"Many men would give much to have your thick, wavy hair. You need no periwig." She eyed the gently curling sable mane that fell to his shoulders.

"Actually, I prefer it tied back. We do things more simply where I come from." He donned his plumed cavalier's hat and cocked it at a jaunty angle. "Do I look the rakehell?" His eyes took on a lascivious gleam.

Brittany laughed, a sweet, melodious sound that never failed to enchant him. "Nay."

What he did look like, she thought, was a most beautifully handsome man, more splendid than any hero she'd every conjured up in her girlhood fantasies. He'd shouldered back his cape in the stuffy interior of the coach, affording Brittany a clear view of his attire. The pure white lawn shirt with its elegant lace ruffle at the neck set off the teak tone of his skin. The short, indigo-blue jacket— the same shade as his skirtlike breeches—had slashed sleeves to show off the full-sleeved shirt beneath, with its silk and lace flounces falling over his hands like foaming waterfalls.

"You said I would dazzle them," she said, "but, in truth, 'tis you who will rob every woman of her senses." Unexpectedly, she wondered if Diana Hartland would be attending.

He took her hand and turned it palm up. His lips tasted the sweet skin, their touch a burning brand; his tongue followed, sending hot desire shooting through her lower abdomen. He raised his eyes, then slowly straightened. "In that case, we shall take Whitehall by storm, shan't we?"

Chapter 24

Thousands of tapers in branched candelabra and hanging chandeliers threw patterns of warm, fluttering light across the dancers on the floor. Ladies dipped and swayed, met their partners, and retreated to the strains of the music, their gowns of taffeta and silk, satin and velvet, in every color of the rainbow, swirling about their ankles.

Gentlemen sported great periwigs and, beringed and beribboned in the latest fashion for men—fashion imported from France through life-size dolls dressed *à la mode*—their clothing eclipsed all feminine attire in its elaboration and effeminacy.

Between dances, the banqueting hall hummed with light small talk and serious dialogue, gossip and diatribe, speculation and fact, jesting and laughter. People partook freely of the variety of foods and beverages set out on tables around the sides of the hall, or sat eating and talking on chairs set aside for that purpose.

Two huge fountains of wine spewed the liquid upward in contrasting ruby-red and sparkling clear. There was also ale, a punch mixed with spirits, and, for those requiring something more potent, brandewine or brandy. Servants were in attendance everywhere, refilling empty goblets and huge platters of food, carrying away dirty dishes and bringing clean, taking cloaks and gloves from new arrivals, removing an accidental stain from an unfortunate guest's gown or breeches, and seeing to the comfort of everyone in general.

Tristan introduced Brittany to many people, and she thought how different it was to see unmasked faces, with everyone dressed in courtly splendor rather than clever or bizzare costumes. Nonetheless, she was in awe of the rich attire of the Restoration Court. As elegant an image as her mirror had revealed, Brittany felt pale in comparison to the many beauties around them. Even those not so fetching were made to seem so with elaborate hairstyles, facepaint and patches, and exquisite gowns.

As the evening wore on, Brittany and Tristan were surrounded by his friends, too many of whom, she thought wryly, turned instantly into her admirers, despite the fact that he introduced her to everyone as his betrothed. In the brilliant and scandalous court of Charles II, dalliances outside of marriage were in vogue, and soon Brittany had many persistent requests for dances.

First she danced with Tristan. Although they barely touched, as decorum dictated, his gaze was warm and assuring and held a wealth of promise. When they neared the resplendent King Charles, however, Brittany held her breath. The king nodded a cool greeting to Tristan, then allowed his gaze to alight on her face with indolent but frank appreciation.

After the first few dances, Brittany began to sense a tension in Tristan, especially when he led her off the dance floor for something to drink.

"Why do you not approach the king?" she asked as they stood on the periphery of the hall, sipping cool wine.

His mouth hardened. "As I told my grandfather I would, I made the first move by attending the ball, but I will not crawl to Charles Stuart to ask forgiveness for so insignificant a slight as a little truth—even angrily stated—when compared to the gravity of his transgression."

Brittany sought to wipe the frown from his face. She put her hand on his arm, and when he looked down into her eyes, she said, "I love you very much."

His expression changed immediately, as when the sun peeks from behind stormclouds. "And I you, sweet. More than you'll ever know.'' He set down his half-empty wine-glass and took her arm.

"But your wine . . . You didn't finish it.''

"We've a long night ahead of us, and I cannot drink more than a few goblets.''

At her look of puzzlement, he explained with a rueful quirk of his lips. '' 'Tis my Powhatan blood. Indians have not developed a tolerance for the white man's spirits. Would you have me climbing into the branches of the candelabra? Or disgracing myself by being sick into one of the fountains?''

"Certainly not, but you've never mentioned it before.''

"There was never any need.''

Sir Geoffrey Peckinpaugh came up to them, barely recognizable to Brittany without his fierce and hirsute Viking accoutrements. He was delighted to see them both. He bowed over Brittany's hand and, after exchanging greetings, said to Tristan, "Everyone is talking about Buckingham's dismissal from court. No one knows exactly why, but the court is abuzz. 'Tis the most popular topic of the evening.''

Before either Brittany or Tristan could comment, several of Brittany's admirers surrounded them. "Come, come, Savidge!'' exclaimed one. "You monopolize the lady's time. Let her dance with us before we expire of broken hearts.''

Brittany smiled at the man's theatrical exaggeration and looked up at Tristan. "I hear a branle starting up,'' he said. "One more dance with my lady and then I will deign to give you a turn, Renshaw.''

Tristan deliberately ignored his growing ire with the king, concentrating on the exquisite creature he'd wooed and won, and would soon make his wife, and one day his countess. With each graceful step, each glance exchanged, he vowed anew that she would never know want or mistreatment again. The intoxicating scent of violets mingled with the clean, female scent that was uniquely hers, and produced a heady sensation within him. The king be damned, he thought, and my grandfather, as well. I would like nothing more than to take her home and make love to her until she is weak and breathless. He bestowed a devastating smile on her and the brilliance of her own was returned. And naught would please me more than to take her back to Virginia and—

You have too many obligations and responsibilities here now, a voice reminded him. Yet, he mused as he automatically moved through the steps of the dance, there surely could be some way to spend equal time in both places, and should they have sons, perhaps one of them would be content to live in England upon reaching his majority and—

"May I have this next dance?" inquired a familiar voice.

Tristan met this sovereign's gaze, but instantly Charles's eyes went to Brittany, as if he expected an answer from her alone.

Brittany sent Tristan a swift, bemused glance, but Charles was already taking her hand and raising it to his lips.

Anger, hot and potent, rose up in Tristan, threatening to send all caution and restraint scattering. Scathing words sprang to his lips, but he bit them back and, instead, couched his ire in courtly rhetoric. "Once more, 'twould seem, the lady must entrust herself into your most *tender* keeping." His eyes were as hard and cold as sapphires. "I *thank* you most humbly, majesty, for providing—and then taking—the opportunity to put all to rights, as only you in your royal magnanimity can do."

The blood left Brittany's face as Charles slowly turned his head until their gazes collided. "The lady is as a rare flower who would never receive aught but the most careful tending at our hands, I assure you. Perhaps she would fare better beneath our benevolent tutelage than that of one who cannot recognize what is before him."

Not a word of apology—no hint of regret—from the man who'd been one of his closest friends, Tristan thought as their gazes held. The king had failed to show any contrition for having gone along with Buckingham's scheme, for making love to Brittany afterward, for the entire night. Oh, how well Tristan knew that public laundering of their private quarrel was unthinkable, but he'd hoped that perhaps—just perhaps—Charles might have shown some sign of remorse . . .

The searing pain of remembered betrayal struck Tristan, tearing open the tender membranes of healing forgiveness, and giving his words the stringent edge of censure.

"You are known for your good nature, your abhorrence of angry words and violence—all this I have been witness to for almost half a score of years. Yet your obvious refusal to—" Once again, years of habit forced him to bite back his words, but his eyes were narrowed in challenge, for his grandmother's people had taught him of honesty and forthrightness.

"I would be honored to join you in the dance, your majesty," Brittany interjected, the fine edge of panic slightly raising the pitch of her voice. She all but shook Tristan's hand from hers in her haste to swiftly separate the two men. She gave Charles a blinding smile she was far from feeling, all her attention turning to him in an effort to divert the royal regard from Tristan.

The king obviously read the desperation in her eyes, for he nodded without smiling. "Shall we?" And he led her to the floor.

As Tristan watched them, fighting the murderous urge to tear them apart, jealousy ripped through him, threatening, for a brief, maddening moment, to rob him of all reason in a red mist of frustrated rage.

"He'll tire of her soon enough," Barbara Palmer said from beside him. He wrenched his gaze from the couple moving through the throng of dancers and looked into the king's mistress's seductive violet eyes—eyes now dark with her own jealousy. "Why don't you give him a taste of his own tonic?" she invited slyly.

The mist cleared as Tristan caught her meaning. He knew Barbara was securely ensconced in the royal affections and favor. Why not, indeed, fight fire with fire, as she suggested.

He managed a tight-lipped smile and bowed to her. "Would you care to dance, my lady?"

They danced within sight of the king and Brittany and, on the chance that they would be noticed by them, Tristan forced himself to gaze with obvious fascination into Barbara's eyes, at her sultry mouth, to be daringly familiar in his movements. Barbara reciprocated. Before the second dance was over, people were beginning to note their heedless preoccupation with each other.

Although it was common knowledge that the gay and intrepid Barbara took other lovers and had long desired Sir Tristan Savidge, Tristan had always behaved discreetly because of Charles's infatuation with her. If he'd felt any attraction to Barbara Palmer, one of the Restoration Court's greatest beauties, that interest had been totally extinguished as soon as he'd met Brittany St. Germain . . .

Until the duchess led him to one of the refreshment tables and he recklessly downed a glass of brandy.

Suddenly Barbara's mouth seemed the most inviting he'd ever seen, her heavy-lidded, slanting eyes the most bewitching, driving out all other considerations as his inhibitions began to melt away.

"Savidge, where have you been all these long months?" asked William Hartland, the duke of Dansworth, Diana's father.

Tristan gave the duke an engaging grin. "The wolf has been hiding in his lair, your lordship, didn't you hear?" he asked, lowering his voice to a conspiratorial murmur.

"Hello, Tristan," Diana greeted silkily. Her gaze, on Barbara rather than on Tristan, raked over her "friend" in open hostility.

As Tristan returned her greeting, however, Roger Palmer, Barbara's unfortunate, cuckolded husband, joined their group. After greetings were exchanged, Roger asked them to excuse his wife and led a reluctant Barbara away.

Not, however, before Tristan watched her full mouth form the words, *I'll be back.*

He glanced at Diana and noticed that she, too, had caught Barbara's silent promise. He dismissed the feral gleam in her hazel eyes and wondered if Diana realized how fetching she looked . . .

"—and Villiers is furious at someone, but neither he nor the king will divulge the reason," William Hartland was saying. "He's cutting a wide swath about London, though he's denied Whitehall and all court functions."

Tristan shrugged and accepted another glass of brandy from the duke, while Diana sipped her punch and watched Tristan over the rim of her glass.

This time the brandy slid down Tristan's throat like liquid silk, and his feelings of utter relaxation and calm helped force Brittany and the king from his mind, dulling his pain and dissipating his anger.

Let them dance until dawn, he thought through a growing fog, and raised his glass to Diana in a silent toast.

Brittany's mouth ached from smiling at all the people to whom she was being introduced. A headache caused by tension was blossoming behind her temples with alarming speed. Yet she and Charles were the center of attention, especially so since Catherine was ill and not in attendance. Brittany was forced to cater to the king.

A host of questions bubbled to her lips, each dealing with the growing rift between Charles and Tristan, but the king gave her no opportunity to raise them as he chatted on every subject under the sun. When they weren't dancing, he was introducing her to still more people.

When Samuel Pepys and his wife, Elizabeth, were presented to Brittany, Charles teasingly accused the up-and-coming officer of the Navy of being enchanted with the countess of Castlemaine. Pepys flushed to the roots of his hair, but his wife took the comment with good grace.

"That lady's affections lie elsewhere," she said sweetly, and Charles laughed with good humor.

"Half my courtiers are in love with her," he observed, and, indeed, at that very moment Brittany caught sight of Tristan leading the beautiful Barbara off the dance floor.

As the evening progressed, it appeared that Charles was reluctant to release Brittany. Whether due to his continuing enchantment with her or out of sheer perversity, she could not tell.

"Your majesty," she began as he led her to a table of refreshments, "will you not heal this breach between you and my lord Tristan?"

He paused in selecting several choice tidbits for her plate. "I will not speak of it again, mistress, but Tristan has a lesson to learn in humility. That it had to involve you is unfortunate, but nevertheless a *fait accompli.*" His dark eyes looked sad. "I was too long in exile, in foreign lands, bereft of my country and my subjects and my rightful crown. Never again will I allow myself to be humiliated or denigrated, treated with anything less than respect, even by a well-loved friend."

He raised a sweetmeat to her lips and, for fear of insulting him, she forced herself to accept it, praying that no one would see and read more into the action than it merited. "I exiled George Villiers from court and extended an invitation to Tristan to attend the ball, offering him a chance to make amends." He handed her a goblet of wine and took one for himself. "And yet he shuns me, can do no more than glare at me from afar." He raised the glass to his lips with a flourish that belied the gravity of his words. "All he has to do is approach me, even now using you as an excuse, and offer one word of apology, one simple gesture."

Brittany replaced her filled plate, unable to eat. She did, however, drink her wine, for she had need of something bracing. Another courtier, whose excess of ribbons and ruffles made her think of an elaborately decorated cake, claimed the king's attention. During this brief respite, Brittany had a chance to accept the failure of this attempt at reconciliation.

A sense of futility invaded her heart, and in that moment she realized that the streak of unbending pride she'd only recently glimpsed in Tristan was part and parcel of his character. Nothing would make him unbend. Not even his love for her.

She suddenly wanted only to go home to bed . . . alone.

Tristan looked down at his half-emptied glass of spirits, beguiled by the deep amber brandy in the crystal goblet. He tilted the vessel this way and that, canting his head in a most serious contemplation.

A hazy voice in the back of his mind was telling him to set the goblet down, but the liquid was so fascinating. It reminded him of someone's hair by firelight, but he couldn't remember whose.

"Tristan?" Diana Hartland's voice came to him as if from far away.

He ceased his study of the brandy. She looked like a midget to him. Small women were nice enough, he thought with utmost seriousness, but she looked like an ant dressed in a gown. Nay, where was her fish's tail? His forehead creased in a bemused frown.

"Will you dance with me?" she asked.

He sketched an inelegant bow and executed a few pas glissés from the courante, which looked to Diana like the shuffling steps of an Indian dance Tristan had once demonstrated for the king. "Just to warm up," he informed her gravely.

Diana decided she'd do better to get him alone. If he made a fool of himself on the dance floor, concerned friends would intervene. Tristan's sensible habit of moderation in drinking was known to all. "Come along, Pale Wolf." She peered into his face to see his reaction to her use of his Indian name.

He gave her an idiotic grin and mumbled something in a strange tongue. Then he let out a low whoop that Diana supposed was a war cry.

She instantly put a small hand over his mouth. "Hush,

love.'' She pulled on his hand and he followed docilely along, past the refreshment tables toward groups of chairs lining the hall.

He stopped suddenly before a tall, bronze candelabrum, inadvertently yanking Diana to an abrupt halt. She turned to find him studying its taper-lit branches with that undeserved fascination reserved for the embarrassed or the inebriated.

She tugged on his hand.

"D'you know, Diana, that this r'minds me of a tree back in V'rginia? Matt an' I used to climb—'' His head lolled back until his bleary gaze overshot the top of the candelabrum and met the ceiling with its allegorical paintings of the Restoration.

The world tilted crazily and dizziness overtook him. He forced his head down and tightened his grip on her hand. "Need ta sit down. Jus' for a li'l while.''

It was just what Diana wanted. She led him to a window alcove from which two lovers emerged—he looking exceedingly satisfied and she a bit less than perfectly arranged. Tristan sank into a chair, pulling Diana into his lap.

She regarded him with a knowing smile, for any man, she knew, was easier to manipulate while foxed. And more than anything, Diana Hartland wanted to be caught in a compromising situation with Tristan Savidge . . . especially by her father . . . before Barbara could return and claim him. What better way to hook one of the most sought-after men at court? Barring that, she hoped the Frenchwoman who'd cleverly attached herself to him would come upon them thusly.

Tristan draped a careless arm about her shoulders and looked up at the ceiling, forgetting for a moment his previous bout with light-headedness. "Nice ceilin', Diana, m'girl . . . isn' it?''

She agreed with innocently widened eyes and drew his chin down toward her. It dropped until they were eye to eye. "Tristan?''

"Umm?" His blue eyes were slightly unfocused, but still possessed the power to make her weak.

"I've—well, I've always wondered what it would be like to kiss an Indian." She blushed profusely, lowering her gaze and then peering up at him from the camouflage of her lashes.

"Indians didn't used to kiss. The white men taught 'em that."

At her pretty pout, he offered, "But now that we know, there's no stoppin' us!" And he laughed uproariously.

She patiently waited for his bout of merriment to subside. When he met her gaze again, she reached up to place one hand behind his head and drew his lips down to hers. " 'Sides," he said just before their mouths joined, "we *have* kissed before . . ."

She should have known, she realized as his lips touched hers with clumsy exuberance, that a man too far into his cups was as useless as a eunuch in matters of lovemaking. Damn, and he'd had barely two glasses of brandy!

When the brief kiss was over, she noted with satisfaction that her lip pomade was smeared over his mouth and cheek. Now, if she could only manage to loosen a bodkin and . . .

His head had slumped against the high chair back. A smile still curved his mouth, but Diana needed his full attention. She put her lips to the strong column of his throat. "Tristan?"

"Aye, sweetheart."

Perturbed, Diana pulled his chin down again so their gazes met. She smiled brazenly into his eyes and placed her hand over his codpiece. That made him start.

"Naughty, naughteee . . ." he slurred with a twist of his lips that looked more like a leer than a smile.

She slowly brought her arm up to reach for a bodkin, causing her breasts to rise slightly with the movement before she sucked in her breath to emphasize the décolletage of her gown. As the pin slipped free, part of her hair cascaded down the side of her face and, in a move that would have turned a pickpocket green with envy, she dropped the bodkin between her breasts.

"Oh, Tristan!" she exclaimed in distress, "my bodkin! And my hair!"

He regarded her as a hound watches its master with a look of canine disgust, for he'd caught the flash of metal as the pin had descended. "For shame, Di . . . You mus' pin it back up, for you look lopsided." She had always been lackwitted, he thought dimly. For God's sake—losing a bodkin down the front of a dress . . .

She reached into her bodice with thumb and forefinger and fished around, drawing his jaundiced eye. "Oh, my fingers aren't long enough, Tristan," she wailed. "It's slipped lower!"

He tried to roll his eyes, but that only produced the same results as tilting back his head, and his expression immediately turned bland.

"Will you help me?" She wrapped her arms around his neck and pressed her lips to his. "No one will see, I promise."

Well, she was giving him free license, he thought through his increasing stupor, and she did have tempting breasts. He tried to remember what they looked like. Hadn't she allowed him to pull her dress scandalously off her shoulders and fondle them? He frowned in concentration. Yet she'd managed to hold on to her virginity, a thing unheard of at court—nay, in all of London. And he hadn't been quite stupid or enamored enough to deflower her.

His head hurt from the effort of thinking, and so he allowed an indolent smile to curve his lips and lifted one hand to her neckline, his other resting around her waist.

Her flesh was soft and warm, and from somewhere deep inside, he felt a tickle of arousal. He plunged his fingers more deeply, his initial hesitation disappearing at her smile of pleasure as she leaned forcefully against his hand, her eyes growing languid and dark with desire.

Tell me that you've never felt passion for another . . .

Brittany's words penetrated the fog of intoxicated bliss,

and his fingers paused in their search for the wonderfully elusive hairpin. Guilt stabbed at the edges of his swiftly fleeing sanity. Wasn't he guilty of the same sin of which he'd accused her?

"Nay," he muttered to his conscience. "*She* was with Charles Stuart . . . my *friend!*" That seemed to make things different.

"What did you say, sweet?" Diana purred, rubbing against his now limp fingers.

He shook his head and was immediately sorry.

He closed his eyes and tried to concentrate on his task. When they opened again, Diana and her lopsided, tumbling blond hair, her hazel eyes, and her pale, voluptuous bosom—God, what overlarge breasts for an ant!—all seemed to blend into one myopic blur. His head fell forward just above his marauding hand, his dark hair against her throat. The healthy, umber shade of his skin contrasted vividly with the alabaster tones of her bosom.

"Tristan!" Diana said sharply. This would not do at all.

In one last heroic attempt, Tristan heaved up his head, essaying to assure her that he, the bodkin finder *par excellence*, would not fail her. His hand wiggled one last time within the warm, scented valley between her breasts, and her hand went to his codpiece, her head wantonly thrown back.

And it was thus that William Hartland, with Brittany right behind him, came upon his daughter and Sir Tristan Savidge.

"What the devil is going on here?" demanded Hartland.

Diana jerked as if burned and made a great show of removing Tristan's hand from her bodice.

Tristan's eyes narrowed as he tried to focus on William Hartland, but the figure standing so close behind the duke caught his wandering attention. "Good evenin', yer grace," he began, and then fell silent.

The sight of Brittany staring at them would have been

sobering to a less inebriated man, but Tristan remained very drunk.

"Where's *Charles?*" he sneered.

"I'm waiting for an explanation—and it had better be a damned good one," Hartland demanded before Brittany could say a word.

"Father, I—we . . ." Diana stumbled to a halt, blushing becomingly and managing to look miserably guilty. "He, Sir Tristan, was attempting to ravish me—"

This last bit of exaggeration caught even Tristan's befuddled attention and he looked from Brittany to William. "Like hell I was, yer grace." He attempted a glower at Brittany. "The king is the ravisher, not I."

"Then what were you doing with your hand down the front of my daughter's gown?" The harshness of Hartland's voice toned down considerably when he realized that Tristan Savidge was drunk—something unusual in the extreme.

"Well, I lost a bodkin, Father, and Tristan insisted upon searching for it—"

"The devil she did. She *dropped* it down 'er bodice and wheedled me into findin' it." Tristan frowned, his head beginning to ache in the worst way. He closed his eyes against the pain, and the dizziness, and the nausea.

"Let me take you home," Brittany said, stepping forward. Overshadowing her jealousy and outrage at his behavior was her anger at his refusal to mend his rift with the king.

"No matter what either one of you says," William declared, "Diana's been compromised." He noticed more than a few witnesses to the scene staring with undisguised curiosity and murmuring behind their hands.

"I'm certain Tristan can make reparation on the morrow, your grace," Brittany told the offended Hartland. "I think Tristan and Diana would make a handsome couple, and then, of course, her reputation would be spared." Diana removed herself from Tristan's lap and Brittany went to take his arm and draw him out of his chair.

He jerked his arm away, his expression turning ugly. "Quite convenient, isn' it, Brittany? You'd like nothin' better'n to see me safely wed so you can continue on as one of Charles's *women.*"

As she raised her hand to slap him, she noticed the rouge smeared over his face, the wilted and crushed lace at his throat, the mussed hair . . . Even more telling was the bleariness of his gaze.

"You are a pathetic excuse for a man," she said softly, for his ears alone. "Marry your Diana and be damned! I'll gladly remove myself from you aegis, your home . . . your country."

She swung away without so much as a glance at either Diana or William.

With unexpected agility Tristan launched himself out of the chair toward her, his face flushed with drunken fury. "Come back here, court trollop, or I'll—"

Before he could complete the sentence, he passed out on the floor.

Chapter 25

Sir Geoffrey Peckinpaugh assisted Brittany in hiring a hackney back to Wildwood. She had the strongest urge to leave Tristan to find his own way home, but after he collapsed on the Banquet Hall floor, she could not bring herself to do it. With the help of William Hartland and Giles Renshaw, she managed to get Tristan safely out of Whitehall.

It did not help matters that she was forced to sit on the same side of the coach as Tristan and support his head and shoulders. If left on his own, the jolting of the coach would have sent him rolling onto the floor. And so Brittany held him in her arms, her gaze unwillingly drawn to the beloved face resting in her lap.

As they passed through the streets of London toward Chelsea, Brittany had more than enough time to think. She was torn between her deep love and the realization that she had no recourse but to leave him. If he couldn't make amends with the king, if he didn't trust her enough to think better of her, then there was no future for them.

But he has every reason to mistrust you after you spent the night with Charles Stuart, whispered a voice.

Her throat clogged with emotion as she remembered the look on Tristan's face when he'd come upon her and the king in bed. As long as Tristan refused to approach the king, he would never learn the truth or understand that she would never have willingly betrayed him.

Images of him invaded her thoughts: tender and gentle,

wooing her patiently; laughingly wrestling with Ikuuk or matching wits with his irascible grandfather; making love to her, his eyes dark with desire; and fierce and implacable when coming to her rescue, whether at the Hunter's Run or in St. Malo. He was a man of many facets, yet, overall, sweet-natured, tolerant, and self-assured. Only recently had he exhibited a tendency to become withdrawn, a frown marring his noble brow.

And at this point in his life he needs the same nurturing he so willingly gave you in your desperate need not so long ago.

"He made a fool of himself—insulted me in a way he had no right to do!" she exclaimed softly.

He was sotted with spirits.

He certainly was!

And why? the voice persisted. *Because he was hurting from what he interpreted as a betrayal by not only you, but the king as well.*

" 'Twas only his pride that prevented him from putting all to rights with the king. He could have easily avoided the pain he inflicted upon himself this night," she whispered in despair.

She closed her eyes and leaned against the squabs. She would send a message to Matt. The *Virginia* was to leave day after tomorrow, and she would be on it.

They reached Wildwood and, after Georgie and Jims got Tristan out of the coach, Ikuuk slung him over his broad shoulder and took him into the house.

"Uds lud," Enis exclaimed. "My lord never drinks more than a few glasses of wine."

"I suspect he drowned himself in brandewine," Brittany told her in succinct tones that invited no further questions.

Ikuuk took Tristan upstairs to his room and, in no mood to offer help, Brittany sought her own chamber and closed the door firmly behind her.

In the morning, Brittany went down to breakfast. She ate alone and was glad of it. As she served the meal, Enis told her that Ikuuk had given Tristan a potion to make him vomit, and although pale and light-headed and suffering from a hammering headache, the master would be himself within the next twenty-four hours.

Brittany finished her breakfast and dispatched Jims with a note to Matt. She went upstairs to pack a few belongings, her mind blessedly numb. She took only the bare necessities, leaving the volume of *Tristan* and the dressing casket Tristan had given her on the table in her room. Her vision blurred as poignant memories assaulted her when she touched the book's leather binding and looked one last time inside the small chest. But she ruthlessly blinked the moisture away.

She informed Enis of her plans, to the woman's dismay, but the determined look on Brittany's features warned Enis not to attempt to dissuade her.

"I plan to stay the night in London," she told the servant. "The ship leaves at dawn and I will be right there near the docks."

When Jims returned in the early afternoon with a hired coach and Matt's reply, Brittany hugged Enis goodbye. "Thank you for everything, Enis."

"But my lord—will you not at least bid him farewell?"

Come back here, court trollop . . .

"I already have," she lied.

She said her farewells to Georgie and Jims and turned to Ikuuk. He had long ago ceased to frighten her, but even now she could not decipher his thoughts. She threw herself into his stong embrace, for he was Tristan's blood brother, as close to Tristan as any natural sibling.

He returned her hug, lifting her off the ground before setting her back down. *He loves you,* he signed.

"He is stubborn and proud and a fool."

Amusement rose in his eyes. *He is. But he is also patient and gentle and loyal.*

"He refused to make his peace with the king, and things can only get worse. I have no choice, for my own peace of mind and contentment.'' She turned away lest he see the anguish in her eyes.

His hand on her shoulder stopped her. She swung back. *When you love someone, sometimes you must put them before your own happiness.*

Her eyes brimming, she met his gaze. ''Ah, our Ikuuk now giving advice on affairs of the heart.'' She stood on tiptoe and kissed his cheek. ''Take care, my friend.'' She glanced down at her left hand. ''And give him this, please.'' She removed the emerald and sapphire ring, the gleam of its precious stones dancing before her eyes.

If you care for me at all, you'll never remove it.

She placed it in Ikuuk's hand and curled his fingers around it, her heart breaking. ''Give him this, for I cannot in good conscience keep so precious a gift.''

She realized belatedly that she would never see the earl again, that she wouldn't be able to bid him farewell. Ignoring a chastising voice inside her, she walked toward the waiting hackney.

''Gemini, 'tis Brittany!'' Janie Neggers exclaimed. Unmindful of the trayful of drinks she was carrying, she hurried toward the door of the inn.

Brittany smiled with genuine pleasure. When Janie realized she held a loaded tray between her and her friend, she laughed and set it down.

''I'll take care of it,'' said a passing serving girl Brittany had never seen before.

The two friends hugged, and Janie held Brittany away from her. ''Let me look at you—lord, you're gorgeous!''

''You look wonderful yourself, Janie.'' Brittany noted the contentment in the girl's dark eyes. Her hair was clean and shining, her clothing neat and mended.

''I've got me a man,'' Janie confided, her eyes dancing. '' 'Is name is Bobby, an' he's head over tails in love with me!''

Brittany laughed with delight. ''That's wonderful, Janie. I knew some man would snatch you up.''

They both laughed again.

"An' I've get yer money stashed away, Britt. It's safe an' sound."

"You keep it, Janie. I've no need of it," she lied.

Just then, a harried serving girl jostled Brittany's arm, and the latter swung toward the tables where patrons were eating. "I'd like a light supper, Janie, and if Maude can, indeed, spare you, have a bite with me."

Janie led her to a small table in an alcove and hurried away to seek Maude's permission. While she was gone, Brittany glanced around, taking in the familiar sight of girls running hither and thither, with trays of drinks and food for customers who stood near the roaring blaze in the great hearth or sat at benches and stools around beaten and scarred oaken tables. She breathed in the familiar scents of spilled spirits, cooked food, and unwashed bodies. Her ears caught all the sounds she'd become accustomed to while employed by the Dobbses. But now the circumstances were different . . . *she* was different.

The front door opened, and the wind eddied in, bringing with it the mixture of odors from the docks and the Thames, just as it had one night almost a year ago. The memory of her first meeting with Tristan Savidge struck her like a physical blow. In spite of the ordeal with Buckingham, she could still remember how tall and capable he'd looked to her, even then. The striking features and stunning blue eyes that bespoke intelligence and compassion beneath his high brow . . . how he'd tricked the tipsy duke and cleverly spared her from being hauled before the king . . .

"Yer back, I see . . . and unharmed."

Brittany's gaze met Maude Dobbs's. The look on the older woman's face was wary. Brittany wanted to ask her how much richer she'd become as a result of her cooperation with George Villiers, but she squelched the ignoble thought.

"Aye. How are you, Maude?"

The innkeeper's wife seemed to let out a silent breath of relief. A hesitant smile started in her eyes, then softened her mouth. "No hard feelings, I see," she said.

"Nay," Brittany answered, *although you helped Buckingham ruin my one chance for happiness.*

Over her shoulder to Janie, Maude said, "Go get the both of you some supper . . . on the house." As Janie hurried to do her bidding, she tried to cover her awkward gratitude by asking, "What brings ye to the Hunter's Run alone? Are ye wantin' yer old job back?" She forced a laugh, although her expression seemed to say she'd be willing to grant Brittany just that to make amends for her part in Buckingham's chicanery.

Brittany smiled slightly and shook her head, her gaze dropping to the table before her. "Thank you, Maude, but I'm not here for work. I leave for the Colonies on the morrow. I-I want only a room for the night and a chance to visit with Janie."

If Maude, who had always been so sensitive to the mysterious girl she'd taken in with nary a recommendation almost three years ago, read the defeat in the droop of Brittany's shoulders, the sorrow in the striking green eyes that raised to meet hers again, she hid it well.

"Well, good fortune to ye, girl. I know ye'll always do well, wherever ye go."

"Thank you, Maude."

"Here we are." Janie came up behind Maude with a curious Katie Dobbs in tow. She set down two trenchers of boiled beef and potatoes and a wheel of cheese. Katie followed suit with two well-dented pewter mugs of ale.

"Well, Brittany . . . 'tis you in the flesh," Katie greeted. "Where's yer 'andsome Indian?"

Brittany had to smile at Katie's excellent recall for a good-looking face. "He's recovering from a slight . . . indisposition."

"Come along now," Maude told her daughter, putting an end to Katie's probing. "Janie and Britt have much to catch up on betwixt 'em." And, with a nod at Brittany, she prodded Katie back to work.

Janie sat across from Brittany, her hazel eyes alight. "I can't believe I'm not eatin' in the kitchen. Lord, I feel like royalty!" She grinned in that impish way of hers before adding, "Maude gave ye the biggest and best room in the house. Uds lud, Britt, 'ave ye got somethin' on the woman?"

Brittany returned her smile, finding her happiness infectious. "You might say that, Janie." Obviously her friend knew nothing about the trick Maude Dobbs had played, using Janie as a lure, and Brittany saw no reason to enlighten the girl.

Janie leaned forward, pushing a mug toward Brittany. "I can't accept yer guineas, Brittany. You must take the money. Won't ye need some in the Colonies? Or to pay yer passage?"

Brittany took a drink of the ale, immediately recognizing it as the best in the house. "I have enough, Janie," she lied again. For, in truth, she had only a small purseful that Tristan had given her for any incidentals she might have needed while they'd stayed at the earl's town house in London. But she did not doubt for a moment that she would find a way to repay Matt after she established herself in Virginia. And certainly Matt would provide her with a letter of recommendation . . .

"Tell me what's happened since Sir Tristan Savidge spirited you away, Britt," Janie implored, her eyes wide with anticipation.

"Later, Janie," her friend answered, her voice subdued. "First tell me all about your Bobby."

Much later, the sounds coming from the taproom below gradually faded as Jack Dobbs ushered out the last of his clientele. Brittany couldn't make out the whisk of the brooms, but she knew that they were being applied with vigorous strokes as everyone pitched in to clean up before retiring.

Her room was, indeed, the best at the Hunter's Run and, she mused wryly, she had no use for so large or luxurious a chamber. Maude's conscience must be positively writhing, she thought with an ironic quirk of her lips.

She faced the street and the waterfront beyond it, exactly as she had when she'd worked here, but instead of a tiny garret window, she was looking out a good-sized, glass-paned mullioned window.

The bell man came by with his bell and called, "Past one of the clock, and a cold, windy morning."

Brittany left her post at the window. She had to get some sleep, for dawn came earlier now than in midwinter, and she'd just as soon not have circles beneath her eyes to proclaim to Matt and all the world just how miserable she was.

A barely discernible knock sounded on the door as she sat down on the edge of the bed. "Britt, are you still awake?" Janie called softly.

"*Oui,*" she answered. "Come in."

Janie slipped through the door and closed it behind her, holding a steaming drink that smelled heavenly. "You should be sleepin', ye know." She looked suddenly concerned. As Brittany gave her a falsely bright smile, she realized that Janie had matured in the last seven months. The girl had always taken it upon herself to be Brittany's protector, a humorous reversal of roles, Brittany had always thought, considering that Janie was quite a bit younger. But now there was a maturity about her bearing, in her eyes and voice, that had been missing heretofore.

Janie sat beside her and handed her the cup. "Drink up . . . 'tis only buttered ale and will help you sleep." She reached out to smooth the long fall of honey-brown hair that lay in rippling waves over Brittany's shoulders and down her back.

As Brittany complied like an obedient child, Janie continued, "Ye hardly touched yer supper. I suspect there's more to yer story." She paused, watching Brittany sip the mixture of ale, butter, sugar, and cinnamon. "D'ye want to tell me about it?"

At the tender concern in Janie's voice, Brittany felt the rise of emotion in her chest and reached over to place the ale on the table beside the bed. "There's not much more than I've already told you."

Janie shook her head. "Yer runnin' from *him*, aren't ye? He's not joinin' you in the Virginia Colony like ye said earlier because he's stayin' here."

Brittany allowed her gaze to meet Janie's, even as she fought the press of tears. "Oh, Janie," she whispered in anguish.

Janie gently nudged Brittany's head down upon her shoulder. "Let the tears come. Now, now, there's a love . . ."

After one last valiant attempt to shake her head in negation, the floodgates burst open, and for the first time since she'd lost the refuge of her mother's love, Brittany cried her heart out in another woman's caring embrace.

I know 'e'll come for ye, Britt. I'm a good judge of character, and I had Sir Tristan Savidge pegged from the first.

In the pearly-gray light of dawn, Janie's words echoed in Brittany's mind as she walked briskly toward the docks. *'E's a fine man, just a mite stubborn and proud, I think.*

Brittany pushed Janie's voice away, glad she'd asked the girl not to come to the ship with her. She hated tearful partings, and their farewell before she'd left the Hunter's Run had been difficult enough.

She allowed her gaze to take in the still, calm waters of the river, a ghostly haze of fog hovering over it. Ships in dock sent their naked spars into the somber skies as they creaked and swayed in the morning breeze. Men were already working on the decks of many of the vessels, shouting or singing bawdy songs as they swabbed the decks and polished the brass trappings, or loaded cargo up and down the ramps stretching from dock to deck. Others, whose dress and authoritative actions singled them out as captains and officers, consulted with one another or shouted orders to the seamen. The smell of tar and wet wood, of a vast variety of different cargoes, of dead fish and garbage washed up along the banks where the water lapped gently, assailed her nostrils and, in spite of the circumstances, Brittany felt the first, reluctant stirrings of excitement at the prospect of traveling to a new land with Matt and Genna.

She stopped and looked for the *Virginia* among the myriad ships. She would recognize Matt, of that she was certain . . .

"So you think to sneak away like the lowlife you are— sneak away before you can be apprehended and made to suffer for the crime of murder."

Shock ricocheted through her as her mind placed that dreaded voice, and Brittany swung slowly to face Charlotte Chauvelin.

She only barely noted Buckingham standing behind the woman, accompanied by two grim-faced men. At the look of chilling triumph on Charlotte's face, Brittany's brain suddenly refused to function. Her recurring nightmare had caught up with her yet again. *Dieu,* she wondered dazedly, how did they know to find me here?

As if reading her thoughts, the duke said, "Your rift with Savidge was the talk of the town by yesterday morning. Lady Charlotte arrived in London just last eve—a most fortuitously timed occurrence—and I guessed that you would go arunning to Matthew Stark."

Brittany found her voice. "You can do nothing to me," she said to Charlotte through stiff lips.

"Can I not? 'Tis absurdly overconfident of you to think so," the woman assured her. "The king of France himself has issued a writ calling for your return to France for the murder of my son."

Brittany's eyes flashed. "I did not murder him! I tried to save him from the fire. Rather 'twas your man Marquet who neglected his duty and allowed the fire to start in the first place. Then, when I would have dragged Raymond from the room, Marquet told me to leave him be, and fled."

"And where were you when the fire started?"

"I—why, I was out for a breath of air." How paltry an excuse it sounded now before Charlotte's malignant gaze. "Tristan Savidge was a witness," she added, her voice sharp with rising hysteria.

"Savidge is no doubt still suffering from the aftereffects of his overindulgence." Buckingham looked at Charlotte. "It seems to me that you're wasting your time arguing with her, Lady Charlotte." He nodded toward the two men and they stepped forward to flank Brittany on either side.

With desperate strength she gripped the handles on her small bag, intending to take at least one of the men down before giving up.

"What is going on here?" a deep voice demanded.

Brittany turned. Matt!

"Why don't you go about your business, Stark," Buckingham advised with a sneer. "This is none of your concern."

With a glance that quickly sized up the situation, Matt answered, " 'Tis very much my *business*, Buckingham. You're detaining one of my passengers. Release her, now."

"Impossible, monsieur," interjected Charlotte. "She is wanted for murder in France."

Matt walked toward one of the men, who'd grasped Brittany's arm. The henchman struck out at him, but Matt ducked and delivered a stunning blow to the man's midsection. A seaman came up behind Stark and engaged Charlotte's second hireling, and a scuffle ensued among the four men.

Brittany backed away, her free hand to her mouth. She shook her head mutely, dismayed beyond measure that she'd involved Matthew Stark—that he might be injured because of her.

She looked around wildly, searching for help, but Buckingham stepped forward and grabbed her upper arm. Their gazes clashed, and without hesitation she swung her satchel toward his head with all her might. He ducked and yanked her arm upward until Brittany felt something in her shoulder crack. Her face twisted with pain and outrage and, gritting her teeth against the agony, she sent a swift kick toward his shin, backing up as she pulled her arm away sharply—

Pulled away to come up against the warm, solid bulk of a horse.

"Let her go."

A sword tip appeared out of nowhere and pressed against Buckingham's throat.

Instantly, the grip on her arm eased as the duke released it. Her bag dropped to the ground and, clutching her aching shoulder, she slowly pirouetted.

Relief flooded through her at the sight of Tristan Savidge astride Gorvenal, Ikuuk beside him on another mount. Tristan's eyes immediately sought Buckingham, his sword tip pressing into the duke's skin to draw a drop of blood that stood out against the snowy lace at his throat in the brightening morning light.

"Call off your men, Villiers, before I settle my score with you here and now, and in a way that will put an end to your debauched existence."

"You wouldn't dare."

Tristan leaned over Gorvenal's alabaster-maned neck. "Oh, wouldn't I? I would have the king's blessing after my grandfather revealed everything to him. After all, I would hardly call your banishment from court the action of a pleased monarch."

Ikuuk had dismounted, and at his approach, one of the hirelings backed off, his mouth dropping open in amazement. Charlotte's jaw worked, too, opening and closing like that of a beached fish, but nothing emerged save an ineffective squeak as she watched the tall Indian help Matt to his feet.

"Enough!" Buckingham roared at the second miscreant who had pinned the seaman to the ground. At the duke's imperious order, the man jumped to his feet and backed away, swiping at a bloody lip.

Tristan swung one leg over Gorvenal's neck and dropped to the ground with ease, facing the duke. He slid home his sword and took Brittany's hand. "Now, Buckingham, I suggest you hie yourself off and send the lady"—he glanced at Charlotte—"back to France."

Buckingham reached inside the jacket beneath his cloak and withdrew a folded and sealed parchment. He tossed it to the ground at Tristan's feet. "Here is something that might interest you."

Tristan arched a dark brow. "I doubt you could interest me with aught now, Villiers."

" 'Tis a decree from Louis XIV of France demanding the return of one Geneviève Elise Chauvelin to face charges for the murder of Raymond Chauvelin."

Tristan began to laugh. Charlotte's eyes narrowed in anger, and Buckingham's expression turned nearly apoplectic.

"Obviously your feelings for the jade have lessened considerably, if you find humor in the fact that you must give her up."

Tristan sobered instantly. "If you ever refer to her thusly again, Villiers, I'll cut out your tongue." His arm went around Brittany's waist, and he drew her close to his side. "There is no one in France who can command her to return for, you see, we were wed last night, and as the wife of an English subject, she is not answerable to French authority."

Villiers frowned blackly. "Just how gullible do you think I am, Savidge? 'Tis plain as day she was running away from you, hardly the action of a new bride."

"She was coming to bid Matt and his wife goodbye," Tristan answered smoothly.

"Then why the baggage? And why did Stark accuse me of detaining one of his passengers?"

Tristan smiled down into Brittany's eyes before his look hardened and his gaze clashed with Buckingham's once more. "Even Matt was unaware of our sudden decision to

be wed last eve. As for the bag—well, Matt's wife left
behind several items she'd loaned Brittany at one time.''

"Even if 'tis true, as cousin to his majesty, Louis can
appeal to King Charles.''

Tristan looked down at Brittany, his eyes warm and full
of love—but also with a question in their measureless
depths. He spoke to Buckingham, but his gaze remained
on her upturned face. "Louis was not particularly receptive to his majesty or his plight while the Royalists were
in exile. I don't believe Louis will get any support from
Charles Stuart.'' He gazed out toward the river. "And,
most especially, in view of our long-standing friendship.''

"Now, why do I have the distinct impression,'' the duke
asked softly, "that all is not right betwixt you and Charles?
Perhaps because you acted the sotted fool at the ball before all and sundry? You—the most *temperate* Tristan Savidge?'' He spat the last words with venom.

"I give you leave, Villiers, to put that friendship to the
test,'' he challenged, a deadly light in his eyes. "And
while you're at it, do continue your plotting and harassing.
I would like nothing more than to see you fall completely
from grace.''

The words hung in the charged air between them before
Buckingham muttered an expletive and turned away to escort the thwarted and furious Charlotte to his coach. The
two hirelings melted into the small crowd.

Matt sighed. "So, now I suppose I'll have to deal with
Genna's disappointment that Brittany will not be on the
Virginia when she sails. I certainly wish you'd make up
your mind, Tris.''

Tristan grinned at Matt. "Genna will be delighted to
learn that if you can find it in your heart to delay sailing
until the morrow, the *Virginia* will have four extra passengers instead of one.''

"What the devil do you mean, 'delay our departure'?''

"Grandfather will pay you handsomely for the delay
for, you see, he wishes to travel to the Colonies to meet
his son. He's on his way to London even as we speak.''

"Ah, I see." Matt nodded solemnly, as if it were perfectly natural for an English earl to abandon everything on a whim and set sail for Virginia.

Tristan looked down at Brittany. "And, of course, Brittany, Ikuuk and I will accompany him. 'Tis only for one year, mind you." He brushed back a lock of windblown hair from her face, then glanced back up at Matt. "We'll all be here at dawn tomorrow." He looked at Ikuuk, standing tall and silent behind Matt, oblivious to the few gawkers who were staring at him. "Why don't you take Ikuuk to the *Virginia* for now? Get him reacquainted with his sea legs. Brittany and I have some unfinished business to attend to, and then we'll return for him."

"Very well." Shaking his head, Matt made his way toward the docked vessels with Ikuuk close behind.

Chapter 26

Brittany watched with mixed emotions as, with the heel of his boot, Tristan ground the letter at his feet into the mud.

"Brittany?"

She raised her gaze to his, torn between a fierce joy because he'd come for her and frustrating disillusionment at the obvious fact that nothing was really settled.

She gave him a level look. "You're very sure of yourself, aren't you."

He squeezed one hand and reached for the other. "Brittany, I—"

She backed away, her eyes dark with disappointment. "And just what is this about 'unfinished business'? You think perhaps to take me to the Hunter's Run or the town house and try to win me over with your ardent wooing?" He shook his head, but she was past caution now. "I'll not allow you to break my heart again and again, all because of your ridiculous pride! How much do you think I can—"

He took her face between her palms and held her fast, his heart in his eyes. "I love you, Brittany . . . more than my life—"

"And what of the 'court trollop'? Do you love her, too? For, according to you, we are one and the same."

Remorse flitted across his features. "Oh, God, those words have come back to haunt me a thousand times in the past two days, to torture me relentlessly with their callous and unfounded insinuation.'' He crushed her to him, ignoring the curious stares of passersby. ''Forgive me,'' he murmured against her hair. ''Forgive me, or I'll never forgive myself.''

She remained silent, reluctantly savoring the feel of his arms about her, shielding her, sheltering her, even as he had since the first moment they'd met in a crowded taproom.

''Be mine, my love, and I'll spend the rest of my life showing you just how precious you are to me.'' His grip tightened. ''I'm nothing without you . . . floundering, soulless . . .''

Brittany relented slightly in the face of his moving confession. She shook her head. ''Nay, Tristan. You're more self-assured and independent than most can ever hope to be.''

He smiled sadly. ''Perhaps a year ago, but not now. My life is irrevocably bound to yours, and I will do anything to prove my sincerity, for Tristan cannot live without his Isolde.''

The stark beauty of his features swept away her breath for the hundredth time, for this extraordinary man, gifted by God with so noble a character, so beautiful a spirit. She, too, Brittany realized with a sudden sense of wonder, would never be whole without him, for he'd taught her of laughter and love and life.

''Marry me, Brittany. Remain with me and accept my love for all eternity.'' His splendid eyes misted with the strength of his emotion, and her heart melted like the last patch of snow in a spring thaw.

''On one condition,'' she whispered.

''Name it.''

''You must make your peace with the king.''

He gazed into the distance, his eyes closing briefly as he drew in a long, sustaining breath. His hesitation lasted no more than the space of a heartbeat, and when his eyes met hers, they reflected only his willingness to please her. ''And so I shall . . . for you.''

She reached up to touch his cheek. "Do it for yourself, Tristan—for the sake of the love you bear him, for what he's been to you and you to him. For honor, for loyalty, for the priceless gift of true friendship."

"So be it." And his mouth descended to meet hers.

Tristan paid a small, grimy urchin to lead the two horses back to the Hunter's Run and hired a hackney to take them to Whitehall Palace.

He was silent during the ride, but held her close the entire time with his cheek resting atop her head, as if he would never let her go.

It was still early and the king only just rising when Tristan was announced. Brittany insisted on waiting in one of the antechambers in the royal apartments. This matter was between Tristan and Charles, and she had no intention of intruding.

As Tristan was given leave to enter Charles's bedchamber, he felt a sense of hopelessness creep into his heart. If Charles was so angered as to ignore him at the ball and monopolize Brittany's time out of spite, how could he, Tristan, ever swallow his pride and apologize for something he still maintained was less serious than Charles's own breach of faith?

But the king surprised him out of his dour ruminations by asking him, "And where is your lovely Brittany?"

"She's in the antechamber, your majesty, by her own preference."

Charles tied the velvet sash of his dressing gown about his waist. "I would wager 'twas at her insistence that you've come to me at long last." He allowed a smile to curve his mouth. "I would ask that she be present."

Alarm screeched across his nerve endings as Tristan turned back to do the king's bidding. Why did he insist on seeing her again? But he stifled his apprehension.

When they both stood before him, Charles motioned Brittany toward a chair. "Sit, mistress, while I have my morning draught. Will you both join me?"

They declined, desiring neither to eat nor to drink in the tense moments before Tristan spoke.

"I will not take up any more of your time than is necessary, majesty," Tristan began.

Charles accepted a cup of mulled wine from a page. "There was a time when you were not so eager to quit my presence. Will it ever be so again?"

"Only if you wish it, sire." Tristan looked at Brittany, as if for support, and she obliged him with a smile that proclaimed her love—and encouragement.

With the promise of their future together written across Brittany's expressive features, Tristan turned to Charles and said, "I tender you my most abject apologies for my behavior the night I . . ." He paused, his eyes darkening at the memory of the scene he had stumbled on when he'd blundered into this very room. "The night I invaded the privacy of your bedchamber like a jealous fool."

Charles guessed what those words cost Tristan and hastened to assure him, "Your apology is heartily welcomed . . . and accepted." He glanced at Brittany, then back again. "You could have spared yourself this moment if you had only approached me with some sign of your regret at the ball, my friend. I had wished most diligently for some such indication that night, for 'twas entirely for your benefit that I held the gathering. But 'twas not to be."

Tristan met his sovereign's regard for a moment, flattered by the revelation, but not enough to prevent his mouth from tightening at the reminder of his own behavior.

"Have you learned your lesson then? Will you acknowledge that no matter how close a friend to the king, a man must yield to his sovereign in all things?"

"Aye."

Charles's dark gaze rested fondly on his friend. "I have always suspected a stubborn streak in you, Tristan, but only in the face of my betrayal and that of your Brittany has it come to the fore." He motioned to Brittany. "Come here, my lovely."

Brittany did as she was bid, refusing to allow her wariness to show. Charles took her hand and held it to his lips, then stood with her, facing Tristan. "You have a woman beyond price—did you know that? Ah, of course you did, for why else would you have plucked a rose from a tavernful of thorns? A St. Germain of the St. Germains of France, so the earl told me."

The king studied Brittany, his fine dark eyes filled with the wariness and melancholy acquired from ten years of fighting and hiding and being at the mercy of others. "And has our Tristan promised to wed you properly? Has he forgiven you for the sin of remaining in my bed even after he discovered us together?"

"I have, to both questions," Tristan answered before Brittany could open her mouth. A warm, wonderful feeling rushed through her at that unequivocal affirmation of his love and forgiveness.

Charles smiled, a sad, wistful smile, but one that also held a hint of self-mockery. "And so you are as loving and forgiving of her faithlessness as my sweet Catherine is of mine." He released Brittany's hand and she moved to stand beside Tristan. He took her hand and held it to his lips, a smile that promised a lifetime of devotion lighting his splendidly wrought features.

"The earl told me, also, that you are going back to Virginia for a year or so?"

"Aye, majesty," Tristan answered.

"I shall miss you. But your return is something I can look forward to, and I welcome the chance to give the first of two wedding gifts while you are here with me."

"Two gifts, majesty?"

"You'll have to wait until you return to England for the second, but the first should keep you content for a lifetime."

Puzzlement flashed in Tristan's eyes, but Brittany only smiled secretly, for Charles alone.

"Do you truly think that your Brittany remained with me that night because she wished it?" At Tristan's silence, he continued, "Look at her, man! She is deeply in love with you—and only you. Nor is she one to be so flattered by my attentions that she would jump into my bed even had such an opportunity presented itself.'' He shook his head, a gentle admonition in his eyes. ''She is as fine and rare as ever to be found, for she would have sacrificed her very honor to save your life.'' He paused. ''Now, I ask you, you thickheaded, obstinate Indian, why would such a jewel ever betray the very one for whom she would have sacrificed so much?''

''I pray you, Charles—do not say it,'' Tristan exhorted suddenly, unable to acknowledge the unexpected and terrible suspicion of the injustice he'd possibly done to both Brittany and the king. '' 'Twill not make me love either one of you more, and 'tis not necessary—''

''You cannot accept the guilt of having wrongly accused us? The two of us who love you so dearly that your face came between us when I still would have had her out of sheer perversity—and she would have surrendered to secure your release from Newgate?'' He put a hand on Tristan's shoulder. ''My foolish friend, being misled by Buckingham was one thing, but you underestimated the depth of our affection for you—and my respect for our friendship. Your Isolde was the exact opposite of everything George claimed she was.''

Tristan looked down at Brittany, and the brilliance of her smile blinded him. Then he was looking at Charles again, a sheepish grin spreading across his face. ''You devil!'' he charged.

''You proud buffoon!''

Suddenly they were embracing, and Brittany quietly let herself out of the room, a sweet contentment seeping through her and settling around her heart.

When they separated, Charles said, ''Now, I suggest you get your affairs in order and take your grandfather and your betrothed to Virginia.'' He raised a roguish eyebrow. ''Before I have a change of heart, Savidge, and do what I've been wanting to do since I first held the young lady in my arms at the masked ball.''

Tristan caught the barely suppressed amusement in the king's eyes, the twitch of a mustached lip, and replied, "Indeed I will, sire. For, as you so eloquently put it, a man must yield to his sovereign in all things."

The two coaches proceeded from Chelsea to London, the coruscating rim of the rising sun just breaking over the horizon in a benign blessing. A wagon loaded with baggage followed close behind.

In the first coach, Tristan sat with Brittany, his arm draped loosely across her shoulders. She felt his gaze constantly upon her and was rewarded with either a kiss or the tightening of his arm when she looked up at him.

She'd never been happier or more secure . . . or more excited.

"Tell me more about Virginia," she said for the third time since they'd left Wildwood.

Tristan laughed softly. "You are more curious than a child. We have an entire voyage across the Atlantic to discuss Virginia—and my family."

At the mention of his family, a frown knitted her brow. "What of your father, Tristan? Do you think he will receive the earl?"

Tristan sobered. "He may be half Powhatan, but he is no uncivilized savage. 'Twill be most interesting to see how Grandfather handles him. He is not one to humble himself, yet he will be at a definite disadvantage being in a strange land, facing the son he disowned almost fifty years ago. I think perhaps, before Grandfather returns to England, he will have learned much of humility."

"He has already humbled himself, I would say, by the simple fact that he has undertaken the journey. I would not want to trade places with him."

"Father would never be aught but receptive to a beautiful woman," he answered with a twinkle in his eyes.

"You know what I mean, Tristan Savidge." She leaned back in his embrace and closed her eyes. "I would truly like to meet Running Deer. She must be an extraordinary woman. Do you think she will approve of me?''

"Aye," he answered softly. "We were destined to find each other, you and I, to join our spirits for all eternity." He traced the sweet curve of her cheek. "Grandmother will love you—not as much as I, of course," he added with a twitch of his lips, "but, then, no one could—or shall."

His lips met hers in a most thorough, probing kiss that sent a thrill of desire streaking through her.

"Will we have a private cabin, my lord?" she asked breathlessly when at last he drew away.

"My little wanton," he chided gently. "You'll make my head swell with your eagerness. Do you think you can wait to be married until we arrive at Jamestown?"

"Oh," she said, the disappointment in her voice obvious. "I thought Matt could perform the ceremony on board the *Virginia*."

Laughter rumbled from deep within Tristan's chest, and Brittany felt the heat of color rise in her face. He pressed her tightly to him and smiled into her eyes. "Only weeks ago I would have given anything to hear you say those words."

For once she was tongue-tied.

"But I thought to wed you in my parents' home—with all my family present—and then, if you like, we can be wed again, in my grandmother's village."

"Would that please you?" she asked quietly.

"It would please me very much."

"Then I should be honored to wed you twice."

He withdrew his arm from around her shoulders and reached into the small purse at his waist. "When Ikuuk brought this to me, I . . ." He paused, emotion closing his throat at the memory. "I thought I'd lost you forever." He slid the emerald and sapphire ring onto her third finger and sat gazing down as it sparkled in the soft morning light.

"I'll never remove it again, I swear," she whispered, and brushed his lips with hers.

He grinned crookedly. "Speaking of Ikuuk, I wonder how he and Grandfather are getting along." They were following in the second coach.

Brittany laughed. "The earl is undoubtedly fending off Ikuuk's attempts to coddle him."

Tristan raised the hand on which he'd just placed his ring and pressed his lips to the soft, scented skin. "I wouldn't want to ride in that coach for all the gold in England. Poor Ikuuk."

The coach suddenly lurched as it took a turn, and Brittany looked out the window. "We're going in the opposite direction of the other coach," she said in puzzlement. "This isn't the way to the riverfront."

"How astute you are, sweet."

She looked at him expectantly.

Tristan sighed and drew her onto his lap. "I see you are also too curious for your own good, wench."

She snuggled against his chest amd reveled in the sound of his deep, even breathing beneath her ear. "Where are we going, my lord?"

"Why, to Newgate, green eyes," he answered, as if that fact were perfectly clear.

"Newgate?" She shuddered with horror but did not lift her head from the pillow of his chest.

"Aye," he mused softly as they turned onto Holborn Street. "We're going to obtain the release of one Oliver Wendall Chalmers and take him to the New World."

"What will Matt say to yet another unexpected passenger?" she asked, as if there were nothing unusual about retrieving an inmate from the bowels of Newgate.

"Matt has learned to indulge me." His mouth curved into a wry smile as the infamous prison came into view.

She looked into his laughing eyes. "Grandfather, Ikuuk, and Ollie . . . This should prove to be a most, ah, *interesting* voyage."

LINDA LANG BARTELL

From the moment she picked up *The Wolf and the Dove*, LINDA LANG BARTELL knew she was irrevocably hooked on historical romances. She says, "Here was an outlet for my love of history and my incurable romanticism. I became an avid reader of historical authors of the seventies while I taught high school French and history. It wasn't until my husband Bob and I moved from our hometown of Cleveland, Ohio, to Michigan that I decided to try to write my own book—and, to our delight, also conceived our daughter, Heather Lauren. That first manuscript is in my basement, but my second one sold, and the rest is history.

"I still love to read historical and general fiction, but I don't have the time I once did, because of my writing, research, and family. I love sports and dancing and am inspired in my writing by music . . . anything from Tchaikovsky to Van Halen."

Linda Lang Bartell is the author of three previous Avon Romances, *Alyssa, Brianna,* and *Marisa.*